ISBN: 9798386549510

Cover design by: Pascale Hutton
Library of Congress Control Number: 2018675309
Printed in the United States of America

Dedicated to myself, for any others who inspired this did so unknowingly.

The Loneliness That Others Call Freedom

by

Steven Vaughan

1

KIM

It was when he told me on our first meeting that he didn't want to have sex with me that I sensed it was going to happen. The falsity of his words was not the issue, in fact, I felt oddly gratified by them because it showed how badly he wanted to get me into bed. The only thing I felt it imperative to express later on was that I was sleeping with him in spite of his bravado rather than because of it and when he asked if that was meant sarcastically, he didn't seem in the least perturbed when I replied in the affirmative. The truth is that I wanted to call it a seduction when in reality it was far closer to a shared understanding, one that seemed so muted it barely passed for consent. I didn't want to think of how this had happened and I'd been unable to establish whether it had been error or frustration or a combination of the two. All I knew was that he'd caught me at the right time, just as I'd grown tired of my intuitions and had rebelled against them in a petulant mist which I seldom ever do. Of course I was going to regret it but it had gone beyond my control and if I've learned anything in my twenty-nine years, it's that inevitability is strangely persistent and difficult to deny.

The holiday was supposed to have been one of spiritual and meditative development and Hayley had sold it to me with fervent talk of primitive living, healthy eating and a wide range of rigorous, daily activity. Through yoga, we would bring both body and mind into alignment which would in turn transport us to the zenith of inner peace. It was exactly what I needed but things started inauspiciously and didn't improve from there.

We were lodged at a reclusive farm on a distant island that took us an hour to reach by boat after a rickety, six-hour flight. My enthusiasm wasn't dampened by this but on learning that we were expected to offer our services as unpaid farmhands for three hours of every day, it certainly started to waver. This explained why the price in the brochure had seemed so reasonable and the quizzical look of the boatman as we boarded his vessel with our heavy luggage in tow. The compliance with which the rest of the travelling party greeted the news suggested we were the only ones to have overlooked this, so I was left with little choice but to set about my duties with an obedient gusto. Hayley, on the other hand, did not.

I'd like to say that her behaviour alarmed me but the truth was that I didn't really know her well enough to say that. She'd been a colleague of mine for a few months but as she was based in a different department to me, I hadn't shared a great deal of conversation with her up to our going away together. Our acquaintance had been formed on the exchanging of paperbacks in the canteen and although her literary knowledge impressed me, I was to learn that this would not be an adequate basis on which to form a character assessment.

She failed to join me for breakfast on the very first morning and this aroused my concern instantly. I tried to convince myself that the reason was jet lag, mainly because I can't lie to others with any sort of conviction unless I've thoroughly rehearsed what I'm going to say. Sure enough, that was met with sceptical enquiry however, I still think that the holiday may have been salvageable had Hayley not repeated the act for three consecutive days. By then, she'd informed me of her intention to 'throw the rulebook out of the window', which wouldn't have been so bad except she'd fallen somewhat short of the full truth there. It was instead her intention to attach a rocket launch to the spine of said rulebook and send it flying into orbit. Diplomatic pleas from the group leaders fell on deaf ears as she flat out refused to offer any sort of assistance on the farm and attended afternoon classes with a frequency that depended on her mood. When this provoked the expected level of irritation from all else present, Hayley responded by challenging them to expel her from the island. Half an hour later, we were bundled on to the same boat that had brought us in and off we went.

Hayley considered this quite the accomplishment (and in a way I suppose it was) although she felt they were 'a little rude about it.' We disembarked and the scribbled list of objectives I'd made on the eve of the holiday burned a hole in my pocket as I stood watching the boat sail back off into the distance. As we dragged our luggage across a deserted landscape, Hayley placed a consoling arm around my shoulder and reassured me that all my expectations would still be met somehow. I knew instantly that this was designed to placate me.

If the signs had been ominous just three days earlier, then it was nothing when compared with what was to come, as the holiday descended into a haze of chaos and debauchery. Not long off the boat, we hitched a ride with a flatulent man who leered at Hayley and petted my knee throughout an arduous and uncomfortable journey. With no intended destination, we escaped at the first sign of civilization and with our finances already dwindling, necessity forced our hand. At best, one could describe the resort in which we stayed as functional and unpretentious, at worst (and perhaps more honestly), it was plain rotten. The taps didn't always run, there were damp patches on the ceiling and the bathroom floor was so sticky that we couldn't remain in a standing position for too long a time for fear of gluey entrapment. This was made all the worse by the vista that presented itself from our window, a dirt-ridden building site full of cranes, cement and flabby builders screaming at each other in a foreign tongue. It seemed hellish but it was all we could afford.

On reflection, I probably saw more of Hayley when she conducted her three-day bedroom protest on the secluded island than I did here. I lost her for five successive nights only for her to reappear the following lunchtime (almost to the very same second) looking pale and confused and asking if I'd seen her stilettoes anywhere. She was comatose in the afternoons and only came alive of an evening when the turnaround was so striking, it seemed as if she drew strength from the rays of the moon. The days began to drag with nothing but my own company and the combination of bustling builders and stifling heat meant I was up and awake far earlier then I really should've been.

She did, however, break routine for the first time this morning by returning to her bed three hours before dawn. She couldn't have slept for more than a couple of hours but when she roused, she looked transformed beyond all recognition and appeared something close to glowing. When I asked how this was possible, she relayed the story of how she'd met the man of her dreams while regurgitating into her own handbag and asked if I would be so kind as to vacate the room later in the evening so that she could 'get to know him a little better.' I didn't have the energy to offer any protest (preferring to sleep instead) and hours later, when I finally left her to it, I departed to a rather excited version of Hayley screaming and whooping from the balcony. She had been reacquainted with her stilettoes.

How chance would have it that on the last night of my holiday, Ricky had finally accepted my Congrelate friend request while I lay waiting for inadequate sex in the bed of another. I had sent the request moments before the plane had taken off on the assumption that I wouldn't have time to think about it once engaged in the pursuit of spiritual enlightenment but think about it I had to the tune of seventeen notification checks a day (what I deemed to be a sketchy estimation). At first, I'd reasoned his rejection away as it wasn't impossible that he might think that Simon and I were still together but even if that were true, it hadn't bothered him a great deal in the relations we'd shared up to now, at least not enough to ever prompt him to make such an enquiry.

Just two weeks prior to today, my Congrelate profile contained thirty-five photographs with my being present on a mere twenty-one of them (yes, I had checked). Yet, in the time it had taken to be escorted off an island and into the most putrid of lodgings, my photograph count had now multiplied into a staggering seventy-eight! When Ricky was ignoring me I hadn't much cared for this as I could easily delete the least flattering of the collection at my leisure but once I knew that he had instant access to these, the terror consumed me. Indeed, some of these pictures were so unpleasant that I struggled to accept their validity and it struck me that only the most hideous of the holiday set had survived the cut. What had happened to the shot Hayley had taken of me with my sunglasses balanced on the end of my nose, stirring a cocktail while looking peaceful and pensive? It was the best of a bad bunch mainly because I didn't know that she was taking it and I was in the shot alone rather than deferring to her comparative beauty. All I had as a result were countless pictures of my looking bloated and sunburned whilst being cradled by lecherous men with asinine expressions. I cursed myself for not deleting all of these photographs sooner but I hadn't done so because I wanted everyone back home to believe that I was having a great time (even if I wasn't particularly). In the end, I found myself lying in the bed of another, frantically de-tagging myself from just about every one of them and praying that Ricky hadn't seen them as an imbecile muttered inconsequential nothings from his bathroom.

"I like to play dress up," is what he'd said to me just two hours earlier by way of introduction and I had to confess, I'd never heard such a preamble before. This, I felt, can never bode well unless you're really into that sort of thing and I wanted to know if this was a line he was prone to using or whether I was unintentionally emitting signs of sordid sexual tendencies. He took me to a bar that he claimed ownership of but nobody seemed to view him with any semblance of recognition, much less talk to him with the sort of reverence one usually does their boss. His flatteries soon became clichéd and no doubt entirely fictitious, so I quickly judged him to be a fool and had to warn him against the prospect of losing my interest entirely. My ultimatum was ignored and he mistook my disregard for keen captivation, disclosing with wild satisfaction how he'd previously slept with something close to three hundred women. Such detail (undoubtedly false) had been devised to impress me but I couldn't think of how he felt that this was ever likely to lure someone or if it ever had before. Women, I explained, would only ever say such a thing in the hope of repelling a man and even then we'd only see it as the last resort, doing so without taking any pride in it. He was as indifferent to that revelation as I'd expected him to be but it baffles me to think of such a clear disparity on this between the sexes, more so when the intended outcome is always much the same.

I took the considered decision to stop listening to him once we were back at his apartment principally because I knew the more he talked, the more likely I was to come to my senses and so I'd looked on tolerantly while he opened two cupboards' worth of pornography and garish sex aids. I wanted to feel something, be it alarm or apprehension but such feelings were not forthcoming, instead, I felt something close to pity and the plot seemed too far developed to simply extricate myself. He strolled back into the bathroom and only then did I shake myself from my lethargy on reaching for my phone and had discovered the full extent of my photographic oversight via social media.

I started to think of what my best friend Claire would do in the same situation. She was famed for her number of carnal liaisons and though I didn't exactly admire her for this, she did have a tendency to come out of them with her pride and sense of self-respect intact. This wouldn't faze her (not a lot did) but it's difficult to really shock someone who sees recklessness as a healthy pastime and seldom considers her own imperfections. Perhaps she never thinks of the worst-case scenario whereas I often do, erring on the side of caution and thinking ill of most people I meet. I couldn't answer logically as to why I'd gone against my usual code of conduct in this instance but sensed instinctively that the outcome would be ruinous and I tried in vain to recall the moment when any of it had seemed like a good idea.

When he finally emerged from the bathroom, I stared at him incredulously thinking that my eyes must have been deceiving me. Standing before me was a fully grown man dressed from head to toe in a costume designed to replicate a female octogenarian. From the wavy grey wig to the large ringed spectacles and the flowery blouse to the ankle-length skirt, he was simply unrecognisable but for his alcohol-induced, raspy voice. A deep red lipstick coated the bridge of his upper lip unevenly, the result no doubt of a hasty application and he edged towards me in a wholly contrived, shuffling gait. He was the epitome of calm without evident inhibition or trepidation and my mood sank towards revulsion as his words of introduction came flooding back to me.

"They were my grandmother's," he said, as if expecting an intelligible response. I could faintly make out that he was grinning lasciviously or at least I thought so as he nodded towards a similar-looking outfit hanging above the cupboard door. I observed this with the same horror which I did him and wished to make it clear that in no way did I intend to array myself in such a costume and that the chances of sexual activity had been reduced to zero.

"They *were* your grandmother's clothes?" I asked rather pointlessly, as if learning of her death was likely to improve my predicament.

"Were," he replied assuredly, "definitely were."

As I strongly suspected, that hadn't consoled me and a chilled breeze licked at my face with an ominous appeal. I looked towards the balcony sensing that I was approximately four floors above the ground and considered the possibility of jumping.

2

SIMON

It is on the sixth attempt of calling that I relent and finally decide to answer the phone.

"I believe you're in possession of some property that belongs to a friend of mine," says the voice that greets me which is male, privileged and short of the authority that one really needs in a situation such as this. Why he felt the need to discard of the necessary introductions I can perhaps overlook but not the tone in which he said it and so I'm left with little choice but to take an instant dislike to him.

"Well I'd like to talk with *her* or *him* in person if I may? Or to put it more simply, not you." He wasn't to know just how much I'd enjoyed saying that just like he wasn't to understand the restraint I'd exercised in not asking for Vanessa directly even though her identity (and much more besides that) is already well known to me.

"Who am I speaking to?"

"You're speaking to Simon," I reply, for I have no reason to conceal this detail, "and seeing as you won't allow me to speak to your friend, would you perhaps care to introduce yourself?" An elongated pause suggests there's some difficulty in answering this question even though I know his name to be Sebastian from the incoming call screen. A muffled discourse then erupts between the two of them somewhere in the background which quickly develops into a jostling contest, the result of which sees Sebastian relegated to the periphery, and quite frankly, not before time.

"Listen, er, hi, this is Vanessa and the phone in your hand belongs to me and I'd really be very grateful if we could work some way out of your returning it to me." Her accent is much changed from the one that I had struggled to place on the car journey earlier (not that she had said very much) and gone was the steady cadence that had been so distinctive, now replaced by a drawl that seemed much less assured.

"It's not a problem," I say, before pausing for a lengthy intake of my Dry Manhattan, the third I have imbibed this hour. "I mean, what I'm trying to say is I'm sure that we can work something out." She isn't quick to respond and probably detects something vaguely sinister in this last remark but the worry of this does not compel me to elaborate any further.

"Well, would you be able to meet me in a neutral venue somewhere maybe?" She asks, as her voice gently inclines towards the end of the sentence in a style I find endearing. "You are staying in halls too, right? The clock tower at the centre of campus is probably the best spot."

So she didn't remember me or maybe more to the point, she didn't remember where she'd lost the phone. Ironically, on a clear day, I can often make out the clock tower to which she was referring from the balcony of my urban apartment. Bleak and unspectacular, it is connected to a world that I had long ago left, one of youth and near penury, ideals and error, certainly a distant cry from the life I now enjoyed (if indeed you could label it so). Her mistake is of course amusing but it's a deception that I see no need to prolong.

"Listen, Vanessa, I'm not a student so that's just not convenient for me. Try thinking of somewhere else and I'll see if I can make it."

More hesitancy is followed by a poorly concealed dispatch back to Sebastian whose influence on proceedings remains entirely unnecessary. I return my attention to the whisky cocktail in hand which now offers nothing more than the icy residue at the foot of the glass that I soon empty into my mouth. Full replenishment, I decide, can wait a little longer.

"Do you know the Plough and Trinket?" She begins, sounding if anything a little miffed. "I'm usually in there from around six-thirty every Friday." I confirm that I do (albeit only vaguely) and that diary permitting, I may just be able to make it. For this, I am thanked effusively and so I neglect to mention how I hadn't offered an absolute guarantee and just submit to her assumption. "Thank you so much, er..."

"Simon," I interpose, as duly prompted.

"Ah yes, Simon, well I'll try and grab a seat near to the door. You'll know what I look like from the photograph on my lock screen, it's a fairly recent one so you'll have no trouble recognising me." Ironically enough, I had already trawled through just about every photograph that I could find of her so I really wouldn't doubt my powers of recognition come the time of meeting.

At this point, the climax of the call feels close at hand but Vanessa isn't finished and so I'm left with little choice but to further humour her.

"So where was it that you found my phone Simon? I mean, if you're not a student then I couldn't have left it somewhere around campus like I thought I did." Her accent is now subtly reverting to its more natural form, a sign that suggests any initial apprehension is starting to ease and, perhaps more so, that she is free from inebriation.

"It was in the car," I reveal, "on the backseat."

"*Oh the taxi,*" she exclaims, like one finding the simple explanation to a long sought problem. "I guess I must have left it behind when I got out, were you the driver?" I lie and tell her that I wasn't. "Well I'm lucky that it fell into your hands then. There was something pretty eerie about that driver although I couldn't put my finger on it at the time and I think I was in a rush to get out of the car. It's all my own fault though, I really shouldn't drink so much."

The ice in my mouth dissolves into a watery slush, numbing both my teeth and tongue to a temporary paralysis.

It saves me from saying too much before I hang up the phone because I really don't want to address her lack of gratitude and pitiful recollection. This same ingratitude was notably absent just hours earlier when I picked her up about a hundred yards south of the high street, alone and unsteady, entering my unmarked car following a series of lengthy discussions with a line of vacant taxis parked up ahead of me. Back then, she didn't seem quite so concerned about my driving credentials and probably sided with the balance of probability when measuring the risk of encountering a nocturnal serial killer against the bonus of a reasonable fare. Perhaps she deserved it or perhaps I really should've drawn her attention toward the flashing mobile phone left behind on the backseat (it was still live) while she remained within earshot but something instinctual prevented me from doing so. Maybe it was the fact that she didn't really say much and I resented how my attempts at conversation fell flat every time despite my questions falling some way short of intrusive. It was difficult to say because things like that shouldn't really irk me (even though they did) but even so, I wasn't about to exit the car chasing after her for the reward of minimal acknowledgement. Besides, the phone in my possession was likely to reveal far more about her character than what she'd been willing to disclose and so I scrupled very little about driving off with it.

Her youth struck me from the moment I set eyes on her (she is around nineteen or twenty years old) springing up from her seated position at the foot of the Council House steps where she was temporarily stationed following her failure to grab a proper taxi. Drunk? Yes, but not excessively so and although her accent was incongruous and intriguing, it was nonetheless clear and comprehensible. She didn't know the city well so I took a circuitous route back to her abode, tentatively taking lefts instead of rights and occasionally doubling back on myself when the mood suited. When I eventually arrived at her requested destination, pulling in to the sparse forecourt of a halls of residence, I recognised the sense of envy that I often felt around the youthful demographic and instantly felt out of place. If she left me a tip then I wasn't to know, for I didn't bother counting the beer-stained coinage that she tossed into my hand and the campus was already out of sight before the phone presented itself, flashing wildly in my rear view mirror.

The accident that followed just mere moments later was entirely my own fault and a better man would've faced the recipient of such carelessness sporting some degree of visible contrition, but that really wasn't me. It was a combination of factors that distracted my attention away from the stationery vehicle ahead of me and before I could recover, I had failed to brake sufficiently at a red light. The collision had been far from cataclysmic but was still enough to leave a small but clear indentation to the rear bumper of the car in front and was certainly enough to suggest that its rectification would be reliant on an expert's touch. When the lights turned to green, I met the frantic gesturing of an irate driver with a self-admonishing wave of the hand and tracked his progress to the side of the road with a submissive indication. Life teaches you that situations such as this cannot end well and usually engender either violent reproach or monetary loss and so after speedy deliberation, and once the traffic in my wake had cleared, I pulled away with haste and didn't dare look back.

My judgement had very likely been impaired by two things in particular, one being the several beers I had shared after work with my colleague Agatha, the other being the mobile phone that Vanessa had unwittingly donated to me, the discovery of which had coincided with the approaching traffic lights. Sure, I'd taken my eyes off the road and could've reacted quicker but try explaining that to someone with the lingering stench of alcohol on your breath and note their reaction, chances are you won't be met with sympathy. Still, I hadn't left the collision entirely unscathed as a fine abrasion beneath the groove of the headlight now served to remind me. It was only around two inches long and arguably invisible to the untrained eye but after several rigorous inspections, I still could not be sure that Kim wouldn't notice. It was her car after all and just a matter of months old and when you're only allowed to use something in the case of an emergency, well you really should take the utmost care. My insurance would only stretch so far and if the truth be told, this wasn't the first time that I'd had such an accident, particularly while driving under the influence.

I like to blame my many bouts of recidivism at the wheel on anything other than the truth, which is that I drink too much and drive too poorly. Living in an apartment that is nothing more than a fifteen-minute walk from my place of work brings with it many advantages but the lack of a daily commute means my driving skills are now more than a little rusty and unlikely to improve under the influence of alcohol. The proximity of my apartment also relieves me of the 'should I, shouldn't I' dilemma of a Friday evening where I observe people falling out of wine bars at eight o'clock, stumbling back to the multi-storey car park and praying that sobriety will meet them at their cars. Agatha is the only colleague that I choose to spend time with outside of work but she's much older me and has a husband to go back home to so my evenings tend to end when hers do by default. Too often, I reluctantly head home to the loneliness of the flat with a restlessness for company that is fast becoming habitual but recently, an act of spontaneity changed things altogether.

It was late one evening around two months ago when I decided to counter the inertia by gathering the car keys and heading out into the city, desperately in search of the excitement I felt for certain I was missing. I wanted to discover a nocturnal aspect of the city that housed me through the daytime, the side I didn't see but often read about and then cruise between the roots of the silhouetted skyline. It didn't take long to realise that I had stumbled upon the town in its most intriguing aspect where the details of the

14

scene were ever-changing and positively unwelcoming. The flickering lights of fast-food restaurants, the loitering gangs, the discarded bottles of beer, the small rivers of flowing urine, a landscape littered with flyers and food wrappings. Everywhere about me there seemed to be a complete abandonment of formality while people zigzagged in and out of moving traffic, took wrong turns down ill-lit alleyways and lost souls sought the sweaty grip of another, clinging to the hope of prospective carnal fulfilment. The menace that permeates this scene is stronger for the fact that you never actually see the violence, though you know it's there, like an undercurrent of imminent attack or a series of sinister algorithms masquerading as a truce. Without question, if I could paint a panorama then this would be it.

Before long, I found myself repeating this twilight excursion on a regular basis like some illicit addiction. Often, I would wait for the light in Kim's room to fade and then stealthily exit the apartment to return to my nightly adventure with the aid of her vehicle. In this alternative reality, intoxicated pedestrians became confiders, mistaking my car for that of a working taxi, and I would regularly collect up to five or six passengers a night. It was a strangely lucrative experience even though I seldom profited, choosing instead to donate my earnings to the homeless guy asleep at the parking bay gates of Gaddis Avenue (the complex where I live) whenever I returned. The money wasn't really a factor for me, it was the company that I craved and I profited from the insights that this host of characters bestowed on me. For reasons I could not understand, my back seat became their throne of confession, a moral soapbox or a sounding board for the boastful and vain. They sought my counsel on a range of different subjects from marital reconcilement to career advancement and worryingly enough, they seemed to take my unqualified opinions and mistake them for the words of one who understood. I avoided large groups for obvious reasons but it was the solitary pickups that I found the most unsettling, like the lonesome wanderer who would inevitably slip into the car at around three o'clock in the morning, fidgety, guarded and largely unresponsive.

A chill begins to set in which forces me away from the balcony and back into the kitchen where I seek out further replenishment. I'd been sifting through the contents of this phone for around an hour now, trying to join the dots together of another person's life but without much success. It is possible that in between the litany of banal photographs, academic emails and flirtatious text messages from our friend Sebastian, that there really is nothing more to discover about Vanessa than the patently obvious. It is also possible that of all the characters fortune could've placed in my path tonight, I have found one without any secrets to protect or scandal to withhold and for this I feel greatly chagrined. But it really is amazing to think how this electrical block of circuits and unfathomable science seems to hold the key to the inner fabric of our lives and our personal identities. These tiny machines which we sleep beside at night and carry about our person like a necessary limb enrich our alter-egos, encourage duplicity and bury our intellect underneath emojis and illiterate text. And yet in spite of this, we'll happily peruse their content when on buses and trains, in workplaces and waiting rooms, seemingly relaxed about the priers and the inquisitives. We tell ourselves that nobody is really interested in the details of our lives even though we like to gaze over the shoulder of another at every opportunity, worryingly complacent, as if we are somehow exempt from the very same intrusion. When you take all of the above into account and yet still, at the height of carelessness, you drink so much that you forgetfully leave it on the back seat of a stranger's car, the best that you can hope for is that it doesn't fall in to the wrong hands. In most cases of course, it is destined to.

3

KIM

Doctor Block seems unsuited to his surname in just about
every way I'd imagined. There is really nothing cold or
detached about him and as far as one could judge from a series
of succinct emails, I had clearly been way off the mark. The
stubble beneath his chin makes a harsh, abrasive sound when
he studiously scratches it and small, wispy grey hairs peep
out from the space between his right sock and trouser hem.
So far, he'd asked the questions that I'd expected of him, yes,
the clinic really was a rather impressive establishment and
the staff that they employed were very friendly (even though
I'd expected nothing less for the five thousand pounds that I'd
invested already). The tour of the building seemed elongated,
where worryingly inactive nurses offered smiling platitudes
and feedback from the patients seemed less authentic than
the actors on their website. Still, it was salubrious and just a
twenty-minute drive from my apartment, factors that I didn't
dare discount.

Doctor Block, middle-aged and no doubt liberal, looks
faintly bemused by my personal confidence but not unsettled
by it. I explained that this was near enough my second time
and that the pertinent details were still largely fixed in my
mind but I got the impression that I was veering off script.
I was curious to learn about his family and wanted to know
how many children he had, how healthy they were and what
sort of a mother was his wife.

"Three, very and excellent," he replies rather reticently

to me, but there are no family portraits to be seen adorning the walls of his office. "I guess it would just seem a little *insensitive* in the circumstances," he says and then reluctantly hands over a picture previously secreted in a drawer.

"They're really very beautiful," I concede, before the picture is swiftly retrieved.

Two days since returning from holiday and still dehydrated, I accept the green tea offered by his assistant who breezes in and out of his office in a swift, perfumed haze. It is also interesting to note that I am still, somewhat inexplicably, finding sand about my person which included a few stray grains now residing between the toes of my right foot. I resist the urge to take my shoes off.

"What I need to ascertain at this stage Kimberley, is why exactly you are here and I mean for us to go beyond the obvious. This is not a clinic that works to time constraints, budgets or reputations, we are here to change lives and the enormity of what we do for our patients is never lost on us."

I wrack my brain for something suitable to say, wary of sounding trite but I have little to offer other than the truth.

"I am here because I am desperate to become a mother and my life will never feel complete until that happens."

To this reply he simply nods, unmoved, undaunted and impassive.

"IVF can be an exhausting process, one that doesn't always produce the desired results. But what I can say is that for someone your age and of your state of health is that the success rate is really quite high."

"It's just over thirty-two per cent to be exact Doctor," I interject assuredly and the nettled glance that he fires my way above the rim of his glasses somehow suggests that further interruptions will not be appreciated.

"Indeed, well, what I really want to know is how you arrived at this point and please do take your time, there are no details that we deem *irrelevant* no matter how trivial they may seem." He couldn't help but elongate the word 'seem' as it coincided with a lengthy stretch made towards a notebook and pen that is just about within arm's reach.

It was difficult to know where to start really as there seemed to be no obvious beginning. It was around three years ago that my ex-boyfriend (Simon) and I decided that we would try for a baby. On reflection, I accept that the timing could've been better with my father fast entering what was to be the latter stage of his life and my love for Simon having been long since extinguished. The prospect of motherhood and new life would, I hoped, help me to deal with my impending grief and ignite what was a dwindling relationship by bringing purpose to all that had become mundane. While these motives were undoubtedly hollow, borne from a fear which I was yet to define, my yearning to become a mother only seemed to grow and as it did, Simon and I drew closer together. Banished now were the jealousies, animosities and old habits that had irked us before, as we embarked upon this adventure, destined for parenthood, with an impetus and a happiness that I had long thought impossible.

They were brief but halcyon days. After twelve months without success, my complacency was interrupted by a visit to a local GP who excelled in ominous pauses and unwilling analysis. There was nothing to worry about, we were assured but further examination would be necessary and an appointment was made with a Fertility Specialist. The tests that followed felt unnatural and degrading and were matched only in their unpleasantness by the questions that accompanied them. Selfish though it sounds, I prayed that Simon was the problem because of all the worst-case scenarios that they could theorise, defects on his side were easier to surmount. I tried to stay positive and to believe in the empty reassurances that were gently passed my way on the back of every test that couldn't yield an immediate result but a gloomy intuition was starting to envelop me. Just days later, these fears were substantiated when the specialist informed me that I was infertile. I was twenty-seven years old. Just days after this bombshell, my father died.

It is of course, considered perfectly normal to question the validity of such results (which I did) and to seek further opinion to consolidate what you dispute (which I did not) when faced with this reality. Even then I realised that it was not the truth of their findings that I doubted but more the injustice of it all that I could not accept. Why had this happened to me and how had I managed to live in ignorance of this condition for so long? There was no history of infertility in my family as far back as I could research and so there had to be a reason far greater than genetics to account for the misfortune.

Blockages were found in both of my fallopian tubes which made it near impossible for me to conceive naturally. Diagrams were thrust at me and pointers extended, all of which did nothing but complicate simplicity, for the science was really quite clear. These blockages were a biological wall barring the sperm on its route to the egg and consequently, ending all chance of fertilization. That this cause of infertility was 'more prevalent than one would think' meant absolutely nothing to me, I felt barren and worthless, a disgrace to womanhood, I was the point at which the circle of life ended with an abrupt halt. What was the value of my achievements in this world when I had failed at the one job my sex was naturally programmed to do? All that lay ahead of me was empty consolation and uncomfortable sympathy from friends who recalled that one distant relative that had defied medical science and conceived against the odds. But they would never understand how I felt because I never dared express it and though I hoped that time would pacify the anger, I really couldn't envisage it doing so. When the realisation kicked in, I turned to Simon for support but all I could see was a palpable relief etched upon his face. To this day, I've never quite known whether that relief stemmed from his unwillingness to actually become a father or if it was simply that the humiliation would now belong to me alone.

One would like to think that the examinations would cease at this point, allowing the barren female time to grieve, but they didn't. Instead, more questions ensued about my sexual history and then about Simon's, which did nothing but promote a festering suspicion between us. It was often the case that a sexually transmitted disease could be the root of the issue (I was informed), lying symptomless within the uterus but once I was found to be free of this, the specialist seemed a little baffled. When he asked after my medical history, I indulged his request without much thought and here he felt that he had finally discovered the cause of my infertility. I had suffered from appendicitis as a teenager which he speculated may well have caused inflammation in the pelvic cavity. This would mean that I had been infertile from the age of fourteen. This diagnosis seemed to pacify his ruminations whereas all I wanted to do was curse this useless scrap of my anatomy, a relic of evolution that had denied me the one thing I had wanted more than anything else in my life.

We discussed alternative options. Surgery seemed unsafe and unpredictable and so I wasn't really very keen on that. Simon, on the other hand, expressed a preference for conceiving naturally, arguing that although the chances of success remained slight, it still wasn't impossible and time remained on our side. I could not share his unwarranted optimism though and it was then that I turned to IVF, judging this to be the safest and most reliable option available.

In spite of my renewed optimism, Simon refused to be convinced and opted to collude with the specialist by focusing on every negative that he could find. Talk of ectopic pregnancies, multiple births and irreversible defects dominated his thinking as he fast became blinded to reason and ignorant of my wishes. While I grieved the loss of my father, my will seemed to die with him and the idea of IVF was abandoned. Just one year later, Simon and I were no more.

The yearning doesn't dissipate of course, if anything, it just grew stronger and before long it started to consume me. I eyed all mothers with new-born babies ruefully, going as far as to invent phantom children of my own to the point where no shopping trip would be complete without filling my bags with toys and accessories. I attended coffee mornings where I exchanged false photographs with 'fellow' mothers of babies I'd never met and regaled them with tales of the joys of motherhood. Beyond that, I also started to view the men that I met with a completely different focus. Did they seem paternal? Would they find my condition off-putting? Could their manhood survive the ignominy of masturbating into a tube? Perhaps all of the above sounds a little disconcerting but the truth is that it was none of these things, I was just grieving. The reality was that I had shared twelve years of my life with Simon and I really couldn't afford to wait that long again.

My best friend Claire came to the rescue. She steered my attention towards a fertility forum where women from all over the world shared their personal experiences with eye-opening candour. Here, I learned that IVF treatment was not only available for married women in stable relationships but to women in many different stages of their lives and personal circumstances. Perhaps most pertinently, a host of singletons extolled the benefits of IVF, recounting their stories effusively, their profiles full of pictures of bouncing, healthy babies, their decisions ratified and made without regret. It was clear that I could do this alone, and if I had the money available, I could circumvent the system and pay for the treatment at a private fertility clinic. The figures didn't seem important, regardless of my means and so I found myself here, revealing all to Doctor Block who didn't seem all that enlightened for the length of my response. Well, he hadn't asked for concision and so I hadn't offered it.

"I don't wish to sound intrusive," he continues, while pushing a hand through an imaginary tuft of hair, "but I notice that you are only twenty-nine years of age and you have opted for third-party sperm donation?" I verify this preluding question with a gentle nod of the head. He readjusts his seating position and then renews his line of discourse. "This clinic aims to assist the needs of our patients whatever they may be but sometimes in doing this, a different route becomes available, one that is perhaps not immediately visible. Well, it's our duty to direct you on that journey and we will do this as painlessly as we are able to do." I begin to sense digression and so I instigate a return to relevance with silent assent. The sand between my toes is beginning to take on an uncomfortable, burning sensation. "What I'm trying to say is that you are still *very young* and in fertility terms you are at an excellent age. We can offer a facility that will freeze your eggs for up to ten years and in that time, conditions may become more favourable towards you having children with a partner who shares your desire to start a family."

"But if one is hungry at breakfast time then why wait until lunch?" I respond, but the analogy doesn't move him and I instantly regret it. "I own a house, a car and my work is lucrative. My body and mind are telling me that now is the right time and I won't allow a possible change of circumstances, years down the line to dilute this sense of certainty." The fact that I part-owned an apartment with my estranged ex-boyfriend (who for the record knows nothing about any of this) is a detail I don't deem necessary to include nor do I admit that my current job is far short of well-paid. Doctor Block can remain in ignorance about some things, I decide, despite his best efforts.

"And you are comfortable in the knowledge that your child will grow up without any idea as to their father's identity? Rest assured that we vet our donors rigorously, of course, but it is something that we ask our patients to carefully consider before we can proceed."

This I felt to be a redundant question. Of course I wasn't comfortable with this but then I really didn't have a choice. Sure, there were men in my life that I had contemplated asking but the quandary seemed to lie in deciding what I really wanted from them. Did I want them purely for genetics or for good character? Would I be happy for them to play an active role in the child's life or would I encourage distance? Even if I opted for the latter, what recourse would I have to stop them from entering the life of my son or daughter if they really wanted to? Babies could often turn a distant father into a doting one, I'd seen it happen and I couldn't take that risk. The fertility forum was engulfed with accounts of this very same subject, mothers told tales of having sought legal agreements with their chosen donor prior to the conclusion of their treatment while others regretted not having done so. It was a minefield it seemed and a costly one at that.

Doctor Block's apparent dissuasiveness was beginning to irk me somewhat and I couldn't understand this position he'd taken as if testing my resolve. How would he, a middle-aged man in pea-green trousers, know what was best for me and why would he even care? Surely the clinic was here primarily to make money and whether they did so morally or immorally really didn't make a jot of difference once the patient was out the door.

"None of this is ideal Doctor," I begin, "but I'm aware that my child would be legally entitled to contact their biological father at the age of eighteen and no sooner. I know of many people who've been raised without the presence of a father and they have matured into fine people, certainly none the worse for the experience." I smile back at him smugly. Though the first part of my statement was true, the second part was pure fabrication as I knew of few people that had been raised in such an environment. Depending on the popularity of my donor, my child, at the turn of adulthood, could soon discover an extended family of half-siblings dotted about the world and this would be something towards which I would be able to provide little empathy. Whether they would be mature or indeed broadminded enough to understand my reasons for bringing them into this world in such a manner I really couldn't predict but it would be cowardly of me to hide behind this fear and then deny a child the love that I had to give.

"Quite so," he returns, while prodding away forcefully at his notebook with the nib of his pen. I notice that he has written literally nothing down. "Now I need to come on to some of the formalities, if I may and do forgive my candour but have you considered the risks that attach themselves to the process of IVF?"

"Well I've read all the horror stories just like everybody else and I haven't found anything worthy of deterring me." My answer seems to cause a momentary unease in him, evidenced in the way he shuffles closer to me and then furrows his brow.

"Yes, I'm sure you have and it's good to do so but it's an insistence of mine to consult with the patient at the earliest possible stage about the form of embryo transfer that they wish to pursue. We, as a clinic, offer both SET and MET as an option, but the choice is ultimately yours. Now, have you any thoughts, preferences or questions on this?"

To translate that into layman's terms, Doctor Block was simply asking me how many embryos I wished to have inserted into my womb once they had been successfully fertilised by a donor's sperm. SET was Single Embryo Transfer, which was the more popular choice for women under the age of thirty-five when they are generally considered to be healthier and more likely to produce better embryos. The advantages of this were very clear, by implanting just one embryo, the risk of multiple foetuses was significantly lower, as was the risk of premature birth and long-lasting health issues for both mother and baby. But some aspiring mothers feel that pinning their hopes on just one, lonely embryo diminishes their chances of falling pregnant and instead opt for MET, Multiple Embryo Transfer. Although the process mirrors that of SET almost exactly, MET inserts two or three embryos (sometimes more) into the womb with the express idea that implanting more embryos increases the chances of successful pregnancy. Despite the mathematical advantages being relatively simple, some experts argue against this method for the reasons listed above and that the reality of mothering two or three babies, as opposed to just one, is a task unsuited to a first-time mother.

I'd studied the arguments for both but even after consulting the forum it remained difficult to resolve on a conclusive answer. Everybody had a tale to tell but on a platform that was designed to support and console, it seemed that nobody was willing to make judgements on others, which was morally fine but personally problematic. For a long time I felt unsure about which option I would select. I started to err towards MET, thinking that I'd play the numbers game (so to speak) but when I thought about it further, I couldn't help but focus on the horror stories that Simon had once referred to. Images of children with deformities, stillbirths, babies born horrifically underweight and the thought of spending the first year of parenthood in a hospital ward looking on helplessly at a sick baby plagued my mind. I wrestled with these hypothetical scenarios but soon accepted that to defy all of the evidence placed before me and opt for MET would be done in defiance of Simon, which would not only be reckless but incredibly selfish. The stark reality was that although I longed for a child, I was also realistic enough to know that I could not afford a litter and the idea of bringing up twins on my own was far from appealing. Logistically, it was impossible, financially even more so and I didn't see the point in offering two or three children a hindered start in life when I could offer an only child the best of my time, energy and resources.

I feel the warm hand of Doctor Block on my own which breaks my line of thought and although it should feel creepy, oddly, it doesn't.

"This is not a decision that you have to make now necessarily," he says in a slow tone that I'd describe as sympathetic.

"No it's okay," I say resolutely, "my mind's been made on this for some time. I want to choose SET. It's the safest and I believe most sensible option."

He gazes back at me, looking vaguely satisfied like I'd just managed to successfully remember his birthday.

"We'll have to check the quality of embryos at the transfer stage and if need be we won't hesitate to transfer more but that decision will be yours." And with that, for the first time today, he actually appears to write something down before inputting further details onto a small computer located on the other side of his office. "And what about your family," he resumes, while still typing away, "what do they make of your decision to pursue IVF? Are they supportive of you?"

Finally, a question that I really wasn't prepared for and I try to conceal my hesitancy. Just how was I to explain that my mother's rather vocal opposition to IVF extended back to the time that Simon and I had come so close to applying? IVF wasn't natural, she had argued and was against the will of God, which seemed difficult to comprehend coming from a woman who had only embraced religion in her retirement. Yes, my mother, whose ecclesiastical studies ranked the politics of the church choir above the scrutiny of the good book, remained steadfast in her hostility towards the idea which meant that above all things, asking for financial help was really out of the question.

"They're delighted," I say, "in fact, they really couldn't be happier for me."

"That's wonderful to hear," he replies, before addressing 'the elephant in the room' and alerting me to some additional payments that perhaps weren't made clear enough in the promotional material. I adopt my poker face and then, when he leaves the office to make copies of some documentation, I subtly remove a shoe and dispense of the sand entrapped between my toes into the nearest bin.

4

SIMON

I am late and unprepared for what had been a rather hastily arranged team meeting and although my tardiness is now generally accepted as customary, it doesn't necessarily excuse it. When you do this sort of thing with the regularity that I do then excuses become redundant and so expectant are they of my belated arrival that all points relating to me have now been consigned to the lower order of priority. Fortunately, as Team Leader, your reasons need not be investigated and as Agatha slides over a copy of the agenda (which of course I do not have) along with a glass of water and an aspirin, I start to feel something close to prepared.

The truth is that I don't like Simon Trice, Learning & Development Team Leader a great deal and do not value the title in the way that I probably should. He's professional, no doubt but prone to nonconformity and I talk about him in the third person sometimes because quite often that's just how it feels. I work for Tanner & Webbing, a conglomerate that specialises in business process outsourcing, offering a wealth of professional services to a range of different companies depending on their business needs. In plain speaking, we secure work by highlighting the areas in which our clients are either too incompetent, too cheap or just too lazy to do themselves. In managing the Learning & Development Team, I am charged with the responsibility of looking after the training needs on behalf of those clients.

The nature of our success is really very simple, we

thrive on the failure of others because that's how we gain our business and when you toss the empty rhetoric to one side, you'll soon see how the dichotomies are hidden in the detail. We put people *first* yet our trade is secured by putting thousands of others out of work. Our employees *matter* but not enough for the top brass to heat the office properly and save us from shivering at our desks in the winter months. We support *growth* but stifle the little man, we believe in *frugality* just so long as that excepts a lavish Christmas party or two at the end of every year. It's not that these things matter of course, nor are they critiques exclusive to us alone but the constant projection of a myth is easily wearying when the outside world does not care for such pretence.

Truthfully speaking, the job does not engage me and I've never professed anything to the contrary. My greatest source of puzzlement comes in trying to understand just how I've managed to attain the level of success that I have rather than actually celebrate the fact. Having joined the company on a temporary basis seven years ago, the powers-that-be mistook my habitual disinterest for a humble ambition. This indifference has gained me an assumed position of neutrality regarding all office matters and as I've taken great care not to build any personal alliances, naturally, I've forged no enemies either. My acceleration up the career ladder has come about as a result of this detachment and mostly at the expense of others who are far better qualified than I am. The hierarchy at Tanner & Webbing isn't interested in forward thinkers and eager underlings who challenge their longstanding practices and once this became clear to me, subsequent promotions just fell into my hands. I don't bemoan this success of course, for I have climbed the ranks relatively willingly but the resentment amongst those I have seemingly displaced is clearly palpable and as a result, friendships at work have been nigh on impossible to make.

Agatha, my Team Secretary, does not fall into that category and is (at least to me) one of life's dearest treasures.

For seven years now, she has mothered me ceaselessly on a daily basis while I've offered little resistance and pretended it is something that I simply endure. Efficient though she is in her role, there are far greater qualities of which she can boast and the warmth that exudes from her person is borderline infectious. The comfort of her middle age seems to personify itself by the ease in which she sidesteps all of those around her, their ill-motives and their mindless trivialities and I value her rational wisdom above the cynicism of everybody else. She is the only person in the office who knows that Kim and I are no longer together, not that I told her of course, she just sensed it and not once has she urged me to confide or share the lurid details. Agatha seems to have a way of coaxing all of that out of you and if she sees wrongdoing then she doesn't seek rebuke. When she talks, she does so wistfully and usually of her two children now living far from the family home (even though I know how she misses them) and I understand that her maternal urgings are only passed onto me through this default. Although both she and her husband Allan often plead with me to call in for dinner some time, I always recoil and make my excuses, though I can't figure out exactly why. Agatha is the only member of the team that I'd dare to call a friend and even should not be reciprocated (although I'm certain that it is) a colleague with a ready supply of aspirin is certainly one to be savoured.

And so to the rest of my squad. Philippa, Carys and Evelyn work as L&D Coordinators and it is they who spend the majority of their time deciding where best to steer their contempt before tactfully settling on either myself or my second in command, Marion. This chattering trio are the hub of illicit information and although competent in their duties, they are seemingly unable to tackle them with the kind of thirst they share for office scandal. It's difficult to add much more of note about any of them really because each of them is indistinguishable from the next and I've never bothered to challenge this observation.

It is Marion who I'd have to describe as the real nucleus of the team for holding things together when my presence elsewhere cannot be spared. She's employed as the Assistant Team Leader (although she deems this too subservient and has since adopted a different title) and I leave many of my management responsibilities to her even though it doesn't technically fall within her job description. I'm fortunate in that her ambition far outweighs her intelligence and she mistakenly believes that sheer zeal will fast-track her career towards a loftier position. It is personal experience that enables me to call her actions misguided, seeing as I've been the victim of a similar deception myself. My Manager, Gavin Crockett (whom I affectionately like to call 'The Croc') skilfully managed to double my workload over a period of seven years while paying me a wage that never quite matched my responsibilities, my bitterness at which means I now have no qualms in doing the very same to Marion. Naturally, I realised the error of my ways once it had become far too late to do anything about it and now I find myself rooted in this role without discernible retreat.

Where Marion is concerned the trick, I often find, is to encourage her aspirations while subtly undermining them and to do so just enough to ensure she understands and respects my authority. I know that she resents me (that much is pretty clear) and I don't blame her for thinking that she could probably do my job far better than I can but her griping is constant and intolerable and has done her fewer favours than she probably perceives. She wastes no opportunity in exposing my flaws to senior management in total ignorance of the futility of this for they secretly loathe her and her endless politicking does nothing more than nag away at them. Now largely irrelevant, her years stuck in the wilderness appear to be anybody's fault but her own, an opinion of which she is happy enough to relay should you have the time and patience to listen to her long enough.

But I would argue that Marion's ambition would be

lessened if she were to discover what a management role really consists of should you strip away the false prestige. If she is made to understand how the price of the ascent causes you to lose all sight and feel of the essence of the job that the company pays you to do. How you no longer feel like part of a team but like some desperate nomad hopping from meeting to meeting without time left to catch a breath. How your desk has now become a point of fleeting refuge, where you seldom grab a ten-minute lunch or dump the shy intern. How your laptop starts to feel like an extra limb as it never leaves your side and the photographs dotted around your desk are the youthful images of loved ones who no longer bear any resemblance. How you suddenly realise that the basics of office protocol are now beyond you, transferring calls, updating voicemail messages and understanding the newly devised lunch rota, all of these simple tasks now require assistance and you blush at your own stupidity. How you finger every new office gadget tremulously as if one nudge out of place will force the machinery to detonate. How in corridors, people start greeting you who you simply don't recognise, talking to you in genial manner as if the conversation is in some way connected to a previous one. No, I would suggest that such instances would cause the most ambitious among the flock to completely reassess their motives, their ideals and most importantly, the cost of their sanity.

For all of her faults and doubtless naivety however, I remain wary of Marion and for good reason. Although management despise her, they are happy to feed her ego and exploit a willingness to do the tasks that they clearly don't want to. What stokes my sense of caution around her more than anything else though, is the very real possibility that in a matter of weeks, we could both be competing for the very same job.

Under the company's perpetual cycle of restructuring, a new post has recently been created and rumour is that the role of L&D Area Project Manager is to be advertised shortly. When the job had been outlined to me quite some time ago by The Croc, to others, it appeared to be the natural progression for someone of my experience, aptitude and inferred application and they hadn't really considered the notion of my not applying. However, I did have strong reservations and these had only wavered at the thought of a pay rise that could give me the chance to own my apartment outright and once I learned of Marion's intention to apply, I was really left with little option but to re-evaluate. The Croc has always been steadfast in his belief that the job is mine for the taking, that Marion is still too inexperienced and that his influence on the panel will prove decisive. But after having viewed an early draft of her mock application, I have to admit that I'm impressed with its quality even to the point that I'm beginning to view her with an increased suspicion. Up until now, I've never seen her as a genuine threat to my personal ambitions (whatever they are) but now the thought of her inflicting the pain of years of subordination onto me keeps me awake at night. I know that I can't allow that to happen and if it means taking on a job that I really don't want in order to prevent that eventuality then I'm quite prepared to do it.

The ostensible reasons for today's meeting are really nothing out of the ordinary. It's not that we haven't touched on the biannual team evaluation or the latest Tanner & Webbing rebrand, we have done so but without any real conviction. What we're really here to discuss is something that up until now has been unprecedented in the company's history, something unforeseen, something deemed unthinkable. The employees have finally reached breaking point, our trade union has spoken and in doing so, has bucked an historic trend of disinterest and compliance. As of today, ballots are being issued and posted out to the membership and the early signs are that the result will be something close to unanimous, the overwhelming majority to vote in favour of collective industrial action.

My personal involvement with the trade union stems back to an encounter I shared with a colleague known simply as 'Print Room Joe' who managed to accost me one morning as I stood waiting for the lift. Florid-faced, rotund and visibly demonstrative, Joe struck me as one of those people that saw any attempt to ignore him as a surmountable challenge rather than a snub and sold the union to me by playing (quite adeptly) on my youthful idealism. There was an instant rapport between the two of us for I admired his candour and pretty soon we were meeting up regularly in the office canteen to exchange literature and share ideas. He was inherently antagonistic when it came to authority, viewing them with distrust and evident hostility while at the same time supporting my personal ascent within the company. He often liked to tell me how the business needed 'more of my sort' inside its management structure and although I was never entirely sure of what he meant, I knew that there was kindness somewhere in the sentiment. When it was time for Joe to retire, it was only fitting that I replaced him as a workplace union rep, finally inheriting the role for which I had been unknowingly groomed. This new position of mine was tough at first and I'd be lying if I said I wasn't daunted but the reality proved much different to the theory. As it turned out, my services were mostly called upon to tweak the fine print of company policies and consult the dog-eared contracts of ungrateful staff members who mostly blamed me for their apparent oversights. The visions I had of leading a worker's rebellion were mostly replaced by these mundane matters and with Joe gone, much of my own tenacity seemed to leave with him. We made plans to stay in touch but we haven't spoken once since he left even though I often think of him and miss his sound advice.

In the short term, nothing much has changed. We call union meetings and then cancel them with the membership unwilling to sacrifice their lunch breaks and the employer even more unwilling to grant us any kind of a concession.

The apathy is palpable, recruitment stagnant and if ever we build any kind of impetus, management responds with fear, falsehoods and promises which are far from binding. Our employer treats us as firebrands while the membership labels us inactive and if a resolution is ever found then it pacifies nobody and both sides resent us for either doing too much or doing too little. It is tough, unrelenting and unrewarding but whether out of loyalty to Joe or a creeping fear that my ideals are beginning to make less sense to me, I still retained involvement in the union.

Although it can be argued that the company restructure will work to my advantage on a personal level, the reality is that this places me in the minority for these imposed reforms are proving just as brutal as they are unstoppable and few are set to escape unscathed. Workloads are increasing, wages are frozen, longstanding members of staff are being forced out through redundancy and then replaced by cost-effective temporary replacements as this 'exciting' phase of change and redistribution is starting to reveal itself as something very different. As stoicism has given way to anger, a growing sense of injustice has spread across the workforce like a rising inferno as the meek have become firm and the indifferent inquisitive. With the masses emboldened and unshackled, the in-house company magazine recently fanned the flames further by printing detailed interviews with smirking shareholders, flaunting their wealth and demanding our reverence. To many, this was deemed to be the very last straw and the workers are finally revolting.

The momentum for strike action has been gathering speed for quite some time now and with our membership numbers having increased substantially in the last few months, a belief in our collective strength has grown with it. Almost overnight, we've been transported from a position of enquiring after change to flat out demanding it and gone is the discretion that once lingered in voices of muted discontent. With mutiny abounding, the union presented these demands to management who refused to enter into any form of negotiation which left us with little alternative but to call for an indicative ballot. The result showed unwavering support for the prospect of industrial action which did at least force management's hand into offering terms that can only be described as derisory. Once these were rejected offhand, a conciliation body entered the fray with the intention of seeking resolution but they too failed when both sides accused them of buddying up to the other. Several rounds of futile discussions then ensued with the stalemate only ending when, against the advice of the conciliators, the union declared that we would be balloting for strike action.

With the inevitability of a yes vote being strongly touted already, teams across the company (such as ours) are now huddling together in last-minute meetings (such as this one) in an attempt to thrash out contingency plans and clarify their legal positions. Perhaps understandably, conjecture now reigns as a host of hypothetical scenarios are up for discussion ranging from the sublime to the ridiculous. Will anyone choosing to cross the picket line face violent repercussions? Is it conceivable that the company could go under if labour is withdrawn for just one day? How easy would it be to put together a makeshift brazier? The team sound fearful but oddly resolute and even if the reasons behind what we are doing remain lost on one or two of them, they seem to suppress their lack of comprehension. But in the midst of this wave of provocation, tension and rumour, what lone dissenting voice should step forward to buck the militant trend and preserve the company's honour? Well it has to be Marion, doesn't it?

My support for strike action ranks some way short of vehement but it would be folly to have outwardly expressed this and so I mostly rely on the presumption of others whenever the matter is discussed publicly. Marion however, fervently opposes the union's position, branding it reckless and her repugnance at the very idea has, if anything, strengthened my façade. Her erroneous beliefs have never been a concern to me but how she has arrived at them is the thing I find most puzzling. Just six months ago, I had no recollection of ever having seen her at a union meeting, still less had she extolled the virtues of the movement and in just a matter of weeks, she had somehow gained a nomination onto the union's committee. Quite how she'd managed this I really can't say as no one admits openly to having voted for her and her tenure so far has offered nothing more than a persistent undermining of the membership's consensus. Baffled though I am at this, I am overtly encouraging for I secretly know the perils of this position (one that I have often turned down myself) and how it will only serve to further sour her relations with the management team. As with so many things, the knowledge of this bypasses Marion completely and she probably hasn't grasped why her fellow committee members consist of lower-paid colleagues and elderly firebrands, the latter channelling their efforts into nothing more than preserving the company's semi-generous pension scheme.

It is only when she attempts to use today's team meeting as a platform to disseminate her personal opposition to the ballot that I feel it my place to interject. I remind her that the union's position on the matter is very clear (and most pertinently, that of the committee) and then perform a swift deviation into the subject of yearly appraisals before my headache gains the better of me and I draw the meeting to a close. No one contests the premature conclusion and perhaps most notably, Philippa, Carys and Evelyn who depart the room leaving their notepads behind them and each of which contains not one line of recorded observation.

Ten minutes later, when back at my desk, I receive an email from Marion asking if I'll permit her time away from her regular duties once the ballot has been returned as the union have nominated her to assist in counting the result. I express no qualms with this and for once I am sincere. Though a second email expresses gratitude at my consenting to this, I also learn that The Croc has already sanctioned it. Seeing how she has spent the last two weeks in and out of his office with an alarming regularity, this news is no surprise to me and though I should feel thwarted, I am typically indifferent.

5

KIM

It was my own fault for sharing news of my intended duvet day via Congrelate and now my last day of annual leave was to be spent in the company of a three-year-old child. Just thirty minutes after that particular post, Alice (who is one of my oldest and closest friends) arrived at my flat with Charlie (my godson) in her arms (looking sleep-deprived and narky) and a host of pitiable entreaties leaving her lips in rapid fire. Whatever the unavoidable midweek engagement was I hadn't asked for she would offer no embellishment and knows too well that I seldom spurn the chance to babysit my godson.

Although Alice often does this sort of thing, on the back of my appointment with Doctor Block, perhaps today just felt a little different and my motives for saying yes were more personal than usual. Love him though I do, there's always something missing when I hold him in my arms and though there was a time I had questioned my maternal abilities, it is now clear to me that those doubts are groundless. Selfish though it seems to view child-minding as a form of practice, it remains the best way of testing one's maternal instincts and while my friends insist on having children, I'll happily make use of them as they do me.

Charlie (who rather endearingly calls me 'Kinlay') never seems particularly enamoured with me despite my best efforts but is still relatively playful. Although Alice assures me that this trait is commonplace, his wincing and wriggling at my every touch has forced me to abandon any thoughts of physical affection and he instead prefers to seek out any breakable objects within my apartment. Only when bored with an article of sturdy furniture does he turn his attention to a boxful of toys that he has previously left behind from past visits, a collection that I've acquired through his own forgetfulness. Whenever Alice comes to collect him, he'll often depart clutching a toy of some description, the purchase of which she will mistakenly credit me for, unaware of how several further items of his are accumulating in various different sections of my flat. Charlie will switch his gaze in a confused fashion between mother and babysitter at this, rueing his inability to expose me while I fraudulently bask in Alice's praise. I'm thankful for this though as it stops me from having to lavish him with gifts bought with money I do not have and this I say while I sit munching away at a half-eaten quiche I've rescued from the fridge that tastes several days past its most edible.

I keep one eye on Charlie who is roaring at a table lamp that he's confused for a dinosaur as I sit here filling out yet another job application form which is my third this week. Not too long ago, I had a thriving career working as an Applications Manager for a community regeneration company but I cannot boast of this anymore. There wasn't much about the job I didn't love, the status, the money, the joy of delegation but most of all, I loved the solitude of my very own office with a desk big enough to store several pairs of shoes beneath it (God, I missed that desk). So when the company became insolvent around eighteen months ago, instead of accepting its demise with grace and resignation, I entered a state of denial and opted to maintain my daily routine in the hope that others wouldn't learn of my sudden downfall. I set my alarm at its regular time, rose and got dressed before leaving the flat as I always had, even pulling in to my usual parking spot outside my former place of work. This charade was eventually broken when, in the midst of my denial, the building was eventually sold and a surly car park attendant threatened me with arrest unless I abandoned my daily ritual. Now, I work in event management on a flimsy contract through a supply agency for a wage that is so paltry, I can only assume it is in some way illegal, an observation I have frequently relayed to the empty-headed consultant at the agency that technically employs me now. She (with her split ends and wild eyebrows) is far from interested in anything I have to say and nothing brings home the true scale of my downfall any clearer than the knowledge that this vacuous creature is probably making far more money than I do (though I swear you'd never guess that by looking at her).

In my former role, I used to earn enough to sustain both myself and Simon and still have a little left over for a luxury item here and there, now, I don't earn enough to sustain myself. Back then, I had been the main breadwinner while he was still at university and now that the inverse was true, I couldn't help but resent how our careers had gone in opposite trajectories. The realisation of this is only further compounded by my growing debt and a woeful inability to readjust my spending habits to something more befitting my lowly income. IVF treatment will likely cost me several thousand pounds and I still have instalments to pay on the new car, household bills, a mortgage, credit cards, outstanding legal fees around my father's will and on top of all that, I still owed Hayley a hefty amount for the holiday.

On the plus side, I have been resourceful and have frequently managed to top up my meagre earnings by selling just about everything that isn't a necessity. The result of which has seen the contents of my wardrobe halve, with some meagre replacements at a fraction of the cost of what I used to own. During times where I haven't been able to find enough of my own possessions to trade, I have instead taken items from the flat that do not technically belong to me and have sold them from underneath Simon's unsuspecting nose. When I've felt particularly daring, I have even auctioned off a number of my father's personal effects which tend to prove far more lucrative than anything of mine. It's a draining experience and never an enjoyable one but in reality, I've had little choice. Sometimes, I consider asking my mother for a loan but the price of her knowing the causes of my penury seems a greater weight to me than the burgeoning debt and so there's really nothing more I can do other than preserve her ignorance.

My father died just under two years ago and twelve months after his passing, I split from Simon. The two events were undoubtedly linked because I truly believe that the latter could not have happened without the former and it was also around that time that my financial profligacy began. I developed an addiction for extravagant expenditure which infected my veins like some malevolent drug, buying a quantity of things that I arguably didn't need. I put it down to grief because it was easy to do and while others jump out of planes, run marathons or turn to drink, I gained the enviable esteem of lowly-paid shop assistants instead.

I'd been with Simon since I was sixteen and had been (mostly) happy but our time together now came with its regrets, none bigger than our decision to buy this flat when we had barely embarked on our twenties. Since the break-up, we've been co-habiting here in what I'd expected to be a temporary measure pending his imminent departure but it's one year on from the split and he's still here. Sometimes it's difficult to understand what really keeps him here as even he must comprehend that our relationship is way beyond revival but still the purgatory continues. Maybe he dreaded the same things that I did, the endless arguments over material possessions, debating the true ownership of the furniture, the artwork, the television and the percolator? Perhaps the thought of walking around the flat sticking post-it notes to every item that you deemed to be your own depressed him just as much as it did me? Thank God we didn't have any pets.

On reflection, it is fair to say that we never did broach the subject about which of us would be better suited to moving out with enough conviction other than a few tentative discussions that clearly hadn't yielded any positive decisions. It didn't take a genius to figure out that both of us were reticent but for entirely different reasons but I'm still convinced that Simon only sticks around in the faint hope of a renewal of our relationship. He wasn't to know that I didn't have the money to buy him out but he certainly earned enough to either make me an offer or move on himself and as of yet, he'd suggested neither. I won't entertain the thought of leaving here though, 228 Gaddis Avenue is *my* home and I have worked hard in building a home that I am proud of with little or no input from him. From day one, 228 had been a project of mine and the visions that I'd had for it had come slowly to fruition. To leave would be to admit defeat and the fact is, Simon does not deserve to inherit this.

We continue to share a joint mortgage on the property which means that neither of us really holds any power over the other when it comes to claiming absolute ownership. I regret this now because when we moved in eight years ago, I could've put my name to the property outright with my career already proving prosperous and Simon still a student but such is the folly of youth and love. Now, nobody is going to lend me enough money to buy out his share or secure a mortgage elsewhere thanks to my appalling credit history, rocketing debts and my shaky employment status and so this state of purgatory is set to be perpetual.

Simon, with his habitual sense of trust and indifference, leaves the task of paying the monthly bills to my charge and continues to transfer whatever amount I ask of him, thankfully without delay. That sometimes I am prone to the odd 'miscalculation' though I do not deny. I will often take the proceeds of my 'blunder' and buy myself something nice to recompense the misery in knowing that the 'rewards' of my employment can no longer do this. Naturally, this has started to arouse some suspicion in him and he sometimes threatens to conduct a financial overview, so that I fear my subterfuge is close to being exposed. In reality, he never gets much further than a few mental calculations and the examination of some bills that I've somehow managed to falsify already. Before long, we become exhausted in each other's company and the investigation is abandoned but I know my luck can only last so long.

Alice and I have known each other since secondary school and in that time, she's seen me meet Simon, fall in love with him, live unhappily with him and then finish with him. She differs from Claire (who completes our friendship trio) in that I've only ever known her sleep with two men both of whom she'd shared steady (if not entirely gratifying) relationships with. It was me who had introduced her to her first boyfriend, Graham, a fellow student in my sixth-form maths class who mirrored Alice's general aversion to everything and so I'd nudged them both together more out of personal amusement than expectation. Alice, a girl with little time for the male gender (her words, not mine) who'd spent many a teenage disco spurning their advances, soon fell in love with him and he with her. The relationship only ended after two years when Graham, in his first year away at university, called to say he didn't want to be with her anymore and hoped she'd understand. Luckily, she did. Days later, she ruefully confided to me how he'd beaten her to the punch by just one day and that she'd actually intended to break up with him herself once she'd secured enough credit on her phone. Simon had always held a theory that their relationship had been one of pure convenience and that he'd seen no evidence of any physical attraction between the two of them in all the time they'd been together. Rumours then began to circulate that Graham was now in a relationship with another man. I discounted this at first just as I did many of Simon's weird theories until I recalled one drunken evening with Alice when she'd bemoaned the fact that Graham could seldom maintain an erection and how the problem had only marginally improved when she had cut her hair. I'm not sure if that was bitterness or just accurate perception (hey, I thought the same of Simon before he asked me out) but after a relatively short period of celibacy, Alice turned up at the flat with Adrian in tow. He, five years her senior (and a close friend of her brother's), had the image of a man on the losing end of a bet that he couldn't back out of and sat submissively by her side that evening in a position he has metaphorically maintained ever since. Despite our cynicism however, they remain together just as unhappy now as they both appeared then, he, dutiful and silent while the ghost of Graham still seems to linger large with her even if Adrian perhaps doesn't know this. Like any relationship that is built from the wrong emotional fabric, there is no demand or expectation of love but there is tolerance and lots of it and in a funny kind of a way, I admire that.

Alice arrives back at my flat half an hour earlier than planned and attributes this premature return to an argument she has had with her sister. She asks how Charlie has behaved himself while readjusting a hair clip and then freeing one hand to pick at a shred of undigested food stuck between her teeth. I reply, but she isn't listening, nor does she notice how her son is now running his tongue along the arm of my sofa, causing small streams of saliva to run down the leather upholstery.

"Sorry if I forced you into changing your plans," she begins and I answer with mild embarrassment because I had no plans to change. "So how are things with you anyway? It feels like ages since we've talked." She's half right in her observation here as although a week barely goes by without her calling me, I seldom get to talk about myself. "You know I really miss double-dating with you Kim. I'll have a word with Adrian if you like and see if he can find someone to fill the extra space, I'm pretty sure he wouldn't mind." It was one thing I didn't miss in truth, sitting in an expensive restaurant of a Saturday evening, eating poor food while Alice and Adrian squabbled over culpability for the poor choice of eatery. We used to joke a lot back then that if we ever ended up anything like these two then we'd walk away well before the animosity became too much. And then before we knew it, we were at that very point ourselves.

"Well maybe it's a little too soon for me," I say, and of course, I lie.

"Too soon? Oh come on Kim, it's been a year now, singlehood doesn't suit you, you're not one of life's loners so don't pretend otherwise." I shrug and feel Charlie brush by my right knee en route to his mother with a leaf he's pulled free from a plant in my living room. "Anyway, did you get to meet any exciting new people on your holiday? I always thought these hippy get-togethers were largely just a front for smoking drugs and having sex by the camp fire." Thinking back to the near miss I'd had while on holiday, I involuntarily shudder.

"There's just a lot going on right now to be honest. Men are kind of on the backburner."

Alice looks back at me with that near-condescending smirk that all tired mothers seem to possess, the one that suggests you cannot understand tiredness unless you have experienced parenthood. She then lifts a pleading Charlie up into her arms and scoffs at him resentfully for impeding on the conversation whereas I just feel indebted to him.

"You know Adrian wants another one don't you?" She says, while inclining her head towards Charlie. "I keep telling him one's enough but he's incessant about it and nothing I say ever seems to resonate with him."

I briefly contemplate telling her about my appointment with Doctor Block and my decision to follow through with IVF but resist the urge. It's not because I want to deceive her or avoid tempting fate but more that I've never met anybody who seemed to resent children and parenting quite like Alice does and I know she will inevitably try to dissuade me. She'd confessed to me how Charlie had been unplanned and that a termination of what would've been his younger sibling had followed some time afterwards, a detail of which Adrian remained in ignorance. Alice bemoaned what childbirth had done to her body (sometimes a little too graphically even though it was always easy enough to intuit) and when she wasn't complaining about fellow parents she was forced to mix with, she'd turn her attention to Adrian, who was by her reckoning, lazy and listless. Much of this is purely for show because in spite of outward appearances, she's some way short of being labelled a bad mother and Adrian, whom she does love in her own unique way despite statements to the contrary, is neither lazy nor listless.

She then makes a half-hearted attempt at racing around the room to gather up Charlie's belongings which are strewn across the floor in standard toddler fashion. As she heads towards the door, she reminds me of her offer to fix me up and leans in for a hug, where I detect traces of unpleasant body odour and more alarmingly, wine. When she thrusts Charlie towards my puckering lips, I feel a sharp scratch on the tip of my mouth and when I open my eyes, I see that he's somehow managed to insert a toy dinosaur between my lips like a guard against a thing unpleasant. As he responds with gurgling laughter, Alice simply says, "we'll soon find someone to love you."

Shutting the door behind her, I notice that it's still early afternoon which leaves me with plenty of time to complete my application. On closer inspection, a new difficulty presents itself when I notice a child's indiscernible scribble has somehow made its way onto the page in front of me. As I'd only taken my eyes off him for a matter of minutes today, I wonder quite how he's managed this and then I toss the application in the bin. I don't consider myself a fatalist but perhaps it just isn't meant to be.

6

KIM

I don't know what it is with Ricky but he has this unfortunate habit of bumping into me every time I'm at my most disorganised and so I really didn't want him to see me like this. Our paths could've crossed any number of times since I'd returned from holiday but for whatever reason, despite his only living on the floor above mine, chance decreed it too simple to let us meet at a more convenient moment. Instead, he mostly tends to catch me on days like today when I'm running half an hour late and have already given up hope of making myself look even vaguely presentable.

My lateness could be explained by a variety of different factors but was most notably due to the mixture of fertility drugs that were currently swimming about my system. The first round of these, which had caused no ill-effects (other than increased water retention), was designed to suppress my menstrual cycle in order to make my ovaries more susceptible to a fertility hormone called gonadotrophin. The object of gonadotrophin is to stimulate the ovaries by creating a greater number of eggs which then offers the fertility clinic a greater number of embryos to choose from at the point where they are fused with the male's sperm. This all sounded fairly reasonable until Doctor Block explained how the hormone could only be inserted to the body via a syringe and that I would be expected to self-administer this without the aid of supervision. He wasn't to know of my illogical fear of needles and I wasn't about to tell him either but while I secretly prayed that the fear would dissipate at the point of injection, it simply hadn't. And so I'd spent the last three evenings of my life performing this routine procedure, injecting myself with quivering hand into my abdomen while gnawing at a pillow and then calling Claire to extol my valour once the process had been completed. The side effects had been unpleasant but manageable, bouts of morning sickness (which I hope I shall have to get used to) giving way to abdominal soreness but as sacrifices go, it meant very little. I could always make the time up at work if I really needed to and Ricky would have to accustom himself to seeing me as a pregnant woman sooner rather than later (I hoped).

"Hey Kim," I heard him call out to me in the parking bay when I'd mistakenly assumed I'd escaped his notice, "you left something behind." Whatever it was that he'd been wrestling with in the boot of his car had been abandoned while he strode up to me brandishing a purple scarf that was littered with sequins. My guess is that he must've thought I'd dropped it in my mad dash to the car and was thrusting it before me by way of return. It was a tawdry garment and in no way reflective of my taste but my protestations melted away the moment I saw him. "Oh and by the way, I'll be posting something through your door later so look out for it when you return home, okay?" I offer a slight pause to encourage some elaboration but, as is typically Ricky, he either doesn't pick up on this or simply ignores the hint.

It is all very much still there, every point of his physical beauty in a faultless formation quite unparalleled to that of anyone I'd ever met. It was a beauty so strong that every line of his face seemed to merge with a remarkable symmetry that did in no way detract from his natural ruggedness. His eyes were so deep and his gaze so intense that I felt something close to submission simply by staring at them, leaving me often contemplating how long it would take for me to grow tired of the sight.

I accept the orphaned scarf with a feigned gratitude

while he neatly repositions his sunglasses and stands stroking a heavily tattooed left bicep with his right thumb and forefinger. While I mutter an inadequate and inaudible reply, one of the other reasons I'd initially elected not to say hello to him (while his back had been turned), came a little clearer into view. I'd noticed that there was somebody with him sitting in the passenger seat of the car and I'd wanted him to leave the boot and pull away before me so that I could gain a better view of them before I left myself. I could only see the side of a delicate head but could make out that it was a girl and that she sat impatiently, strumming the fingers of her right hand rhythmically on the dashboard. I do not push for an introduction for obvious reasons (and she seems happily aloof anyway) and in the uncomfortable seconds of silence that follow, I am forced to juggle all reasonable explanations as to her identity without conjuring a clear answer. Was she his sister? Did he even have a sister and if he did, what reason would she have for being so unsociable? She was certainly very pretty in a conventional sort of way so I guessed she could be related. Her face didn't seem familiar to me and although a horde of women seemed to plague his Congrelate page with flirtatious comments, I didn't recognise her to be one of them.

Her presence had deflated me slightly as Ricky departed the scene with an outgoing farewell of, "see you later, Congrelate friend. Hope you enjoyed the holiday, it certainly seemed like you did." Perhaps he was being sarcastic or perhaps he wasn't but I couldn't always tell with him as he was a difficult boy to read. On the one hand, I felt uncomfortable in knowing that he'd seen my holiday photographs but also encouraged in that he'd taken the time to actually look at them. This sense of discomfiture was nothing new between us though and it made me recall the night we first became properly acquainted. I'd nearly put my foot in it then in addressing him by his full name which he quite rightly pointed out I had no way of knowing. I saved the day by pretending that I'd picked up some post for him in error which I'm not sure he really believed but it still seemed a better option than admitting I'd spent two weeks assiduously trawling through his Congrelate profile prior to formally meeting him. That research had yielded little information but I didn't have to wait very long for all that to change.

Ricky moved in to our apartment complex about eighteen months ago. We'd exchanged pleasantries most mornings as his parking space was four down from mine and through a combination of good fortune and immaculate timing, I'd managed to synchronise our daily routines and call it coincidence. As a result, a short time passed before our daily flirtations moved beyond the stage of smile and hint and this would be due to an incident of legitimate chance.

My relationship with Simon was deteriorating fast at this point and I'd wandered home alone one evening after we'd become separated at a party that we'd attended together. It was only on my return that I realised I was locked out of my flat which left me with two options, either call Simon and drag him away from the party, feeding him ample excuse to throw resentment my way, or spend the rest of the evening sleeping in my car. Thankfully, Ricky crossed my path at the last moment. As I explained my predicament to him (while vainly attempting to feign sobriety), he responded with sympathy and offered his apartment as a more comfortable alternative. Although outwardly I offered weak resistance at the thought of imposing, inwardly I felt no such dilemma.

The first thing I noticed was just how different his apartment was to mine. Although it wasn't quite as big (just the one bedroom, he informed me) it had an abundance of living space and more impressively, two balconies (although my lone balcony is sun-facing). He hadn't moved in that long ago and it was still mid-renovation with the interiors either covered in wrapping or stuck in transit. This would prove to be a strange metaphor for Ricky's character as I learned nothing of his inner workings and little more of his exterior. It was all largely due to the inherent skill he had for evading answers and switching the focus away from himself whenever I searched for greater insight. For example, I learned that he worked as a journalist but had no idea whether he was connected to one publication or whether he freelanced and if such an occupation was as profitable as his apartment suggested. My enquiries didn't lead anywhere and I was both baffled and intrigued at his habitual ambiguity and wondering if he sensed that. I left that night having told him everything there was to know about me and not having learned anything about him.

I wanted to sleep with him that night and really couldn't fathom why I'd been so quick to recoil just moments before nature had been due to take its course. At first, I assumed it to be some lingering loyalty towards Simon that had prompted this decision but really I hadn't thought of him at all, nor acknowledged any guilt in my actions to that point. It left Ricky looking perplexed and his glittering eyes turned wistful as he'd muttered the words, 'but I don't understand.' And how was it possible for him to understand when just seconds before that, his right hand had been making steady and unerring progress up towards the curve of my breast while our bodies had started to entwine? And then, when everything had pointed towards the inevitable, I had pulled away from his grasp and offered by way of explanation, 'yes I know Ricky but the time isn't right for us both to understand.'

To this day, I've no idea why I said that or what it even meant but ever since then, I've wanted to tell him that I've never considered what happened between us that night to be a mistake and that I hadn't rejected him. I wanted to assure him that I thought of him perpetually and that his touch enlivened me in ways I'd long since recognised. Most significantly, I didn't want to cheapen or betray the chemistry that bound us together by obeying a rash desire or giving the false impression that it really didn't matter. The truth is that it did, especially to me, and the longing to put all of that into words weighed heavy on my heart.

I decide to keep hold of the scarf for now as I may find an opportunity to return it to him and maybe that could lead somewhere. Perhaps there will never be a 'right time' to tell him how I feel, for there will always be a sulky girl in tow or an ex-boyfriend sleeping in the spare bedroom of my apartment. Fate could still spare me of course, but it won't be too long before my life and prospects could look very different and I cannot say with confidence that Ricky will want to join me on that journey.

Traffic is horrendous and I arrive at work more than half an hour late. Despite travelling this route on a daily basis, I somehow managed to make three wrong turns and pull into the car park looking a tad dishevelled as confirmed by a peak in my rear view mirror. I recognise Lucy (a colleague from the marketing team who seems to have fewer friends here than I do) pulling up into the space beside me, looking equally flustered and although we barely know each other, we exchange the routine pleasantries. It isn't long into this civil greeting that I notice her attention is drawn towards something on my backseat and I see that she is focusing on Ricky's scarf (which I'd deposited there in a rush). It is evident that she really likes it as she circles the rear of the car and presses her nose gently against one of the back windows.

"Wow, I just love that scarf," she says, now cupping her hands against the window to gain a clearer view. "You really need to tell me where you bought it from."

There really is nothing but sincerity in her voice.

7

SIMON

"Hey Sport, am I okay to come up?"

I say no instantly. I could've supplemented my refusal with further reasoning but the truth was that he'd already taken a liberty in asking.

It is 7.15 in the morning and The Croc has treated me to this entirely unnecessary wake-up call via the intercom that fed into my apartment. There were two reasons why I wasn't going to allow him entry that I adjudged to take precedence above the general principle. Firstly, that I'd specifically requested we meet at the office just after 7.30 and secondly, because I didn't want him to confirm what I suspected he already knew, that Kim and I were no longer together. I didn't doubt for a moment that the prospect of ogling her before work was another motive for arriving so punctually but our strength of distaste for him was one of few things left that we could still agree on.

"Let me in, Sport, I want to say hello to Kim."

I really can't abide his terrible use of nouns and much more besides, especially so when that someone is stood outside of your flat so early in the day. When I catch up with him downstairs, his manner has changed to one of irritation as he paces around the perimeter of his car, clutching at a mobile phone and gesticulating wildly. The poor soul on the other end of the line has fast become the recipient of a harsh, peremptory rage and his anger seems to comically intensify with the strain of his repetitions. The Croc wants to make it clear that the blame lies squarely at the feet of his counterpart, that a poor reception is no excuse for his instructions being unheeded and that his patience is now beyond recovery. Cutting the call short, he finally catches sight of me and starts to walk towards me. He is wearing a look of mild deflation and I notice that his tie is hanging loose around his neck, resembling a snake under heavy sedation.

"Hey Simon," he shouts, although I'm now mere yards away from him, "you remembered the sat nav right?"

I tell him I have and it's a good thing too seeing as The Croc is notoriously bad with directions and even worse at following instruction. Most people with directional flaws would think about purchasing such a gadget for themselves but as many come to understand with The Croc, he really wasn't 'most people.'

The common perception of the man shared among those that didn't know him as I did was one of industry, success and fierce dedication but I had learned that this was simply a myth that he had happily perpetuated. In reality, here was a man with little talent that had maneuvered his way into a position of power through a combination of charm, audacity and plain good fortune. This success (if indeed you could call it such) had been assembled on the backs of others through skill and swerve and while the battlefield of in-house politics had seen his adversaries metaphorically perish, he somehow managed to keep the blood from his hands. Flitting between contempt and reverence depending on the company, he too often mistook his own charm for wit and focused his energies on the value of delivery above substance. People saw him as meticulous and maybe in a way he was but he really had to be because he didn't cope well under pressure and he lacked pragmatism. He was pitied by some, despised by others but I was aware of few who ignored him.

With his youth far behind him, a compulsion to rouse envy in some and veneration in others meant that no expense was spared in trying to exhibit the apparent splendour in which he lived. The falsity of his character was matched by his physicality and two rows of teeth with an artificial glint clashed against a bronzed skin tone that was anything but authentic. The blinding gleam did at least deflect focus from the ill-fitted hair transplant, the plucked eyebrows and all other poorly concealed signs of cosmetic enhancement that completed this tawdry look. Standing at a diminutive five foot six, he seemed to resent his size which in turn manifested itself into an overt and self-consuming paranoia. Perhaps that, and the memory of all those he'd so skilfully trodden on to gain his position of power, fused to form an echoing reminder of just how fragile success could be. It seemed to spawn dishonesty, moral ambiguity and, I suspect, a mild impotency in every sense of the term.

As a result of this, working for him hadn't always been the easiest of occupations and though I often wondered how I'd managed to stick it out this long, the quest for answers only ever seemed to muddy the waters further. What I really wanted to know was why he'd asked me to accompany him today at some business exhibition miles away from the office when we both knew my time would've been better spent back at work, getting on with the job that he employed me to do. It really didn't take two of us to sit at a stall all day in some draughty mezzanine, liaising with representatives from other companies in the vain hope of acquiring new business. Fortunately however, I'm a patient man and I knew it wouldn't take long for The Croc to reveal the truth.

"Have you had any more thoughts on the L&D Area Project Manager role yet Champ?" He starts, once the painstaking trivialities have petered out between us. "Word is that the screening process is moving into phase two and it's time to lay the cards on the table. I mean, you know my feelings on the subject, I've always maintained that whoever gets the job is going to be really rather lucky but..."

This appeared to be the latest instalment in a long history of discourse that we had shared on this matter and so I temporarily switch off. The Croc's attempts at pressuring me into applying for the job had been tantamount to a personal fixation, one that had been so persistent, it had initially surprised me. If I'm being honest, back then, the role didn't really appeal to me and The Croc probably believed that if he dangled the carrot in front of me often enough, then sooner or later, I'd make a grasp for it. This early indifference had obviously aggrieved him but once I'd perceived this frustration, it merely offered me an incentive to further indulge my (mostly) sham apprehensions. Perhaps not fully realising the skill of my own pretence, I'd somehow managed to convince The Croc that what I really lacked was self-confidence and not ambition. It forced him to change tack and for a time he'd done little else but shower me with compliments and glowing, personal endorsements. After all, I'd always known that I held the best hand and that hadn't really changed from the off because the last thing that The Croc wanted was for Marion to take the job. Much like me, he sensed the impending disaster that that could spell and although we had very different reasons, self-preservation was probably the strongest. I knew that even I couldn't lose a one-horse race and there was nobody else in the company that came close to matching my experience. The more I thought about it, well, the less I thought about it. The Croc often talked of the monetary gain the job would bring with it and living with Kim just wasn't working out anymore, if indeed it ever had (since the split) This new job would give me the opportunity to call her bluff by enabling me to make her an offer for the apartment because I wasn't going to wait forever for her to do the same.

I'd managed to drift off into reverie (and not for the first time when in the company of The Croc) but this digression of thought is suddenly and sharply interrupted by a sense that his usual pattern of bluster and pretension is not pursuing its normal course. I try to recall my attention to the point at which I'd trailed off from the conversation. Had he really mentioned a 'screening process?' Come to think of it, had he not said 'whoever gets the job?' What was 'phase two' and why at no point up to now had there been any reference to a 'gradual sifting process'? I am disconcerted by this but then the bombshell really hits.

"So there I was down at HQ last week Simon, schmoozing with the powers-that-be and all of a sudden I get this brainwave. Why not open the job up to external candidates? Now Miles and Isabella weren't so keen initially but I'm pretty persuasive when I know I'm in the right and an hour later, they're both cursing themselves for not thinking of it sooner."

"External candidates?" I blurt, unable to hide my disbelief, suddenly unwilling to prolong the pretence any further.

"Yes, external candidates, clever don't you think? If we end up appointing one then I'll have to be credited for that no matter how much it's likely to stick in Isabella's craw. It's creating competition, Simon and competition is good."

Competition wasn't good for me, that much I'd resolved already and I didn't like where this conversation was heading.

"But you're still backing me for the role, right? That's what you said, that's what you've always maintained." This wasn't so much a question but a feeble plea, the goalposts were being shifted and I hadn't seen it coming.

"Well, maybe my position up to now has been a little misleading," he says, ponderously.

"Misleading?" I exclaim, breaking free from the shackles of astonishment. "You couldn't have performed a bigger U-turn if you'd intended to, it's practically treachery!"

He muses over that last response for a moment, tapping his fingers lightly on the steering wheel and then pursing his lips as if to imply his next return will be nothing if not carefully controlled.

"Listen, Simon, the appointment panel will consist of a group of three. Firstly, there's Miles, who sees you as his preferred candidate and then there's Isabella, who sees Marion as her preferred candidate and then, well then there's just little old me left with the casting vote. Maybe it's a luxury, maybe it's a burden but as things stand I can most definitely confirm that *I* am undecided."

Though I know what he is saying, I cannot fathom his reasons for it but The Croc quickly establishes where the bargaining must begin. "You're still repping for the union, right?" He enquires, while staring straight ahead into non-existent traffic. I nod in corroboration. "Well, speaking personally Simon, I've always respected the work you do there (this was a lie) but you know, there are those in the management structure at Tanner & Webbing that don't look on such an association as being an entirely *good thing*. Now think about this forthcoming ballot. It's regrettable and when these things happen, well, some would say there are no winners or, at least, there aren't many, not in the long run anyway. So if this vote for strike action goes the way we're hearing that it's likely to, then it's going to make us look weak and rather foolish and that doesn't reflect well on the company. Management do not appreciate being put in that position Simon and I think it's fair to say that if they are, they'd all be rather keen to hold someone responsible for it and that someone won't necessarily be the right person. And that pertains to you because your loyalties as a union representative are being questioned here and this isn't tittle tattle either, this is coming from the highest echelons of the company."

"So you're asking me to resign from my role in the union, right?" I respond semi-dismissively.

"No, not exactly Simon," he starts cautiously. "Quite the opposite, in fact, I advise you to maintain that allegiance to the union, if anything, strengthen your influence and do so quickly."

"But why on earth would I want to do that?" I ask, with some exasperation. "It's clear that such a move would only count against me, perhaps irretrievably if everything you've just said is to be believed."

"Because it's the only way you'll be able to safeguard the future for you, me and hundreds of others. Look, it's clear you're not getting this so let me explain more clearly." Like an actor turning to the audience before performing the soliloquy that will define his career, The Croc steadies himself and extracts a deep intake of breath. "This strike action cannot go ahead, no, scratch that, this strike action *will not* go ahead. Have you ever asked yourself what possible good it is likely to achieve? A few extra pounds in the pockets of those that wouldn't even know how to spend it? A further day's leave for them to fritter away idly? Better working conditions for the meddlers to exploit? Once that door opens Simon, once it's just slightly ajar, then it becomes impossible for us to close it. See what they fail to understand is that these short-lived gains aren't really sustainable because what we give with one hand we will only take away with the other. When the shortfall has to be addressed, we'll be forced to recoup the money from somewhere, putting more out of work along the way, which only creates an environment of loss and instability. Then our backers start to get anxious and they're turning to our competitors as if the last twenty years meant nothing to them. They say there's no loyalty in this game Simon, but some loyalty *is* rewarded."

"But I fail to see how I fit into all of this. Even if what you say is true, there isn't any way that I can prevent it from happening."

"Oh but there is, at least, it's in your interests to find a way, so I advise that you do." He imparts that suggestion in a provocative manner and although it's becoming rather difficult, I try to ignore the sinister overtones that permeate his response.

"My interests?" I ask in surprise. "You don't honestly believe that I would be held accountable if our members were to vote in favour of strike action do you? That just doesn't make sense."

"No, you wouldn't be held entirely accountable Simon, not to them anyway but like I said, some loyalty *is* rewarded."

"I still don't understand." And this was true, I really didn't.

"I need you to make sure that the ballot is returned with a positive result for the company Simon, one that sees the very notion of a strike utterly and thoroughly quashed."

"But you know I can't do that, how would I even..."

"Now, I've given this some thought but ultimately the mechanics of it will very much rest with you. Due to your position with the union you'll have access to the branch office, the place where the ballots will be counted. I need you to utilise your position to the full and find a way of sabotaging the vote. Like I say, I don't care how you do it, that's for you to decide but if you *can* pull this off then it's something that you won't end up regretting. Look, I understand that it's a lot to take in but I have faith in you to do the right thing here. Remember Simon, when I'm sat on that interview panel, I really want to give you that job so give me the opportunity to do that otherwise I can place a pretty solid roadblock in the course of your career. It's harsh I know but there's really no other way."

As a rule, I don't often respond to threats but feeling weakened by the vulnerabilities he's exposing, my capacity for debate is ignited and forces me onto the offensive.

"I can't believe you're asking me to do this, Gavin. You could've asked anyone else to do it so why me and why now? I've never offered you anything but loyalty and now you're leveraging my ambitions against me."

"Well I really don't see it like that," he replies, in a tone that just exudes glibness. "Look, don't mistake the position that you're in as if it's one that others wouldn't kill for because the truth is that people have done far worse before in order to achieve far less. Just do as I ask of you Simon because if you don't, I'm certain you'll regret it."

A paralysis of thought takes over as injustice wrestles with disbelief and shock defeats clarity. In the background, at the periphery of my consciousness, The Croc is casually adjusting the station on the car radio to something he probably thinks more fitting before whistling out of tune to a song I loosely recognise. I instantly realise the quandary I am facing here and just like so many times within this last year of my life, I feel the depth of a wound dealt by my very own hand.

Despite a history of flawless machinations and manic self-preservation, I hadn't seen this level of ruthlessness from The Croc present itself quite so overtly before. None of this had ever been about me, the truth was that I was just as dispensable as all the others he'd mentioned, working jobs they didn't care about while aspiring to things they mistakenly believed they really needed. The only difference between them and I was that their naivety could be excused whereas I could be heading into a trap of my very own making.

The immorality of the task he was asking me to undertake disgusted me but less so than the thought that I'd be acting under some obligation to him. I owed him nothing, despite what he believed, so there was really very little for me to consider if I looked at it from that angle. He didn't understand the sacrifice he was asking me to make because he had no integrity and naturally assumed that I shared his lust for all things gained at the expense of others.

The rest of our journey is predictably muted and for once, The Croc seems to relish the silence, no doubt assuming that I'm contemplating his proposal. This is partly true because I didn't want to vocalise what I was thinking and give him the impression that my participation in this project was simply minus a plan to execute it. I make a call to Agatha back at the office and instigate a needless conversation simply to avoid further dialogue with him and by the time I hang up, we are at our destination.

8

KIM

I'd managed to gather what Ricky posted through the door at my flat before Simon had been able to see it and thus avoid an awkward confrontation. Although he no longer held any claim over me, an explanation as to why a fellow male resident of our apartment complex was slipping correspondence through our letterbox (addressed only to me) would've produced more questions than answers and Simon's inferences wouldn't have been too wide of the mark. Disappointingly, it had simply been a note informing me that he was now on holiday for the weekend and that a cleaner called Daisy would be due at his flat this evening. The note went on to say that due to a mix up with the cleaning company, she had no means of entry and I would have to pass the key (that he included with the note) on to her when she called at my flat later on in the evening. The fact that it was Friday and that I could have made other plans obviously didn't occur to him but even if I had, chances are I probably would have cancelled them anyway, such is my infatuation and such was this opportunity.

I'd made up my mind about what I was going to do from the moment I'd read the note and had waited patiently for around an hour for Daisy to return the key to me after she'd completed her cleaning duties. In reality, Ricky hadn't left me much choice or at least that was what I told myself when, not too long after she'd left, I found myself turning that very same key in the lock of his apartment and making my way inside. It was just possible that he knew I was going to do this and that the mishap with the cleaning company had been a mere ruse designed to lure me in to his flat. It didn't seem logical exactly but maybe this was just a way for Ricky to circumvent his own reticence and to allow elements of his home to show me something of his persona that he clearly couldn't tell me himself. I also figured that my apparent rejection of his advances had maybe injured his vanity more deeply than I'd imagined and that he could be gambling on my stumbling across something that would enlighten my perception of him.

On entry however, I notice instantly that the flat isn't quite how I remember it and now bears little resemblance to what he had inherited on moving in. Gone are the loose furnishings, the piles of nondescript boxes and the pale, naked walls now transformed into a bright and tasteful living room. A giant television takes up much of the space by a front window which, I assume, blocks much of the natural light and a rudimentary games console takes central placing. The wall adjacent to it is partially obscured by three uneven rows of pristine-looking paperbacks by authors I'd barely heard of and sporting autobiographies from athletes I definitely hadn't. The artwork scattered about the place carries no particular theme and is, on closer inspection, simply covering patches of faint discolouration on the walls. The bathroom and the kitchen offer some contrast to the minimalist approach of the living room though. The former looks positively ornate, with gilded taps and marble flooring, while the kitchen looks sleek and contemporary with gratifying lighting. These were the only rooms in the flat that were likely to leave an impression on me, from their matching upholstery to the space used so effectively and I couldn't help but think that the elegance of both oozed a clear femininity. All in all, despite the varying aesthetics, everything felt clean and relatively coordinated and although Daisy could probably take the credit for that, my guess was that she probably didn't need to do a lot whenever she was here as Ricky clearly didn't spend a lot of time here himself.

Naturally, my self-guided tour takes me into the bedroom which is, by contrast to every other room, disorderly and untidy. This space appears off limits to Daisy and her cleaning colleagues, for there are various items of clothing strewn across the furniture, the bed is partially made and a general state of flux pervades it. A quick inspection of two sets of drawers does not produce anything of note other than some unused contraceptives, bodybuilding supplements and a comb densely clotted with thick strands of hair (which doesn't even look like Ricky's). I move over to the dressing table and pick my way through a variety of grooming products, applying different aftershaves about my neck and then inhaling the aromatic cocktail. There is what looks to be a football shirt resting on the back of a chair. I slip into it and it fits me better than it should and also contains the lingering but not totally unpleasant scent of body odour about the arms and neck. For reasons that aren't immediately clear to me, I half-undress from the waist down and climb into the bed.

In a way, I wanted to pretend that this situation wasn't as it seemed, to detach myself a little to introduce a dose of normalcy. And in doing so, I hadn't realised right away exactly what was happening or what I was doing, or at least the compulsion to deny the absurdity of it all had taken precedence. With my eyes closed, I could sense Ricky lying right beside me, leaning towards me and then climbing on top of me. I tell myself I'm no longer in control and that these aren't my hands and that this is not a substitution for something that I covet. I push the bedsheets further down and pull my knees up closer to me and there is suddenly a triangular surgical curtain veiling my lower half while my underwear completes its descent from my ankles to the floor. The small of my back writhes against the unforgiving mattress and the bed no longer feels adequate for this operation. I know instinctively that all is lost if I even contemplating stopping and so with this in mind, I take the nearest pillow and rest it over my perspiring face to fully protect the illusion. Everything succumbs to this selfish pursuit of gratification with the inevitable result of a climactic discharge and it suddenly dawns on me that I cannot remember when I last did this.

Time passes for I don't know how long before I start to hear what seems to be the sound of a fist pounding on a door along with a woman's voice I only faintly recognise. Sure enough, it was Daisy and so I quickly reapply my jeans and then stumble back towards the entrance of the apartment. It turns out that on leaving her second cleaning job of the night, she had happened to walk by Gaddis Avenue and notice that a light from Ricky's apartment remained on. Certain that she had not been responsible for this, she had returned to my now empty apartment to see if she could retrieve the key and then came here to further her investigation. I lie and tell her that yes, she had left the light on and that I'd seen this on my way out of the complex and maybe she would've believed that had I not still been wearing Ricky's football shirt. She looks me up and down, brimming with suspicion and I offer no further explanation, praying that her inspection will not take her beyond the threshold. Thankfully it doesn't, she leaves and I spend the next few moments wondering what I would've said had she insisted on entering and found my discarded underwear still lying on Ricky's bedroom floor. This was a bad idea.

9

SIMON

Last Friday, an inebriated student mistook the car that I was driving for a taxi and I (like so often before) allowed this deception to continue without thinking of the consequences. One week later, a mobile phone that she had unknowingly left behind was about to bring us back into each other's company and give us both the chance to maybe challenge our first impressions. Had her initial cruel assessment of me lingered long in my thinking (she had described me as 'eerie' you may recall), then I probably wouldn't have met her tonight nor would I have if Allan's on-going sciatica issue had not flared up again, forcing Agatha to cancel on me to tend to him instead.

I arrive at the Plough and Trinket (the meeting point of Vanessa's choosing) in a reluctant mood ready to return the phone and maybe take a drink by way of recompense. The pub is as anticipated, quirky but unexceptional, with eye-stinging artwork, waxed beards and a long line of beer taps, the titles of which all looking as though they are steeped in innuendo. It was obvious to see how I (standing there in full work attire) didn't fit in with the bohemian clientele which probably explained why Vanessa recognised me so quickly, introducing herself with a delicate hand and a tentative line of enquiry before a fuller conversation proceeds.

Vanessa's beauty strikes me immediately as more understated than obvious, with an attraction that perhaps you'd be forgiven for not immediately observing. I say this because her features seem to lack that smooth equality of line and length that is bestowed on others via the lottery of nature and in its place was a visible but not unpleasant imbalance. Her hair is both thicker and darker than I recalled, shoulder length and tumbling from its roots and her eyes (lurking beneath a pair of faux-designer glasses) are accurately placed above a small, slender nose. It is this point of delicacy from which all her features seem to encircle and contrast in their apparent normality for it looked youthful yet refined when compared to all else about her face. And it is difficult not to be drawn to this subtlety of beauty because it was clear to me already that she lacked the gift of confidence to harness its power which is a character trait that I've always found endearing. None of this is reflected in her personality though, for she is animated and demonstrative, upbeat and impassioned, flitting between reticence and verbosity depending on the subject. When speaking, her diction is eloquent but furiously projected with an urgency to reach the point at the expense maybe of the chief details. She didn't remember me, I figured and for this I am thankful because the Simon who was driving the car that night never had the luxury of eliciting any of the above.

The evening should've ended there and then really with the phone having been retrieved and thanks imparted, but it didn't. Already, in my short time at the Plough and Trinket, I'd noticed how six or seven different people had passed Vanessa by, each of them stopping to say hello before exiting into a back room. At first, I didn't make much of it and just assumed it was a friendly exchange shared between regulars until I caught sight of one of them waving and beckoning for Vanessa to follow them. A host of different things ran through my mind at that point but the Plough and Trinket Book Group wasn't one of them. When Vanessa asked me if I cared to join them, no doubt borne from courtesy rather than expectation, I could only say yes if I wanted to remain in her company. So I did, leaving a surprised (but at least not visibly so) Vanessa with little choice but to lead me across the room and into the literary sanctum.

Initially, the group seem tolerant of me if not exactly welcoming and so I try to respond in kind despite the challenging circumstances. After routine introductions, I sit there looking ill-equipped before Vanessa offers to share her heavily annotated copy of Joyce's *Dubliners* with me and I scour the inner recesses of my brain, trying to recall a time where I may have studied the book in question. I needn't have worried though for I quickly deduce that Vanessa's scribblings seem more designed to impress her literary neighbour rather than to offer any pertinent insights, not that many of her notes are actually legible. Before long, I find myself nodding away concurringly to a litany of banal interpretations of the text voiced by different members of the group. What is most bemusing to me however, is trying to establish quite how Vanessa has managed to enter into friendship with such a motley crowd as this. She was the youngest of the group by some distance and looked totally out of place in the midst of this ensemble that consisted of the intellectually stagnant and types who probably considered this the highlight of a week lacking in social activity. They didn't seem to be bad people admittedly but very much the sort who are perpetually incompatible no matter the environment and the back room of the Plough and Trinket probably gave them opportunity to feed off each other's eccentricities. When, after an hour, we finally reach 'The Dead' (the final story of the collection), one female sexagenarian marks the feat by placing a clammy hand on my own and then proceeds to stroke it with anything but a tremulous touch. This made me feel both confused and repulsed but somehow it seemed congruent to the general atmosphere and while Vanessa simply diverted her gaze elsewhere, I just submitted to the awkward initiation.

In the aftermath of Book Group, I share my stinging observations with Vanessa who tries desperately to defend their quirkiness before eventually conceding that I wasn't far wrong. She goes on to explain how she'd only joined the group on being new to the city as a student and had seen it as the ideal way to combine her love of reading with the chance of meeting new people, even if the choice of literature was a little bland and she'd made nothing more than passing acquaintances.

I learn a great deal about Vanessa as the evening progresses and much of what I learn impresses me. At nineteen years old, she is a student of classical music in the first year of an educational exchange program that will conclude in three years' time. She opted for this course on the back of a burgeoning reputation as a childhood prodigy, a notoriety that then secured her a government-backed artistic grant which pretty much covered her course fees in their entirety. In addition to this, she will spend each year studying in a different country making the downside (she admitted) quite difficult to find. Of her family she spoke infrequently but described the affection of her parents as 'stifling'. She revealed that she had two older brothers, one who worked in pharmaceutical science and the other an architect and I noted that she was mildly puzzled at my curiosity about them as if she was unused to this casual line of enquiry. When I asked what her relationship was to Sebastian (the meddling friend of hers who had spoken so obnoxiously to me on the phone last week) she offered an ambiguous reply which did to some degree inform me that this was a subject which she didn't care to discuss.

I liked how she didn't interrupt me when I spoke, how she was inquisitive and never condescending and how she deemed it gentlemanly for me to buy her drinks without expecting one in return. In reality, she knew nothing of me and that meant that I could present myself in the way that I wanted rather than trying to be someone I thought she might want me to be instead. This was not the same girl who'd tried everything to avoid conversation with me when I had picked her up just one week ago and at no point did I answer the internal need to fully reveal myself. When I asked whether she'd like to meet up again for a drink, it really didn't surprise me that she responded by assenting and when we embraced and exchanged numbers, nothing felt contrived or in the least untoward.

It's not until I reach home that the enormity of what had just happened fully registers. In a few weeks' time I will be turning thirty, having just asked somebody out on a date for the very first time in my life, accomplishing a feat that I should've consigned to my adolescence. When I first met Kim, things transpired organically in the way they often do as teenagers, in spite of all the nerves and apprehension that falling in love for the first time inevitably brings. At the age of sixteen I was besotted and a cruel snub would've crushed my self-esteem into irretrievable pieces. At twenty-nine years old, there didn't appear to be quite so much at stake anymore. Had Vanessa recoiled at the suggestion, I'd simply have reflected on the multitude of reasons that made the very thought of the two of us being together an absurdity, safe in the knowledge that I'll probably never feel for anybody what I once did for Kim. But for now, all that remains is to raise a glass to the Plough and Trinket Book Group, even though an invitation to return would probably go unanswered.

10

SIMON

<u>BALLOT RESULT</u>
Yes – 180
No – 50
Spoiled/Unclear – 7

The mood which greets the news of a positive vote for industrial action at Tanner & Webbing is not as jubilant as had been expected and is met instead with hesitancy and caution. Those who claimed to have predicted such an outcome do not celebrate their prophecy nor do they talk of their contribution with any notable fervour, even the most outspoken of dissenters appears pensive in the wake of their accomplishment. Pockets of elation spring up here and there but they still seem muted and already there are questions producing nothing but confused responses.

I felt just as underwhelmed as everybody else but for entirely different reasons. The result had been undoubtedly resounding with seventy-nine per cent of the membership having voted and seventy-six per cent of those voting in favour of strike action. In electoral terms, one could label this a landslide. The emptiness that I feel is not a shock to me and so I portray the look of one unfazed, easily mirroring the general bathos. Perhaps it is Agatha who best depicts the consensus of the office by absorbing the result with a deflated shoulder shrug and not allowing the news to disturb her daily duties. She goes on to reveal how she'd only voted yes in trust of my convictions and although I find this to be a sweet loyalty, it lies with me uneasily in ways she must never know the reason for.

11

KIM

Claire lost her virginity at twenty-three and I was deeply upset when she did as she did it for all the wrong reasons. She did it because she was scared of losing someone, she did it because she was drunk. The decision she made at twenty-three was to sleep with a married English tutor and it was a choice that would shape her sexual behaviour from that point on. By the age of twenty-five, she'd lost count of the number of men she'd had sex with and neither ill repute nor venereal disease seemed enough to prompt her into change.

She was used at twenty-three by an older man who only sometimes bothered to take his wedding ring off and preferred to drop her at the bus station rather than drive her home. He made her wash the smell of perfume away from her face and neck before she entered his car and when the mood so took him, he was sexually aggressive and liked to punish her for his own infidelity.

It was he who ended the relationship for reasons that he never disclosed. Claire assured me that his wife's pregnancy had not influenced his decision but even if that was so, he had at least been kind enough to return items of missing underwear (washed and ironed) by post.

And it was because of this man mistreating her in the way that he did that Claire was now unable to attach any value or significance to the act of sexual intercourse. When it came to men, Claire simply saw them as a means to an end and if any of them were foolish enough to think it was *they* who held the cards, she seemed to enjoy it all the more. It didn't matter to her if they believed she swooned at the chat-up lines they fed her because sincerity wasn't necessary, if anything, it just held things up. If they bragged to their friends about her, be it false or fair, then so what? She was in love with the idea of being talked about and if the facts got a little tangled and rehashed then it really wasn't so important as long as she remained the centre of attention in the story.

So when she told me that she'd bumped into her first love once again in the supermarket yesterday, I was immediately intrigued. He was older, he was larger and his demeanour was that of a man who knew despondency well. Now she described him as a picture of sadness, an homage to regret. He spoke to her like a man forlorn in a tone that lacked the confidence he once seemed to ooze. And yet, the embers of a once-known passion glowed within her still. I knew instinctively that she would see him again no matter what I or anyone else thought about it. When I asked her why she would do such a thing, she simply replied, "because I love him."

12

KIM

After starting to believe that maybe it would never happen, it had taken just one Congrelate conversation for Ricky and I to end up in bed together. He had no way of knowing just how long I'd coveted this and probably thought that our moment had passed, consigning it to the annals of fate just as I had. Our story wasn't finished though and what went on to happen comfortably surpassed my previous experience when I had lain alone in his bed, fulfilling my desires with visions of what could be.

I started by telling him that it just wasn't necessary, that he didn't need to do it because I was pretty safe about these things. Without telling him the whole truth, I really didn't think I could make it any clearer. He laughed before he insisted and recited a tale of how he'd once caught an ex-girlfriend pricking his contraceptives full of holes prior to having sex with him. In addition to pleading with him to agree to start a family with her, she'd been doing this for months without his having any knowledge of it and the episode had clearly horrified him. I didn't say but I guess I kind of understood and although the conversation was perhaps unseemly, it wasn't to prove ominous, for what transpired between us was anything but regrettable.

When you sleep with someone for the first time it is never quite how you imagine. Be it better or worse it is always different and it seldom equates to what you have foreseen. I often think back to the first time I slept with Simon, how uncomfortable I had felt in taking his virginity and allowing him to think that he had taken mine. There were others that came along after him (but still during our time together) that he knew nothing of and whose actions in the bedroom in no way reflected the mild-mannered characters they had so skilfully portrayed before the act of consummation. I thought of Adrian, the budding tattoo artist that liked to use my body as a sketchbook and then of the ever-urbane Nathaniel, who chose to interrupt proceedings at the height of our intercourse to take a call from the wife I didn't know he had. Most of them hadn't mattered much to me beyond my own gratification but I could at least now state with certainty (and by the benefit of comparison) that Ricky had proved to be the best of them all.

In truth, I hadn't anticipated any less but where I'd expected to find traces of restraint and inhibition, there was instead a symmetry to our lovemaking that seemed pleasantly assuring for two so unacquainted. The ease into which our bodies converged meant that no act felt like encroachment, no urge too bold or sensation too wild and we simply proceeded without challenge or hindrance. The conviction to his lovemaking was matched by a contrasting softness as he obeyed every cleft and groove of my body with a startling sensitivity that sent me into near rapture. Even as we lay together, basking in that gentle fatigue before sleep, I felt a heart that beat in sync with my own and I longed for the night to extend that blissful, eternal rhythm.

I awoke to find a rather altered Ricky from the one I had fallen asleep beside as if the hours of brief slumber had brought about a sharp transition to his mood. Gone was the man who had made love to me with such strength and confidence and in his place lay one unmoving, staring at the ceiling in an unblinking trance. This change to his character had been so great that I felt reluctant to rouse him and it forced me to lie estranged from him, quite in the shadow of this powerful abstraction. With my curiosity piqued, I eventually felt compelled to break the silence by returning to a subject we had touched upon earlier.

"So why was it that you didn't want to have children with the girlfriend you mentioned earlier? Did you not love her? I mean, I guess I understand why you broke up but it sounded like she told you about wanting to start a family before you found out about what she was doing behind your back." Breaking momentarily from his far-removed state, he turned to face me and offered a probing look like one deciphering the motive of the question.

"Because I never wanted to be a father, that's why."

The answer, (though undoubtedly clear) hadn't seemed like enough so I ignored his usual inclination towards reticence and continued probing.

"So it wasn't the deception that bothered you but the thought of fatherhood?"

"Well I guess it was maybe a little bit of both," he replied, fidgeting slightly and clearly a little irked.

"And do you feel the same way now, about having children I mean?"

"Yes, absolutely, more so than ever." He affirmed this in a tone both calm and definitive but I remained unsatisfied and so I gently squeezed his arm just above the elbow to goad him into further detail. It caused him to flinch involuntarily but did prompt him to indulge me. "Look, Kim, I didn't want children then and I don't want children now. I don't see a future with children in it and I'm happy with that. I don't want to hold something in my arms and pretend to love it or to understand it's worth while waiting for some special bond to form that I instinctively know is never going to happen." His eyes returned their focus towards the ceiling and although he sounded a little exasperated, it wasn't quite anger.

A sense of deflation had surged through my body at that point and taken up habitation somewhere inside my ovaries. Settling for a safe place between confession and concealment, I didn't reveal anything because I hadn't really judged if my current predicament would ease or alarm him. His words could've been bravado but they shook me nonetheless and it was beyond my comprehension to think how anyone could be so vehemently against the idea of parenthood. So instead, I lay unmoving, disguising my discomfiture, only this time it would be Ricky who pierced the mood of stillness with a line of questioning I had far from expected.

"Kim," he began, somewhat pensively, "can I ask you something personal? It's not that you have to answer if you don't want to or anything but I feel like it's something that I'd be better for knowing, something that I really *ought* to know."

"Sure Ricky," I answered, meeting his enquiry with a visible disquiet. "I don't have anything to hide from you."

He paused for a moment, unaware of this untruth, before his focus seemed to switch from one of preoccupation to a deep, solid scrutiny. Still he didn't stir, conversing with the ceiling as if it were somehow mediating the conversation.

"Have you ever slept with somebody that you didn't love? Somebody that you could never love? Somebody whose love you could never really be worthy of?" Only then had he turned to face me, staring so intently, that every last remnant of scheme or design seemed to drift away from me. It felt as though this was a sinister sorcery, a control that he was mindful of along with the difficulty I encountered in attempting to repel it. I studied the glare that exerted this influence for any signs of remorse, embarrassment or even humour but detected nothing of the kind. It became quite clear that he was about to offer no retraction.

"You know that it's impossible for me to answer that Ricky," I replied.

"Why?" he then asked with an evident frustration. "It's just like you said, you've no reason to hide anything from me, I'm not here to make any judgements."

"Because I don't want to lie to you," I said, "and I'm scared of saying something that I'll never be able to retract."

"But you know how it feels to hurt somebody, right? I guess that's what I'm asking, *that's* what I'm really curious about." His query was presented with an urgency that seemed to be gathering speed. I wasn't sure if I was being tested or interrogated but I knew this didn't pass for conventional pillow talk and I certainly didn't enjoy this pursuit of unnecessary details.

"I just don't understand your interest in this Ricky," I responded, albeit a little reluctantly, "and I don't see the point in recalling my past for the study of others. Mistakes, regrets, they hold no interest for me, they've made me what I am so I waste little time reflecting on them. I'm only concerned with what I can change, the here, the now, whatever's gone before us both is out of our control."

An elongated pause greeted that last response and so I lay relieved, fatigued and indebted to the silence. Had I said too much? Had I said too little? It was difficult to discern for Ricky had returned to his former state of inertia, focusing on something overhead as if some greater presence had once again taken command of his mind.

"I used to spend a lot of time thinking about the hurt I inflicted on other people," he continued, "so much so, that it would often keep me awake at night, the guilt would just consume me and I could never figure why. I was selfish, manipulative and deceitful but oddly enough, nobody wanted to accept this. Instead, they saw my defects as weaknesses, like some harmless compulsion they'd be capable of curing and all of them relied on a sense of human decency that they assumed I had. But you know, the truth is that I never wanted or needed to change and no matter how often I said this, my honesty always seemed to be ignored. Once I recognised this, everything became easier. I knew that the blame lay with them, not me and so I started to punish those around me for this blatant and recurring oversight. I don't feel that guilt anymore and I can't tolerate people that believe in happy endings."

I watched as the rhythm to Ricky's breathing became convulsive and unsteady, losing its regular pattern and falling out of sync with the measure of his words. I turned towards where he lay, cupped his head between my hands and met that piercing gaze with a resistance I had never yet been able to accomplish. Through those beautiful eyes, I knew that I was looking at a damaged soul much like my own but like most things in life it was still salvageable.

"I'm not sure that happy endings exist, there are always too many loose ends and it all just sounds too simplistic," I offered, unsure if Ricky was even chasing a response at that point. "Do you know the type of person that I want to be with? I want to be with someone and not really know them, I want to be excited by what they could be and not long for what they were. People say a sign of loving someone is the ability to finish the other's sentences but that's precisely what I don't want. I want the mystery that imperfection brings and not some false ideal."

Ricky seemed buoyed by that answer and withdrew my hands from his face.

"Listen, Kim," he said, with a look of intense entreaty. Gone were the signs of his inner turmoil, vanished just as quickly as they'd appeared. "I just want you to know that I'm trying really hard to be honest with you here and I hope that you can see that. None of this is an act and you probably know of me now all you're ever going to. I guess what I'm trying to say is that if this is the only chance we ever have of spending the night together then I've got no issue committing this to memory, no issue at all."

I thought this a beautiful thing to say because I didn't see an ending but rather a beginning. There could be no return now to what we were, no more subtext and furtive glances, his confessions had confirmed this and where others had probably felt daunted by the strength of his admissions, I felt quite the opposite. I wanted him to know that they brought me closer to him and strengthened my affection. I sensed that this was it, the moment where my strength of feeling moved beyond regular definition and into an unknown, where all the shortcomings of earlier passions would lie exposed. This was what others told you that you would one day feel and yet, there was still recognition in the revelation despite it being so new to me. It was really so simple, I was in love.

I fell back to sleep next to an unmoving Ricky, knowing instinctively that when I woke again, he would no longer be there alongside me. True to this prophecy, when I opened my eyes, he had gone but the aftermath didn't feel as lonely as it should have. My eyes traced the objects that lined his bedroom, some which I remembered and others that I did not. It seemed roomier, cleaner, lighter and more homely and I couldn't decide if all of this had changed since I last lay there or if I was simply viewing things from an entirely new perspective.

13

SIMON

"Hello?"

"Hi Simon, it's Kim."

"Oh, hi Kim."

"How are you?"

"I'm fine, what's up? It's nothing serious is it? Is everything okay with the flat?"

"You're never in these days anyway, it seems like I always have to call you to conduct a conversation."

"I've had a really long day, Kim, I'd prefer it if you could leave the heavy stuff for another time if possible?"

"Look, you remember that it's two years since the death of my father, right? Well my mother has arranged a small family gathering in order to commemorate the occasion. It's nothing formal or anything but I thought it right to ask you if you wanted to come. My father did care a lot about you."

"Does your mom know we've split up, Kim?"

"I've told my mother everything. Of course she does."

"Will Declan be there?"

"I've not spoken to him but I imagine so, why's that important?"

"Of course I'll be there. When is it?"

"It's next Sunday afternoon."

"Yes that's fine, no problem."

"It's just going to be close family there but that's how my mother sees you I guess. You were a big part of both their lives and I want you to understand that. It's just (voice becoming muffled) such a hard time for me right now and I need people around me that show consideration for my feelings. I hope that for one day we can cast aside any hostility that exists between us?"

"I never meant to hurt you Kim, you know that don't you?"

"We don't need to drag all this up again."

"I agree. That's the last thing I want. Are you okay? You sound upset."

"Simon (weeping now), I can't talk about this memorial just now, it's left me in such an emotional state, I don't think I'm fully with it."

"I understand. We can talk about this tomorrow, if you like?"

"Yes, tomorrow (still weeping)."

"Good night Kim."

"Good night Simon."

It's odd to think how despite still sharing a living space together, Kim opts to call me rather than extend the invitation in person, as if the act in itself would be seen as a concession. It's not really a measure of how far our relationship has declined because it's been this way for quite a while now and we tend to avoid personal interaction like it's some tacit clause written into a divorce agreement.

I said yes to the offer of attending the memorial even though the prospect of spending the day roaming around the perimeters of Kim's family like the ghost at the feast isn't the most appealing. I haven't seen or spoken to any of them since the break-up, which is another of the rudimentary laws of separation that one simply has to adhere to, no matter the difficulty of the undertaking. That didn't rest easy with me for they had been a fixture in my life for twelve years, treating a younger and more inhibited version of myself with dignity and kindness and then assuming a position of silent neutrality when things between the two of us had soured. It's a given, no doubt, that Kim has publicly conveyed a version of the break-up to them that greatly favours her, passing the fault onto me wherever possible, so my reservations can perhaps be understood. Perspective seldom favours the narrator of course so maybe had I been in her position, I would've done much the same.

In an odd way, it had been the death of her dad, Barney, that brought about the end of our relationship although it didn't become clear to either of us until much later. In the very same week of his passing, Kim learned of her infertility and the proximity of these two tragedies blunted her sense of clarity which the luxury of time would surely have prevented. And I say this because there is simply no other way to explain the remarkable transition of the woman I had fallen in love with into someone that I didn't recognise in such a short space of time. Perhaps she was driven by the notion that one must replace death with life but I've no doubt that when the fertility tests showed that the problem lay with her, that was the point where her rapid descent into irrationality began. Deny it as she did, it was obvious that she was grieving and what had been a somewhat casual approach towards the conceiving of a child up to then was quickly usurped by a frantic vigour to become a mother. Whilst I stood by, stuck somewhere in between consolation and protestation, I recoiled at the suggestion of IVF and tried to highlight the alternatives, all of which were roundly dismissed. She must have known that I was merely placating her but it didn't seem to matter, she knew I couldn't walk away in the midst of such tragedy and so her obstinacy defeated my logic. We broke up one year later.

On reflection, the news should've hurt me more than it did and I should've been capable of echoing her sense of loss with a modicum of sincerity. Perhaps I could've made her understand if I'd been selfish enough to impose my true feelings on to her at the time but there simply wasn't room for self-indulgence and whatever I did feel, I too often downgraded. The truth is that I longed to be the one at fault because the thought of becoming a dad had failed to captivate me in the way that it did so many others. I couldn't abide by the theory that parenthood was something that one simply grew into because my parents had failed me and I have never forgiven them for it. Although it wasn't clear to me at the time, my relationship with Kim had always been my riposte to the two of them (my parents), my way of showing that their failure and neglect was in no way inherent nor was it a fate that I was destined to repeat. Back then, my dreams both numerous and pure didn't seem so flawed and I often felt that they were tangible and still within my grasp. A baby, I felt, would've made those coveted goals impossible or at best deferred them and while my ambitions remained attainable, I couldn't allow a child to hinder them.

In weak moments when I'm prone to melancholy, I sometimes wonder what might have been had we somehow managed to defy biological science or had Barney not succumbed to dementia. I can't be certain that things would've turned out the way that they did but I strongly suspect that the inevitable would only have been delayed. The way that Kim and I ended things lacked the finality that it deserved as we'd been together the whole of our adult lives and I still could not recall the day, the time or the parting words that were exchanged. We had both earned our swansong and yet instead, it felt as though we had acted out our final scene together only to turn towards the audience and realise that nobody was watching us anymore.

14

KIM

"Hello?"

"Hi."

"Who is this?"

"What?"

"Who?"

"Simon, it's Kim."

"Hold on a minute, I'll go outside."

"Okay."

"I said hold on a minute."

"Yes, I said that's fine."

"Sorry."

"It's fine Simon."

"What? No, not you, I just bumped into someone. Right, who is this?"

"Simon, it's Kim, did you not recognise my name or number on your phone?"

"Oh, hi Kim."

"Simon, have you taken my number off your phone?"

"No, I haven't."

"Where are you? It sounds loud."

"It's not serious is it Kim? Are you okay? I can come straight back to the flat if it is?"

"No, it's not, well, it isn't gravely serious."

"I've had a really long day. I'd prefer it if you could leave the heavy stuff until another time if possible."

"Simon, please don't start being unnecessarily

defensive with me, I just need to inform you of something. You remember that it's two years since my father died? Well my mother has arranged a small, family gathering in order to commemorate the occasion. It's nothing formal or anything but I thought it right to ask you if you wanted to come. Now you've not been formally invited so please don't feel that you have to attend but it would be unfair of me not to give you that opportunity."

"Of course I'll be there Kim, when is it?"

"It's just going to be for close family I think, most of whom you've never met, she really wants that close-knit family feel, you know?"

"When is it?"

"It's next Sunday afternoon, at least I think it is. My mother was indistinct about the details. Why, does it clash with something you already have planned?"

"Yes that's fine, no problem."

"She understands though Simon, if you can't make it I mean, she really does understand."

"Kim, I'm repeating myself here."

"I'm just saying. You know this isn't a particularly easy time for me and a bit of consideration for that instead of your being so curt every time would be appreciated."

"I never meant to hurt you Kim, you know that don't you?"

"Simon, please don't drag all of this up again, you don't sound like you're fully with it."

"Can we talk about this when I next see you?"

"I'm happy to talk about the memorial if you want to come but I don't need any emotional bombshells being dropped in my lap at this time and neither do my family. I really need you to be conscious of that."

"What?"

"It doesn't matter."

"Kim? Hello?"

"I need to go, Simon. Good night."

"Kim?"

I'd been left with little choice but to call Simon seeing as our paths seldom seem to cross these days and even when they do, it's often by accident rather than design. Perhaps I hadn't been clear enough but I'd known about my father's memorial for quite some time now and had withheld this detail from him for reasons that he could neither know nor understand. This wasn't due to some unnecessary acrimony but more so because I felt it easier to perpetuate his ignorance rather than enlighten it. My first reason was that I hadn't yet told my mother nor indeed any of my immediate family of the break-up on account of the interrogation that I was likely to receive once the news had been announced and a memorial for my dead father was hardly going to be the best time. That said, by way of an alternative, the thought of spending the day with Simon, flaunting an imitation of togetherness, struck me as a grim pretence too far and one that I simply couldn't entertain. My family (and most notably my mother) would be perceptive enough to see right through that charade and so it wasn't really fair to ask Simon to aid me in that subterfuge. Equally however, I didn't quite know how to divulge the details of our separation in a manner that would convince any of the guests that we were well and truly separated. The few in my life that already knew had all listened to the sorry saga willingly enough but seemed unable to accept that there was no cataclysmic conclusion to report after spending so long together and tended to view the split as a hiatus. The fact that we still lived together didn't make them any more credulous but the decision had been a mutual one and despite rumours to the contrary, was not inspired by an illicit dalliance that either of us could be accused of.

I couldn't transport any of them back to a specific day that I had fallen out of love with Simon because that day did not exist. The act of separation was not immediate but was a protracted severance, like a task on a list of things to do that one had simply forgotten to carry out. Sure, I could elaborate on the IVF situation and the wedge that this had driven between us but Simon's unwillingness to have children (although significant) was a detail that had simply accelerated the process and magnified our unsuitability. Now, we owed it to ourselves to seek something better in our lives and for me that process had already begun.

It dawned on me prior to calling Simon that there was one other option that I'd yet to consider, which was to invite Ricky to the memorial in place of him. That, in one single act, would present the separation to everybody and take the onus of explanation away from me, knowing that nobody would dare ask about my relationship with my former boyfriend when in the company of what could possibly be my new one. Simon would be upset of course but he would spare himself the humiliation of attending once he'd settled on an excuse that would prove credible enough and I would only contest his decision half-heartedly.

Whatever I decided, I felt certain that my mother would arrive at the truth and once she did, she would be heartbroken because she openly adored Simon. For whatever reason, she has always wanted me to end up with someone a lot like my father which I find inexplicable considering how she felt anything but love for him. In Simon, she saw someone that mirrored her husband's personality and her praise of him was unwavering. Perhaps just like my father, her fondness for him stemmed more from a lack of imperfections than it did from an abundance of discernible qualities for had she taken the time to form a more thorough review of his character, his deficiencies would surely have unravelled before her. For example, my mother had no idea how Simon often drank excessively, a problem of his that became ever more prominent towards the end of our relationship nor did she see how quickly his clarity of thought eluded him once the drink took hold. She also had no way of knowing how his moods would typically fluctuate under the influence of alcohol, be they wistful or macabre and although the former was initially endearing to me, I grew to loathe this state of mind far greater than I did his gloominess.

It hadn't always been that way because there was a time when things were very different and I still missed the boy that I once fell in love with. Back then, my friends would call him 'Sensible Simon' because of how risk-averse he was and his manners, like his ethics, were solid and selfless. He didn't drink or curse or pride himself on falsity and this I deemed a welcome relief at an age where boys are generally inclined to the opposite. He was creative but with restraint (although that would later change) and I often relied on his sense of perspective in domestic situations when Claire and Alice were at war with each other. He valued youth and loathed responsibility but in an odd way, it was perhaps because of this that he would go on to fail at becoming the partner that I needed him to be in our later years together. The change was not immediate but the progression of our relationship was undoubtedly stalled by what seemed an incessant longing for former times that began to subsume his thinking and arrest his ambition. It was a regressive yearning for a period of our lives that I had no wish to revisit, much less repeat, and once our neutral ground disappeared out of sight, so too did any hope of reinvigorating our love.

With all that said, as suitable partners go, I knew that my mother wouldn't take to Ricky and that his numerous qualities would probably be lost on her. It was infeasible to think that she would embrace him in the same way that she had Simon or that her misinformed opinion would work in his favour. For a start, she felt a natural aversion towards any man that took pride in refining his appearance and Ricky was undoubtedly attentive to the way he looked. She wouldn't see his robust, natural beauty, for she would only focus on his embellishments and in her eyes that would amount to vanity. If she admired Simon's tact and sensitivity, then Ricky's candour would alarm and quickly unsettle her and though

I think she'd recognise his enigmatic draw, she'd be deeply
cynical of the mysteries that lingered about his character.

But extending the invitation to Ricky was really
only half the story as there was a question of far greater
importance that I really needed to ask him. Like the revelation
of my break-up with Simon, this I felt reluctant to do against
the backdrop of my gluttonous relatives while the vol-au-
vents are being passed around and my mother's range of
drinks are being unanimously censured. I simply *had* to tell
him and I had to tell him soon while I still had a buffer of
uncertainty. He needed to know exactly what parenthood
meant to me and just how integral to my future happiness it
is before I ask him if he will do me the honour of fathering my
first child.

It's not that I'd forgotten his misgivings on the subject,
I remembered them all clearly, it's just that I didn't believe
them. In truth, I'd heard it all before as it's the type of thing
men tend to say around women when they suspect the
maternal fires are already aflame and they flee the inferno
instinctively. But Ricky had let his guard slip in the moments
after our sleeping together and had revealed to me something
of his true character, a spirit akin to mine, a man well capable
of love. What would be the point in examining the profiles of
a host of sperm donors that I knew very little about, I figured,
when a man who fitted the mould of everything I wanted was
already in my life? He was beautiful, healthy and intelligent,
with characteristics I could vouch for and for a sacrifice so
simple, he could offer me the greatest gift of all and, perhaps
in time, a gift that we could share. Because that was really
what all of this was about, giving a child the opportunity of
knowing their own father without assuming that my need
to become a parent was greater than the need of my child to
fully understand and establish their own identity. It would
of course remain dependent on Ricky's wishes and perhaps
beyond donation he would crave no further involvement but
I had seen children melt the hardest of hearts and I sense that

he would make an excellent father be he distant or near.

The enormity of this decision had not been lost on me and I wasn't foolish enough to think that a positive response from him would be immediately forthcoming. I wanted him to answer honestly rather than in haste and so perhaps the confines of the family home in which I'd been raised would not serve me very well. Lastly (and perhaps most significantly), I still couldn't face the thought of my mother finding out about this course of IVF, as she, the God-fearing widow, had once described my initial flirtation with this as 'impatient and unnecessary' to all who would listen. It was a view she would consolidate by rhetorical debate with her sycophantic friends and more often than not, this would be followed by lengthy laments of how her grandmotherly credentials were sadly going to waste (and all of this said without a trace of irony). It is safe to say that I am not looking forward to my father's memorial.

15

SIMON

'Forget the Past, his fate and fame shall be
An echo and a light unto eternity!'

The choice of that line from Shelley's 'Adonais' struck me
as an odd one primarily because it seemed a tad banal and
because he'd never expressed a fondness for his work in all
the time I'd known him. It was centrally placed (but without
accreditation) on the front page of an invitation to Barney's
memorial that I find by accident while tidying up the flat.
Posited beneath a pile of Kim's effects, it was as though she
hadn't intended for me to find it (even though it was addressed
to us both) but even if she had secreted it, it didn't much
matter now.

    I'd always found the atmosphere at the Pleydell
household rather difficult to assimilate with in the time that
Kim and I had spent together which meant that the idea
of attending a memorial for her late dad caused me some
trepidation. Kim's childhood differed from mine in just
about every way imaginable and although we both sought
distance from our parents, our reasons for doing so were in
no way comparable. Kim had wanted for nothing growing
up and her parents had raised her with an admirable and
enviable freedom in a home that was rich with expanse and
luxury. That they could afford such liberality was not in
question and their wide-ranging affluence was both financial
and philosophical, underpinned by a moral flexibility that

is the privilege of wealth. But for all her inherited riches, I would argue that none of this served to prepare her well for adulthood and did not cultivate her character in the way that it should have. She simply didn't understand the unique advantages that had been afforded her and this had arguably affected her sense of limitation in later life. Too often she would flit from one goal to another with an animated but fleeting passion and although she was undoubtedly talented, her fiscal security would always act as a safety net, eliminating risk and devaluing her achievements. I envied her upbringing because she just didn't realise how lucky she was but instead of cherishing such good fortune, she had chosen to detach herself from it for reasons that were both illogical and lamentable to me. She couldn't have wished for two better role models than her parents and although she wasn't related to Declan by blood, I couldn't quite share in her opinion that he was somehow the villain of the piece. The protracted legal wrangling over Barney's estate hadn't helped matters of course but if this memorial could go some way towards engineering a familial disarmament, then Kim still stood a chance of righting her obvious mistakes.

I should have reproached her for all of the above and challenged her unwarranted criticisms back in the days where she still loved me enough to value my opinions. I didn't do this because she knew better than anybody that my resentment was not aimed solely at her and that my sense of injustice went way beyond wanting what I could never have. By contrast, although we both did seemingly all that we could to keep our history at arm's length, Kim will always find herself on the cusp of reconciliation should she choose to seek this, whereas I cannot conceive of anything less appealing than burying my discontent towards my parents.

The term that society would use to best describe my mom and dad would be 'functioning alcoholics.' It's a trite phrase assigned to those who make it through their day-to-day activities with few outward signs of the true damage that this excess is causing both to themselves and those around them. I didn't much care for the common perception of alcoholism for it didn't match my own experience, the father often seen as the brutish, violent patriarch and the mother weak, repressed and utterly browbeaten, at least to say that it didn't match my own reality. My parents are habitual drinkers and have been so for as long as I can remember. As a child, my weekends seemed to consist of an endless stream of guests filing in and out of our house at all hours of the night. There was seldom any reason to celebrate but that didn't stop all manner of people imposing themselves on our family home, a group largely made up of lecherous older men (always family friends) who toed the borders of tactility and their screeching wives with garish, ill-fitting attire and gin-coated lips. There were tears and loud music, dancing and discord, innumerable breakages and asinine debate. You don't mind it as a child because it's all you really know and you embrace the liberal nature of your parents allowing you to stay up later than your friends at school. You can be forgiven for assuming that this is all somehow normal but of course, it isn't and the older I became, the more I began to realise that my parents' behaviour was the exception and not the rule. Although the partying didn't grind to an absolute halt, in time, the numbers started to dwindle. Maybe their friends moved on or just grew tired of their debauched lifestyle (it was never openly discussed) but my parents were unwilling to do the same and their revelry was substituted with sullen, lone drinking, the two of them continuing to imbibe into the early hours without the staying power of former times. The mornings that followed were predictably worse than ever with the daytime spent trying to shake the inevitable lethargy and counting down the hours until the brief respite of another drink returned them back to whatever high it was that they thought they were attaining. As far as I know, none of this has changed.

    As I entered my teenage years, I quickly realised that my parents' predilection for excess had been passed down to me and that this destructive gene was indeed inherent. It is knowledge that I live with every day. It goes beyond the lure of alcohol, presenting itself in the form of various obsessions that have, from time to time, plagued my life. My parents' lives still centre around their binging because they've never found anything to replace it with and I lack the endurance to offer them an olive branch. I differ from them in that I often like to balance on the precipice and test my self-control but that vision of the depth of my plight is always just enough to pull me back.

The bulk of my reproach is reserved for my dad, a man who has failed in his duty to protect his family and has instead succumbed to his own indulgences, time and time again. In truth I hate him, for he is the antithesis of everything I want to be and he remains both a terrible dad and a feckless husband. Conversely, my mom has made various attempts over the years to break away from the alcoholic drudgery, all of which I've supported but all of which without success. The older I've become, the easier it is to sense the unhappiness about her, from the craterous eyes to the crippling inertia, evidence that she is tired of this debilitating lifestyle and wasteful repetition. She's left him several times but has always returned to him after what is more often than not, a futile hiatus. My mom, being an only child, has no other family to turn to so will inevitably arrive at my aunt's door (my dad's sister) who then spends the ensuing days resolutely defending him and subtly shifting the blame of their brief separation on to her. My dad knows that she just isn't strong enough to cope without him and does nothing but revel in this when the inevitable reconciliation occurs, usually with my mom in tears and professing culpability. Back when I was a child, I used to pity her but now her weakness does not elicit any such response from me. I left home, moved in with Kim and, at least in that respect of my life, I've never looked back.

Now, I don't really have a relationship with either of them that I can speak of and my life is easier because of this.

Mom likes to call every now and then, mostly at a time that she knows I'm unavailable and her rambling messages are always devoid of any real thread or content. When we do speak, the summary of every call largely amounts to the same, nothing has changed, she will say (as if that's somehow a positive thing) and I'll just hang up the phone and feel no better for it.

Returning the invitation to the place of its possible concealment, I focus once more on the simple couplet that adorns it. I know that if I were to die then I'd want something more thought-provoking than that but I'm not sure who'd feel qualified to make that decision. Kim? My parents? The Croc? It doesn't bear thinking about and is impossible to call but then it's difficult to encapsulate a life in just two lines. Death provides a sentimentality that is seldom offered the living.

16

KIM

When my mother called me this morning to talk over the final details of my father's memorial, I really hadn't expected the two bombshells that she was about to drop. Firstly, that she was in advanced discussions with a potential buyer for the family home and that she was confident that the sale would be completed in the next week or so. Not only this (and perhaps more significantly), she went on to say how she felt it only fitting that I should receive a share of the agreed sale price and that if accepted, she would transfer the said amount over to me once the sale had been completed. While she then digressed into explicit detail of how suitable the property was likely to be for the prospective buyer, I managed to form a quick calculation in my mind as to what my share would amount to. It was difficult to contain my elation when I arrived at a figure of forty-five thousand pounds and although my mother had been initially reluctant to verify the sum, she later conceded that it was 'very much in the ballpark'. My mother could not comprehend the significance of the news she had just relayed to me without my having to reveal to her the uncomfortable truth of my financial situation and so I disguised my relief as happiness for her. This sum of money would not only clear the mounting debts that I had incurred but would also enable me to take on full ownership of 228 if Simon can be convinced to sell me his share of the property. In doing so, this would sever the last tie that I shared with him and with nothing left to link us both together, my life could finally begin again. Yes, after months of sleepless nights and days filled with endless worry, salvation, I felt, was on the verge of being secured and this through the unlikeliest of sources. All I have to do now is stave off the creditors with solid assurances that my mother's word is gospel and hope they take the money from the sale of a house I don't own as valid security. I thanked her ebulliently while she mistook my tears of relief for ones of sadness, telling me how she just couldn't stay in that house any longer and apologising for making me upset. I didn't correct her but I did pass on my bank account details.

My mother then deemed this an appropriate time to 'remind' me that Declan was planning on saying a few words at my father's memorial this coming Sunday. When I replied that I had no knowledge of this, she reluctantly conceded that she may well have forgotten to tell me but that her intention to do so had been ample. Perhaps to her, a failure to alert me of my adopted brother's intention to take centre stage on Sunday wasn't a significant detail but to me, it felt like an oversight too far and bad memories of the eulogy he'd delivered at my father's funeral still loomed large. That day, in spite of the strongest of entreaties, he stood before the grieving congregation and offered up a tribute that was rich in merriment and jest, highlighting the quirks of my father's character and nothing of his virtues. To me, it was a breach of decency that placed a church full of mourners in an uncomfortable position but that's Declan for you, no one else matters when he wants to have his way and the sentiments of others are just collateral damage. The result of all this now means that I too will have to prepare a speech as I know how uncaring it will look if my father's only child is to pay no tribute to him at his memorial.

At this point, it's important to clarify why I do not share a relationship with Declan and how there is nothing to suggest that is ever likely to change. My parents adopted him when he was just three years old and I remember him as a placid child who was often unresponsive to affection or instruction. These unusual traits were linked to an early diagnosis of autism and although this condition inhibited him, it wasn't solely responsible for the distance we were accustomed to. The truth is that I never saw Declan as my sibling particularly as the age gap between us was so great (I was fifteen when he joined our family) and while my parents lavished him with his every want and need, it left little room for me to do the same. But contrary to what you may think, I never resented Declan for the affection my parents bestowed on him because I knew it hadn't come at the expense of any love for me. He was a product of their loneliness, a second sorry attempt at parenthood and they were somehow foolish enough to believe that it could actually work. That Declan would be burdened in later life by the weight of their failings was very much a given but it was the aftermath of my father's passing that went on to reveal just how damaged he really was.

My father battled bravely against dementia for three arduous years before eventually succumbing to the disease. He'll be remembered as a healthy man who was principled, prodigious and intellectually gifted but the illness tore through his capacities in a manner so swift it seemed almost unreal. It was a plight made worse by its severity and too often towards the end of his life, I gazed into his eyes in search of the power that they once emitted and saw nothing but an empty scrutiny. I didn't want this version of the man who had raised me to tarnish my memory of him but however hard I tried, I couldn't see past the harsh regression of his faculties or the lifeless touch of his hands. I knew I couldn't help him, not in the way he needed anyway and I began to realise that much like him, I had ceased to serve a purpose. Although it pained me in ways I couldn't possibly describe, as his condition worsened, I had to remove myself from the indignity of his final days and accept that I had done all that I could. As with a book with an inevitable conclusion, I owned no wish to see it through to its bitter end and I wasn't at his bedside when he eventually died.

It was at the height of my father's illness that my mother informed me that she was starting to make some progress with the rewriting of his will, a will he had created some seventeen years previous. My initial reaction was one of confusion; I didn't see what right anyone had to go against my father's wishes, especially when one considered he'd been of sound mind when the original terms had been committed to paper. But my suspicions had been aroused and it soon became clear they were not without foundation. The will had been written prior to his adoption of Declan and as a result of this, the document made no reference to him whatsoever. This enabled me to deduce who had been the true source of the redrafting of the will, the one person who stood to lose most by the imminent death of my father.

I guess he hadn't been brave enough to stake his own claim and so he had artfully hoodwinked my mother (with her credulous nature) into supporting his mercenary cause, thinking that this somehow legitimised his sense of entitlement. She argued that my father had always intended to offer absolute parity in whatever he bequeathed and that the timing of the will had been a most 'unfortunate occurrence', but my resistance had been immediate. I raised the objection that if Declan's memories of my father were as dear to him as he professed then surely they were reward enough? It was he, after all, that had received the greatest gift one could ever ask for, a family that had taken him in and cared for him when his own mother had left him abandoned and destitute. But where one expected to find gratitude and humility, there was really nothing more than avarice and selfishness by one who coveted the spoils of things to which he had no right.

To this day, I level no reproach at my mother for the part she played in it all even if her twisted sense of diplomacy got the better of her. Though a little scatty, she isn't malevolent and it was clear she'd been manipulated by one so knowing of her emotional shortcomings. I still regret the legal wrangles that followed and the position that they placed her in but once Declan's motives had been exposed, I was left with little choice but to defend my father's wishes with a faithful resolution. It was a defence that proved more costly than I could ever have imagined and many of my father's possessions have since been sold in trying to recoup the money that I have spent in fighting to retain ownership of them. But if it was vindication that I felt with the outcome, then I've known no weaker form and even now, with time since passed, there is anger and regret when I think of Declan and the ill feeling that his conduct has caused. It was because of this grasping, egregious pursuit that the memorial is taking place twelve months later than originally intended and although he should've sought moral reflection in the year that has passed, I've seen no evidence to suggest that this has happened.

17

SIMON

My intention had been to work from home today but it is scuppered on realising that Kim has beaten me to it. Sitting at the breakfast bar in our apartment, she is dressed too casually for a day in the office and is already punching away at her laptop with the look of one fully absorbed in whatever it is that she is doing. At first, there is nothing to suggest that our customary silence will be breached (which suits me well enough) but Kim decides to break the impasse.

"There's a scratch on the front of my car Simon, do you happen to know anything about it?" I keep my back to her while she asks this and then tell her that I've no idea what she's referring to. It had taken her much longer than I'd anticipated to notice the abrasion underneath the headlight that I'd caused while driving drunk and had subsequently failed to inform her of. "What I'm saying is, I've not had a bump in the car because if I had, I think I'd remember doing it." This approach was typically Kim, accusatory but only in a very subtle way, trying to lure me into a confession by sealing off my means of escape. The time for confession, however, had long since passed.

"As would I," I reply, affronted to some extent, "why on earth would I crash your car and withhold that information from you?"

"It just doesn't add up, that's all I'm saying."

"Well, maybe neither of us are to blame? Maybe someone backed into it on their way out of the car park and just didn't bother saying anything. It's only a small scratch, anyway."

"And how do you know that it's only a small scratch? A moment ago you didn't know anything about it and I've not mentioned its size." She asks this with inquisitive eyes resting just above the rim of her laptop, gazing at me in the way a parent does a child after patiently unravelling their lies. It's a look I know well and I briefly consider owning up but there is something deeper than the shame of a confession that compels me to resist.

"Well I don't know how big it is but seeing how neither of us can recall it happening, I'm guessing it's been there for some time and hasn't been significant enough for us to notice it."

While she ruminates over this false theory, I notice that she's surrounded by piles of (what look to be) bills that are stacked beneath a series of makeshift paperweights. I don't consider this particularly noteworthy but for whatever reason Kim obviously does and when she sees my attention shift towards them, she starts to gather them together in a hasty fashion. Her focus is then momentarily diverted away from this as she attempts to fold her laptop, realises (after several attempts) that the hinge is broken and then abandons the operation altogether, leaving the case at an oblique angle.

"It just doesn't seem fair, that's all, and claiming through my insurance is going to be problematic when I try to explain how I'm not responsible but I don't know who is. It's not like I'm the only one who drives it either." She was right of course and in more ways than she probably realised.

"Well if you need me to contribute in any way then I'd be happy to. We're both insured on the car so..."

"No, thank you," she fires back at me, a little too insistently. "Just leave it with me. I think Alice has a brother who should be able to help so I'll call her when I find the time." Even though this isn't really a compromise it still feels like it's something close to it and so I leave for work without facing further cross-examination.

It wasn't unusual for us to spend our limited time together these days quarrelling over money, in fact, it often seemed like we seldom did much else. The car itself had always been a point of contention, primarily because I didn't own it and so every request to borrow it would have to be linked to some form of fictional necessity. And even though I tend to fill it up more than she does, I never say anything by way of remonstration, just as I don't when she 'mistakenly' consumes food that belongs to me from our refrigerator. As a list of singular gripes they don't amount to much but I hated how our home was now the scene of domestic demarcation and how it came to be that I now slept in the spare room as if it was somehow expected of me after the split. The alternative was never entertained of course but it was simply one of a multitude of sacrifices that I had made for Kim that had too often gone without thanks or recognition.

In all honesty, I never wanted to buy the flat in the first place but still I had yielded after Kim had pleaded with me to do so when my role in the relationship was simply to accede to what she wanted. This decision (made under clear duress) left me impoverished and ultimately dependent on her with my only source of income being that of a part-time job in a book store while I studied for my degree. By this time, Kim was already settled in to her new career working long hours and covering most of the costs while I internalised the shame of being the secondary earner. Though she would often say how this didn't bother her, I was unconvinced and I felt at meal times, when we would sit down to discuss our days, that there was an obvious air of dismissiveness in her share of the conversation. But I couldn't match or even understand the gusto that she had for her job, likewise she could never comprehend my preference for study over lucrative employment and when I graduated and had long left the book store, my thinking didn't change. I couldn't allow my method of paid employment to define who I was and the longer I resisted this, the more I yearned for the freedom of former times.

Things had changed too quickly for me but I could still think back to the earlier days of our relationship, a time when our ideals and aspirations were in tandem. It was upon leaving college that we decided we would take a year out of our studies to save enough money so that we could find a university where we could study together. This gave us enough time to carefully consider a variety of different courses at a variety of different universities, thumbing through numerous prospectuses before entering the next phase of our lives. It should've been a year of exciting transition but it didn't transpire that way and instead, we entered a state of limbo, the repercussions of which would be lasting and definitive. This was partly because during that summer, Kim secured a short-term position at a regeneration company and impressed quickly, as, in just a matter of weeks, she was offered a permanent role at the firm. Naturally, I didn't expect her to accept this and so I continued complacently planning for our future until it became clear that her language and behaviour were starting to change. 'Maybe we should just delay the move away another year,' she would say, or 'I'd rather earn money trying to figure out what I want to do with my life than spend three years working towards something I might not even want,' and then eventually, 'Simon, I'll never stop you from doing whatever you want to do.' Once she accepted the role, the dilemma that I was facing should've been harder but the thought of trying to construct a life without her was something that I couldn't contemplate back then. In an attempt to make the best of it, I enrolled on a course that I didn't want to do at a university that I didn't want to attend which was much closer to home and carried with it much less academic repute. It would mean I spent the next three years telling myself that I didn't really have a choice when walking the air-conditioned halls of a modern hub of learning instead of something ornate as I'd always envisaged.

In retrospect, I now attribute much of my unhappiness to the sacrifices I made during that pivotal year of my life. Our relationship would never have survived our being so very far apart but like all errors made in youth, perspective arrives too late and I was powerless to change anything. She is ignorant of my regret I'm sure and though I tried for many years to divert any fault from her, I did so more from personal denial than I did from ever really believing it.

After graduating, I reluctantly resigned from my job at the book store and secured employment at Tanner & Webbing so that I could contribute more financially to the apartment. Contrary to what I'd expected, my sense of ownership did not increase with my greater outlay and Kim maintained a tight control over just about everything, my opinion being seldom sought. She had fallen in love with Gaddis Avenue from the moment we moved in and saw it not just as a reward for day-to-day endeavours but as a material symbol of her success. It is because of this affection that I remain baffled as to why she's never made an offer to buy out my share of it and now I'm beginning to wonder whether there are reasons that I'm just not privy to that could explain this reluctance. After all, the status quo wasn't helping either of us, she clearly doesn't enjoy cohabiting with me any more than I do with her and though there had been a time where I'd have been happy to rid myself of the memories and the daily grind of our discord, circumstances had now changed. No longer do I feel any great desire to sell 228 and even less so to sell to Kim. Although the flat itself was once nothing more to me than a place to live, I now saw it as home and I have grown to like living in the city more than I thought I ever would. I liked being surrounded by the bars and the restaurants, the speed and the noise, I like sitting on the balcony of an evening and walking in to work every morning. In an odd sort of a way, I owed this transition of feeling to Kim, this had been *her* dream and I'd inherited a way of living that I could no longer conceive of giving up. I guess it's strange how life works out sometimes and if I were to make her an offer, this would be dependent on a number of tenuous factors, most notably, my being appointed to a role that I would only be able to gain via reprehensible means. That particular dilemma is in itself however, not yet at the point of conclusion.

18

SIMON

The first email that I open up on my arrival at work is marked 'urgent' and looks to have been sent to all staff on behalf of management. Its content reads how last week's ballot result had now been declared temporarily 'null and void' and that an investigation is currently underway to determine its validity. It offers no further detail other than to say there will be 'more news to follow', akin to a TV newsflash that will clearly serve to pacify nobody. This inevitably leads to a tranche of questions within the team, some of which are directed my way by those that mistakenly assume my role in the union entitles me to a deeper insight.

After fifteen minutes of this I find I have a headache and no feasible line of retreat and in the midst of the furore, I notice I have a missed call from The Croc. Unsurprisingly, he's working from home today but there is something grave and ominous to the voicemail message he has left. In it, he reveals that Marion has been placed on 'indefinite gardening leave' for reasons that he cannot disclose and in a tone that sounds disturbingly similar to the email received this morning, he asks me to refrain from speculation about the reasons why. It dawns on me that I hadn't actually seen Marion since the morning of the ballot count and I start to consider whether the two events could be somehow linked. A part of me knows that this is simply impossible for reasons that are still to reveal themselves but that doesn't much help in quelling my internal conjecture. The only reason that I can think of is that it may have been a procedural move to take her out of the firing line until the inquest can be concluded depending on how wide-ranging that could prove to be. It doesn't add up but even if it is just mere coincidence, I still have a team member out of action and a workload that will need redistributing. When I attempt to return The Croc's call however, it inevitably rings out.

19

KIM

It is still a little painful to remove the mobile phone from my left pocket as I head towards home inside the steady shuffle of afternoon traffic. Under the instructions of Doctor Block, I'd successfully retained water for three hours leading up to my latest ultrasound scan this morning (which had produced entirely positive results) but I hadn't been able to relieve myself fully yet and now every jolt in the road posed a serious problem. If only there were bumper stickers to explain this predicament (I consider) while crediting fellow drivers with a courtesy they probably don't own and prepare myself for the impending flood.

I had every reason to feel upbeat though as my pelvic ultrasound (a far less invasive procedure than its vaginal counterpart) had shown good follicle growth which now meant that the dosage of gonadotrophin I pumped into my body could be reduced. For a collection of reasons, I considered this a good thing as I didn't enjoy the process of self-inoculation and I wouldn't miss the side effects, if indeed they ceased. It was still early days, I had to admit but on removing my ill-fitting medical robe, the sound of a whistling Doctor Block from the other side of the partition had told me indisputably that all was well. He didn't word it so effusively of course but he had no reason to, there is still a long way to go yet and I am barely over the first hurdle.

'DONOR 3675 has now been added to the database,' is the rather glaring message that greets me from my mobile phone once placed on the dashboard. I am now approaching what Doctor Block calls the 'second phase' and unlike much else so far, I will retain a certain amount of control over what is about to happen next. This 'second phase' requires me to find a suitable sperm donor and although Ricky remained my preferred choice, I still need a backup plan in the event that he refuses when I put the question to him. Fortunately, I now have a contingency option right at my fingertips in the form of an app that gives me access to an online donor catalogue containing the profiles of hundreds of different sperm donors from all around the world. This also means that at the tap or swipe of my finger, I can access the personal details of any potential donor, weighing one's credentials against another and doing so remotely with just the aid of a mobile phone. The beauty of the app lies in its simplicity and ease of use for it really seems to do just about everything for you. For example, if any one profile matches your specifications (whatever they may be) then you can elevate that donor above the masses and add him to a personal 'wish list'. This league of preference can be amended at any time which not only enables you to separate the weak from the strong but also to engage both family and friends in the decision-making process. Further to that, I've even set it up so that every time a new donor joins the database, a notification will be sent to me directly, as is the case today with DONOR 3675.

I am not naïve and I know how this method is likely to invite detractors but I don't see how it differs very greatly from the general concept of internet dating. If anything, one could even argue that the app's advantages outweigh that of its internet counterpart for no dating site can guarantee that the profiles of their singletons are entirely truthful without affectation or ambiguity. The donor catalogue however insists on a thorough screening process, one that explores the motives of every man wishing to contribute and involves a vast and rigorous health check. Should the sperm be accepted, the donor then provides a full list of his credentials, which include everything from height, weight and ethnicity to non-innate, personal details such as hobbies, academic attainment and religious denomination. So I figured that the donor catalogue was very much designed for someone like me because it cuts through the timewasters and spares me of the relationship gauntlet that I am just so tired of running. I can locate the same features in a man that would draw me towards him in the flesh but without the drawbacks of his actual personality or the hidden mental scarring that seems to reside in so many of them. Here, there is no such thing as ghosting or infidelity or profile photographs designed to lure and I can choose a man on the elements that really matter before attempting to create human life.

The only negative is that, if anything, there is perhaps too great a choice which in itself makes the act of selection feel somewhat onerous. I didn't like the idea of culling potential donors by elevating certain qualities above others because I really can't decide which should preside over the other. I don't know if blood groups are really that important, whether some groups are better than others and even if they are, is it better to match them or to look for an opposing type? Should my donor be an athlete or a scholar? A boxer or a bookworm? Although I don't like sports personally, that doesn't necessarily mean that I don't own that particular gene.

So quite naturally, I find myself looking for flaws in the profile of DONOR 3675 because it's easier to do that than focus on the positives. Looking at his profile, there doesn't seem to be a great deal that really stands out for him other than his PhD in Biomedical Engineering and that he is of 'Nordic origin.' He's six foot three which is a definite advantage for a male but not so much for a female and images of a tall, ungainly daughter, towering above all the boys that she desires, start to flash through my mind. A lack of inherent femininity is not usually a just cause of resentment for a daughter to carry against her mother but in this situation I *would* be in some way responsible. Once again, I know I am overthinking it but this kind of scenario leaves you with little choice but to do that, swiping away on your phone at profile after profile, hoping that some character trait will just leap out at you, uselessly comparing each to Ricky.

I pull into the nearest fast food restaurant to eat my first meal of the day and relieve my bladder if toilet conditions will allow. According to the app, I currently have eighteen donors on my 'wish list' and already I'm starting to think that maybe I've opted for five or six too many. In the grand scheme of things it is an embarrassment of riches but it is still ironic to think that none of these eighteen donors truly understand just how perilous their positions really are. It is empowering, it is Darwinian but it is also imperative that whatever decision I make, I leave myself with no regrets. I have too many of those already.

20

SIMON

I agreed to meet Vanessa at the Plough and Trinket again despite my best efforts to suggest an alternative venue where the clientele wouldn't leave me feeling quite so self-conscious. We'd been exchanging text messages for a number of days now and although it was difficult to gauge exactly where things really stood with her, I'd definitely detected signs of a mild flirtation. I couldn't say with certainty that aspects of our electronic dialogue hadn't been lost in translation but that was perhaps to be expected when considering the gulf in age and how the nuances of her character were still unknown to me.

Once inside the pub, I eventually find her pocketed away in a partially concealed corner of the room, sharing a table with six of her friends in dangerous striking distance of the pool table. It is evident right away that despite my assumption to the contrary, we would not be spending the evening alone together once I introduce myself and nobody makes any attempt to leave the party. I disguise my irritation in the way I'm prone to do but have to concede that I am secretly disappointed at this. I wonder if their presence has maybe come at Vanessa's request, thinking that maybe she just doesn't feel confident enough to be alone with me right now. I ponder this as it isn't unreasonable to assume that maybe she wants to glean my intentions through the eyes of her friends, but this pondering doesn't last long.

"I need a favour Simon," she whispers to me once I've

shuffled in alongside her and have completed introductions. "Can you order my drinks for me tonight? I've left my ID at home and the bar staff here won't serve me without it." I ruminate on the absurdity of this request for several seconds before I feel her hand reach for mine underneath the table and then her fingers knotting themselves clumsily in between my own. It is obvious that she is tipsy already despite the hindrance that a lack of identification should really have presented and is evidenced further by her theatrical gratitude when I say yes. I then remove myself from the table to order drinks at the bar and try not to let it irk me when Vanessa doesn't join me.

If her friends are embarrassed by my presence then they are good enough not to show it as the night wears on and I get on reasonably enough with all of them, except Sebastian. His reception of me is somewhat cooler than the rest and although I didn't really mind that, I didn't particularly cherish it either. In truth, I felt relieved to meet him in person because it now gave me the chance to simply confirm my initial opinion of him. Sebastian doesn't strike me as unique in any way even though that probably isn't his fault and I've met many of his sort before while at university myself. He's the type who is always present but never really there, the bland undergraduate at the end-of-term party, the one who always remembers the previous night's transgressions. And true to that archetype, Sebastian is personable where necessary and deferential where profitable and that seems to be whenever Vanessa is close at hand. Whenever she excuses herself, the pithiness and prickliness returns and I saw none of the artistry or idealism that really should be resident in one his age. No doubt earlier tonight, he had been convinced by everybody else to join them, ostensibly because they valued his company and not because he used his parents' money to buy rounds or because he answered all the questions on the pub quiz machine. There is really very little that is endearing about him and so it doesn't in the least surprise me that when the rest of Vanessa's friends eventually depart for the night, that he decides to stay.

It is pretty clear that Sebastian has designs on Vanessa and that she is cognisant of this. To her credit, she manages his fixation impressively by turning positively boyish around him and so the boundaries are obvious if not explicitly stated. He resents me for reasons I understand and no doubt views me as the shadowy outsider whose backstory he doesn't believe and whose future happiness may come at the expense of his. In his eyes, I am the person that simply doesn't value what I am about to gain and he knows he cannot verbalise his sense of injustice without running the risk of losing her from his life entirely. I can empathise, I suppose, and so I remain lenient with his low-level contempt and uncomfortable probing because I would've done the same to him had our roles been reversed. If being with Vanessa means I have to tolerate a boy with an infatuation too often at her side, then I can just about accept this.

It takes two hours of dialogue (heavily perforated by Sebastian) before we finally manage to escape him and engineer some time alone. Grabbing Vanessa as she exits the toilet, I whisk her away into the sparsely populated beer garden, no longer caring if he detects that the phone call I claim I have to make is a mere pretence. After all, it is he who has prevented this from happening all night and so the rules of whatever game it is that he's been playing up to now apply to him as much as me.

No longer within the confines of the Plough and Trinket, Vanessa seems visibly liberated, like one free of her shackles and begins to dance and sway in front of me, sashaying her diminutive figure between the glare of the pub and the half-light of the garden.

"My sonata, my beautiful sonata. Simon, put your phone away and listen to my sonata." The tune that she hums as she glides an imaginary bow across the strings of an equally imaginary violin is indecipherable to me. I'm not absolutely sure if one is supposed to dance to a sonata or if Vanessa realises how her voice seems several octaves too high, but it doesn't feel right to intervene and so I simply stand and watch, feeling oddly captivated. She is drunk and looks utterly absurd but also elegant as she sways to a rhythm with a youthful panache that only the carefree can know, and before I know how, the chaotic tune falls silent and she is in my arms.

I yield to the inevitable with an ease I at once remember. Even though I hadn't pictured it happening this way, it feels better for its spontaneity and the lack of contrivance seems to strip me of any apprehension. In the intuitive moments just seconds before we kiss, where vulnerability is usually at its weakest, I feel something close to empowerment or at the very least, validation. I have wanted this to happen from the moment I first set eyes on her, even if I hadn't realised it right away and I had felt aggrieved more deeply than I cared to admit when she had sat in the back of the car and shunned me without even knowing it. I had wanted her in ways that night that I didn't dare visualise because those visions were then illusive but tonight, I leant in to kiss her with the confidence of a tacit reciprocation. Our lips meet gently at first but then settle into their natural undulation while my hands work independently, sliding from her shoulders and down to her slender hips. The beauty of the moment lies not in its sensuality but in its intimacy and I try to absorb the softness of her touch and the warmth of her body as I press it closer to me. Our embrace relaxed, we slowly release and I submit to a bashful silence while her saliva still rests on my tongue and we look for suitable wording to close the scene. We do not find this however, and the impromptu sonata returns along with her unrhythmical dancing as she slips away back out of my arms.

"Yours is the phone that rings in the middle of my masterpiece," she then says, with her back to me, cocking her head slightly over her right shoulder. I ask her to repeat this because it doesn't make any sense and as criticisms of my character go, it certainly wins on originality. She chuckles coquettishly, which does at least suggest that the comment has been made in jest, and the humming ceases as she starts to dance away from me again. I don't mind this because in the absence of that haphazard tune is a sweeter harmony that seems to sound in the air around us, resonating, belonging to just the two of us. When we go back inside, we find that Sebastian is no longer there.

21

KIM

Hi Kim,

Sorry to hear about your dad. I won't be around for the next few days as I'm going away on holiday. Really need some time alone to clear my head and put things into perspective. Don't worry about the flat, it's all taken care of this time so Daisy won't be bothering you again.

Ricky

x

I hadn't seen Ricky since sleeping with him and this latest text message had been his response to my formally inviting him to my father's memorial. As answers go, I considered this conclusive and maybe for the best as it wouldn't have been fair to have thrust him into that environment while there were still so many questions about the status of our relationship that I needed answering. In his defence, I hadn't given him enough warning and I could've offered more detail but the cynic in me noted that this was his second holiday in a very short space of time.

I hadn't expected a flurry of effusive communication after we had sex because that wasn't him but I'd be lying if I said that I hadn't expected more. Perhaps he felt embarrassed about opening up to me in the way that he had after we'd slept together and had attached too much significance to the things he'd said or maybe he just felt guilty for leaving me the following morning without saying goodbye. It was futile to speculate, I had little to go on and his exchanges up to now (via text message) had been sporadic at best.

Not seeing Ricky hadn't been for want of trying and although asking him to my father's memorial had not been ideal, it wasn't my only attempt at trying to engineer a date. In fact, such was my willingness to see him that I'd spent every morning of the last week or so loitering around my car in the Gaddis Avenue complex waiting for him to emerge. The result of this was that I'd been late into work three days out of five and that I also learned how Ricky was now operating under a different diurnal schedule than he had been before.

The realisation that I wanted Ricky to act as my donor had been significant and because of its enormity, I knew that I couldn't really share this with him without talking in person. I didn't have the luxury of time that I once thought I had and his words on fatherhood still echoed in my mind like a siren I couldn't switch off. But still I needed an answer and so I sought an alternative method of acquiring this through the means of text messaging and my fertile imagination (if that pun can be forgiven). I decided to substitute my current situation with that of a fictional pair of friends, 'Lizzie and Ryan', to see if I could gain a clearer perspective on his views on sperm donorship. I explained how Lizzie, twenty-something, intellectual, of stable disposition and irrefutable good looks, was also hopelessly barren. In order to rectify this problem, she'd approached Ryan (a man whom she deeply but unrequitedly loved) to ask if he would assist her through the process of IVF by providing a dose of his reproductive stock. Now Ryan, in the midst of his uncertainty, had come to me, struggling between the urge to do the right thing and a nagging uneasiness at the prospect of becoming a father by such an unconventional method. I wanted to help in any way I could but the stalemate was precarious and so I turned to Ricky and asked what he would do if he were Ryan. His response to the question was flippant in his habitual way and void of any interpretable compassion. 'I'd probably leave the country,' he said and I waited for a while before responding to that with a laughing emoji that met no further reply from him. The following morning, he had clearly done just as he suggested.

At this point, I had contemplated telling him the truth but had settled for inviting him to my father's memorial instead, thinking that maybe the mood of the day would generate the dialogue I desperately needed to share with him. I didn't just want to confess to the nonexistence of the characters I'd invented, but to explain (in terms that he would understand) how I recognised the struggle that Lizzie faced and how it was synonymous with mine. I also wanted to say how his attitude had upset me but after four or five rashly deleted attempts at texting this, I gave up. Deep down, I knew that I was being foolish, that Ricky had no designs on becoming a father and I didn't have time to wait for him to maybe change his mind. His position on the matter had never been anything close to unclear and whether I used metaphor, entreaty or name substitution, it really made no odds. To argue otherwise was purely self-delusion. His opposition to the idea was more than mere bluster, it was insurmountable, just as it had been once before with Simon and so there was little point in challenging him or engaging any further. I accepted it then and found a way of moving on, and now I had to do the same. On so many levels I felt I couldn't understand Ricky but at least when it came to this, I knew that his position was rooted in truth and that was something that I couldn't often say about him. The pain was piercing but I would remain steadfast because none of this prevented Ricky and I from actually being together if we still wanted to make that happen and as long as I had the donor catalogue, choice did at least remain plentiful.

22

KIM

My mother had preserved my old bedroom with a remarkable
dedication and everything remained exactly as I recalled it.
With every nook and cranny dusted and maintained, nothing
appeared out of place and a soft scent of melancholy drifted
lightly over me from within the four walls. So devoted must
she have been to this act of preservation that it seemed
designed to encourage my regression and I couldn't help but
feel as if I were fifteen years old all over again. Although I wept
intermittently throughout most of my father's memorial
today, my waterproof mascara had proved invaluable and my
face did not resemble the smearing, streaky mess I feared it
could have. This stroke of good fortune (or prudent choice,
depending on how you judged it) complimented my black cut-
away dress and the balance between elegance and propriety
had thankfully been achieved.

My mother revealed to me today that the sale of the
house had officially been completed. Although this meant
that my lenders would finally be silenced and my financial
problems would take a huge step towards resolution, the sense
of relief I was expecting did not reveal itself. Today was not the
day for such thoughts and my mother had perhaps been right
in admonishing me earlier when I had raised this subject with
her, pushing me instead in the direction of elderly relatives
who did nothing but share episodes of my youth that I could
not remember. This, the family home, the home in which I
was born and raised, would soon be gone from my life and

consigned to the dark and dusky mire of my memory. I cannot picture the family that will inherit this place but maybe they will walk the halls as I once did, dreaming only of the future while thinking nothing of its past, and one day it will all catch up with them, as it had done today with me.

I catch sight of my dressing table, once a silent witness to my every whim and worry, where times of anguish detached themselves from episodes of brief happiness. Photographs adorn the rim of the mirror, scattered untidily around the edges like a jagged row of visual bookmarks, forming the story of a life once mine. Central to them all, a picture of me with my bare arms clasped about my father's neck, he looking vague and uneasy while my eyes gaze back at the camera full of vigour and mischief. It was the only photograph I could find of my family, the rest were a montage of Claire, Alice and myself in the fledgling years of our friendship, proud of a bond that we had no way of knowing would still survive today. Studying my surroundings with renewed interest, I find the prettiest picture yet buried beneath some old sketches of mine in an overloaded drawer. It is of me and Simon from our first holiday together, standing arm in arm with bronzed faces and broad smiles. The two of us look like the embodiment of youth without care or concern, and it takes me back to a time when our love was effortless and innocent. Indeed, it was at this very table that I would sit for hours when I first met him, trying to make sense of the poems and the letters that he'd so dutifully written for me. His writings then were a wonderful homage and though I didn't always succeed in understanding his expression, there was nothing on this earth that I cherished any dearer than their innocent beauty and humbling reverence.

I feel my phone vibrate and find I have a message from my cousin Gwen, who enquires in an awkward fashion as to how the day unfolded while apologising for not being here in person. I so wanted it to be Ricky but while he remained on holiday, I continued to receive the wall of semi-silence or occasionally, if I was lucky, the barest of text messages containing the weakest of platitudes. When he told me that he'd gone away in search of some perspective, I had desperately wanted to believe him but a part of me remained incredulous. After all, what answers could space provide for him that close proximity to me could not? In my experience, distance is something that a man acquires when faced with a problem he's reluctant to address, hoping it will somehow resolve itself without him being implicated. In reality, it does nothing but leave you in limbo which is just what they want, for once you dare make an approach, this act of intrusion will not be forgiven and the breach will be used to justify further retreat. While some women may relish such a challenge, I wasn't one of them and perhaps Ricky knew this, which is why he didn't bother indulging me with conventional flatteries.

It is important to add that he hadn't yet mentioned my invasion of his flat and I couldn't help but think that this was somehow attached to this tiresome stand-off. Had Daisy revealed my secret and if she had, how had Ricky reacted to the news? I had to concede that it was possible and that either he didn't care enough to seek my explanation or he couldn't bear the thought of listening to my excuses. Either way, our having sex had come after the incident in question so I guessed that if she had said anything to him then it must have been after the fact, otherwise I doubt he would not have touched on this while we lay in bed together. But even if Daisy had remained silent, then it was perfectly feasible that my allusions to babies and to motherhood had been a little too persistent for him and had jarred against his singleton principles. It was even possible that he'd seen right through the ruse that was 'Lizzie and Ryan' and realised that they were mere substitutes. Without revealing this, I couldn't put him at ease by saying that I no longer needed his sperm, I just wanted *him*.

If Ricky had been perturbed by anything I'd said then I was at a loss to understand why he hadn't told me so but that wasn't what bothered me most of all. If I'm being honest, then on a day like today, when I was marking the occasion of two years since my father's death, I really would've appreciated a message of support from him. It didn't need to be maudlin or even heartfelt, just a quick line to say that he was thinking about me or that he hoped I was bearing up, anything at all to suggest that he was thinking of anybody other than himself. Instead, I'd received nothing and although there was most probably a perfectly reasonable explanation, it still hurt.

Thinking of such things wasn't likely to make my day any easier, a day that had begun at five-thirty this morning, a full three hours before my mother had risen and now one that was drawing to a close two hours after she'd retired. Hers had been a fleeting yet impactful performance, leaving everything for me to do, disappearing whenever she was needed and then returning at timely intervals to absorb the praise on offer. She'd been oblivious to the many stresses that had plagued my day, like the caterers delivering to the wrong address or the gazebo that collapsed with every gust of wind and the general disorder that emotive family events tend to conjure up. On reflection though, it didn't matter greatly as I often clean up my mother's mess and had expected nothing more from her today.

In a strange sort of a way, it was Simon that I felt for and I guess that was part of the reason as to why I'd been so hesitant about inviting him. Putting all that had happened between the two of us to one side, my father's death had shaken him in ways I hadn't initially noticed and like most things he isn't able to control, it isn't long before they engulf him. The two of them had shared a close relationship and it was a bond that I'd been comfortable with seeing how Simon had always yearned for a father figure that was the antitheses to the one he actually had. Although it was part of a history that he didn't like to talk about, his upbringing had been a troubled one and I suspected that family events like these brought back unwelcome recollections for him.

With all that being said, my sympathy could only

stretch so far and he'd managed to test my patience on a number of occasions today. Our first argument centred around my failure to reference Declan in the speech that I made, as if it had been in some way deliberate or ill-motivated. This was 'callous' and 'unnecessary', he said, as if our history together entitled him to make that statement and then he rounded on me further for emphasising my mother's uselessness too often for his liking. His anger had barely subsided before he was rebuking me again, accusing me of failing to disclose the details of our break up to those present and bemoaning the position that this had placed him in. I didn't see this as a source of much concern and told him so but it fell short of appeasing him and so he spent the rest of the day in an ill-temper, responding to my every word with silence or rebuttal. This failure to control his passions was typical of Simon and exposed his immaturity for having a clear lack of emotional disguise. It didn't make him interesting or amiable, it just made him appear grave and volatile and when these moods were supplemented by drink (as they had been today), he would often become really quite unpleasant to be around. This combination of factors had given me good reason to avoid him but with my relatives still thinking that we were still together, the day had been spent fending off their enquiries about what they all seemed to call a 'lovers' tiff.'

If Simon had been difficult and my mother invisible, then Declan had proved to be the third component in this trio of disharmony. Even though relations between the two of us were certainly irrevocable, I did at least expect an image of unity when hosting the wider family, if only to relieve me of absolute responsibility. This had clearly proved a sacrifice too far for him and for the duration of the day, we hadn't exchanged a word either pleasant or foul. His speech (much of which I missed due to other pressing duties) had been met with the perfunctory level of acclaim that such an event demands and the mourning ensemble offered humour and solemnity at the obligatory cues. I felt for them in truth, because they saw through his charade just as much as I did and so the path was left clear as he returned to the house at the conclusion of his speech to wallow once more in his detachment.

I peer again about my old bedroom and realise how there's nothing here that seems to belong to me anymore and my presence feels like an intrusion on a life that is no longer mine. I didn't know it then, but these photographs that I now hold in my hands were already showing the thread of my destiny and although I don't believe that any of it was preordained, I also don't believe that I held much control over the path that I took. My parents shouldn't have adopted Declan and I shouldn't have felt compelled to love Simon by the sheer strength of his love for me and my father shouldn't have died years before his time. But if just one of these events had not occurred, then my sense of perspective would not be as it now is. My mother is moving on and I'm glad that she is leaving this ill-fated house so that the ghosts of my childhood can linger a little longer, free to haunt those who inhabit here afterwards. Looking into the mirror again, I notice that my mascara has started to run.

23

SIMON

Today had been the saddest of days for it reminded me just how much I cared for Barney, the respect I'd always held for him and how much I missed him. Two years on from his passing and the sorrow still ran deep and although his memorial had been a fitting tribute, the task of honouring the memory of such a remarkable human being was always going to be a challenging one. I say remarkable because I'm yet to meet another quite like him and although enigmatic figures have blessed my life at various different times, none of them have left such a lasting impression on me as he had.

It's difficult to know where to start when describing Barney for he was a man of vast personal qualities with an intellectual acumen that one could only admire. When I first met him, he was lecturing military history at a local university but opted for early retirement in order to pursue a writing career under the same subject. As to whether this decision had proved successful or not, that probably depends on how one defines success, but this transition visibly invigorated him and he would talk about his writing far more effusively than he ever did his academic career. His talent was unquestionable and while he savoured the comfort of the semi-detachment of his later years, his anecdotal prowess seemed to grow over time as well. I'd never met anyone with a penchant for verbal illustration quite like him, who nourished other people's insight where they seemed to lack it with a mastery of subject matter and impassioned delivery. He loved people and saw intrigue in their nuances but his notoriety was such that while he sent no invitations, he would still receive an endless stream of visitors at the Pleydell estate. None were turned away because their intrigue needed satiating and all they really wanted to do was feed off his erudition and not leave disappointed. These encounters served him just as much as they did his audience for they increased his understanding of the workings of the human mind, its limitations and its singularities and so he never fell prey to idle judgement or slack definition.

I always felt that you could trace the source of his genius back to his study, a room which he often inhabited from day's beginning to end. Rarely did I catch sight of him outside of there, in fact, never did a man look quite so contented as he when entrenched in his vast array of historical literature and half-built model railways. Though to an outsider the room probably appeared quite the dusty cubicle full of clutter and tat, everything resided where it belonged and nothing strayed out of its appointed place without his notice or permission. It was here that his breadth of interests was most keenly displayed and where Barney could recall the inner detail of hundreds of books with an incredible precision.

I attached a great sadness to his death for dementia had wrestled these mental faculties away from him in the cruellest of ways and though strength had seeped from his body, his greatness still shone in my eyes. Altered though it became, his bearing remained one of distinction and although he'd often forget who I was, I always had the pleasure of reacquainting myself with him at our next time of meeting. Kim saw his passing as a blessing for reasons I understood but could not conform to, and I instead remember him fondly as he was, thinking of that study and the man who reigned there.

With these memories being most prominent, I couldn't resist returning to that study at the first opportunity today and had stolen away from the mourning crowd, determined to pay my respects in a private ritual within the confines of this revered chamber. Navigating my way through the Pleydell residence with an acute recollection, I found the room easily enough but the scene that was to greet me wasn't one that I instantly recognised. The change to the study had been so significant that I at first assumed I had located the wrong room. Drab, solitary and lifeless, it was stillness that now took precedence, infusing every inch of the room and clinging oppressively to any avenue of daylight. Resembling the aftermath of a successful heist, any objects left were now displaced, the walls were now bare and the ceiling ruptured. An air of dilapidation filled the space and no article before me seemed to betray any sign of life. The neglect appeared so great, that the room now resembled a tomb, where all had given way to a deep and lengthy silence. After reaching for a light switch that didn't work, I stood there disconsolate.

In former times, the focus of the study had been a huge model railway system at the room's epicentre. This network of tracks, bridges and backdrops once stood like a human organ feeding colour and animation into all that surrounded it. The result of hours upon hours of arduous enterprise, here Barney would stand directing this miniature world as its omnipotent conductor while unwittingly tangling himself in an abundance of wires. As trains weaved by in snake-like fashion, meticulous detail sprang out from everywhere and each time I visited, some new feature would reveal itself to me that had previously escaped my attention. Even now, in the midst of such scarcity, I could still picture him hoisting above his head a young Declan, who would gaze at the replica locomotives with something close to wonder while the two of us made small talk about his daughter or the progress of my degree. It was apparent even then that Declan really shared Barney's passion for this room and all of its contents and much of the work of the model railway would come from his hand when he grew older. I couldn't count the times that I had called in on them as they sat reconfiguring household items with the object of including them in this simulated landscape and now, there was nothing.

The desire to stay and reminisce dissipated quickly. As I hastened to leave, I somehow managed to stumble over what appeared to be a still and lifeless limb sticking out from underneath Barney's old writing desk. Whomever it belonged to hadn't flinched at all but it quickly became clear that the foot belonged to someone who had joined me in my ritual. Sat inanimately, it was Declan, partially concealed by the semi-darkness and his commemorative garb.

When my momentary surprise gave way to realisation, I tried to initiate conversation by apologising for my intrusion but I needn't have said anything. Distracted and unresponsive, he was evidently wearied by the pleasantries and stale sentiments that had blighted his day up to that point and merely retained his focus on the floor. I knew I couldn't say anything fitting and so I didn't feel in the least offended when just seconds later, he got up and departed the scene in haste without bothering to engage. Today, he probably felt more alone than anybody, a young man still in his teens who had lost a parent and when he'd found a place to sit alone with his thoughts, I'd unknowingly encroached on his solitude. It had only been an hour or so earlier that Kim had closed a long speech before her entire family, a speech that made no reference to him and had overlooked the part that he had played in Barney's life as if it were of no importance. It was cruel and shameful of her to do this, as I had pointed out, but she'd remained steadfast in her denial that this was ever her intention. I hadn't been convinced of this and had sought Declan out in the aftermath without success in order to explain my own position. Breaking up with Kim had liberated me to some degree and I was no longer constrained by a loyalty to her that was simply unconditional. Now, I wanted to explain how I'd never sided with her in the Pleydell family politics that followed Barney's death and to acknowledge Declan's right to feel aggrieved with what had happened. I wanted to defend my reticence, to explain how I'd fought his corner even though it hadn't been my place to intervene and to state how my silence had never meant complicity. But most of all, I just wanted to apologise.

It was sad to see the distance between Kim and Declan and sadder still to say that it had always been that way. At seventeen years old, he still is as he was then, silent and subdued and no doubt cognisant of the fact that my relationship with Kim had always prevented any kind of kinship forming between the two of us. I strongly suspected that he remained affronted with me because of my perceived loyalty to her and also because I had never quite mastered how to speak to him without talking as if he were a seven-year-old child. I'd never done that purposefully of course but that was just the way I saw him, the young boy hanging off Barney's limbs and toying with model train sets. He had grown significantly since then and wasn't quite a boy anymore but those visions still remained my clearest of him and were difficult to shake.

Once Declan had departed, my appetite to remain in the study pretty much left with him. Too much of this day already had been spent in recollection, inspired no doubt by my surroundings which had done nothing but feed my nostalgic temperament. It was good to see members of Kim's family that I hadn't seen in years even though it was clear from the outset that she hadn't told any of them about our separation. I instinctively went along with it because I didn't have much choice and just transmitted this untruth to everyone who asked for the rest of the day. I couldn't fathom her reasoning for doing this though and the mood of the occasion meant I couldn't press the case too hard. It had also been a shock to learn that the Pleydell estate in which I stood had recently been sold, making it unlikely that I would ever step foot in this house again. This news brought with it melancholy, for my memories of this residence were of simpler times when death and separation did not plague my thoughts as they did now. If anything, they had dominated my thinking today which was perhaps the clearest sign that the inaugural chapters of my life were at an end. The future still feels far away somehow so maybe the next period of my life will be parenthetical.

The tears that escaped me today were not of grief but more of anger because Barney had left my life too soon and his illness had prevented me from conveying my respect for him in the manner that he deserved. His death had been my introduction to mortality in a very real sense, jolting me from the complacency of youth in the way that only loss can do. My memories of him will remain though and if ever a man be judged by his willingness to overlook the failings in others, then Barney was undoubtedly the greatest of men.

24

SIMON

Today is the day that The Croc has chosen to make his triumphant return to the office in a brazen display that lacks only fanfare. Like a political prisoner freed from incarceration, he strides about the floor in his robust way as if the reasons for his exile have been anything but self-imposed. Back is the tactile demeanour that makes everybody uncomfortable and although he tries to conceal it, the lack of welcome from his subordinates has left him looking vaguely chagrined. Understandably, he's keen to know just how I did it but I cannot indulge this curiosity within earshot of others without implicating myself. As I absorb his praise reticently, he starts to lambast the enquiry for 'infringing on his duties' and enforcing his 'semi-hiatus' as if the sacrifice he has made in any way matches mine. There are now just a matter of weeks left to prepare me for my new role of L&D Area Project Manager (which he has already promised me) and I want to believe in his assurances that his promise remains intact. When we meet alone in his office, his handshake is cold and clammy and there's a palpable relief everywhere about him. There is talk of new beginnings.

The investigation into the strike action balloting process has finally concluded, providing evidence of fraud, inefficiency and flagrant misconduct. Although enquiries are still on-going, the union has been left with little choice but to declare the result invalid after an injunction from Tanner & Webbing. Rumour has it that an anonymous letter initiated the enquiry which did, on further inspection, produce damning proof of a wider and more sophisticated deception. This means that the union is now forced to sit tight until the formal inquest can be completed, a process that could take months, by which time the impetus will be well and truly lost. The workers, it seems, have been defeated.

So how did I do it? Well, the anonymous letter had quite obviously been a work of my own hand, inspired in part by my ingenuity and more so by the glaring deficiencies of the union. The first blunder that they made had been to override the counsel of the appointed conciliators and to push on with the ballot in spite of their advice against it. To outside observers this portrayed confidence, while murmurings from the inside deemed it impetuous. Either way, the union spurned a potential ally at a point where they could still have been of use to us and the validity of our argument dwindled with their support.

One accusation that my letter contained concerned the distribution of the ballot itself. I explained how I had been witness to a number of papers being handed out to members during the working day which not only contravened the ethos of a secret ballot but brought into question its legitimacy. This had, I wrote, generated a climate of fear and intimidation, in which clear examples of voter persuasion had been seen by others too frightened to speak out. With that in mind, it was now questionable as to how many of the ballot papers counted reflected the decision of the voter in its truest form.

The letter I had penned had simply been the start however. Its design had been to arouse suspicion in those that were looking to find fault while handing them enough ammunition to cast the net of their inspections a little wider. With the result having already been counted and declared, I knew that those tallying the ballot had most probably carried out their duties well, with little reason for their integrity to be questioned, least of all challenged. Only a negative result would've brought with it a far deeper scrutiny and a voluble dissension from the wider membership who had always seen the outcome as nothing more than a given. My only option was to somehow gain access to those papers in the hope that any inspection undertaken would find enough evidence to suggest that the vote had been tampered with. All I needed was a steady nerve and a large slice of luck, fortunately, I had both.

Gaining entry to the union's branch office without being observed had proved far less trying than even I had suspected. The office was really nothing more than a rundown, windowless refrigerator in the bowels of the Tanner & Webbing building, donated to the union three years ago as a placatory measure by senior management. Its existence went largely unnoticed, except for staff members conducting illicit affairs or the geographically challenged and it was because of this that I'd managed to gain entry one evening without worry of detection. Once inside, I couldn't quite believe the sight that greeted me. There, on a desk ahead of me, were three large trays each distinctly marked 'Yes,' 'No' and 'Spoiled/Unclear'. Inside each of these were the returned ballot papers that correlated with the decision labelled on the front of the tray. As I remarked inwardly how chance could not have been any kinder, I set about my work with gusto and it was here that my methods became a little more complex.

Prior to my accessing the branch office, I'd taken the time to study the ballot paper I'd received to see if there was any possibility of my being able to replicate it. It struck me that each was distinctive only by a unique number positioned at the foot of the page with a hyphen either side of it. If one knew how to copy the design (as I did) then the opportunity to duplicate any ballot paper would be relatively easy and so I set about doing just that. I first took twenty-five ballot papers marked No from the No tray and then reprinted these papers anew each with the same unique number at the foot, only this time marking them as a Yes vote and placing them in the Yes tray. I then took twenty-five ballot papers that were marked

Yes and destroyed them while returning my original No papers back to the No tray. This meant that I had now successfully duplicated twenty-five ballot papers so that if someone were to inspect each tray on suspicion of fraud, it could be safely interpreted that the Yes vote had been falsely increased by duplication.

My second act of chicanery was to take a handful of ballot papers that were clearly marked Yes before purposely spoiling them so that no clear voting preference could be determined. Instead of placing them in the Spoiled/Unclear tray (thus making them redundant) I instead returned them to the Yes tray. This would be vital evidence in the findings of the investigators for it would allow them to assert that those counting the votes appeared to have been a little too liberal in their definition of a Yes vote.

My final duplicitous deed was to mark a number of ballot papers with tiny yet distinguishable marks of ink at the tip of the page, just visible enough for the naked eye to discern. This would act to imply that certain voter's decisions were being monitored and tracked on their return to the counting table (which my letter alluded to), something which would of course be strictly prohibited. If this revelation were to be aligned with my previous accusations of voter intimidation, then it would again prove a difficult charge for the union to answer in the face of such 'evidence'.

The deception worked perfectly. The investigative body, torn between a duty to probe and their habitual reluctance, were granted access to the branch office and once inside, they simply couldn't fail to find the evidence that I had so skilfully left for them. In being so meticulous, I had prevented them from labelling my exploits as mere oversight and in acting alone, I had placed no one in the uncomfortable position of having to lie about their involvement. All questions would be answered truthfully and the best of it was that none of those were ever likely to be directed my way.

I conceal all of this from The Croc, who is evidently

stuck between a willingness to learn more and the valid paranoia that knowing too much carries with it. If I was to elaborate then I'm sure it would take several explanations before he'd be able to comprehend it and I don't have the time or the energy to simplify everything for him. He notices how tired I look before linking the cause of this back to Kim and I excuse myself before the conversation can take a lascivious turn. For once, he was right in his observation, I hadn't slept well for a number of nights now and I could trace much of my insomnia back to him and what he'd forced me to do. Last night in particular, in the midst of my latest bout of nocturnal restlessness, I lay awake and sought to justify what I'd done in the hope that it would somehow return me to a state of peaceful slumber. It was the third night in a row that I'd tried this but it had taken me until the eve of my triumph to fully understand my anxiety. As opposed to what I'd initially assumed, it was not a sense of guilt that was the cause of this distress but the complete and utter lack of it, a vacancy where self-censure would usually reside. The ignominy of cowering to a man that I deeply despised should've shamed me and left me longing for confession, no matter how belated, but it simply hadn't. After all, could I really blame myself for the negligence of the union or for the longstanding contempt with which the management of the business viewed its workforce? Both sides of the argument throughout the entirety of this dispute had been driven by a dangerous combination of ego and pugnacity, so it was far from remarkable that conciliation had not been achieved. My motives were rational by comparison for they were born of necessity and I hadn't done anything that anybody else in the office would not have done if their careers had depended on it, just as mine had. Hypothetically of course, lots would deny it but that's the thing with denial, once you've convinced yourself, everybody else is easy.

With a clear diary ahead of me and my thoughts elsewhere, all I really want to do this afternoon is sit at my desk and get to work on my application while avoiding anything too pressing. Armed with pointers offered by The Croc and no Marion around to unsettle these plans, I don't foresee any problems but it is barely thirty seconds into the operation before Agatha interrupts me.

"Hello Simon," she starts pensively, unaware that her soundless approach has startled me somewhat. "I've got a letter for you here and the phone has been ringing for you all morning." Her voice then gently descends into a whisper. "Malcy Kearns from the Supply Chain Team has been, well (quieter still), he's been suspended. You better get his contact details as it seems pretty serious and he's asking if you'll support him."

My reaction is one of regret. Why hadn't I resigned from the union like I intended to? One brief but incisive letter was all it would've taken but I'd been so preoccupied with other things that it had completely slipped my mind and so I still remained listed as a workplace representative. Then I thought of Malcy Kearns. I had to wrack my brains at first to recall who he was, fact is, we didn't have too many dealings with Supply Chain and they, as a team, tended to keep themselves to themselves. The only face I could attach to the name was that of a middle-aged, nervy-looking man who blushed every time you made eye contact with him. I had shared little or no dialogue with him up to now and if I'm honest, I hadn't tried to. Although it didn't really seem to fit, he was the only male member of that team but his reputation about the office was hardly one of dissent and impropriety, quite the opposite in fact.

"And he's requested me specifically? I mean, before asking for anybody else?" I enquire of Agatha, not realising she has left my side and has returned to her work station.

"Yes," she replies, looking about her, a tad perturbed by my lack of discretion, "that's what I'm led to believe."

Did I owe the union anything? Most probably the answer to that would be yes perhaps I did owe them some

measure of compensation after what I'd done but Malcy
Kearns? Why would someone unknown to me invest such
faith in my ability to represent him? It doesn't add up but
I guess no harm can come from my looking into the case
and if it appears too onerous, then it will prove the perfect
opportunity to relinquish my union duties and pass on the
reins to someone more fitting.

I realise I didn't shut the door behind me when leaving
The Croc's office and so I'm treated to the image of him
leaning back in his chair and saluting me, faux-militarily. The
tiredness turns to nausea and I put my application away.

25

KIM

TEXT MESSAGE ALERT

DONOR 2781 has now been added to the database

Age	28
Height	180 cm/5'11 ft in
Weight	75 kg/11.5 st
Ethnicity	Caucasian
Hair colour	Light brown (originally blond, receding)
Eye colour	Blue
Build	Slim, regular
Blood type	A +
Allergies	None
Age of parents	Father 60 (alive), Mother 59 (alive)
Religion	Atheist
Occupation	Sedimentologist
Education level	MSc (Master of Science)
Hobbies/interests	Geology, reading, playing tennis/chess
Screened for	Cystic Fibrosis, HIV, Hepatitis (B&C)

For more detailed information about this or any other donor, please log on to our website.

When the profile flashed through on my phone this morning, I just couldn't shake the feeling that there was something about it that I recognised. I knew no sedimentologists (whatever one of those was) so this air of recall seemed strangely unfounded but still the nagging persisted. The answer, like so many of life's best revelations, came to me while driving home after this flickering memory had beleaguered me all day. Hastening from the car and back into my flat, I turned my bedroom upside down looking for the one item that would validate my faint recognition and simply couldn't find it. The desired article had eventually been located at the foot of a mountainous pile of clothes in a part of the flat that I seldom frequented. It was a CD and one that accounted for one of the most bizarre episodes of my life to date. This CD was a product of loss and a culmination of circumstances that I'd been forced to link together. Once inserted into my laptop, I buried myself beneath the bedsheets (while still fully clothed) and then revisited my strange encounter with Mabel, the spirit medium.

Two nights ago, I went to bed around my usual time but awoke with a start in my living room in the early hours of the following morning. Although this hadn't happened to me for a while, it was at one time a regular occurrence that intensified just after my father's death, when I was eventually coerced into addressing the problem. I had been prone to sleepwalking (or to call it by its more scientific name, somnambulism) since my childhood and my nightly excursions would seemingly increase during times of personal struggle, forcing me to lock all windows and doors before retiring in order to protect myself. Combatting the problem as a child had been relatively easy once my parents came to understand what the issue was but as an adult living in in my own apartment several floors above the ground, the perils were everywhere. So my return to this evening ritual two nights back gave me cause for some alarm as the length of time that had passed since my last foray suggested I had at last resolved the problem.

Simon first became aware of this in the weeks that followed my father's passing. He said that the sight of me sitting in the living room one evening conversing with my dead father had convinced him that there was something more to it than merely sleepwalking. In all the time we'd been together, he'd never experienced my doing this and didn't seem to understand that I had just receded into a former behaviour, one that I had successfully managed to control before and would do again. Instead, he buried himself in stacks of books on the subject, seeking theory and remedy and then arranged a series of expensive and ultimately fruitless sessions with a sleep therapist. They cured nothing. My nocturnal outings continued to the point where I was sharing a one-way dialogue with my father every evening and Simon had started to feel like he was intruding on something whenever he tried to wake me. 'It's probably down to grief,' he would tell me and recommended counselling but I knew that if I followed that option, I'd have locked myself into an endless discourse with a paid professional who would've skilfully elicited a litany of things about myself that I kept locked away for a reason.

But it was after a chance encounter with a strange old lady in a beauty salon that my approach changed course entirely. How we had broached the subject of my sleepwalking I can't recall but she was nonetheless convinced that my flat was haunted by a lingering spirit who was dragging me from my bed every night to relay messages that it was imperative for me to heed. Furthermore, it was in my best interests to communicate with this phantom while in the presence of a woman that she knew well, or otherwise run the risk of the spirit becoming embittered. Naturally, I countered this with scepticism but she was insistent that this contact of hers would not only offer solace but would be able to translate my exchanges into an earthly context. Moments later, a business card for a spirit medium was thrust into my hand, supplemented by a plea of urgency to go visit her. I vowed that I would (well, she made me do that) and then made a pact with myself never to return to that same salon again.

I didn't know much about spirit mediums other than the odd television show that I'd stumble across every now and then in which pony-tailed weirdos seemed to prey on grieving adults by contacting their dead relatives and family pets. It was creepy and tasteless and went against every logical element of my character but I had to concede that it was also a little fascinating. Unlike the out-of-work actors that these low-budget television shows employed as gullible members of the public, I was, to a degree, just who they were trying to depict. I was single, in my mid to late twenties and still recovering from the loss of my father. So in a fleeting, sombre moment, I contacted the spirit medium from the business card and then drove over to meet her in person the following day.

Mabel lived on the fifth floor of a high-rise flat in an environment that exuded anything but affluence. She was younger than I'd expected, maybe around forty years old, strikingly overweight and verbally succinct. Her abode met pretty much all of my expectations from its lavender-scented rooms to low-hanging wind chimes that dangled from every ceiling and emitted an ominous tolling despite there being very little draught Once these were adroitly avoided, she led me to a shabby-looking teepee that was stationed in her kitchen. As I stepped over a snoozing black cat at the mouth of entry, I quickly realised that Mabel left little room for parody.

She began by asking what had brought me to her and so I told her all about the supposed presence in my flat. I wanted to know if this 'spirit' was actually that of my late father, to which she replied that it was difficult to say but that it was most probably not him. Was it a male voice? I said I didn't know. Did I recognise the voice? See my first reply. Had I tried to converse with the voice? No, well, yes but I didn't realise that I was doing it. Did the presence act in a repetitive fashion, returning on certain days like anniversaries or birthdays? I replied that there was no repetition or significance to any of it and became convinced that I wasn't really telling her what she wanted to hear. Mabel considered this briefly before rationalising that I most likely possessed a spiritual gift and that the spirit could be looking to use me as a connection to someone in the physical world. She then said that such a scenario (and indeed such a gift) was in fact surprisingly common and that I needn't be alarmed by it because if the spirit did have any evil intentions then I would've been well aware of this by now. When I suggested that the explanation could be one of unrealised grief, she countered by saying that I needed to separate this entirely from the visitation of the spirit.

Mabel knew the real reason as to why I was there and obviously sensed that the tale of a visiting spirit was a mere ruse applied to deny the fact that I desperately wanted to contact my dead father. She was half right, I really did need her to facilitate a connection with him beyond the grave but not for the reasons that she had probably suspected. I wanted to speak to him because I yearned for the advice that he had failed to bestow on me while he was still alive and perhaps more pertinently, I wanted him to act as my personal seer. She revealed to me that it would be impossible to dictate who would come through from the spirit world if we sought to make contact or what information they would offer. But when I pressed her, she sighed begrudgingly and then declared that she would try.

I was warned about my negative energy from the get go. Apparently, such forces could deter members of the spirit world and make the environment inhospitable for them. I tried to comply with her warnings while her body began to writhe and contort in a rickety motion. The pure absurdity of her behaviour was the only thing that prevented me from laughing while she hummed and she yelped and her limbs appeared to act independently from her brain. There was no protocol specified for this so I didn't know how best to react and while she slipped further and further into some sort of a manic trance, I was left with the hope that this was all part of the show. It took about a minute or so for her to regain composure (I pick up the purring of the cat on the CD during this) and the bodily flailing eased away. It was then that she told me that someone from the other side was speaking to her and that I now needed to maintain my focus more than ever.

Naturally, it wasn't my father but what I'd quickly learned about spirit mediums is that they seldom accept when they are on to a loser. No, I didn't have any idea who cat-loving Freda was, much less did I recognise Clyde, the Naval Sergeant, both of whom were lovely people I'm sure but even within the spiritual world, I still wasn't prepared to heed guidance from those I didn't know. Eventually, an old gentleman with a hat stepped forward although Mabel couldn't quite determine what his name was. 'Barry? Basil? Bartholomew?' She had speculated wildly before I'd interjected with his real name, Barney, to save her the trouble of trying to elicit this information from me in a tedious fashion. Yes, it was my father Barney, she exclaimed, in a tone that still appeared less than certain and all the while what I really wanted to ask her was how my father owned the ability to break through from the spirit world but couldn't introduce himself properly. Vague, physical descriptions ensued, yes he did wear glasses and yes his health had deteriorated before his death, two things which were hardly out of the ordinary for elderly people that pass on to the other side. He was affluent and successful, she had boldly stated, but then I didn't really think that this was difficult to surmise having listened to my dialect and diction for the best part of twenty minutes, being a child of the middle class as I was. The generalities continued while my father must've stood somewhere on the periphery, diffident and reluctant to contribute. I remember feeling tempted to leave at that point, to just dive out of the cramped teepee without a moment's notice as my knees were aching and space was at a premium before Mabel began clutching at the temples of her head on both sides. When the wailing returned and then ceased again, she asked if my father's death had been caused by a fault to the brain and as I froze, finally on the margin of belief, with a tear or two escaping my eyes, Mabel knew that she needed to ask nothing more about him.

I recovered myself quickly because I didn't want to hear my father's platitudes from her, I knew that he loved me in his own bizarre way and that he wanted the best for me as most parents do. That wasn't why I was there. So I urged her to ask him of my future, specifically, was I likely to be married and perhaps more importantly, would I bear any children (by this point, you will recall, I was aware of my infertility). This irked her gravely. I was beginning to learn that spirit mediums don't really like to be interrupted, much less let you steer the topic of conversation. My father had simply replied with the word 'yes' on both counts and it was then that my sense of unbridled relief clashed against my growing scepticism. A future marriage was not beyond the realms of possibility but children were a long shot and I had briefly considered revealing my infertility to her to gain further assurance on the validity of his prediction. But perhaps I wanted to live on with this hope in my mind because I opted not to press her, thinking that if I did, both my secret yearnings and the legitimacy of this whole affair could be exposed in one reply. It was what my father said next to me, without prompt or pattern, that resonated beyond all that had gone before it.

He said that the father of my first child would be recognisable to me as consisting of the following.

That he would be someone who my mother would not

approve of.

That he would be a student of transformation.

That his affection would be something which I would never truly own.

And that was it. Though I pressed for more detail, I was silently defied and moments later, my father appeared to slip off back somewhere into the ether without notice or adieu. He did however offer one final warning on his way out, something I hadn't noticed at the time, but today, listening back to it for the first time in a long time, I suddenly heard. 'The danger lies closer at hand than you think,' he said.

Yes, Mabel the medium really had been kind enough to record our time together that day on a CD which had the phrase 'Do Keep the Faith' handwritten across its face. This transcription cannot capture any of the visual aspects of that day, nor the swift fluctuations that I exhibited as I drifted between indifference, cynicism, hope and trepidation, all in one sitting. It is however, at the point of conclusion, where this tale finally links to the misty recollection that I referred to earlier.

After my father had passed on for this, the second time in my life, Mabel then reached for a pack of cards, picking out just four from the deck. I had no idea what sort of a tangent she was heading off on but I do remember how each of the cards that she turned over showed just one number. 2, 7, 8, 1. As I listen to it now, she enunciates these numbers clearly into the recording equipment and then says in a rather ominous tone, 'remember these numbers Kimberley either collectively or singly because one way or another, these are the numbers that will shape your life.' It was then that she had reached for a fifth card from an entirely different pack and had slowly turned it over to the face with an air of poise and effect. At the time, I had thought to myself that it must've been some sort of tarot card because it didn't contain any suits or numbers, just a picture of a man sitting on a large throne with a crown upon his head. Underneath this image was the word 'JUSTICE' in big, bold lettering. When I enquired as to what this card meant, Mabel replied with one simple word, 'accountability.'

In the context of the meeting that day and considering the questions I had asked of her, perhaps the numbers 2, 7, 8, 1 could well have been the closest that Mabel came to any sort of intelligible clairvoyance. It is no doubt credulous of me to admit, but I felt I owed her something because in spite of my cynicism, I had obviously held on to the CD for a reason. I've added the numbers up to a total of eighteen, thought of door numbers, telephone numbers, birth dates and door codes but I have never seemed to find their relevancy.

Now, I look at DONOR 2781. Although his profile is fairly suited to what I'm after, there's nothing about it that really leaps out at me but still I add it to my 'wish list' on the back of Mabel's rather bold prediction. There's a likelihood that she is wrong of course and is really nothing more than a charlatan of the medium community, legitimised only by my willingness to connect all of the dots myself. I rue my own weakness sometimes but I rue even more that chance meeting in the salon with a woman who probably should've minded her own business rather than inserting herself into mine.

26

SIMON

While sat waiting in a logo-ridden coffee shop, I can't help thinking how this isn't such a good idea. I'd arranged to meet with Malcy Kearns, the colleague who'd asked for my counsel following his recent suspension from Tanner & Webbing for reasons that were yet to be disclosed. I am slightly anxious because I hadn't made any effort to call him to ascertain the facts yet under the ostensible reason of not wishing to prejudice my approach and so I sit in ignorance. In reality, I just hadn't made the time and so I fidget pensively while images flash through my mind of tearful exchanges with a man I barely know, with my offering nothing in return but soft consolations. When Malcy finally arrives, this sense of foreboding only seems to deepen when I grasp his hand for the first time and cannot decide to which of us the perspiration belongs.

My initial investigations into the character of Malcy Kearns provided more questions than they did answers. On a personal level, he was considered polite but not exactly likeable, fair but not forthright, reliable but insecure. His subdued approach bothered some but stimulated others who felt comfortable divulging their concerns and their prejudices to him without ever labelling it companionship. In his mid-fifties, he is balding and short with a slender build and a deferent posture like the manner of one accustomed to following instruction. As he stands there, with a letter of suspension in a quivering right hand, I have no reason to suspect this man capable of any wrongdoing but intrigue alone means that I cannot turn back now. I ask for the details, I encourage concision and direct him towards the beginning of his story.

"It was my twelve-year anniversary at Tanner & Webbing just six weeks ago," he starts in a slow and wistful tone, "and since day one, I've worked as part of the Supply Chain Team. The job isn't glamorous, the pay is unremarkable but I've always done everything asked of me and am proud to say that until recently, my tenure has passed without incident. Now, for reasons which I cannot wrap my head around, my integrity has been called into question and I need your help in proving my innocence."

I resist the urge (though admittedly a very strong one) to remind him of my previous request for brevity. He is struggling to look me square in the eye which I know instinctively to be a bad sign and although he more or less repeats that introduction verbatim from some handwritten notes in front of him, it doesn't seem important to focus on that right now.

"It seems that we share a mutual friend, Simon, do you remember Joe Goldrick? He used to work as part of the printing team but left the company a few years back. Well, it was he who recommended you to me after I bumped into him by chance. I told him of my situation and he talked very highly of you, he talked very highly indeed."

I couldn't help but smile. Print-room Joe, the man who had acted as my mentor and introduced me to the union movement on that fateful day so very long ago, was still making his presence felt, even from afar. I guess things really do come full circle after all.

"I need to know what happened Malcy," I reply in a fit of urgency, overriding the sudden bout of nostalgia. "It's the details that I'm after here, not the sentiment, okay?"

He apologises profusely before straightening his glasses and pushing the handwritten notes to one side.

"Very well. I was recently approached by Marion McKensie, a colleague of yours from the Learning & Development Team." I interject to clarify that I'm actually her line manager (for reasons which are in no way important) before the oversight is acknowledged and he continues. "She asked if I was a member of the workplace trade union, adding that I could only be of use to her if I was not. I confirmed that I was not a member nor had I ever been. She then went on to ask whether I would be interested in acting as an Independent Scrutineer for the forthcoming industrial ballot. Now I'm not sure if you're aware of what that role entails Simon but you may have noticed my name on the foot of your ballot paper?" I had to confess that I did not and that I had not. "Well, it's really quite simple, the Scrutineer's job is to oversee the counting of the ballot papers when they're returned to the ballot table. As previously established, the Scrutineer cannot be affiliated with the trade union in question and this is designed to encourage neutrality. The Scrutineer ensures that all guidelines are adhered to, that all ballot papers are secured away safely and that a written report is made available upon request following the declaration of the result. For a variety of reasons, I decided to reject her offer politely yet firmly but Marion seemed oddly persistent in my agreeing to do it."

"What do you mean exactly by 'oddly persistent', Malcy?" I probe subtly, which seems to perturb him, like he's unable to understand my emphasis on something that he previously deemed irrelevant. He mulls over his next response with the deliberation of one uncomfortable with the detail of his pending admission.

"She just wouldn't accept my refusal. In the end I'd say I consented more out of weariness than anything else but it's fair to say that I regret it now. At first, I thought her kind and friendly enough but once we sat down at the counting table, she became deeply hostile and we disagreed on everything. She continually rejected my authority and treated me as if my presence was nothing more than a hindrance. It was confusing and a little disheartening but I was still determined to carry out the task I had agreed to take on."

"It's almost as though you were asked under false pretences," I add, thoughtlessly.

"What do you mean, Simon?"

"It doesn't matter," I reply, but then he really isn't to know just how acutely involved I am starting to sense I am likely to be in all this.

"A few days after the result had been declared, I received a message from Mr Crockett asking me to come to his office. I met him without trepidation as I've done so a hundred times before only this time, he asked me not to sit down and then suspended me on the spot with just this letter by way of explanation. This letter!" he yells, whilst waving the epistle frantically above his head. "Twelve years of service and the best that they can offer me is four paragraphs, twenty-eight lines and not a word more, that's all I'm worth to them apparently." He slides the letter across the table to me and then takes off his glasses so that he can massage both his eyes before burying his head in his hands. I pretend to study the letter's content and offer thoughtful-looking head inclinations in the manner of one absorbing the details. It is my turn to avoid eye contact.

"What did The Cro... ahem, what did Mr Crockett say to you Malcy? I mean, he must have offered some reason as to why he was suspending you." Thankfully, his reply is closer to composure than it is to hysteria.

"He said that a thorough investigation into the ballot count had found evidence of a number of improprieties. He then added that although the investigation was still ongoing, I was heavily suspected of misconduct and if that could be proven then I'd probably be sacked. That letter you have before you seems to suggest I've somehow manipulated the vote but the accusation isn't clear. If they really believe in their charge against me then where is my motive Simon, just what did I have to gain from doing such a thing?"

He isn't to know the futility of his questions and I quickly recognise the need to fortify my ignorance while making sure that I don't inadvertently shift the spotlight onto myself. That same spotlight however, could be thrust in the face of another, one who currently had no means of defence and had already been implicated by Malcy himself.

"So let's just say that someone did manipulate the vote and that someone wasn't you," I begin, contemplatively. "Perhaps it was someone that you worked closely with. Someone also estranged from their employer at this present time. Now I'm not asking for hunches here Malcy, so speaking plainly, do you believe that Marion could be responsible for any of this?" He considers this only briefly, betraying the fact that this isn't the first time he has done so.

"Well, I suppose it's possible, yes, as she was the only other person who had access to the ballot papers. But I don't see why or how. We barely left each other's side on the day of the count and she even helped draft my report."

I appeal to Malcy to think a little harder on this but it is to no avail. It is clear he isn't the sort to incriminate another to save his own skin and although the idea of pinning this whole thing on her does carry an appeal, it is pretty obvious that Malcy is looking like the fall guy here. That said, discarding my own involvement for a moment, it also seems inexplicable to suggest that she wasn't somehow involved in all of this, even if I couldn't yet figure out how. Although I hadn't seen her for a while due to her being temporarily forced to refrain from duties (which was admittedly starting to make a lot more sense now), there were just too many coincidences, too many unnatural quirks to her behaviour in the weeks surrounding the ballot that suggested my suspicions were unlikely to be unfounded. From her sudden thirst for union activity, to the silence that now shrouded her hiatus, all of it carried the scent of something I wasn't meant to understand.

Even with all of this in mind, trying to turn this whole thing around onto Marion still carried with it a sizable risk and if it was to backfire, I could unwittingly implicate myself. Furthermore, there was a clear conflict of interest here as I am still her boss and we are both applying for the same role within the company. By measuring risk against reward, I guess the decision was really very simple and the only way to secure my safety would be to throw my guns to the ground and retreat with speed.

"I want to be clear with you Malcy," I resume, after an elongated pause, "because I need you to think very carefully about your next move. The situation that faces us here is not one of right against wrong or good against evil, what we are actually dealing with is damage limitation. You question the validity of the evidence against you and feel that it can be disproved but from what I know, the outcome of the independent investigation has been clear in its findings and crucially, they are impartial. Now my instincts may side with your honesty but I'm not confident that this alone will establish your innocence. Someone is guilty here and unfortunately, in situations such as this, the burden of proof lies not with the accuser but very much with the accused. This means that the charges they present need not be irrefutable, far from it in fact." I watch while Malcy attempts to file a response but anger halts delivery, frustration foils thought and his words fall victim to an avalanche of injustice. As difficult as the next five minutes of my life is likely to be, it is no time to wilt. I have to sell a lie as if it were a truth and banish any notion of hope along with it.

"Please Simon, I'm asking you because I'm desperate so if you can't help me, if you *won't* help me, then at least steer me towards somebody who can. I'll talk to the union, I'll seek legal recourse if I have to, I'll do anything it takes but I can't just let them ruin my career because of something I haven't done."

"Listen Malcy," I return pointedly, "I'm limited in what I can do here because my work as a representative of the union only extends to members of it and so you'd be asking

me to work independently of them. You know the job that
I do and you know what the company expects of me, so I'm
sorry if what I'm saying isn't what you wanted to hear but
what you're asking of me is just impossible." He doesn't really
have a defence against this and I begin to bask in this shred
of sincerity. His neutrality hadn't helped the union with past
disputes against the employer and had this industrial action
succeeded, he would still have shared the spoils, regardless of
his non-union status. This gave me the right to shut down this
conversation without having to explain myself further but
as I was entirely responsible for the woes of which he spoke, I
felt that I owed him an ear at least. "Malcy," I continue, while
adopting a slightly softer tone, "there will be other jobs…"

"It's not about the job Simon," he states assertively,
as if I haven't quite grasped the point. "You don't seem to
understand that this isn't just about me, it never has been. I'm
being scapegoated here and nobody is listening."

This isn't true. I was listening to him but only in the
very same way that I had listened to The Croc when he assured
me that this would be a victimless crime. I am placing myself
at the centre of everything and working my way outwards
while sat opposite a man now facing a looming ignominy
for which I would be responsible. I hadn't foreseen this
because I'd wanted to believe that I was the victim and not
the architect and although this fallacy is unfolding before me,
this realisation is unlikely to change anything. My livelihood
now rests on Malcy's failure to recognise the true agent of
his downfall and although it is a tenuous safety net, it is
imperative to remain on the safe side of it.

But there had been something in those last words
of his that suggested he was on the verge of some form of
a confession. I hadn't recognised this instantly but I now
sensed disclosure resting on his lips, a residue of revelation
that was only being heightened by the pause that had since
ensued. He'd definitely alluded to the involvement of another
and hinted at the existence of a back-story that he was now

weighing in his mind as to whether he should reveal.

"I haven't told you everything Simon," he resumes in a precursory tone. "The truth is that I do suspect that somebody else is at the heart of all this and I have evidence that may prove my suspicions to be correct." I am now attentive in the very real sense for the first time today. I guess that he is alluding to Marion, it could only be Marion and if it wasn't her then it had to be to someone who had been acting under her direction. He looks to his right and then to his left before leaning in closer in a conspiratorial pose. The redundancy of the move isn't lost on me as there is barely anyone else around, much less likely are there any Tanner & Webbing agents in the vicinity. "It turns out that I am not the only one who is being investigated by the company right now. Some time ago, I can't remember exactly when, senior management turned up at the office without any warning and took me aside to ask a number of questions that seemed to centre around the business practices of one man in particular. I answered as honestly as I could even though I felt a little coerced and did so on the understanding that my identity would be protected. Problem is that I now know that it wasn't, or at least I think it wasn't and I believe that my decision to partake in that process may have turned a very powerful person against me. That person is Mr Crockett. It is Mr Crockett who is also under investigation."

27

KIM

Claire arrives at my flat half an hour later than expected which on her terms is as close to punctual as one can hope for. It is Friday night, she is already intoxicated and I have no idea who buzzed her in.

"I thought you weren't coming?" I ask rhetorically while exhibiting my irritation and dreading the impending embrace. Quite naturally, she's unable to detect this and grabs hold of me excitedly, kissing me full on the lips.

"You know I wouldn't miss this for the world," she says before breezing by me and heading straight into the kitchen. It is there that she inspects the contents of my refrigerator with a thorough scrutiny before depositing two bottles of something no doubt strongly alcoholic inside of it. "You never have any wine these days babe," she shouts back at me, all legs and torso with her head screened behind the refrigerator door. She's right in her observation but the fact is that it would be unsafe for me to drive and replenish my stock after locking lips with her just now.

"I don't keep wine in the flat anymore Claire, I'm trying for a baby, remember? That's why you're here!"

"How could I forget?" she replies while waving a bottle back at me and returning a spare glass to a place to which it never belonged. Already, her angles are all askew and I sense that I could be in for a very long evening. "Oh well, I guess that's more for me then."

I'd spent way too much time over the last couple of

weeks loading up the sperm donor app on my phone before I finally conceded that things were getting a little out of hand. My 'wish list' contained too many donors already and the task of whittling this down to something more manageable was proving more arduous than I'd expected. Originally, I had hoped that the perfect donor would just spring up at me even though I didn't know what it was exactly I was looking for, but this hadn't proved the case. I soon came to realise that the ideal just didn't exist and once I'd accepted that, I found myself overlooking many of the details that I'd initially defined as flaws and the numbers on my list began to multiply. As a result, the donors were now becoming difficult to differentiate and I now started to mistrust my own judgement. Fortunately, the donor app contained a link to the full website where (for a modest additional fee) I was offered access to a more in-depth service showing everything from explicit medical histories to a donor's quality of eyesight. This was good in theory but not so in practice as I didn't understand the use in learning how someone's grandfather had died of alcoholism at the age of seventy-eight or if this condition even had any genetic link. And then, even if it did, would this be any more concerning than, say, if a donor's grandfather had died at the very same age of a heart attack or a stroke or if they had a second cousin with a history of depression who took his own life at the age of thirty-six? It all seemed superfluous and yet I found myself scrutinising every detail and then discarding scores of donors in a show of appalling hypocrisy.

I knew I wasn't getting anywhere fast and it was then that I turned to Claire. Despite us being the best of friends, it is also fair to say that we seldom think alike and yet, more often than not, we tended to arrive at the same conclusions. I cannot call her logical but I trust her instincts and although she's one of life's oddballs, she is *my* beautiful oddball, trusting, loyal and brutally honest. But I suspect that when I'd told her about my commencing IVF treatment and she in her selfless way had offered to help, she probably didn't expect this. Perhaps she thought of an antenatal class here, babysitting duty there, a shoulder to cry on should the treatment prove unsuccessful but definitely not this. Instead, I texted over to her my log-in details for the website and asked her to select the top ten donors that she deemed the most fitting for me. Starting from scratch, I pledged to do the very same with the intention being that we would pool in our results together on this very evening and see if there were any matches to be found between our selections. If we could find just one suitable donor then the search would be over, I would look no further and I would commit myself to what could be the father of my firstborn.

It placed Claire in a unique position being the only living soul (outside of the medical profession) to know anything about this and, initially at least, she seemed thoroughly underwhelmed. 'But I just don't get it Kim,' she had explained over a lengthy telephone conversation, 'you've rejected every guy that I've ever recommended to you so I'm at a loss to understand why you'd suddenly trust my opinion on this matter?' She raised a valid point but I didn't have time to quibble and anyway, it wasn't like I was asking her to pick out a future husband.

I asked Claire to bring with her printed versions of the donor profiles she'd selected while I had shortened my electronic 'wish list' down to the same amount on the website. My initial plan had been to do this at her house where I could ensure some privacy but once Simon hadn't returned to the flat before six o'clock, I knew from habit that he wasn't likely to be back any time before midnight (with it being a Friday and all) and a late venue switch had been agreed. With an urge to get down to business, she snatches the laptop away from me, makes a critical observation about the strength of my password and replenishes her glass. What follows is a series of gasps, whoops and indecipherable mutterings, where my attempts to interrupt are met with a dismissive wave of the hand or a conquering hush. This leaves me with little more to do than stride about the living room in an anxious state like a prisoner on the verge of a potential discharge, uncertain of his captor's clemency.

"Okay Kim," she begins after what seems to be an age, "let me go through these one by one and I will start by commending you for such an eclectic choice. I'll be honest and say I really didn't know what I was expecting to find but some of the men on here sound H-O-T (yes, she really does spell it out like that) and I don't think either of us would stand a chance of meeting them in a bar and convincing them to fertilise us." I urge her to respect the gravity of the task at hand and again, I'm batted off. "Now, your first choice, Donor 7177," she resumes, while shaking her index finger determinedly at the screen, "he's got a lot going for him, but he really isn't for you."

"And would you care to elaborate as to why that is?" I ask.

"Of course you may my dear. Look, he's clearly very well-travelled and on the surface that's a good thing but there's a risk that comes with that as well."

"I think I'm going to need a little more than that," I prompt with genuine curiosity.

"Okay, well, he carries an adventurous gene right? You don't want your only child upping sticks at the first opportunity and leaving you to pine over them with nothing but your premature loneliness for company."

"That's just ridiculous Claire, please be serious about this."

"Is it? Okay, well how about number two? Now it's obvious he is beautiful but this also poses a very real problem for you."

"Really? How so, Claire?"

"Look, you want a beautiful child, I mean, I get that but if you follow the IVF route again for a second one, then you put huge pressure on yourself to make sure that the beauty of the second child equals the first. You really don't want the younger sibling sat at home of a Saturday night without a date while their elder brother or sister is out there turning all the heads."

"What?" I ask, while trying but failing to disguise my perplexity.

"Just bear with me Kim," she insists and I find myself with little choice but to do so while she clicks from one profile to the next with an alarming rapidity. Seconds later, she pauses briefly to consider expanding on a particular profile but contemplation is brief and she decides against it. "Now, I do like this one Kim but he really does sound far too intelligent."

"And that would be a problem how exactly?"

"I just don't think it would work, you with a precocious child correcting your grammar and making you feel uneducated, we both know how you hate to be wrong."

"No I don't," I object, albeit unconvincingly.

"Oh but you do Kim, you honestly do and I love that about you. While I'm at it, is there any reason why so many of your chosen donors are over the age of twenty-five?" I concede that I really hadn't noticed that there was such a trend. Claire continues. "Hmm, maybe you're focusing on the age thing subconsciously, like one of those innate prejudices that you often read about. Some of the guys in this database are like twenty, twenty-one, they're just kids and although they might come across as total dicks in their profiles, there's still a good chance that they'll mature into fine human beings one day, as would their offspring."

"And is there anyone at all that merits Claire's seal of approval?" I enquire angrily, miffed at her flippancy.

"Well I haven't assessed every one yet hun."

It is difficult to stomach her jocular tone because deep down, she knew how important this was to me. I didn't conceal what I was doing from anyone because I was ashamed, embarrassed or laden with misgivings, I did so because I couldn't bear the thought of sharing this with someone who didn't understand. It was Claire that I'd confided in the first time around, when Simon had submitted to his doubts and my mother had threatened to disown me and while the dream had ebbed away from me then, Claire hadn't wavered. So her attitude tonight had not only disheartened me but had left me feeling saddened, confused and a touch humiliated.

I opt to excuse myself and head to my bedroom rather than create a scene. She doesn't notice that I've left her and continues to talk to me as if I were in earshot but her words are nothing more than what I guess to be a muffled critique. In around three hours' time, she will probably fall asleep on my sofa, leaving me unable to wake her. When I eventually do, Claire, at the height of her self-pity and painfully slow recovery, will pledge to make it up to me and from there a blazing row will ensue. The argument will wake Simon, who will then learn everything that I'd worked so hard to keep from him and that was a risk that I simply couldn't take. I figured that the only way to extricate myself from this mess would be to rely on a tried and tested method, something feasible that Claire would willingly believe or at least not contest. Perhaps I should tell her that my mother had just called me in the middle of one of her monthly mental breakdowns, forcing me to play the doting daughter and leave right away to drag her back to sanity? Claire knows my mother well and so she wouldn't think to question the legitimacy of the story and that way, I could drop her home en route and just ignore her drunken ramblings for the short journey. With this decided, I return to the living room but notice instantly that Claire is now silent and locked in deep study. She hasn't passed out as she is still sitting upright, staring at the laptop in a transfixed fashion, virtually unmoving.

"Hey Kim," she shouts, breaking the silence, "go and grab my bag from the kitchen will you? There's something here that you really need to see."

I do as she bids and bring it to her. She sinks her left hand into the bag and roots around for a few seconds before producing several pieces of paper. They are the printouts of her selected donor profiles and I watch while she carefully sifts through them before pulling out one specific profile towards the back of the pile. She takes this piece of paper and holds it next to the laptop screen, the glare of which now reflecting across her face and her eyes seem to flit between the paper and the screen in a frenzied, pendulum motion. "I knew it Kim, I just knew it, I said all along that we are just too alike."

"What is it?" I ask hurriedly while seating myself beside her on the arm of the chair. "I can't see what you're referring to."

"We've got a match Kim, I think we've found your donor!"

I grab the paper from her while she turns the laptop towards my line of sight which is still resting on her knees. Her incredulous tone belies her outward confidence and my instincts tell me that she's probably wrong and her vision blurred by the wine that she's already imbibed. But in actuality she isn't and between the glare of the screen and the ink on the page, she really hasn't been mistaken. I am looking at the profile of Donor 2781.

I then fall prey to disbelief with a wild notion running through my mind that Claire has somehow managed to pull a cunning ruse on me. Her facial expression (no doubt identical to mine) suggests otherwise, though she too did not expect this (in spite of what she'd said) and the air of flippancy about her has quickly vanished. Donor number 2781, the man I'd elevated to my 'wish list' on the back of a tenuous link to a spirit medium whose legitimacy I had questioned and yet struggled to ignore. This man, who hadn't particularly stood out and had only found inclusion by my failure to deny the sense of providence that surrounded him when many others had perhaps seemed better suited. And yet here he was, this imposter of logic, this fixture of fate, having safely attained the backing of my best friend whose reasons I'm sure would probably amount to much less sense than my own.

"You seem... relieved?" Claire poses the observation as

a question. The words, whatever I intend to say, remain stuck in my throat. "What I mean is, either way, there's no finality about any of this if you don't want there to be. Nothing *has* to be decided tonight."

But Claire is wrong. The truth is, if it isn't to be decided tonight then it probably never will be and this very same scenario will just end up repeating itself on a weekly basis before every single donor has been considered and then rebuffed. That was how it had come to this already and although Claire hadn't seen this struggle, I know that she'd grow to resent me if I pulled her into this endless cycle of indecision. The object of the evening has been met but still I feel disquiet and relief in equal measure and that doesn't escape Claire's powers of intuition. "Why do I get the feeling that there's something you're not telling me?" She probes, which then compels me to plead for patience while I make a brief return back to my bedroom.

I reappear with CD in hand, equipped with the rather fragile assurance that all will make sense should she take the time to listen to its content. I enlighten her with the details of my nightly walks, to the lady in the salon and then on to Mabel and the teepee in the kitchen, before ending with my father's possible re-emergence. Claire takes another large gulp from her glass of wine and then looks at me, bewildered. I insert the disc into the laptop and hit play.

She listens dutifully enough without sign or sound escaping her like an invited voyeur and offers no input be it sarcastic or scathing. At the climax of the recording however, her critical faculties return.

"Can you believe that?" I ask, uncertainly.

"Well, frankly, no," is her response, "and you'd do well to think the same." She places her glass of wine on the coffee table in front of her and then optimises the use of this free hand by running it through her hair, deliberating. "I'm not sure I really know where to start. What was all that about a spirit roaming the rooms of your house? Who were these other people that she *claimed* to be communicating with? You can't honestly tell me that you believe any of this stuff do you, Kim? Come on, you're a sensible person, there's no science to any of this at all, it's just hocus pocus."

"Well I admit I was perhaps a tad disbelieving at first but…"

"Just a tad?" she cries. "Who exactly is this woman? Everything she said just sounds like the wacky ramblings of some chain-smoking hippy who overcharges the stupid at the annual fair."

"Look, I'm not saying that she was right about everything, clearly she wasn't but there's a lot in what she says that I can't explain as much as I would like to. I mean, how could she possibly have known about my father's illness?"

"Kim, that man she claimed to be communicating with did not sound like your father."

"But you don't know that it wasn't him anymore than I can say that it was." I say but I know how I'm not really preaching to the converted here. Claire just sighs loudly at this, stands up and begins to pace back and forth.

"And how does any of what your *father* said pertain to your choice of donor?"

I ignore the contemptuous overtones that permeate her question because I really had given this some thought over the last few days, in fact, I'd thought of little else since reuniting with the CD.

"It pertains to what he said in a way that goes far beyond coincidence, I can assure you. Now think back to what he said when he described the character of the father of my first child. He said that it would be someone that my mother would not approve of. Well, in Donor 2781's profile, it quite clearly states that he's an atheist. My mother, hollow though her Christianity may be, would never accept my first child being part-created from a heathen."

"I'm assuming you have more than this?" Replies Claire, looking back at me now both unfazed and unmoved.

"Okay, well let's look at the next part. He also said that he would be a student of transformation and 2781 is a sedimentologist."

"I don't know what one of those is Kim."

"It's a geological science that studies the evolutionary process of all types of sediments." Yes, I had researched this during the past week.

"So he spends his days playing with rocks and gravel then?" She says with a slight chuckle that I choose to overlook in preference of having her ask me to elaborate any further on this. "And what about the last thing he said Kim, something about never being able to own his affection?"

"Well that's the clearest and truest of them all," I state confidently. "How could I win the affection of a man that I would never, ever meet? Donor selection is totally anonymous."

"But surely the same would apply for any donor that you selected from the database, you can't say that's specific to 2781."

I admitted that was true but it still could not explain how Mabel had managed to produce the numbers 2, 7, 8, 1 on four separate cards in that very same sequence and then present them to me.

"And what about this other stuff Kim, why would your father leave you with such a stark warning? And what was all that about some tarot card?"

I tell her to ignore this because Mabel clearly tended to shoot wide of the mark at times and then I eject the CD to prevent further cross-examination. Claire is unconvinced but I remain steadfast because deep down, I've already decided that she isn't going to talk me out of this.

"Well if that's what you want then obviously I'll support you," she offers solemnly with a discernible air of defeat about her. "I'm just worried about you, your hormones are all over the place at the moment and I want you to make a rational decision."

"Rational?" I say, at the point of exasperation. "There's no rationality to any of this Claire, do you think this is the way that I wanted it to happen? Do you think this is the way I dreamed and envisioned it to be? I wanted the clichéd fairy tale just like everybody else but this is the closest I will get to a happy ending. Now that I've accepted that, I really need you to do the same."

Claire apologises, blaming in part the wine but mostly herself for failing in 'adequate sensitivity' and although my outburst had perhaps served its purpose, I still regretted it slightly. Her motive has always been my best interests (even if that wasn't always clear) and so it was pointless retaining any anger towards her. I recognised the absurdity of the situation I found myself in and had attained some level of comfort with it, but for her it was different. She had responded to the task without her maybe realising just how heavy a weight I was putting on her shoulders.

"Come on then," she says, her arm over my shoulder. "Let's select you a donor."

I guess it should feel slightly more significant than it actually does but still, we do it together. With her hand literally over mine, I click on the option that reads 'Choose Donor' before my decision is confirmed and seconds later acknowledged. Claire celebrates the moment by vaulting herself around the living room, punching and kicking the air like a rhythmless cheerleader, wildly shrieking as she does so. In stark contrast, I ratify my bank details at the request of the website and try to deny the incongruity of the scene.

"I can't wait to be Auntie Claire," she says breathlessly in the midst of her booze-riddled din. "Just think of the fun that the three of us are going to have together Kimbo, we're going to make some memories."

With impressive alacrity, she quickly transitions from prospective auntie into home renovator, offering ideas as to how the flat can be refurbished to suit the baby's needs. A wave of suggestions flow forth as items of furniture face up to their relocation and colour schemes are tentatively proposed. Names are advocated for and then dismissed, visiting hours requested and baby showers discussed and never, at any point, is the idea of the IVF process failing me ever touched upon. And yet, for all of this, I still find myself nodding along somewhat dispassionately for reasons that I can't quite define. Other than the feeling of excitement that I expected, there is really nothing more than a sense of mild relief that fails to justify or elevate the moment. There is no significance, there is nothing beyond the ordinary, but there is a grim absurdity that gnaws away at me and leaves me feeling exposed. Thinking back to the rhetoric that spread itself across the walls of the fertility clinic, there was never any focus on this particular moment, all reference was abstract, a sentence consigned to the foot of a paragraph. It didn't prepare you in any way for the lack of magnitude and maybe rightly consigned it to its natural place, one of a series of events that led you in hope to the conclusion that you actually sought. In the hours that I had spent searching for my perfect donor, I had also tried to convince myself that tonight would prove momentous when in reality, Donor 2781 could be doing any number of things right now in any part of the world. I felt guilty for his ignorance and yet also incredibly thankful for it.

"And the best thing about this flat has to be its size," continues Claire, while she gestures uninhibitedly. "What I'm saying is that this is perfect *baby size* because it's really very small and the baby is never going to be far from sight. Oh and by the way, I'm running on empty here darling." I refill her glass once more and then we move out to the balcony where the two of us stand arm in arm, gazing out on to the glittering landscape of the city. "I do wonder what Simon is going to make of all this though Kim, I really do."

I tell her not to spoil the moment.

Two hours later, Claire wakes up from a brief nap in my front seat when I pull up outside her house and she rejects my offer to see her safely inside.

"This is really happening now isn't it?" She says in a groggy tone.

"Yes it is," I reply, turning towards her and stroking at her fringe in a vain attempt to straighten it while she fumbles unsuccessfully with the seatbelt. "And I'm going to need your help because if it doesn't happen this time then I'll go the full three rounds if I really have to."

"I know you will Kimbo," she says with a protracted yawn, "but you avoided my question about Simon earlier."

"Because it wasn't really a question Claire, that's why I didn't answer."

"He needs to know Kim. You live under the same roof and secrets like this aren't the easiest to keep, especially when you start waddling around the house with a bowling ball in your abdomen."

I strike at her side in mock alarm but she doesn't flinch, the excess of alcohol having raised her pain threshold. I notice she isn't leaving the car.

"He doesn't need to know anything just yet Claire because there isn't anything to know. I just think we both need detachment, him from me, me from him and maybe a child would be the only way to break the deadlock. I just can't afford to focus on him right now and I guess I'll say what I have to when and if I need to and that's all there is to it."

Claire kicks the car door open more forcibly than I'm comfortable with having finally freed herself from the constraints of the seatbelt. She leans in for one final embrace.

"You know what Kim," she whispers to my ear in a toxic haze, "we'd make a great lesbian couple you and me. Well, you, me and the baby I mean. Just give it some thought."

"Get off with you," I say through a fit of laughter, "I'm far too glamorous for you and you'd hate to play second fiddle."

She denies this of course but on both counts, I can assure you, it's true.

28

SIMON

Picking up from where we'd left off, I decided to call Malcy today instead of meeting him in person, assuming that he would speak more freely outside of such a public environment. Our last conversation had ended at the point at which he'd revealed to me how he'd been questioned as a witness as part of an investigation against The Croc and it was therefore natural to conclude that on realising this, The Croc had turned his vengeance upon him and had facilitated his suspension from the company. Malcy hadn't stated this quite so plainly of course but if he hadn't wanted me to delve any deeper then he simply wouldn't have mentioned it nor would he have agreed to resume our line of discussion.

Today, I am far more tolerant of detail than I was just a couple of days previous and allow him to start by offering a summary of his role within the company without interruption. Working as part of the Supply Chain Team, Malcy was chiefly responsible for sourcing suppliers that could respond to the various needs of our vast number of clients. In this position, he would be entrusted with identifying which suppliers the company should opt for by weighing up a variety of factors which could include pricing, training locations and quality of content. Perhaps most significantly, once all these factors had been carefully considered, Malcy would then be expected to offer a personal recommendation as to the selection of the supplier to his manager. From there, a contract would be drawn up and signed by all parties to confirm the agreement, with Malcy's manager being the final signatory. That duty belonged to The Croc. However, it appeared that The Croc had been signing off on contracts without reading them and had been coercing Malcy into choosing suppliers that were nothing more than his own personal preference. In order to cover his tracks, he had asked Malcy himself to sign many of the disputed contracts on his behalf, a detail that seems to have originally prompted the internal inspection of the company's tendering process. The results of this were quite clear, prices were not adding up as they should've been and that had created the credible assumption that some suppliers were being favoured over others despite evidence suggesting that they were far from cost-effective and that their standard of delivery was simply insufficient. The powers-that-be at Tanner & Webbing could not ignore this and wanted to examine the 'goodwill gestures' that our suppliers were offering, speculating as to whether they could be the source of their preferential selection. If found to be true, and the line of wrongdoing could be traced back to The Croc, then the consequences would surely be beyond his powers of disentanglement and his career would be buried alongside his reputation.

"What's important to remember here Simon, is that I'm only ever working under the instruction of Mr Crockett and whatever concerns I've raised have always been dismissed out of hand. Sometimes he dictates my choice of supplier, other times he amends it but by compelling me to add my signature to the contract, he technically absolves himself from all responsibility. What's worse still is that the financial shortfall to the company doesn't seem to bother him and he just acts as if we've money to burn when I really don't think that's the case."

Malcy has entered into a confident rhythm of discourse already, one that I'd not witnessed when in his company at the coffee shop. I go on to ask about the suppliers in question and whether we have any professional or historical links to any of them.

"Well, we always try to push business towards our trusted sources," he replies, "but they've little way of knowing if we've overlooked them and are mostly thankful for our business. Whenever Mr Crockett has vetoed my recommendations, it's almost always in favour of a supplier I've barely heard of and due to his position, he doesn't need to offer any explanation."

"Look, it's pointless beating about the bush here Malcy," I start, decisively. "Do you believe that Mr Crockett is receiving personal benefits in exchange for offering business to certain suppliers? If so, was his decision to suspend you influenced by a need to remove you from any internal enquiry that may have exposed that?"

"I can't be certain, I mean, a part of me doesn't want to believe it because it sounds so evil but it's clear that questions are being asked of him at senior level and I'm not sure how he can answer them honestly without injuring himself."

The line goes silent for a few seconds while I stop to make some notes, partly because I haven't made any so far and I don't want to seem inattentive. Malcy waits respectfully for me to finish and when the silence exceeds the necessary allowance, he proceeds in a near whisper.

"I tell myself that someone of his stature wouldn't need to do this but if he's capable of one crime then he'd be capable of another and when I think back to the way he spoke to me on the day of my suspension, well, I start to wonder."

"Why do you say that Malcy, did he allude to something that day that you feel may be significant? Remember, any detail could be important here, no matter how small it may seem."

He pauses briefly again and I sense that he's unwilling to respond to my speculation.

"No, well, not that I can think of anyway. It's hard to explain really as it's not so much about the words that he used but more the manner in which he used them. They were loaded with venom and he had this vengeful look about him, one that I've never seen before and really wouldn't wish to again. Maybe he'd seen my speaking to the enquiry as an act of treachery against him, something that he couldn't find it in him to forgive but I didn't have a choice Simon and I only told the truth."

I say I understand and really I do because I've seen that vengeful look and heard those venomous words and observed the consequences that followed for the people he reserved these for. They were his enemies, his challengers and those who exposed him (just as Malcy had) and none had survived to topple him. That The Croc is guilty I have no doubt, for he is driven by personal enrichment and his loyalty to Tanner & Webbing will not extend to prioritising them above his ego. I am also now certain that his decision to suspend Malcy is entirely linked to the evidence he could share with the enquiry and Malcy's absolution depends on either removing or discrediting The Croc. The next step for me will be to garner more knowledge about the investigation itself and to find out whether it's as serious as it seems. Only once I've established that can I begin to discover just how any of this is connected to the sabotage of the ballot and how intrinsically linked I am to all of this. One thing is for sure however, there is far more to this than poor judgement and mere negligence and The Croc threads this series of events together like poisonous stitching. These enquiries will lead to uncomfortable answers but the thought of this is not enough to repel my curiosity or tame the thirst I have for greater insight.

"I may still be able to help you yet Malcy," I say semi-tentatively, "but in order for me to do this you have to be patient and it's imperative that you don't talk to anybody but me. Is that clear?"

"Crystal clear Simon, thank you. I'll talk to no one else, I promise you, not that I see that being much of a problem anyway."

"Really, why's that?"

"Because I don't have anybody else."

29

KIM

I come round from the anaesthetic feeling nothing more than a little groggy which seems to surprise everybody present. Bedbound, I spend the next half an hour chatting with a male medical assistant who monitors my return to full consciousness with an admirable diligence and seems to understand my slurry diction. He is softly spoken, effeminate and most likely undervalued in his current capacity and talks effusively about anything other than his present profession. When he departs, the anaesthetist takes over the bedside vigil and spends the next ten minutes or so searching for any lingering effects of the anaesthetic. When convinced that the outward signs are positive, I am then wheeled off to the recovery room where lukewarm tea and unbuttered toast await me. My throat is sore by this point and once reunited with my phone, I am able to determine just how utterly unflattering the surgical gown that they have draped all over me really is.

On arrival at the fertility clinic this morning, a clean-shaven Doctor Block had explained the procedure to me succinctly. It would be a relatively painless procedure lasting no more than around twenty minutes, in which a small needle would be attached to the end of an ultrasound probe that would then be inserted through the wall of my vagina. The purpose of the insertion would be to collect a number of eggs from my ovaries which I had been stimulating through my two weeks of gonadotrophin injections. From there, these eggs would then be transferred to an embryologist who will perform the act of insemination by the sperm of my chosen donor away in the laboratory. Unpleasant though it sounded, I was relieved to learn that I would at least be fully sedated throughout the process and although after-effects were to be expected, they proved to be nothing beyond my pain range.

As I wait patiently for Doctor Block's return, I start to worry whether the time he's taking is a cause for concern or nothing more than a regular delay before boredom defeats me and I drift off to sleep. It is then that the drugs in my body lay siege to my senses and a wild, illogical dream plays itself out in my mind. Naturally, it is my mother who plays the central character, leading me, her unwilling accomplice, into the bowels of a tall building where we attempt to perform a heist. Once the resistance of the safe is overcome, we take to our heels with the spoils of the theft and speed away from the scene on foot with impressive haste. It soon becomes clear that we are not alone though and with our crime detected, we are now fleeing an angry mob that stamp and scream in our wake. My mother warns me not to look round and to face right ahead but, true to real life, I end up defying her. As I look over my shoulder, I see the mob gaining ever closer and at the head of them, my younger brother Declan, his face full of snarl and hate. I notice that my pace begins to slow as my mother speeds on ahead, almost out of sight and as the plunder from the heist starts to spill from my hands, Declan gains on me. The harder I try, the slower my feet seem to move and as I finally relent and accept my impending capture, I turn to see Declan and realise he is armed with just a baby rattle. It is then that I return to consciousness.

If I wake with a start then Doctor Block is good enough to pretend not to notice. I find him sat at the foot of my bed, nibbling away thoughtfully on a pen, crossword in hand. So engrossed does he appear to be with this cryptic conundrum that I'm unsure at first as to whether he's even noticed my stirring and only when he addresses me do I learn that he has.

"Just bear with me one moment Kimberley," he begins distractedly, without hiding the clash of his attention. "Forgive me but you looked so peaceful just then that I didn't wish to wake you. Now tell me, how the devil are you?"

My answer to that particular question would depend on just how graphic a response he was chasing. My genital area is sore, my stomach aching and there's a taste in my mouth which falls some way sort of pleasant but other than that I am largely okay. I consider asking just how long he'd been sat there or whether this vigil of his was standard medical protocol but opt instead to tell him that I'm fine in my stoic fashion. He gets up from his seat, fails to secrete the crossword about his person and then pulls up another chair next to the bed. In place of his surgical attire from this morning, he now wears a faded blue jumper (which is far too long in the sleeves) and thin, grey jeans that pinch at the thighs.

"Now, it is perfectly natural in the aftermath of such a procedure for you to experience some vaginal bleeding or the odd stomach cramp here and there. If this does happen then there's nothing to fear, so just take the medication that is prescribed to you and all should be fine." I tell him that I'm well. His concern seems merely perfunctory and it doesn't quite cover what I really want to know. Just what was the outcome of the operation, and was it successful?

"Successful?" he repeats back to me with what sounds like affected confusion. "Oh yes, most definitely I would consider it so. I anticipated no challenges at this particular stage and thankfully, none presented themselves."

"And how many eggs did you collect Doctor?"

"Well, in total we collected ten eggs."

For a few uncomfortable seconds I wait for him to elaborate further, unwilling to interject and I can't define the silence that ensues. His initial positive assessment seems somewhat weaker than his hesitation and a fear quickly grows within me. In the brief but onerous quiet and with nothing to feed upon but fear, my intuition is screaming concealment of truth and his routine brevity doesn't seem so habitual anymore.

"And is that the necessary amount?" I enquire cautiously, imploring him to expand on his paucity of information with a worried look.

"Necessary?" he repeats, as if to provide himself with thinking time. "Yes, quite so. We usually endeavour to collect around eleven or twelve eggs but we'll work with what we have and hope for the best."

This doesn't sound good to me. Why have they only drawn ten healthy eggs from my ovaries when I had done all that they had asked of me? Have I failed to inject myself correctly in the midst of my fear of needles or has the ultrasound offered a misleading picture of my insides? Maybe Doctor Block has been intentionally pithy in his responses up to now and has used this as a method to control my spiralling optimism? The panic starts to envelop me and visibly so it seems for the good doctor is quick to retrieve his line of address.

"Listen Kimberley, it really isn't about the quantity of eggs that we collect but the quality. We will do all that we can to achieve the desired outcome but there is always that element of chance, good fortune, whatever you may call it, that plays a pivotal part in this. As it stands, we are no further away or indeed any closer to that outcome but we will work assiduously in the coming days to give you every chance."

"So what happens now and just how long will I have to wait to find out?" I mistakenly assume that he considers my question before replying, when in actual fact, his attention is occupied by an unannounced guest at the point of entry to the room. In a show of remarkable and frankly uncharacteristic punctuality, Claire, my chauffeur for the day, has now joined us.

Claire, in her typical whirlwind of sound and colour, fails to even notice Doctor Block who still sits dutifully by my bedside and she breaks into a lengthy tirade covering everything from the clinic's extortionate parking fees to her mother's reluctance to spare the car. Undeterred by this invective, he introduces himself, albeit tentatively, leaving Claire to respond in kind.

"Oh hi there Doc, I'm Claire," she replies, emboldened by his visible discomfiture. "So how long are we expected to wait before we've got ourselves a little bun in the oven then?" I watch as he attempts to translate the metaphor, his face awash with speedy rumination.

"Well, as I was just about to explain to Kimberley, the eggs that we have taken are already in the incubator and ready for the next phase."

"Which is?" she inserts, without a modicum of restraint, leaving me scowling at her. Unabashed by this he readily continues.

"Essentially we'll mix the sperm with the eggs and leave them to culture for a day or so. We'll monitor them closely to see if any have been successfully fertilised and then choose the best of those that we have for transfer into the womb. In all, it will take around five days." Claire nods along with this trying to indicate comprehension while I shoot a look his way spelling unequivocal apology. Doctor Block removes his spectacles and starts to clean them delicately on the sleeves of his jumper. "Now, Claire," he resumes while repositioning his glasses onto the end of his nose, "it is your job to look after the patient for the rest of the day, I assume you are the designated driver?"

He assumes correctly.

"Oh yes Doc, that's me and a very safe one too if you don't mind my saying, I'm renowned for my driving skills as it goes." And she was in truth, only she was perhaps renowned for her lack of skill rather than her depth of it. Fortunately, she doesn't feel the need to disclose how she only passed her test on the eleventh try, has a tendency to ignore road signs and doesn't even own a car herself.

Claire continues her conversation with Doctor Block

while I begin to gather my things together somewhere in the background. I try not to listen in to what they are saying, however, two things soon become clear, one is that Claire is starting to flirt with him and the other is that Doctor Block is also showing signs of a mild receptivity to this. A combination of this latter observation and the lingering anaesthetic accelerate the nausea and my desire to leave grows urgent. Doctor Block beats me to it, makes his excuses and departs, cutting his conversation with Claire short, much to my relief.

"Right babe," she says, turning to me, "we really need to think about getting you home. Now just tell me where I can and can't touch you as the Doc said you might be a little leaky and if I get any stains on my mother's upholstery then she's going to kill me." I tell her I don't need any help just yet and continue what I'm doing. She doesn't seem to mind her apparent redundancy and starts to fiddle with every bit of medical apparatus she can lay her hands on. "You know that Doctor's pretty hot Kim, I mean, it's weird to think that just under an hour ago he had his head between your legs, armed only with a wand and a torch."

"Don't be disgusting Claire," I admonish her. "He's got four kids and it's called an ultrasound probe for your information."

Laughing at her own smuttiness, my rebuke means nothing to her.

"Okay, I'm sorry babe but he's seen parts of you that many men haven't. Hey, do you think he could loan me these stirrups?"

30

SIMON

Judy from the Supply Chain Team had matched my expectations in just about every way on first meeting her. Shy, tremulous and a tad distrustful, she'd failed to conceal her surprise on discovering my identity but had still repressed her curiosity with an admirable restraint. Perhaps it was my level of seniority that had eventually won her trust, for if she was confused by my motives then she did well not to question them and responded to my probing with something close to fluency. This, I soon considered fortunate, as it quickly became clear that Judy knew more about Malcy's situation than I'd originally assumed.

It had taken days of subtle enquiries and carefully timed interceptions to finally yield a positive result in my pursuit of finding someone that could help both corroborate Malcy's evidence against The Croc and attest to his good character. In order to cover my own tracks, I had started by sending a reluctant Agatha in to the Supply Chain Team so that she could gauge the mood and build a line of contact but this endeavour hadn't borne any fruit. Instead of the vocal outrage I'd expected of them at the plight of an esteemed colleague, she had instead met a shared reluctance to say anything of relevance and left with the distinct impression that her presence had been unwelcome. Undeterred by this (while accepting that the onus really should've fallen upon myself), I then decided that my best course of action would be to email every member of the team under a sensibly designed alias, offering them complete personal discretion should they wish to cooperate with me. Three days later, I finally received some positive news when a colleague of Malcy's by the name of Judy replied to my email. Her response was concise but not without hope, revealing a deep dissatisfaction with the way that he'd been treated and perhaps most significantly, alluding to some information that she felt could well be of use. She agreed to meet with me providing certain terms were agreed upon, and I responded with little hesitation. I wasn't disappointed.

Armed with an array of revelations, she began by disclosing how she'd first been made aware of The Croc being placed under investigation some months back and that she'd been all too willing to assist senior management in their enquiries. The request for her assistance never came however and Judy stated ruefully that the reasons for this were in fact twofold. Firstly, because management had never formally approached her (probably assuming her to be too inferior to know anything of any substance) and secondly because a certain Malcy Kearns had discouraged her from whistleblowing. It was typically him, she had said, in not wanting her to become implicated after he had been interviewed and unbeknownst to her, he had perhaps sown the seeds of his own downfall by pleading so successfully. I didn't share her view that this selfless act seemed worthy of extolling but there was very little point in countering this opinion publicly. Not only had Malcy confided in her numerous observations of The Croc's blundering and blatant malpractice but she herself had witnessed the same and found tangible relief in discovering that senior figures had finally decided to act. Crucially, she had responded positively (after some persuasion) to my request that she prepare two statements, one in support of Malcy's character and another that would help expose The Croc for a history of negligence and wrongdoing. Not only this, but I also gained a vow from her that she would be interviewed in person if the need presented itself (as certainly it would).

Judy closed the meeting by quizzing me on a variety of different things all relating to our mutual friend. His health was fine, I replied, yes he was keeping his spirits up and no, I didn't see this whole thing ending negatively (though she maybe didn't buy that). It was clear that she knew very little about his involvement in the ballot, of a potential conspiracy against him or that this had been the ostensible reason for his suspension from the company. I was happy to mislead her on this in what was a tame deception because Malcy remained increasingly jittery in the conversations we'd shared. With disciplinary proceedings against him seeming inevitable, he could do nothing more with his time other than wait for the call and he took each day without news as a sign of inaction, spurring ominous thoughts. Our case was beginning to build however, and I found myself relying less and less on a veneer of bravado and more on a burgeoning sense of optimism.

31

SIMON

Hey you. Hungry. Lunch? x

This is the poorly punctuated text message from Vanessa that interrupts my journey back to the office this afternoon following an arduous meeting with a client that hasn't gone well. After a lengthy and ultimately futile discussion that ended with my decision to take our business elsewhere, the option of listening to Vanessa bemoaning the hardships of student life seems like a welcome relief and so I promptly redirect the taxi and call Agatha to say that I'll be working from home for the rest of the day.

We meet in a restaurant that was once recommended to me by The Croc and although that alone should've acted as a deterrent, my first impressions leave me pleasantly surprised. I don't need anything too elaborate where Vanessa is concerned, just the type of place that lies fairly centrally between one that is expensive enough to impress her but not excessively so, as the difference would probably be lost on her anyway. In that respect, this under-heated and sparsely attended eatery is just the ticket. I locate a table close to the door so as to assume a 'Croc Watch' position on the off chance that he appears.

Vanessa is wearing a grey suit jacket, beads and a T-shirt with an indistinct band name displayed across her chest. The jacket appears frayed at the edges and has stitched elbow pads that only come into view when she slips her arms free at the sleeves as if to take it off and then, after a brief moment of indecision, decides against removing it. She is in a typically gregarious mood and begins by haranguing me for selecting a restaurant that falls outside of her budget. That she knows I will pay for her is of course a given and this mock reproach is purely to establish the fact but I enjoy watching her little performance and hold out for as long as I can before telling her not to worry about it.

We've been seated for around five minutes when I excuse myself to go to the bathroom and leave my order with Vanessa. From there, I take the time to catch up on a few emails and notice how several other men (all dressed like me) are scrolling through their phones in a distracted fashion, offering meagre responses to pressing enquiries. Ostensibly at least, we are all in the middle of a 'business lunch' and the corridor leading up to the toilets becomes a suited thoroughfare. When I return to my seat, I notice that there's a commotion of a different sort taking place about three tables away from ours and that Vanessa is enraptured by the scene. A young couple are embracing amid clamorous applause and a wedding proposal has been made and accepted in the time it has taken me to relieve myself and apply an out-of-office message. I try to act vaguely enthused by what has happened though it is evident to all but Vanessa that I, like every other man in here, am a little embarrassed and so I choose to remain seated while she strides over to the happy couple and offers her personal congratulations. When the coast is clear, I tell her I have to exit temporarily to make a quick call. On the way to my temporary refuge outside, I accept a free glass of champagne, courtesy of the newly engaged twosome.

32

SIMON

"So why didn't your relationship with Kim work out in the end then Simon?" Vanessa asks this while fingering the rim of her glasses and then removing an imaginary speck of dust away from the lens. We are now somewhere near the middle of our main course and Vanessa, having developed a taste for champagne from the earlier celebrations with the happy couple, has moved on to her third glass. The question doesn't catch me off guard because I've been expecting it but the timing could perhaps have been better. I'd mentioned Kim in passing once before because I felt I had to and she was a topic of conversation that would be impossible to avoid moving forward. We'd not had the chance as of yet to really talk about her at length though and Kim still had absolutely no idea of Vanessa's existence. I should've prepared better for this moment having spent the last year telling the few who had listened how the ending had been amicable while convincing myself that the resentment I was feeling was really nothing more than a natural sense of loss. Some saw through it and others did not but Vanessa's verdict was worth a little more and the last thing that I wanted was for her to feel pity for me.

"We were together for twelve years," I begin, "so it probably isn't fair to ask why it didn't work out because in many ways, it really did. Besides, is it really that important?" My answer, as I dreaded, feels woefully insufficient.

"I'm just interested that's all. I mean, I guess you must

have loved her otherwise you wouldn't have stayed together for as long as you did but then I read about these couples all the time who stay together for convenience long after the love is gone. It's really not that rare." She returns her glasses to the bridge of her nose and makes several attempts at repositioning them satisfactorily before giving up entirely and placing them on the table. At the risk of sounding trite, I tell her it is far too complicated to discuss over dinner when in truth, I feel as though I'm being lured from the trenches into a battle I cannot win. Still, she doesn't relent. "Tell me everything Simon. I'm intrigued. Tell me how you met her and how you fell in love."

How does one explain all this in simple terms to the teenager with limited experience who probably feels obliged to ask such a question at this stage of our relationship? Could I express any of it in words she'd understand or that wouldn't make her feel jealous or comparatively inferior? I somehow doubted it.

We met in an English Literature class at the age of sixteen, in our first year of Sixth Form College. We didn't share any mutual friends to begin with and so our interactions were initially limited to a passing hello in a corridor where the presence of her friends always made an enhanced dialogue impossible. That was probably for the best as even then I was daunted by her beauty and had been so since I'd first laid eyes on her. Back then, she didn't need to exhibit or accentuate her beauty nor did she need to answer to her self-defined imperfections. From her enamel-like skin to her faux-bohemian clothing, she was practically free of embellishment and as flawed as the rest of us and once I'd resolved to be with her, that obsession soon consumed my life.

I recall that it was December and a heavy snowfall meant that few students had made it into class that day and so I finally took it upon myself to sit next to her when all around us were empty seats. I'd spent weeks playing out various interchanges in my mind hoping that when the chance came, the scene would pan out just as I'd anticipated. I needn't have worried. She was as amiable and as smart as I could've hoped for and when the inclement weather stopped her daily bus from taking her home, I offered to walk the way with her instead. By the end of the journey, I was infatuated.

The Christmas holiday that followed prevented any personal interaction between us until the resumption of the new term and I was limited to the odd text message here and there when I couldn't decide if I ever said too much or too little. She used to talk a lot about a club called Scally's where most students at our college seemed to converge every Wednesday due to their lenient door policy and liberal pricing system. It wasn't really my scene but I lied and said otherwise when she invited me to meet her there one evening and I couldn't quite decide if there were romantic undertones in the way that she had asked. It was much later that night, when she glided towards me in the middle of the dance floor and kissed me for the very first time. It was intense and it was magical and it felt as though we'd done it a thousand times before and right then I knew that I was in the presence of somebody who was about to shape my life.

The cynics will tell you that everybody thinks that way when they fall in love for the first time at the age of sixteen with nothing to compare it to but there is something beautiful in the assertion, especially when you know that you will only ever experience it once. Kim would be my first and to this day, I am yet to meet anybody capable of stirring such a volcanic tide of longing and desire within me as she did then. The greatest compliment that she paid me was really very simple, she returned my love.

But I don't quite know how to say any of this to Vanessa without making it obvious that the present can never outweigh the past and so I sanitise the truth and simply tell her how synchronicity brought us together and that the comfort of routine had kept us there. My overt reticence on the subject leads to a temporary lull but Vanessa detects this and probably knows that it will be impossible to reopen this line of questioning at a later date.

"And so how did it all end?" She resumes, pushing her empty plate to one side and placing a napkin on her lap out of sequence. "Between you and Kim I mean. Did you fall out of love or was there somebody else? Was it peaceful or acrimonious?"

I could refuse to answer and consider doing so but it's only going to delay the inevitable and then create an unnecessary taboo. Vanessa is not deserving of the truth just yet but then perhaps she doesn't want that and maybe she merely wants to clear this hurdle between us before the passage of time makes it insurmountable. I take a moment to ponder before replying.

"We just drifted apart I suppose, like people do. One morning you wake up and you realise that you're just fed up of lying to yourself and all of a sudden, the alternative doesn't seem so frightening anymore. Ah, you know how it is." Truthfully speaking, she probably doesn't and it is wrong of me to assume otherwise. After all, what can she possibly know about adulthood having barely entered its domain herself? Can she be made to understand how it feels to be in a war of attrition with one you once loved and then to have that strength of feeling usurped by one equal in its bitterness? Maybe I can explain how rationality absconds and how a warped sense of strategy takes over, how you project this as reason when in reality it is anything but. Can I tell her honestly that the highest of the highs is really worth the lowest of the lows? No, it would be impossible because only experience can teach you that and it will do so in a way that every ballad, every anecdote and every movie cannot adequately do.

She appears relatively satisfied with my response or at least sufficiently distracted when the main course is replaced by the dessert. When the waiter is out of eyeshot, she starts to stab and probe at her pudding before reaching for her mobile phone to take a photograph of the culinary ensemble in front of her. I'm not really sure why she does this but then she seems to do a lot of things that seldom make sense to me.

For whatever reason, I get a strange thrill from watching her eat as she does so with an eagerness that borders on intensity as if the taste of every new bite will differ from the last. She isn't a ladylike eater (if indeed one can be distinct from their male counterpart) and the bones of her jaw seem to grind away in a jolty, perpetual motion. She is completely uninhibited by my staring at her and this charming spectacle is only briefly interrupted when I recognise one of the suited toilet-dwellers from earlier, who walks by our table and offers me a nod of tentative recognition. Vanessa is visibly intrigued by this and asks how I know him and doesn't seem remotely satisfied when I explain how I don't but that we'd briefly shared a passing exchange before the meal. Indeed, so perplexed is she by this seemingly insufficient response that she falsely attributes this behaviour to some weird custom only to be understood by men much older than her that clearly lack the social means to generate true conversation. She could be right of course but I tell her all the same that not everything in life needs to make sense and thankfully, she continues to eat her dessert and asks no further questions of me.

33

SIMON

After a chain of inquisitive emails had all seemingly dropped into the abyss, I am able to report with some joy that much like with Judy, my perseverance has been rewarded once again. A loose connection I made some years ago in the Human Resources Department (we'll call him Ken for now although that isn't his real name) returns a favour of which he was never actually indebted and produces a log of evidence that I have been striving hard to acquire. Ken reveals (in a private email) how The Croc has been working under a performance management review for some time with his capability being both tested and challenged under a scrutiny which would at best be seen as undermining and at worst, a prelude to his dismissal. Not only that, but accounts have been audited, clients interviewed and a forensic examination of the Supply Chain process has also been carried out. With that in mind, Malcy's testimony against The Croc has been deemed somewhat fortuitous by senior management who seized upon the chance to add further flames to a steady growing inferno. With an unblemished character and years of close proximity to the accused, Malcy adds an element of legitimacy to their case against him which they believe to be imperative in deflecting any accusations of a management witch hunt. Confident that his evidence alone will prove to be conclusive, Malcy is soon fast-tracked into the position of lead witness with the case then essentially resting on his ability to testify. It is here that Ken's understanding of events appears to fail him however and although he disguises this as a duty to discretion, he isn't to know how successfully I am already beginning to adjoin the missing pieces of the puzzle. He can't tell me much about the reasons behind Malcy's suspension because he simply doesn't know other than to say how the chances of The Croc being exonerated have now significantly increased. This, as he understands it, is not the result that senior management necessarily desired and with the case now on the verge of collapse, it is clear that whatever ugly stain now blots Malcy's character, it has helped turn the tide of events back in The Croc's favour. All it needs now, I remark, is for Malcy to find a way to return to the fold with his honour intact to which Ken agrees but really doesn't see happening. Essentially, without concrete evidence from any witnesses, the case will crumble. Despite inner urges to the contrary, I hold my tongue and offer no further comment.

I close my laptop, ending our electronic dialogue once Ken has descended into obligatory platitudes and just after he enquires about the health of my long-term partner, 'Katy.' I am jubilant but with this jubilation comes a heavy dose of fear for I am speedily approaching the point of no return. So far, I have acted with discretion but I know I can't control the whisperings of others and details of the questions I am asking will surely fall into the wider domain very soon. Should they do so, I am not quite sure how I will spin it. Maybe if The Croc does find out then I can simply lie and say how this was nothing more than an exercise to ascertain what Malcy knows before dissuading him from challenging his employer's decision. Perhaps he won't quite believe this but unless I act on the information I hold, I still remain relatively safe.

As the picture of The Croc's skulduggery becomes ever clearer, I curse my complacency and cowardly myopia for failing to see it sooner. Nobody works any closer to him than I do and although these revelations haven't shocked me, they do reveal how I am not in his confidence quite to the degree I once thought I was. This situation has embroiled me now and

I feel like one toiling away at the earth with a shovel in hand, recoiling from the rewards of my efforts and wincing at the ugliness of my discovery. I sense the sacrifice that is coming. The net is indeed closing in.

34

KIM

"I get the feeling that maybe I'm just a tad overdressed?" is what I ask of Alice as we emerge from her car and stare out at a desolate, grey warehouse that I assume to be our destination. My godson Charlie is already several paces ahead of us, his face illuminated by the gaudy lettering, blinding and askew. The twenty-minute journey that I probably could've avoided ends with Alice reassuring me, "you look beautiful babe, the hotties inside are going to love you."

The grim austerity of the building's outer framework is spectacularly conflicting with its interior as we enter a world of colour, noise and garish-looking playthings, all of which are punctured by hordes of screaming children whizzing about the place like lemmings stuck on fast forward. I'd heard about these kinds of places before (mainly from Alice) where adults load their children full of sugar in the hope that it will tire them just enough to enable mom and dad to fulfil that afternoon engagement for which they couldn't find a sitter and didn't dare cancel. I observe mothers sitting around the perimeter of this multi-coloured coliseum, gratefully engaged in adult conversation while a smattering of fathers carry children above their heads into the den of fun like apes releasing their young into the wild. Perhaps unsurprisingly, I feel totally out of place.

I make the sensible decision to sacrifice my high-heeled shoes as I lead an awe-stricken Charlie into the hub of activity while Alice departs for catering. As I hoist him into a rainbow-pebbled ball pit, I feel the hem of my wrap dress ride up above my thigh and although full exposure is avoided, the adults around me do well to ignore the incongruity of the scene. Within seconds, Charlie is submerged and completely out of sight and so I linger around for a protracted length of time, rooted and uncertain of playhouse etiquette. When Alice finally calls me over, having located an empty table, I quickly realise that the meal in a fancy restaurant that I'd anticipated this morning has been well and truly substituted for a soggy tuna melt and lukewarm soda water.

"What I'm trying to say to you Kim, is that if I was single and looking for a hook-up then here would be the place that I would do it. Some of the dads in here have got a lot going for them, nice cars, great jobs and if you can handle the baggage and the weekend access, then you're onto a good thing."

It pains me to hear Alice talking like this, in the dialect of a character from a sappy daytime drama (that jobless motherhood enabled her to watch), while espousing the joys of material gains that she had never once longed for. That I am taking relationship advice from the girl who's had just two sexual partners to boast of in her life (one of whom is now rumoured to be gay) I can just about accept, but this obsession with my singledom seems entrenched in something deeper than the urge to see me happy.

"Ah yes," I begin, not even bothering to disguise just how tiresome I find this trait of hers. "Stolen smooches in the soft play area, if only Jane Austen were still around to write such a scene into one of her novels."

"You're too dismissive," she scoffs back at me. "In fact, that's always been your problem, you cannot see beyond veneer. I mean, look at me and Adrian. I could be with a better-looking guy if I really wanted but when I see him walking about the house in his socks and underpants, he doesn't look any worse than he does when he's dressed up for an evening out. Now picture a guy that you really like and strip him down to his pants and socks, strewn across the sofa like a bloated whale, it's a terrible disappointment when you see that for the first time but you keep your judgements to yourself."

Strangely enough I do agree with this to some extent even though I picture Ricky and find the image in my mind far from repulsive.

Still, there is much to dismantle in that last statement but I decide against pursuing it constructively and opt instead for silent assent. Alice, buoyed by this (and typically undeterred), vacates her chair, positions herself directly behind me and says, "you know my offer still stands about setting you up with somebody, right?" As she brings her mobile phone into my eyeline, ready for the inevitable hard-sell, I notice the unpleasantness of her body odour and this isn't for the first time.

"Now this here is Ged," I am informed while she swipes away furiously at a procession of photographs from his Congrelate account, none of which are registering. "I think you'd really like him. He fights fires for a living and plays lots of different sports so he's super fit. I think he's had some issues with a crazy ex-girlfriend of his who's lingering somewhere in the background but since the police got involved I'm told that things have smoothed considerably." Utterly flustered, I have no time to formulate the most meagre of replies before Alice is at it again, frantically tapping away at her phone and moving nimbly on to the next candidate. "Not interested? Well, that's okay, I haven't showed you Jason yet, just bear with me a moment, ah yes here he is. I think he does something really boring in computers for a living but he's one of the funniest guys you could ever wish to meet. He still lives at home with his mother as far as I'm aware and he doesn't drive either, oh and while I remember, he's a little on the short side so maybe don't wear heels like these if you do go out with him, yeah?"

That last comment prompts me to take my shoes from the table and return them to my feet. Knowing how you cannot interrupt Alice whenever she's in full flight, I hope that my exasperation will somehow transfer itself telepathically but no such luck. Is this what it's really come down to I wonder? Having to choose between a man who is one restraining order away from becoming a newspaper headline and a midget who will dictate my choice of footwear? Just how many personal defects is one expected to ignore? Whatever I am worth, I feel it has to be more than this and when I plead for Alice to stop, she does so reluctantly and returns to her seat, miffed but unabashed.

"Well if you don't like either of them," she continues, "then you may want to keep your head down while you're here." I ask why, though in reality, I'm already expecting the answer that I receive. "Because they both have children Kim and I often see them in here."

I exit to buy some vending-machine coffee.

I take a quick detour on my route back to Alice and spend a minute or so trying to locate Charlie in the rainbow jungle, thinking for a moment that I spot his blond head popping up above the play pit, before I realise just in time that I'm mistaken and manage to repress a wave. Handing Alice a coffee on my return, I see that her mood has now evidently declined and she looks vaguely chagrined about something for which I assume to bear some responsibility.

"Do you think Simon ever cheated on you Kim?" She queries solemnly, as if picking up the seamless thread of a former conversation. I compose myself and marvel at her ability to segue so magnificently, thankful that her temporary sulkiness does not pertain solely to my rejection of her matchmaking efforts.

"I don't know Alice," I begin, inwardly praying that Charlie will emerge from his colourful retreat and prevent me from continuing. "I guess it wouldn't matter now even if he did but for what it's worth, no, I don't believe that he would ever have done that to me. Why?"

She fingers the rim of her polystyrene cup with an ominous reserve as if weighing the importance of articulating her next reply.

"Well, this may sound crazy to you but a couple of months ago I became convinced that Adrian was having an affair." She is right, that does sound crazy to me and for a number of reasons but even though she probably deserves as much for the way that she treats him, it seems beyond unlikely. Adultery isn't his style because he's far too craven for that and Alice is pretty open about the violent recriminations that he will face should he even think about transgressing. "It all started when I noticed how something looked a little different about him and I couldn't quite put my finger on it. He hadn't lost weight but he hadn't gained any either and as I buy all his clothes for him, he couldn't have adopted a radical new look without my knowledge. Then, one day, I find a tub of hair gel deposited away in the back of a bedside drawer and I think to myself, 'why is a man who is so indisposed to self-grooming suddenly deciding to use hair gel?' It didn't make any sense. I knew he wouldn't tell me if I asked him outright so I had little choice but to investigate myself. So I start off with the standard things one usually does when suspecting that their partner is having an affair, I check his phone messages, smell his clothes, scan his social media accounts, but it didn't really lead me anywhere. Naturally, I assumed it had to be someone that he worked with as he's seldom home of a weekday evening before seven o'clock and whatever he's been making in overtime, well, he certainly hasn't shared with me. The obvious candidate, or at least the only candidate was this bitch called Hilary that he introduced me to at his office Christmas party three years ago. He always assured me there was nothing going on between them but I could never be sure and I know she hasn't forgiven me for the drink that I threw at her."

"Hold on a second there," I intercede. "You're telling me that you threw a drink at one of Adrian's colleagues because you once believed they were having an affair? That's insane." Although Alice can be eccentric, I have never known her to be violently so nor have I known her sense of doubt contaminate her rule of logic in such a way.

"Details babe, mere details. Anyway, for the last six months he's been coming home even later on a Wednesday evening as he often joins his friends for a game of five-a-side football and it was this detail that eventually led me to the truth. We were walking through the park with Charlie one weekend and a stray football rolled over towards us. There was a group of about five lads asking us to return it to them and I mistakenly assumed they'd stop calling out at us if I ignored them and just collect it themselves. But they didn't and so Adrian reluctantly walks towards the ball and then makes the lamest attempt at a pass that I have ever seen, slicing at the ball wildly and sending it several yards wide of his intended target. Now Kim, I was raised with three older brothers and I know a football player when I see one and Adrian clearly hadn't kicked a ball in his life, much less was he honing his skills at this sport on a weekly basis. I knew then that I had found my breakthrough."

She takes a brief moment to recompose herself and pushes a strand of hair behind her left ear with a tremorous hand. It's difficult to judge where this point of brief hesitancy stems from, be it a reticence to complete the full story or a passing concern that she will somehow omit a pertinent detail. I suspect it is probably the latter.

"It seemed to take an age for the following Wednesday to come around," she resumes, "but when it did, I dropped Charlie off at his uncle's house and then carried out a meticulous plan to stake Adrian out at his place of work. On reflection, I probably wasn't thinking straight at the time but without any solid evidence to confront him with, I had to find something tangible, something irrefutable that would prevent him from improvising his way out of it. So I find a suitable vantage point behind a parked car on the street where he works and at around six o'clock, I spy him leaving the office with Hilary in tow. I follow the two of them at a safe distance while denying an insatiable urge to bring matters to a head there and then and eventually they arrive at a bar and go inside. For the next ten minutes, I pace about the car park rehearsing what I'm about to say, trying to gain control of my anger and order my thoughts. Already I'm thinking further ahead, picturing the ways that I will happily destroy his life once the scandal has been exposed, devising my exit strategy and picturing him tearful and pathetic as I walk out of his life for good."

She interrupts her narrative to light up a cigarette with the air of one used to semi-rebellion. The security in the building, young, lax and indifferent, strain a neck here and there but then decide against intervening, probably still reeling from past requests to desist having been flatly ignored by Alice. I decline an offer to partake and allow her to resume.

"Well, such was my sense of fury that I didn't really take in my surroundings as I entered the bar and charged over towards Hilary who was sat alone at a table, filing her nails. I picked up the nearest glass that I could find, ready to repeat the dousing of the Christmas party and headed in her direction but before I could execute my attack, she let out a wild shriek and started waving frantically, looking to divert my attention towards the activity behind me. As I turned around, I noticed that there were families all about me sat at tables eating meals or carrying trays of drinks and children dazzled by the lights of endless arcade machines. It was then that I realised this was no regular bar but was in fact a bowling alley and it didn't take me very long to pick out Adrian either. As I followed the line of Hilary's gesticulations towards the alley lanes, I saw him stood at the head of one of them, ready to take a shot, perched like a model of concentration. I watched closely as he fizzed a ball down the aisle with a gloved right hand, clattering numerous pins in the process before returning to his seat. Several of his colleagues were huddled around him and it was odd to note that they were all wearing matching attire and if I wasn't mistaken, Adrian even had his name emblazoned on the back of his bowling jacket. I was stunned. In all this time that I'd convinced myself that my partner was conducting some illicit affair, he was doing nothing more than hanging out at a bowling alley full of spotty teenagers and ugly shoes."

"Wow Alice," I say, trying to repress my laughter and wondering if I have interposed too soon. "You know, if only you'd have consulted me at any stage during this fit of paranoia then I could've told you that you were acting irrationally."

"I was just so ashamed Kim, a little at him but mostly at myself for thinking that he was capable of doing such a thing. When we came home that night, we had this really heated argument but I don't see how I was to know that he and his colleagues had formed a bowling team? They'd been playing together for a while apparently and all in the name of post-employment revelry but he wasn't the only one of them with a wife back home and I bet the rest of them all knew about it. When I asked him why he hadn't just told me the truth in the first place, he said he couldn't because he knew that I'd consider it unmanly and deride him for it just like I always did everything else and then he suggested that I'd probably have preferred him to be having an affair anyway. The strange thing was, for once he was right but obviously I couldn't possibly admit that."

"And the hair gel?" I ask, trying to thread the story back to its origin. "What I mean is, did you ever find out if it was his or not?"

"Oh yeah well I've since thought about that. Turns out it probably wasn't his after all. My brother Carl stayed with us for a week not too long back while his house was being fumigated so it probably belongs to him. I guess it's kind of ironic when you think about it."   But I don't see it as ironic in any way at all. It was reckless and immature and in no way befitting of a twenty-nine-year-old mother of one. I contemplate relaying this opinion to her but when she's in a mood such as this, nothing will ever resonate, so I figure what's the point?

"I'm thinking of leaving him Kim," she resumes,

somewhat mournfully. "I realised that's why I was so disappointed about the bowling thing because however ridiculous it may sound on the surface, deep down I really wanted him to be having an affair. That way, I could've ended it all and the decision would've been an easy one."

"You're too hard on him," I declare and not for the first time either. As long as the two of them have been together she has forever been either on the cusp of leaving him or seriously contemplating doing so and it has never happened yet. I didn't see the point in staying with anybody that made you unhappy and Adrian seems to be the cause of her unhappiness even if he is in no way responsible for this. Truth is that Alice secretly loves him very much but sees the strength of this attachment as a weakness in herself and so she chooses to resent him for it and the poor man suffers continually because of this.

"Do you think that I should leave him? I often wonder what it would do to Charlie but then my parents divorced and I'm pretty sure it didn't mess me up. Your parents stayed together right? Heck, you're just about as messed up as the rest of us aren't you babe?"

She is right, my parents did not divorce but that isn't really the full story and she well knows this. In reality, they never should've married or at least, they never should've married each other. I knew from an early age that something had never been quite right between the two of them and as time wore on, I soon grew to realise that it wasn't just something, it was everything. Unlike Alice and Adrian, my parents were two different people struggling to assimilate with one another while clinging to some antiquated notion that marriage was a vow you didn't break no matter how unhappy it made either of you feel. While divorce may have seemed a sufficient remedy to others, it wasn't so for them who saw no honour in marital collapse and ascribed it to weakness and failure in those that exercised that right. When I think back, I'm pretty sure that the decision to adopt Declan emanated from a misguided belief that it would somehow bring them closer together and of course, it didn't work. After all, how could it? My parents were selfish in that they used the fact that they had two children as an excuse to stay together because neither of them possessed the courage to walk away and strike out independently. Although they were successful in their chosen careers, they failed in their first duty as parents and substituted the love they couldn't impart with material rewards. Simon often liked to tease me about the luxury of my childhood but he never understood the emotional bankruptcy within which I was raised. Sure, I can't deny that I was maybe a little spoiled but nobody can have everything and when you have so much, it's easier to long for the little that you never had.

I contemplate articulating all this to Alice but soon realise the futility of the operation and simply advise her to do whatever it is that makes her happy. It's not the answer that she wants from me of course because she simply wants to amplify all her problems but I don't feel sufficiently qualified to counsel her on relationships right now and my parents' marriage will form no fair comparison. When things were at their worst with Simon, I seldom confided in her and yet that restraint was a courtesy she had never offered me in return. Perhaps if I had done so, my relationship with him would never have lasted as long as it did but while Alice and Adrian remained together in spite of their unhappiness, the grounds for my own separation never felt justified.

We talk intermittently for the next half an hour or so before Alice decides it's time to leave and sends me out into the toy jungle to gather up Charlie. Clearly satisfied with his day's endeavours, he clambers over a couple of space hoppers before accepting my embrace without any sign of his habitual resistance and by the time we reach the car, he's asleep in my arms. Perhaps I too am wearied by the day's events and thinking unclearly when I suddenly resolve to finally confess all to Alice about my IVF treatment. If there is to be a right time to reveal this then the temporary lull created by a sleeping child in my arms is probably as good as any and the burden of concealment certainly needed to be lifted.

"Listen Alice, I really should've told you this before and it probably won't come to anything but..."

"Ah, you look so cute together," she observes, interrupting me and nodding at Charlie. "Maybe next time you should bring him back here yourself, you know, just the two of you. God knows it would give me a rest and you can test out your parenting skills before you make the inevitable mistake of taking the plunge yourself."

With my fleeting impetus lost, I opt against resuming my line of personal revelation as I'm reminded of just how undeserving Alice really is of much of what she already has. She doesn't know how much I envy her for aspects of her life that she doesn't seem to value and how that hostile indifference that she frequently exhibits prevents me from disclosing my most onerous of secrets.

I'm not prone to gloomy meditations but when I am, I often like to think of how Alice would react to the news of my sudden death. She knows nothing of the physical toll on my body that my IVF treatment is taking right now nor does she know of Ricky or my accumulation of debt and it is doubtful to assume that anything I do tell her registers in any way. Sometimes, I even go so far as to imagine Alice's eulogy to me and picture the crowd at my funeral all running private bets and estimating the time that it will take before she reverts to talking about herself. I don't like to be flippant about such things of course but I often can't help it.

When I am back home at Gaddis Avenue, my phone buzzes in my pocket and I see a message from Alice.

Kim, I totally forgot but I think you wanted to tell me something??? xxx

Exhausted and unwilling, I simply say:

Alice, I'm just really, very lonely.

She doesn't reply.

35

SIMON

I hung up the phone abruptly on a tearful Vanessa who was certainly worse for wear but nonetheless coherent as the usual formalities were dispensed with. It was Sebastian of course (well, who else could it be?) and in a way it was really all my fault because I'd seen this coming and yet I hadn't warned her. I trusted Vanessa but I'd never trusted him and I hadn't felt comfortable with the lustful way he looked at her, his constant close proximity or the way in which his hands lingered too long upon hers. I knew that in my absence he was fluent in his distaste of me with his slurs and his conjectures and his ill-motivated assertions, and that Vanessa's defence of me would be meek by comparison. It had all inevitably led to this, Sebastian, no doubt enlivened by the stimulant of alcohol, forcing himself upon her at a party and thoroughly vindicating my foreboding.

The fury engulfed me in a transformation so swift that I barely even felt it. Perhaps, had Kim been awake, then she would've reasoned successfully against my taking her car and driving while still intoxicated in the middle of the night but in truth, I doubt I would've listened. Excluding my recent misdemeanour, I'd often found that I drove a little better when under the influence of alcohol as my concentration levels tend to rise even though the dent at the front of the vehicle remained evidence to the contrary. It had also been a while since I'd driven through the city at so late a time (as I habitually liked to do) as since meeting Vanessa, I hadn't ventured out once on a nocturnal round and the urge to do so had seemingly ceased. This evening, that predilection returned as adrenalin fused with my destructive tendency among the din of angry horns and the hazy fog of lights. One accident while driving in such a state and everything would fall apart for me and yet, somewhat against the odds, I reached my intended destination entirely unscathed.

What happened when I arrived at the party remains indistinct and the following chain of events are linked only by a series of fleeting recollections. The first of which was that of a tall man standing at the door of the property who urged me to be calm as I entered the house at speed without the necessary invitation. Once inside, I asked around for Vanessa's whereabouts but couldn't glean anything from the unintelligible responses proffered by drunken students who seemed miffed at my intrusion. The party had evidently passed its peak and costumes were either partly discarded or consisting of stray articles that would not have belonged to the original ensemble. It took a while before somebody seemed to understand what I was saying above the musical racket and pointed me in the direction of the back door. It was there that I found her sitting on a pile of clothes in the back garden, sandwiched between two friends, with her head resting on the shoulder of one of them and holding the right hand of the other. Dressed in a burlesque costume that looked both rumpled and gaudy, there was a forlorn quality about her that I didn't recognise and a red hue sagged below her eyes to indicate that she'd been crying. Stripped of her vivacity, she looked youthful and pathetic and felt limp in my arms as I led her through the house and back to the car, my progress briefly interrupted by her two friends who quarrelled with me like two obstinate drunks in the mistaken belief that their argument became more conquering the louder they became. I didn't wish to reason and so I simply pushed past them and continued towards the exit.

I belted Vanessa in and pleaded with her to not throw

up, listening without confidence to her slurred assurances and then made my return back to the house. It was there that I finally caught sight of Sebastian, standing across the room and remonstrating with the girl who'd been holding Vanessa's hand in the garden, before turning his petition to me as I made my way towards him. Amid the clamour that ensued, there was a cacophony of broken glass, the hurdling of limbs and voices ringing out like alarms. The furore itself was brief but intense and the casualties that followed formed no clear distinction between those that intervened and those that didn't. After about a minute or so, I shook myself free from several arms of restraint and headed back to the front door where my exit was met with much less protestation than had been my entry.

The next thing that I recall is being back at Vanessa's dorm and desperately wrapping her hair around my fists while she vomited convulsively into the toilet. This volcanic onslaught was so unforgiving that I felt angry at my redundancy and repulsed by the scene in equal measure and I baulked even further at the violent contortions of her slender upper body. I couldn't tell if this was drink or something more sinister, whether the cause had been self-induced or not but it hurt to see the tear-stained face that eventually turned back to me, aching with regret like the torture were never-ending. When the rhythm of the nausea finally abated and Vanessa offered me a much-needed respite, I noticed that there were bloodstains on both of my hands.

Despite being wounded and fatigued at this point, I still managed to carry a prostrate Vanessa to her bed in the hope that she'd be able to sleep off her evening's excesses. Naturally, it took a while for her to reach a state of slumber as the previous exertions clung to her like the dried bile did to the corners of her mouth but once she fell asleep, she did so peacefully. A quick rummage about the room produced a moderately strong bottle of gin, which was my only company as I sat at her bedside in an uncomfortable chair and tried to make sense of what had happened. I noticed the spare bed lying adjacent to Vanessa's and briefly considered jumping into that before deciding against it, figuring that her fellow student wouldn't take too kindly to the intrusion should they return. I set the alarm on my phone for the early morning so that the car could be returned to the Gaddis Avenue parking bay in readiness for Kim's daily commute and then I fell asleep.

I awoke to find the bottle of gin was still in my hands but it was all but empty. The spare bed that I'd opted against sleeping in remained vacant but the sound of a tap left running in the bathroom forced me to get up and turn it off before returning to Vanessa. She was lying on her back and breathing heavier than before and so I repositioned her onto her side to see if that would alleviate the problem. As I did this, though she remained unconscious, I sensed that she was trying to say something and that a barely audible sound seemed to be escaping her lips. What she was saying wasn't clear but I didn't want to wake her and so I drew closer in, unsure if it was an instruction intended for me or something else. It was then that I made out exactly what she was whispering, she was repeating the name, 'Sebastian.'

36

SIMON

The silence from Judy had become unnerving. After a fourth
email had gone unanswered, I introduced daily visits to
the Supply Chain Team as part of my routine, each with an
ostensible purpose and all of them without result. On enquiry,
nobody had seen anything of her and although I sensed
that I was being misled, the impression that I left with was
that I was free to speculate just so long as I didn't expect any
answers. At this stage, it was still too early to tell if Judy had
succumbed to the pressure and betrayed her convictions. As
chance would have it, I was about to find out.

But this wall of silence does not relate to Judy alone
as it also seems to have extended itself to Vanessa as well in
recent days. Since seeing her home from the party the other
night and then subsequently nursing her back to sobriety, I'd
not heard from her once and every text or call has been met
with no reply. It's difficult to define how I really feel about
this because Vanessa is of an age where a certain amount
of flightiness is nothing out of the ordinary but I didn't see
myself as one of her peers and feel that I deserve a little better.
I'll reach a point where my patience wears thin eventually or
she'll decide that she needs a lift somewhere or an expensive
lunch. Then, no doubt, this hiatus will come to a swift end.

"That looks a little sore Simon, are you sure you're not in
pain?"

I tell Agatha that it's nothing as she hands me the
latest edition of the Tanner & Webbing internal magazine

and notices the swelling on my right hand. This morning, I was again unable to form a fist when trying to clean my teeth and although the skin around my knuckles is now much less inflamed, it is noticeably misshapen. Fortunately, the laceration on the right of my neck remains outside of her line of vision.

I start to flick through the pages of the magazine with little attention to its content until one defining image suddenly leaps out from the page. It is a photograph of The Croc, gleaming with the visual falsity for which he is renowned while grasping the hand of a female colleague in congratulatory fashion. There, stood beside him, sharing in this joyful moment while looking both vague and incompatible is Judy, celebrating the news of her recent promotion.

Wilful disbelief envelopes me entirely as I stare at this sinister revelation and fight to deny that my fears have been realised. I close the magazine and push it to one side but the visual deceit has now internalised and the picture lingers in my mind like a stuttering, cinematic projection. A sense of nausea takes up immediate residence.

"Agatha," I call, while clutching at the corners of my desk to maintain my equilibrium. "Where in the building would I find the Communications Team?"

"They're on the fifth floor," she answers after considering briefly, "but they've only been operational for about a week or so. From what I'm hearing, it's a bit of a mess up there at present and best avoiding." I take leave of my desk immediately.

It is natural that my course should take me via the Supply Chain Team where I head once again armed only with my laptop as if that somehow legitimises my presence. Once there, I stand against the door pensively and try to recall my composure, observing Malcy's former colleagues as I do. It is clear that he is now erased from memory, his desk bearing no discernible signs of its former occupant and arid plants fight for space with uneven piles of paper upon it. But there is also another desk adjacent to his that is now unoccupied that I hadn't originally noticed and this is distinguished by the orderly fashion of its former inhabitancy. This desk shows signs of a departure far less acrimonious than Malcy's where success has elevated its former dweller all the way from Supply Chain to the Communications Team of the fifth floor.

This newly formed team differs from Judy's former unit of employment in just about every way. The Communications Team is the latest apple of Tanner & Webbing's eye in a fruit bowl that is forever spitting out one sour fruit before replacing it with another. In what is an old idea rehashed by an overpaid and underused executive, a collection of the company's most aspiring employees will now be huddled together in this department, offered an inflated wage and set a number of unattainable targets for the small price of their sanity. In two years' time, when the team ceases to exist and with the weak now separated from the strong, the latest round of staff cleansing will be complete and the cynical yet cyclical process will continue to thrive under the pretence of gentle evolution.

In this new department there is no need to conceal my presence because I am largely anonymous before this flurry of activity, where people scuttle around disconnected wiring and juggle over-packed boxes in hurried, interweaving paths. I can make out Judy from afar, pacing around the periphery of the action in what seems a desperate attempt to look busy and useful. Although she is only a matter of feet away from me, she may as well be a million miles for whatever impression I formed of her has certainly been way off the mark. The bitter irony of this misjudgement is that it was reflected and surpassed by another who now stands to lose more than anyone for this indulgent oversight. He never told me so but in his own inimitable way, it is pretty clear that Malcy is in love with her and if I pressed for a confession then I'm sure I'd have got one from him. This, I perceived not only from his willingness to protect her at the cost of his own integrity but

STEVEN VAUGHAN

more so from the blatant elevation of his spirits whenever he or I alluded to her. And now, it will fall on me to expose such foolishness by telling him how the woman he loves has struck a deal with the only enemy he has probably ever made in his life, for reasons he will never be able to understand.

I lurk around furtively for about twenty minutes before the opportunity presents itself to finally catch Judy alone. Having stealthily tracked her across the concourse of the floor, I somehow manage to slip into the same elevator as her and before recognition prevails, the doors have closed behind us and we are stood in semi-solitude.

"Why did you do it Judy?" I ask as the upward mechanism of the lift jolts into motion and we begin to ascend floors. She looks back at me more perturbed than panicked, like one who expected this to happen but probably not so soon and certainly not here. "You know how Malcy feels about you and you know how his career rests on evidence that only you can share. He deserves an explanation."

"I'd prefer to have this conversation with him if it's all the same to you?" She snaps with an irritation that she has no right to display. She then edges daringly towards the keypad of the lift and I briefly consider hitting the emergency button to take control of the situation as you see people do in movies. I don't though and she merely selects a different floor either to protract the time spent in the escalator or to choose a quieter floor on which to continue this. "I'd really rather not do this here," she continues with exasperation, "and I can't say that I appreciate this."

"When you answer my questions you can call time on the conversation Judy but until you do, then I'll be happy to wait for as long as it takes."

She backs away from me and folds her arms across her chest. I get the feeling she is buying time and preparing what she's about to say but if that be the case, then I won't let her deception extend to me.

"I just changed my mind Simon. I offered no guarantees,

I gave you no promises and you have no justification for accosting me like this. Malcolm would be horrified to learn of what you're doing right now."

"No Judy, Malcy would be horrified to learn of your betrayal of him. Somehow, Gavin Crockett got wind of the fact that you were about to expose him just as Malcy once was. Then, he did what he does to every human being that crosses his path, he found your weakness and he exploited it." I pause briefly to take breath as my tone begins to rise volubly and I find myself now standing over her in an imperious posture. "He offered you this job to buy your silence didn't he? That was the price of your betrayal and now you are too cowardly to admit it."

"No, that isn't true, you cannot say that to me..."

"I say what I like to liars Judy. You've sold out a man that loved you, that put himself on the line to protect you and all for the sake of a better job and a new title to boost your ego. Not only this but you have done it all to protect a man that deserves no loyalty, not from you, not from anybody and he will sever your allegiance just as quickly as he acquired it."

"No Simon," she repeats, almost imploringly and then endeavours to shoo my words away with both her hands. "Stop this now, stop what you are saying to me!"

"Just admit your treachery. Confess it to me now. I want to hear your reasons."

She turns her back to me and faces the floor and I detect that some form of a confession is about to follow.

"I have to say that this is all a bit rich coming from you," she begins, in a softer tone now like a solemn preface. "Yes it's all very rich for you to accuse me of treachery." Turning around now, she takes one step toward me and the contrast in her face and her deportment is truly stark. Until this point, I have struggled to attract her line of sight and thought this to be simply a reluctance to face my accusations but the dilated pupils and contemptible stare tell another story. There is something eruptible to that glare and it is a look that I have seen in others when the persecuted becomes the persecutor. I begin to feel an instant discomfort. "I know what you have done," she continues. "I know that you worked in league with Mr Crockett to somehow sabotage the ballot and all for the very same reasons that you choose to condemn me for. It was you who struck a deal with Mr Crockett so you could secure some promotion that you were after and it's pointless pretending that it wasn't. Just where were your principles then Simon? Probably in the same recesses of your character as they were when you learned of Malcolm's fate and how he was set to pay the price for what you'd done. Which reminds me to ask you, just how does he feel about all of this exactly? I'm assuming that a man of such solid principles has taken the time to tell him?" My jaw begins to feel as if it's wired shut, my heart throbs violently and for whatever reason, the pain in my right hand resurfaces. "No, of course you haven't. Heaven knows what nonsense you've filled his head with whilst you've steered his attention away from the truth, you gutless, cowardly man. It is *you* that is responsible for Malcolm's downfall because it is only you that can prevent it and although you've probably had several chances to do so, you have no doubt resisted every one. Yes Simon, you don't fool me, not in the very least, so let's not pretend that you are motivated by anything other than guilt. Now, you've had far too much of my time already."

Seconds later the surge beneath my feet comes to a halt, the elevator doors open and Judy departs through them, pacing away from me with the steadiest of gaits. I make a vain attempt to call after her but it sounds weak and tentative and is lost within the rhythm of office clamour. She doesn't look back.

I have little time to collect my thoughts though before my phone starts to ring and rather eerily, it is Malcy's name that appears on the screen. I jump back into the lift and step out at the next floor which just happens to be one that I do not recognise.

"Hello Simon, are you okay to talk?"

"Of course," I reply, even though he's literally the last person that I want to talk to right now and I regret answering. "Listen," I say, "I'm glad that you've called because I really need to tell you something before anybody else does, I just need to work out where to begin..."

"You sound out of breath Simon."

"It appears that events have transpired Malcy and I want to prepare you for a bombshell that could be about to hit..."

"You're not wrong there. I can't say it didn't come as a shock to me either."

"Listen Malcy, I can explain but you have to put yourself in my position before you make any judgements here okay? I had little choice."

"You've received my email then Simon? The one I sent you this morning?"

"Email? What email?"

"Oh right, you haven't then. Well, I received a letter in the post from the company today and they've made me an offer, a clean break as it were."

"Go on," I compel.

"Well it seems like some sort of waiver and if I sign it, they'll expunge any mention of what has happened from my record and pay me notice. I guess essentially, I can walk away from all of this and forget it ever happened."

"Malcy, are you absolutely sure that's what it says? This doesn't make any sense to me."

"Yes. I've scanned you a copy and attached it to the email, go take a look when you find a moment."

I stride frantically down a thin corridor, not really sure where I'm going and tug at various door handles in my search for a vacant room, disturbing numerous meetings. I eventually find one on the fifth attempt and then connect my laptop to the nearest port. In the time it takes to load, I place the phone down, pull open a window and lean my head outside into the open air. Staring out across the city, I realise

I'm several floors higher than usual and so try to make out my apartment block from this much greater vantage point and then fail in this endeavour. I suck polluted oxygen into my lungs and do a quick mental calculation of how long it will take me to reach the ground if I vault out of the window right now.

I recover quickly enough from this departure of my senses though and sit myself down. I shake as I tap away at the keys and mistype my password several times before eventually logging in and I put Malcy onto silent so that I can access what he's sent me without being disturbed. Judy's words still ring in my ears for our conversation had revealed many things but what was most alarming to learn was that The Croc has betrayed me, or he has at least intended to in telling her of my involvement in sabotaging the ballot. What I don't yet know is why he's done this but I suspect he's either learned of my encouraging Malcy to stand against him or something even more sinister is afoot in which he has purposely implicated me. My secret has clearly not been revealed to Malcy however, which comes as some relief, as just moments ago, I came so very close to exposing myself to him. Although this refuge can't last long, I have every reason to cling to it.

I access the email to which he refers and quickly scan its content. In the style so customary to Tanner & Webbing, it is both brief and legally evasive, for they know that Malcy will not have the means to scrutinise it professionally. The devil (as always) seems to rest in the detail but he appears to have grasped it accurately enough and another difficult conversation is about to ensue.

"Don't accept the offer Malcy," I begin, having taken him off silent and returning the phone to my ear. "You know that if you take it then they're going to put this whole thing to bed. They'll leave you responsible for what happened and The Croc will walk free."

He pauses for a few seconds to consider his next response which tells me immediately that our perspectives are already at odds.

"It isn't perfect Simon, I know that but it's my future at stake here and I need to think rationally."

"Malcy, I urge you to reconsider this, they're offering you a pittance and we both know why. It's you who is the victim here remember and if I can't prove how Mr Crockett framed you, then I can at least make management believe that he had motive to do so."

"But Simon, you have given me no reason to believe that any of what you say is true. You tell me to be patient and I comply, you ask questions of me and I indulge you with replies, but seldom do you explain to me your confidence. Why is it that you believe I have the slightest chance of being exonerated? Please do list your reasons because I haven't seen them."

"Just give me one more week. Give me five days and I promise that if I haven't delivered for you what I've promised then I won't stand in your way whatever you decide."

"No Simon, my mind is made up and I'm going to walk away from all of this. Even if I stay and choose to fight the allegations against me then it's far from certain that I'll be vindicated and I could end up with nothing. Then where does that leave me? What employer is going to take on a middle-aged man with something as ignominious as this on his record? How do I look people in the eye and try to explain to them what happened without them thinking me a liar and a fantasist?"

I have no idea where he is drawing this sense of resolution from. Not so long ago, when he sat before me looking meek and browbeaten, I sought this steely defiance from him without success and now, in a cruel turnaround, he has my future in the palm of his hands and doesn't even realise it. Of the bitter irony of this he must remain unaware but I can't keep up this weak façade much longer without spinning one last desperate lie.

"I can't support that decision Malcy and the reason I

can't support it is because if you do this now then you will ruin somebody that you care very much about."

"I don't believe you."

"Maybe you don't but you do believe Judy, right? Judy, the woman that you love, the woman who has put her career on the line to stand in support of you? She has offered evidence that implicates Mr Crockett on the understanding that you will fight the charges against you but if you accept this offer then there's no going back for her. She'll not have the luxury of an exit blessed with dignity Malcy, her career will be finished and you will be the one responsible for that."

More silence ensues but this is a beautiful silence which encapsulates the moral dilemma that he is facing far greater than mere words can express. For all of his ethics, Malcy is clearly no different to the next man when it comes to a common weakness, the illusory hope of an unrequited love.

"I never asked for her to be involved in any of this Simon, I only ever wanted to protect her and now you have taken that one intention away from me."

"But you still can," I say, fervently, "just one week Malcy, that is all I ask. Give me this, invest your faith in me just this one last time and that trust will be fully and unequivocally rewarded. On that you have my word."

There is another deafening hush.

"Okay. I'll give it one more week before I go back to them. Not a minute more though Simon and I really mean that."

I click off the phone without saying goodbye for I now have little time to waste. I pace back over to the window and try to order my thoughts but these immediately turn to The Croc. It still isn't clear exactly how much he knows and Judy could only reveal so much but he wouldn't have linked me to what happened with the ballot quite so overtly unless he felt threatened in some way and the fact he hasn't foiled me publicly suggests he has a plan. Judy is not acquainted with the depth of my knowledge so maybe her betrayal has really done nothing more than bring about the inevitable conclusion a little quicker than I anticipated. With the final chapter at hand, I head straight to the office of The Croc.

What greets me there is the sight that I expected, a desk unoccupied and a chair vacated but it matters very little. I am willing to wait and whatever apprehension I once envisaged was likely to accompany such a moment doesn't seem as prominent now. From the first day that I walked through the door at Tanner & Webbing and was introduced to the man who I would go on to serve, this moment seemed somehow preordained. It had to be, for it is simply unfathomable how we've managed to coexist without one of us breaking or bringing about the demise of the other long before now. It is a downfall of which I once dared to dream and now it feels as though it is finally within touching distance. Although the circumstances leading up to this have not been ideal, my motives have never felt purer.

I sit myself down in his chair, look out towards the far corner of the floor where my team are working diligently and notice how everything looks like a throng of subordinate activity from here. It struck me some time back that maybe I was a little short-sighted when I first decided to help Malcy and that I'd far more to gain from this whole affair than I first thought. I figured that if The Croc could be eliminated from the picture entirely, then his own role at the company would then become available and this was a position where the mechanics were well known to me but perhaps more importantly, the politics that came with it. Is it possible that the reason he'd initially primed me for the role of Area Project Manager wasn't so much because he recognised my potential but more so because he saw me as a threat and wanted me safely removed? Has he seen the dormant seeds of my ambition finally being reaped while recognising that I too share some of his inherent cunning? Perhaps so, but he hadn't acted quickly enough and now his little empire is on the verge of collapse. All I need to do is simply reach out and take it. A clearer and more profitable destiny has revealed itself to me and this throne of tyranny on which I now sit has never seemed quite so attainable as it does right now.

The truth is that I hate him and I hate how I am forced to turn obsequious in his company and feign interest in the facile things that he says. I hate having to pretend that his counsel is important to me and can't bear the thought of having to spend another fifteen years spurning invites to his home and the weddings of his daughters. I hate him personally and even more so professionally and more than anything in the world, I hate being labelled as his protégé. Gavin Crockett, the man who typically flees the trench at the first sign of conflict will be offered no clemency from me. The scars from this battle will be all his.

But as confident as I feel, I know that my own position in all of this is by no means certain and that my fate does not rest entirely in my own hands. Fact is, if Malcy changes his mind and chooses to walk away with the company's offer then it leaves me exposed and although I can still share everything I know about The Croc with those investigating him, it is really worth next to nothing without Malcy being there to publicly validate it. In that scenario, The Croc will get away with everything and, knowing of my treachery as he now does, he will surely come after me. If Malcy does choose to reject the offer however, and see events out to their bitter end, then that leaves The Croc with two choices as far as I can see. Either he accepts the evidence that we've compiled against him and resigns from his position with immediate effect or he elects to fight the charges and face the ignominy of a protracted departure. Whatever decision he makes will not necessarily bring about Malcy's full exoneration as he still has charges to face himself (around the ballot) but while they remain simply allegations, they cannot be used to discredit him as a witness against The Croc. It is also possible that The Croc will stand resolute and choose to defend himself but if word of his misdemeanours is to be shared publicly, then it is unlikely that senior management will allow the integrity of the business to be undermined so blatantly, that being of significantly more importance than the fate of a middle manager such as he. Crucially for me, there is no physical evidence linking me to the distortion of the ballot and so any accusations that The Croc can make linking me to such an act are unlikely to be considered, especially when made by someone so discredited as he will then be. Certainly, Judy now knows something of my involvement but whatever The Croc has told her is purely circumstantial and there can be no logical motive attaching me, a trade union representative, with the spoiling of a ballot calling for industrial action. After all, I've made no confession to him about what I did or how I did it and although I've never denied my own chicanery, in reality, an accusation without solid proof isn't going to stand up. Most likely, the company's deciding body will not have too much time for conspiracies linking The Croc to the spoiling of the ballot but that will perhaps be an argument for another day and Marion will sing like a canary if her future at the company depends on it. Her involvement in this sorry affair still remains something of a mystery but she is undoubtedly implicated and perhaps only via a confession from her can Malcy be absolutely saved.

And in Malcy's debt I remain (even though he still doesn't realise this) as my livelihood is now entirely dependent on him keeping his word. This wasn't so when he originally came to me with a hopeless case of which I was the cause and he mistook my initial signs of diligence for a noble faith in the pursuit of truth. He wasn't to know that gaining his pardon has never been my primary objective and didn't see the hypocrisy whenever I condemned The Croc's moral bankruptcy and staggering hubris. He is right in surmising that his position remains a dubious one but my assurances to the contrary are now built only on necessity while he remains my unknowing martyr.

As I wait patiently for the arrival of my adversary, resolution now starts to wrestle with apprehension. I stand up to draw the blinds of the office together and then return to the desk and open up my laptop to check on The Croc's whereabouts. My hope is that I haven't missed him but this, I realise, is a futile act, knowing how seldom he likes to update the shared calendar. I attempt to make myself comfortable by leaning back in the chair and placing my feet on the desk, purposely kicking several family photographs over onto their faces. I picture how this office will look with my own personal effects neatly placed about it, with my name above the door and jacket on the coat stand. These visions work to strengthen my current state of resolve and so I sit and so I wait.

37

KIM

"Hey, this is Brian, what's up?"

Distracted though I am, I can't have called the wrong number. For a start, I don't even know anybody called Brian and Claire's number is saved into my phone contacts list.

"Er, is Claire there?"

"She certainly is, may I ask who's calling?"

"It's Kim."

"Oh, hi, just hold on a moment and I'll grab her for you." I hear Brian call for Claire's attention followed by the hushed remnants of a short conversation between the two of them. I have no idea who he is or why he's answering her phone but in Claire's world this doesn't pass for extraordinary. In between the background chit-chat and general sounds of frivolity, I can only surmise that she's in a bar somewhere, most likely participating in a liquid lunch.

"Hey, Kimbo darling, what's up?"

"Who's Brian?"

"Brian? Oh, he's my boss, well, my senior, I mean the man immediately on top of me, look, does it really matter?"

It doesn't but I laugh anyway because it's clear that he's still well within earshot of that remark. As usual, I'm spending lunch sitting in my stationary car to avoid eating out with colleagues I don't particularly like who tend to eat at restaurants that I can't particularly afford. The canteen used to be my preferred haven but since returning from holiday, I've done my best to avoid seeing Hayley because I still owe her money for most of it. Instead, I sit shivering in my front seat without the aid of the heater, knowing that should I turn the engine on, it will very likely blow my cover. Needless to say, I'm counting down the days until my mother saves me from this ignominy and my penury comes to an end.

"Listen Claire, I'm booked in for my egg transfer at the clinic on Wednesday and I really need you to be there with me." Indiscernible noise ensues. "Claire?"

"What day is that again babe?"

"Wednesday!" I shout, perhaps unnecessarily.

"Wednesday, Wednesday, now let me see, hey, I thought it was next Wednesday hun?"

"No this Wednesday, *this* Wednesday, it was always this Wednesday. I saw you write it down Claire." Which of course she had being one of life's eternal jotters, living in an apartment that is a sea of post-it notes and crumpled self-reminders, some of which like to attach themselves to the soles of my shoes and come all the way home with me on occasion.

"Did I? Hey, don't leave that there."

"What?"

"Oh no, not you honey." She decides not to finish the sentence.

"So?"

"Transfer, next Wednesday, yeah I'm there with you babe."

"No, this Wednesday Claire, this Wed…"

"Yes of course this Wednesday, this Wednesday, no problem, hang on." She excuses herself to go to the toilet in a declaration so loud that it slips through muffling fingers. "Sorry babe, just needed to get away from Brian there. Anyway, just give me some time to work on a valid excuse to get out of work that day and I'll be there with you." That won't be too much of an issue, I think, seeing as Claire works fairly flexibly, a necessity on account of her being so habitually disorganised. Sleeping with her boss (which she may or may not be doing in this case) is also a helpful aid in this endeavour.

"Thank you."

"Will you be expecting the full-on chauffeur experience again Kim?"

"Well I can drive there but I think you might have to take the reins on the way home, it's likely that I'll be a little dazed and maybe a little sore."

"Cool. Just text me the details Wednesday morning and I'll see you then, my little mother-to-be."

I remind her not to tempt fate and call me that even though I secretly love it when she does.

Five minutes later, knowing that I've now missed the lunch exodus, I return to my desk and most pertinently, the warmth of the office. As I exit the car, I'm reminded of the ugly bump that still remains at the front of the vehicle and how I haven't made any real efforts to repair it yet. It isn't a priority of course and I really should get Simon to pay for it seeing how I'm almost certain that he's responsible for it. But at this moment it would be an unnecessary expense because once the sale of the house comes through, I'll have the money to buy a new car, one with heated seating so that my lunchtime ritual will be a much more comfortable experience. Gone will be the days of vending-machine lunches and ignoring Hayley's phone calls and frankly, it can't come soon enough.

38

SIMON

The Croc doesn't greet me with any palpable alarm as he enters his office and while there is perhaps a vague look of perplexity at the sight of my being seated behind his desk, he barely even checks a step. Instead, his attention seems primarily taken up by a small pack of sushi that he is eyeing and fingering with an evident distrust.

"I do hope I haven't kept you too long Simon," he begins, while simultaneously removing his jacket and placing it on the hanger beside the door. A decision on the sushi quickly follows this and it is tossed into the bin.

"You talk as if you were expecting me?" I reply, and remain seated where I am.

"Well of course I was," he says assuredly, while rummaging through the pocket of his jacket for some elusive object. "I've got eyes and ears dotted all about this place and it pays to be on top of things." He doesn't ask to change places with me and opts instead to pull up a guest chair, seating himself on the opposite side of the desk. "Anyway, I'm guessing that this little confab you've got planned here relates to a certain Malcolm Kearns does it not?" I simply nod by way of verification. "Well in that case the floor is yours, fire away Champ." He raps his knuckles on the desk as he says this so that his verbal invitation is partially obscured. Passive-aggression marinates his words in a typical attempt to trivialise the moment and although this act unsettles so many others, I have witnessed it far too often to wilt as they do.

"I'll begin by telling you what I want Gavin and I'm going to say this in plain and simple terms for the benefit of clarity. I want the offer you have made Malcy to be taken off the table and for him to be allowed to return to work with all charges against him dropped." The Croc leans back in his chair with the posture of one who is vaguely distracted and takes a brief moment to inspect some dirt underneath the fingernails of his right hand.

"Are you saying that the offer the company has made is ungenerous?"

"The figures involved are irrelevant here and I can speak confidently on his behalf when I say that it will not be accepted." He rolls his eyes nonchalantly and looks totally undeterred as if his first line of bargaining has met with a resistance much anticipated.

"Simon, Malcy's worked here for what, twelve years? I like him, everybody likes him because he's quiet and trustworthy but he's never been respected and he certainly isn't the future of Tanner & Webbing. In reality, he's just a middle-aged man without a wife to support or children to provide for and the money that he makes here, well, he'd just as easily make elsewhere. And so with that said, it would be awfully foolish for any man to put his own career on the line in order to protect him. Simon, you *do* have a future here and a bright one at that. You *are* respected, your opinion matters and unlike him, you have the advantage of youth on your side. Now surely that is far more important than some frivolous allegiance to a man who cannot benefit from your loyalty?" It is staggering to see just how easily The Croc can segue from severity to flattery as if the transition is in some way organic. Like everything with him this is simply a skill, a gentle ruse that plays on one's own egoism because he understands the power of vanity and gratification better than anyone I've ever met. "Maybe you need a little more time to think about things Champ?" he returns, misconstruing my brief silence.

"Quite the opposite," I say, "my mind has long been

made up and it's clear to me that you confuse my motives. I'm not here to bargain with you Gavin, I'm here to give you the opportunity to right what you have wronged. We both know that this is far bigger than Malcy Kearns."

"No Simon, I'm afraid it is you that has misunderstood. I'm advising *you* to recommend the offer that the company has made to Malcy Kearns as I believe it will be in *your* best interests to do that." His pattern of inflections does not go unnoticed but I deem them more bothersome than relevant and so I continue.

"Well, if you refuse to do as I suggest then you leave me with little choice but to expose you and I will tell you plainly that none of what I say is bluster. I urge you not to underestimate the weight of evidence against you or my willingness to disclose all that you have worked so very hard to conceal."

"Ah ha, so it appears that revelations really are afoot? Well in that case Mr Trice I beg you to elaborate." He doesn't look troubled as he sits there in an idle pose like one mildly annoyed at having to exercise his formal obligations before the real drama can commence. It is evident that he has been expecting this.

"My charge against you is simple, that you wilfully and methodically hatched a plan to oust Malcy Kearns from this company in order to preserve your own position here. When senior management placed you under investigation for a history of failings and blatant wrongdoing, you became aware that Malcy possessed damning evidence against you, evidence that he'd already started to share and that he wasn't the only one. Knowing that the leadership of this company were on to you and already looking to dispose of you, news that the workforce were set to vote on potential strike action could not have come at a more opportune time. You conspired with Marion, getting her to cajole Malcy into the position of Independent Scrutineer for the ballot count with the sole intention of manipulating the vote from the inside and

THE LONELINESS THAT OTHERS CALL FREEDOM

allowing him to take the fall for it. Once he was in place, you then blackmailed me into helping you corrupt the vote and relied on my ignorance, as an innocent man was already in place to bear responsibility. When the vote was scrutinised for a second time after the company had been tipped off, Marion was no doubt quick to implicate Malcy, blaming him entirely for all that had happened. Then, with him suspended from the company, you trusted that the investigation against you would surely collapse seeing that the lead witness was both discredited and deposed. Now, I challenge you to tell me that any of what I've just said is either false or unfair."

Even though I pieced together that string of events internally quite some time ago, my relief in conveying them feels something close to liberating and so the revelations pour out of me like an admission discharged. Whether this appears perceptible I really can't say and so I sit there confidently, daring The Croc to counter me while secretly hoping for his immediate surrender. Instead, he offers what seems a rueful grin and ponders briefly before answering.

"Allow me to congratulate you Simon on your powers of deduction but despite being in the vicinity of the truth there are details which either you have omitted to mention or that you remain in ignorance of." As he rises slowly from his chair, a joint in one of his arms creaks loudly but doesn't deter his progress towards the blinds in the office that I previously drew together. He slowly reopens them and the clerical landscape of the rest of the floor is once again visible to me. "I made overtures to Marion some time back and directed her to find a role in the union that would enable her to exert some influence from within. What I needed was someone who could act as an infiltrator at a time when the workforce was becoming increasingly restless so that I could remain a step ahead should the union decide to accelerate their threat of industrial action. She proved useful at first in gathering some intelligence and before too long, we were able to forecast which way the ballot was likely to go before it was even put to vote. In addition to this, and certainly more crucially, she was then able to negotiate her way on to the ballot count itself and although she didn't know it then, potentially save my career. She didn't understand why I placed so much importance on the identity of the Independent Scrutineer but after much persuasion, she eventually convinced Malcy to undertake the role.

I originally intended for Marion to work alone so that she could frame Malcy under my instruction without her actions being traceable to mine. But it soon became apparent in the days leading up to the count that her resolve was weakening, her pragmatism was waning and I sensed very clearly that she would be unable to do what I had asked of her. In truth Simon, you were my back-up plan and in essence, I gambled. I didn't have any margin of error here but somehow, between the two of you, I still felt that my plans stood a fair chance of success. This was prudent of me as Malcy carried out his role of Scrutineer a little too diligently and any late attempts by Marion to implicate him had been thwarted by his conscientiousness. At that point, it really wasn't clear whether you intended to intervene or not and when the result of the ballot was declared, I feared that you hadn't. It was only when news of the enquiry into the result emerged that I realised you had in fact succeeded where Marion had failed."

I sense that The Croc is at the height of his oration now with his focus back on me and his glare is one of confidence and conceit. Equally however, there are thin black lines of perspiration on either temple which looks like an unsightly fusion of hair dye and ill health. The tie is loosened.

"You look alarmed Simon? Well, you shouldn't be. The truth is that Marion was no harder to convince than you were and ambition is a powerful thing. I made her believe that she'd get the Area Project Manager job ahead of you if she helped me and although that was never really my intention, I still have the power to make this happen if you create difficulties for me. Do remember that she still hasn't spoken yet and I've kept her out of the firing line for a reason but all it takes is a little prompting from me and she will happily turn the focus on to Malcy and maybe even you. She just needs to believe that her aspirations will be gratified and she will say whatever I ask her to."

"And what about Judy? Are you certain that her new role will buy her silence too? You clearly did for her just as you promised to do for Marion, only this time it was more than just the lure of promotion you had to offer. Somehow, you received word that I was digging into your affairs, of the questions I was asking and the progress I was making and so you tested her ethics and got the result that you wanted. But she is the only ally that you have left now because management see you as a blight on this business Gavin, a business that you have cheated and profited from while mistakenly believing that your hands remained clean. Once I present that evidence to them, with the help of Malcy, they will remove you from this company just as swiftly and as ruthlessly as you did to him."

It is at this point that I expect to see some signs of agitation from The Croc as I wrest the upper hand from him with a confidence and strategy that he cannot have foreseen. My words, being bold in both thought and delivery, were submitted so viscerally that it is impossible to misconstrue their meaning or intention and yet he remains unfazed and simply purses his lips with a thoughtful pause.

"It seems that you are chasing some form of a confession from me when I've told you enough already and that your mind is still set on pursuing this in spite of what I tell you." He briefly halts to stifle my attempt to interrupt him with a raised hand and an oblique gesture of the head. "You are free to do as you wish but I'll warn you now that I've never responded to threats and I've no intention of changing that position for you or anybody else. Look, let me put this to you in a different way because it's obvious that you still don't understand. Yes, management *have* been monitoring my performance for some time and my job has become far from easy as a result but I've lasted this long for a reason Simon when many others haven't. Sure, some of my practices have been ill-conceived and I've not acted with the level of integrity that others would perhaps expect but in many ways that's why I'm here sitting in this office and everybody else is out there on the other side of this wall scrambling after scraps that I toss them.

Now, cast your mind back to the union's indicative ballot and how the prospect of strike action was more or less confirmed by its result. The consensus among senior management was that they'd been more than reasonable in their negotiations but that they were left with little room to manoeuvre any further. They were concerned about the damage that widespread industrial action would do to the company, that it would make Tanner & Webbing look weak and leaderless and embolden our competitors. It was collectively decided that they couldn't let this happen and so it was that they then came to me. I'm not sure why I was chosen but I'd like to think that they saw qualities in me that they saw in no one else and were confident that I could do as they asked without implicating them in any way. And so we struck a deal.

They said that if I could find a way of burying the strike and then of nullifying those responsible for it, such a feat would not go unnoticed and would work out favourably for me in my own investigation. At that time, they were not aware of the extent of the evidence that Malcy and Judy had against me as their probing hadn't really advanced beyond the preliminary stage but I was of course. Even with that promise in mind, I knew the difficulty that they would face in ignoring such evidence once it was shared in a more formal setting and so my position still remained a little tenuous. By this time, my plans were already in place to offer Judy that promotion with conditions attached but Malcy remained a problem. But it then occurred to me that if I could find a way of fulfilling their request while implicating Malcy at the very heart of it all, then I could effectively save my own skin and enhance my standing in the eyes of senior management. I knew it wasn't going to be easy but I've always been resourceful Simon and thankfully, your ambition and your naivety played right into my hands. I chose you because I see that merciless streak of ambition that courses straight through you and frankly, it's as prevalent now as it was when we first met. It's what drew me towards you back then because I saw myself in you and I wanted to harness those enviable traits. I took that craving for power and indulged it for my own gain and although you didn't cover your tracks quite well enough, the very idea that you had your sights set on replacing me didn't come as a shock. Marion, Judy, your contact in the HR department, they all picked a side Simon and they picked the right one too so don't waste your time thinking that they ever had any loyalty to you. Management will not be pursuing any case against me because I've done what they asked of me and now they are in my debt. In removing Malcy from the equation, I've simply made it easier, easier for me and easier for them as they can bury this whole thing now without his intervening and causing an unnecessary furore. Frankly, it's the only way that you and I can both come out of this unscathed."

It was inevitable that he would bring this back to me because fear is often his only recourse when logic and truth defeat him. Despite what he says, we share no similarities because he is anathema to me and if he thinks otherwise then he has never truly understood me nor recognised the contempt that resides under every word I've just about ever said to him.

"I'm still in possession of the truth," I declare, "and should Malcy decide to share what he knows then your position is perilous but mine is far from it."

"No, you're mistaken again in believing that this will end favourably for you if you force the hand of senior management against me because this truth that you possess is nothing more than an inconvenience. It staggers me to think just how long you've worked here and that you still don't seem to understand how intrinsic the chicanery really is. It's the culture of business Simon, the culture of *our* business and though you may believe that you can challenge it, that endeavour will not get you very far. Now I told you that management were indebted to me and I told you why that is, so if you were to challenge me and engineer my removal from the company then you would effectively end your own career. Whether I stay or go, I will find a way to implicate you, I will help them place a target on your back and pin not only the mishandling of the ballot on you but every other mistake you did or didn't make. I will expose your antagonism to the true values of this company so that everyone who matters will know how you put yourself ahead of the greater good and all in pursuit of something that you cannot even cherish. I don't believe that deep down you really want that Simon, in spite of this bravado but I do believe that secretly, you long to become everything you claim you are trying to defeat and so you have my word that if Malcy accepts the company's offer, then the promotion that I offered you remains yours. It is risk against reward Simon. Our secrets can be our bond, so persuade him to say yes, or pay a heavy price for your naivety."

I long to interrupt the silence that follows because it makes me feel uneasy and seem less in control. The Croc, on the other hand, seems to luxuriate in the lull, for he knows what has inspired it after feeding me that slow and steady poison and batting off my threats with a disarming ease. He has incited an internal conflict between morality and ambition by placing me in a position where one has to come at the expense of the other. My line of attack has stalled and he knows this well enough as he begins to toy with his expensive cufflinks in a habitual manner of his that I have seen so often before, exuding total confidence. I rise from my seat to fully face him.

"I'm afraid you are gravely mistaken if you think that my career means more to me than my honour Gavin. I don't know what you think you see in me but I've never subscribed to your values and we are not alike. If I leave here, I leave on my own terms and with my conscience intact."

"You'll need to convince yourself of that before you stand any chance of convincing me. We both know that you are far too cowardly to follow through on any of your principles otherwise you wouldn't have found yourself in any of this mess to begin with. No, you can pretend you are many things Simon but I stand by what I said, we're cut from the same cloth me and you and the sooner you accept this, the less you will feel so troubled by it."

Without quite knowing how, we appear to have exchanged places now and The Croc seats himself back at his desk while I take up his former position on the other side. It was just minutes ago that I entered this office feeling proud and imperious, ready to wage war on a man who is my enemy and didn't even know it. Perhaps I mistook my vanity for righteousness because now I just feel weak and indignant and certain that a wound has been inflicted that will prove difficult to heal. If there is a balance of power then I am left in no doubt that it has shifted.

The Croc makes a brief attempt to resume his line of discourse before stopping himself so that he can flip back the family photographs that I overturned earlier. I expect an enquiring look to accompany this particular act but it doesn't come.

"What I'm trying to say to you Simon is that I can overlook this temporary insanity that you've subjected me to today if you let me do what's needed."

"And what about Marion?" I ask, although I'm not quite sure why I only raise this now. The Croc leans back in his chair in the pose of a poker player not bothering to conceal the strength of his next hand.

"Well, I'm afraid that Marion is really nothing more than collateral damage here. If you choose to work with me, then I can make her exit happen and all suspicion around the ballot will leave with the two of them, even if their guilt is not explicitly stated." He allows neither time nor room for contemplation of this as he gets up from his chair and heads back towards the door of the office. Removing his jacket from the hanger, he slips one arm after the other into the sleeves and opts for one last address before leaving. "Listen Simon, and do try to remember this if nothing else. Idealism is great but it doesn't pay the bills."

I briefly consider pursuing him when the door shuts behind him even though anything I've left to say would be nothing more than needless repetition. None of this has played out as I envisioned nor have my charges been met with the belligerence that I expected. In reality, it isn't the lack of a verbal onslaught that has perturbed me but the confidence with which The Croc made his riposte, as if the whole thing was somehow predetermined. I witnessed his exposure of the filthy, corrosive system that is Tanner & Webbing and although I responded with anger at his labelling me a part of it, I know deep down that my chagrin is rooted in recognising this truth and not because it isn't justified. After all, it isn't so long ago that I'd stepped through those revolving doors in entry to this building for the very first time, exchanging the comfort of the book store for this glossy, corporate ogre. With the scale of the transition, I should've felt overawed and faintly revolted by the tide of sharp suits and the immediate sense of ambiguity but the homogeny eventually absorbed me. I told myself back then that this environment would never change me and this vow I have upheld, for it has simply elicited elements of a truer self that were so much easier to ignore in my young adulthood. Nobody at Tanner & Webbing had any interest in my back story and even had I told them, it would not have set me apart from them in any meaningful way. The Croc didn't snare me, I had trapped myself and the result of this self-generated predicament will be the banishment of values I at one time held dear, dressed as a reprieve.

39

KIM

I haven't seen or spoken to Hayley since our disastrous holiday together and this, in absolute honesty, has been by design. As she works on a different floor to me, maintaining my distance at work has been easy enough but the endless stream of messages and emails had started to plague my conscience. What intrigues me most about Hayley (and believe me, there are many things) is her persistence and I can't quite determine whether she feels responsible for my frosty silence or simply overlooks it. Maybe everything to her is really just a conquest though and our relationship was really no different to the ones she'd had with the men that she'd pursued on our holiday, odd, mildly fulfilling and in the long term, unproductive. So this morning, when I finally broke the silence and agreed to meet for lunch, it did perhaps inform me that I was no longer mad at her for ruining my holiday.

"So much has happened to me since we stepped off that plane Kim, you just wouldn't believe it." I suspect that I probably would but I don't intervene. Hayley looks much like she did the last time I was in her company, sexy, svelte and carrying with her that natural elegance that both frustrated and beguiled me. Although the canteen is full, you'd be forgiven for thinking that all eyes are on her, which leads to no end of affectation and energetic intensity to every tale she tells. "I think we really need to start thinking about what country we're going to visit next," she continues, typically undaunted, "we had such a great time together didn't we?"

It's clear that there is no trace of irony to what she says and while the very thought disturbs me, my liver also balks at the suggestion.

"Well, I'd love to Hayles but I'm desperately short of money right now so there's just no way I could afford it."

"Oh that's okay babe," she counters with embellished sympathy, "it's the company that makes the holiday after all, not the expense." I sigh quietly and then catch sight of Jillian, an affable colleague of mine who waves back at me from across the canteen. As I return the greeting, Hayley switches focus sharply, scoffs audibly and then states disdainfully, "I really hate that bitch." Part of me wants to enquire why this is so but as I'm pushed for time and convinced that the basis for such hatred is most likely trivial, I don't pursue it. Hayley resumes. "So how are things between you and that ex-boyfriend of yours, Steven is it? It all sounded rather toxic when you last spoke of him."

"It's far from simple," I say, making no effort to correct her and feeling slightly uneasy with the focus now on me. "He still loves me but I don't love him, in fact, I've found someone else."

"Ooh, tell me more, tell me more," she insists excitedly and I instantly regret saying anything. I stop to consider how I'm about to phrase this because as far as I'm aware, Hayley is yet to see me with my guard down and she doesn't rank high on my list of confidantes.

"He's an enigma," I answer, "a beautiful enigma and that's what every girl wants, right?" Every other girl yes but not Hayley it seems.

"Oh I've had my fair share of them," she replies indifferently, "you'll find that very few of the male sex are truly enigmatic though, at least, not in the true sense of the word. Just dig a little deeper honey and you'll often see there's no real mystery to them at all, they're just uncomfortable with their own emotions and I'm pretty certain it's innate. Sure, you can ask them to express the way they feel but I guarantee you'll end up disappointed because their aloofness is an intellectual necessity and not a lifestyle choice."

I laugh a little too energetically at this even though it's clear that Hayley isn't talking flippantly and I start to recall the qualities that drew me towards her in the first place.

"It isn't like that, what I mean is, he isn't like that. Look, I know it sounds silly and perhaps a little trite but I've never felt like this about anybody before. It's scary and frustrating but I think I like the complications." There were countless others that I should've been confessing this to, friends that better understood me, ones who are hesitant to judge but right now, Hayley was my only outlet and I could at least rely on her honesty.

"Listen hun, it sounds to me like you're doing all the work here so try taking a step back and surveying all your options. It's much easier to land a guy when you stop trying so hard and far more rewarding."

"But surely that depends on what you want from the guy?" I offer timidly, not entirely sure where I'm heading with this. "Not everybody wants the same things, our needs differ just as our expectations do. Look, I didn't tell you this but while we were on holiday, I very nearly slept with someone. I barely even knew him and what I did know I didn't like but it made me realise that I was worth a little more than that. I'm chasing something more substantial but it's difficult to define exactly what that is."

"But you had a good time, right, on the holiday I mean?"

"I enjoyed *some* of it."

"Oh come on Kim, have you not seen the photographs? You're smiling on every single one of them."

"Those photographs are hideous Hayles, I really can't bring myself to look at them."

She is naturally irked by this and pauses to meditate for a second or two before slowly crossing one leg over the other as if the act were to signify a testing self-censorship.

"As it happens, I've got a funny story to tell you about

those photographs Kim, one that may well prove my point after all." She then looks about her as if wary of continuing, embracing her inhibitions in a move that seems totally out of character. "It was sometime around the middle of our holiday when I received this message via Congrelate from some random guy I'd never even met before. He said he'd seen the photographs of the two of us and that he thought I was beautiful and he spent the best part of the days that followed begging me to go out on a date with him. Now as a rule, I don't do eccentrics and I was far too busy on holiday to really bother with him but he was charming and persistent and my social calendar wasn't exactly brimming when I got home so I relented and accepted his offer."

I suppress my laughter more successfully this time as Hayley, the girl who took wilful promiscuity to another level on our vacation, now expects me to believe that she is an advocate of sexual circumspection. With a reputation that is practically viral, I doubt that this mystery man used those photographs for anything other than a means to verify the rumours that are probably rife in male circles.

"But how could he have seen those photographs of us if he'd never even met you?" I ask, as if the details are in any way important.

"Because we shared a mutual friend, that's how."

"And who would that be?" I enquire while feeling a tad disturbed at my developing interest.

"Well isn't that obvious Kim? It was you."

I feel the urge to interject but Hayley isn't pausing for breath anytime soon.

"I guess I was intrigued by him at first because it was a pretty ballsy move to just approach me in the way that he did but he turned out to be the most disingenuous man I think I've ever met." She interrupts herself at this moment to leave her seat and retrieve a half-eaten salad that somebody has discarded on another table. This, she doesn't eat but merely pokes at with a plastic fork for several seconds before pushing it aside with the look of one frustrated. "Oh where was I?" I tell her somewhere in between the holiday and the first course in a restaurant and she doesn't laugh. "Well I think the alarm bells started ringing when we were back at his apartment and instead of being greeted with a nice glass of wine, I was shuffled out onto the balcony while he proceeded to tidy away his girlfriend's things."

"So he had a girlfriend?" I exclaim, a little too audibly, while realising that I'm asking lots of questions without learning anything of real importance.

"Sure he did, several most probably, but then, is there any appeal to the ones that don't?" I find this question stimulating and want time to consider a reply but Hayley it seems has already decided for me. "I found him perplexing more than anything because I couldn't decide why he felt the need to try and hide her existence from me as if such a discovery were likely to deter me. I mean, sure, I had my misgivings but I wasn't going to abandon the whole affair and head for the hills through some warped allegiance to sisterhood, though perhaps I really should have."

"And you didn't feel uncomfortable sleeping with him once you'd discovered that he wasn't single? Who is he Hayles? He really doesn't sound like anybody I would know or even want to know." I was trying to steer her towards telling me what I wanted to hear but try as I might, she was unwilling to follow my directions.

"Why should I? She wasn't any of my business until *he* made it so. I pity her more than anything but if you choose to fall for a guy like that then I guess you always get what you deserve."

This is a side to Hayley that I dislike. That she is reckless and insensitive I am willing to overlook just so long as it affects herself and no one else around her but to carry that level of disregard towards others makes me feel uncomfortable of our acquaintance. What frustrates me more than anything is seeing the qualities that she possesses, beauty, wit and confidence, and knowing that this isn't quite enough for her. It is as though whatever she achieves always falls short of what she actually wants and that the real joy lies in disposing of what she's gained once the novelty wears off. And then I start to wonder, somewhat digressively, if Simon could be the mystery man to whom she is referring? After all, she doesn't know what he looks like and couldn't recall his name correctly, so improbable though it is, it also isn't beyond the realms of possibility. But thinking along those lines will bring just about every man in my life under the radar of suspicion and even if I do that, Simon will undoubtedly find himself somewhere near the foot of that particular list. This is too elaborate for him because he isn't that vindictive and he has always been intimidated by assertive women (as Hayley indisputably is). Furthermore, he just isn't that cunning and it would be impossible to believe that even Hayley would've failed to identify him and draw the connection between the two of us. For these reasons, those speculations are quickly discarded and I am saved the ignominy of sharing them by Hayley's free-flowing narrative.

"He even cried after we had sex," she reveals, scoffing at the recollection. "I mean, can you believe that? I watched him curl into a foetal ball and sob like a baby and when I asked him to explain, all he could say was how he loved his girlfriend but the sex with her just wasn't working for him anymore. Clearly, he didn't find that sense of guilt quite so consuming when he was ripping my clothes off but lust has a funny habit of overriding restraint. By that point it really didn't matter though as I'd made my mind up not to linger and although I try not to think about what happened too often, I still shudder when I do."

I ask myself if conversations such as this once passed for revelry in my youth, where racy subject matter was simply an empowering show of femininity and not the cause of embarrassment that it feels like now. I've never been what one could call a prude but I don't like where this is heading, with Hayley now attracting attention from people sat at other tables which happens to include a nervous-looking Jillian. She is only a matter of yards away from me and certainly within earshot of all that has been said and so one can safely assume that any esteem she held for me is swiftly dwindling by mere association with Hayley.

I have no more time for this, I decide, and begin to gather my things in readiness of leaving. It was a bad idea, Hayley and I are just too different and although I don't regret giving our friendship a second chance, I do regret not realising this sooner. As she leans in to kiss me goodbye, I respond reluctantly and try to offer as little warmth to my embrace as the moment will allow. With her arms clasped around my neck, I try to step back in retreat but she fails to disengage and is instead fingering the material that is draped around my neckline.

"Did I lend you this scarf Kim?"

I take a brief moment to study the garment in question, a purple scarf with little grey sequins that I don't much care for and have only worn today as it was the closest thing to hand when I left for work this morning. More to the point, I can't quite recall how I came across it and I don't remember buying it but I'm certain that Hayley didn't lend it to me and so I tell her this. "You know what's funny," she continues, "I used to own one just like it, identical to this design in fact, but I lost it somewhere and I can't remember where. Silly of me really as I used to wear it all the time." She leans in once more but this time pulls the scarf towards her nose and inhales deeply. "That's strange," she reflects, a little nonplussed, "I can definitely smell my perfume on this."

The canteen, despite its wide expanse and liberal ventilation, feels suddenly claustrophobic as the air disperses from my lungs in a sharp and violent gust. My heart then starts to throb with powerful reverberations that pound against my temples as if looking for escape and my throat contracts in a way it often does when terror takes hold. Like a passenger stranded on a plane that is nose-diving towards its inevitable fate, the impact is nigh and I am powerless to stop it.

"Hayley?" I begin, mustering a greater courage than what she could possibly imagine, as deep down, I know already what she's about to say. "I need you to tell me the name of the man that you slept with before you go any further."

Although she pauses for what is only seconds, it feels like a tragic eternity.

"Oh sorry Kim, did I not say? His name is Ricky."

Of course, it is the very same scarf that he returned to me in error on that day in the Gaddis Avenue parking lot, believing it to be mine. I didn't want it then but I've maintained ownership of it ever since because it reminds me of him at times when there is nothing but distance between us. It is a vestige of the man I love and I've absorbed its scent with what I now know to be a faint and false recognition and as I realise for the first time its true owner, the revelation turns my stomach.

Hayley either cannot see the damage of her words or simply chooses to ignore their obvious effect and so the anecdote resumes.

"It was funny because one of the first things he did was make me promise not to tell you should anything happen between us which I have to say confused me somewhat. When I asked him to explain, all he could say was that he thought you really liked him and that he didn't want to hurt you if he was able to avoid it. Can you believe his audacity? Don't worry, I set him straight on that one Kim, I told him that you *had* taste so that couldn't possibly be true but he just found that amusing. Seriously, it was like his vanity was so strong that he was just incapable of hearing any negative remarks without believing them to be marinated in humour." She stops briefly to throw another piercing stare in the direction of Jillian who, if nothing else, is doing an admirable job of pretending she isn't eavesdropping. "I can't even begin to explain what a relief it is to finally get to tell you about all this Kim. I've been meaning to say something ever since we got back but you've been so detached and I didn't want to put all the gory details into an email." Hayley then decides to move her chair right alongside mine in a manner that seems oddly collusive and her tone lowers measurably. "I haven't even told you the worst of it yet. It appears that Ricky didn't just leave me with a deep sense of self-loathing and regret that night, he also, well, he passed something onto me and this was something that I *really* didn't want." I briefly contemplate whether her elongation of the word 'really' is an attempt to denote humour or discomfort but of course, none of that matters anymore. She cannot now be stopped and there's a stronger urge within me to remain silent, embracing the exterior calm, my outward stoicism. "He gave me an STD Kim."

I've always known that there are others in Ricky's life and it has never much concerned me just so long as I don't spend any great length of time really thinking about it. Perhaps I have convinced myself that what we share transcends all of that but if I'm guilty of this, then the fault for this delusion cannot entirely be my own. I have trusted him as a confidante and much of that trust was preceded by his sleeping with someone that he knew to be my friend. The act in itself is not the most troublesome aspect of this sorry affair but to think that I've been used as a means of gratifying some sordid, sexual gain leaves me feeling nothing short of exploited. If Ricky feels no remorse for what he's done then he has no reason to conceal it from me but the fact that he has never told me suggests otherwise. Already, it is difficult to see any way back from this and that is heartbreaking for a number of reasons, the most prominent one being that his exile from my life is something I'm not quite sure I'm ready to comprehend.

I don't know the Ricky that her lurid allegations describe and this makes it significantly harder to attribute such behaviour to him. With one so prone to embellish as

Hayley undoubtedly is, I start to wonder if her true motives have initially escaped me and that her plan all along has been to oust me from his life by painting such a repellent picture of him. This isn't implausible for I have seen the lengths that Hayley will go to attain the things she wants (especially when guided by desire) and once she has tainted him with my revulsion, the path will then become relatively clear for her.

That being said, I know that pertinent questions remain unanswered and that my willingness to believe the worst in Hayley is perhaps illogical. For example, if the scarf did not belong to her originally then why does it smell so clearly of her perfume? And if her intention is to deceive me, how can she have linked my acquiring the scarf all the way back to him in the first place (albeit inadvertently)? In addition to this, the nuances of his behaviour to which she had alluded are far too concise and exact for me to label them a mere coincidence, much less can I ignore them. I think back to the time we slept together, recalling how introverted he became in the aftermath and though I'd seen this frailty as something deep and beautiful, it was perhaps nothing more than a weak attempt at self-reproach. None of this intimacy had been reserved for me alone but then, I wasn't in a position to verify this assertion. Did he perceive my wants and needs and then exploit them and if so, how many others have fallen prey to this calculated deception? Hayley is probably right, there have to be others, some prettier than me, maybe others less so and perhaps somewhere in the background, a girlfriend of sorts that feels about him as I have, even if that love is not returned. I have, after all, surveyed his apartment from the inside and noticed a definite feminine quality about its style which maybe revealed the influence of a woman in some form or another.

Now, it all seems so clear to me and a sense of foolishness is defining itself more acutely by the second. I could curse myself for not seeing things for what they really were before but the clues were cleverly concealed and my emotions had been manipulated. There is a skill that has underlay his actions up to now and it seems that he has always been several chapters ahead of me, controlling the narrative and protecting himself. Had I posed the right questions still it wouldn't have mattered because of my willingness to dilute his every truth and dress the doubts in mystery. That's what happens when you love someone I guess, you ignore their imperfections and focus on the faintest of qualities even when you know that you've exaggerated their value.

I want to express all this to Hayley but her inability to self-censor prevents me, much like the certainty in knowing that she won't understand how any of this feels. Instead, I make my excuses and leave the canteen, find my car in the parking bay and lock myself inside. Back in my now regular lunchtime ritual, the tears inevitably start to flow and I only have the sequined purple scarf at hand to halt their path. I bury my head in my hands before deciding to drive home to Gaddis Avenue and ignore several calls from colleagues along the way.

40

KIM

For the second time in a week, I find myself lying horizontally with my feet in stirrups. The staff here at the fertility clinic know me well enough to make small talk even when unnecessary now but still it feels slightly disconcerting when the medical contingent apply the same convention while their heads are in my genital area. I try to regain focus but it's difficult to know where best to look and so I link my fingers between Claire's, smile at her faintly and immerse myself within the moment.

The horror of my meeting with Hayley yesterday, along with a natural trepidation about today's procedure, meant that I didn't sleep a wink last night and gloomy prophesies presented themselves in the form of nausea. A straight-thinking Kimberley would deem the sickness to be psychosomatic, a physiological manifestation of my many mental ailments but that Kimberley seems alien to me these days and I don't feel her presence very often. Instead, I wept, cursed and indulged in the very real fear that all wasn't well and nothing was going to work out as I had hoped. The sickness felt consuming but it did at least serve one very productive purpose, by stopping me from walking over to Ricky's flat and confronting him with the revelations that Hayley had presented to me. I simply couldn't do it and the thought that such an emotionally fraught confrontation could in any way endanger my prospects today thankfully proved enough of a deterrent. I stayed in bed, I stared at the ceiling and counted the clock down until the morning while simultaneously ignoring the many phone messages left by my consultant from the supply agency, no doubt admonishing me for yesterday's desertion from my place of work.

The last time I was here at the fertility clinic, I left mildly disappointed having only produced ten eggs from the collection phase of my IVF treatment. This morning, it became clear that I probably should've listened to the reassurances of Doctor Block for despite their shortage in number, five of the eggs obtained had now fertilised successfully and were considered ready for transfer. The purpose of today is to take one of these eggs (or to give them their correct title, 'embryos') and to transport it into my womb, where, with a bit of luck, Mother Nature will take the reins from science and reward me with motherhood. What I didn't realise was that the choice of embryo would be mine to make, so when Doctor Block handed me a photograph of each of them, it was a dilemma that I simply wasn't prepared for. All I could do was try and replicate what I assumed every other woman did in this situation and so I thumbed through every picture with a false scrutiny. Just why exactly did this burden of selection now lie with me and how could I make this decision without a prepared criteria? The reality was that there was nothing to choose between any of them as the images were blurry, vague and indistinct, making a solid preference virtually impossible. Under the weight of this pressure, I did something that I probably shouldn't boast of, I made Claire decide for me.

In Claire's defence, she didn't cower from this responsibility in the same way that I had, preferring instead to study each photograph with an avid circumspection. I of course had no idea what she was looking for nor did I understand what she found in the successful embryo but I considered it self-defeating to question her about it. Neither of us had the right to play God but I was happy for her to assume that role if it meant that I didn't have to. I would instead think about my five beautiful embryos, one of which would now be offered the chance of life and in the absence of a husband, I could think of no one better to share this moment with than my best friend.

Claire has spent most of the day seated at my side looking visibly overawed by the whole experience. This has prevented her from saying a great deal (which I have to admit makes a pleasant change) and the facile line of questioning that I expected of her seems to have been replaced by pertinent observations. This sense of etiquette (welcome though it is) has faltered only once, when the medical team informed her of a necessary costume change. They were happy for her to accompany me but she could only gain entry to the operating room by agreeing to replace her fashionable attire with the customary faceguard, hairnet and surgical boots. Her horror at this (although undoubtedly embellished) displayed itself in accusatory claims before she finally relented but I really didn't appreciate this blip in her conduct. As if sensing my disappointment, she tried to reconcile me by offering to film the upcoming procedure, which of course drew nothing from me but the threat of physical recriminations.

The set up in the medical room doesn't differ drastically to how it was when my eggs were collected apart from a couple of very noticeable things. Firstly, there now appears to be a crowd that has gathered at the base of my modesty, each member of which has taken the time to offer introductions. I hear names and fancy titles which are no doubt designed to legitimise their presence but the formalities are tiresome to me and wholly unnecessary. As always, it is Doctor Block who is acting as the fulcrum here and my focus remains on him while he directs those around him in the manner of one relishing the centre stage. To his left (and my right) there is an ultrasound screen that is positioned at an angle so that both myself and the medical staff are able to observe it. Opposite to that, there appears to be some kind of a serving hatch through which various bits of equipment are passed to and fro as the procedure progresses. The staff are good enough to provide a running commentary of their actions as the transfer develops and even though this isn't necessarily for my benefit alone, it still adds a sense of fluidity which I find very soothing.

The first thing that they do is place a speculum into my vagina in preparation for the entry of the catheter (which is passed through the serving hatch to a crouching Doctor Block). The catheter contains my embryo and is inserted slowly through the speculum while my attention is diverted towards the ultrasound screen. On there, I can now see the progress of the catheter inside of me which is really just a thin, white line making slow progress before it suddenly recoils and then emits a clear, white dot. That white dot is my embryo. He withdraws the catheter and hands it to a member of staff back through the hatch, who then nods and mumbles something by way of confirmation to him. The process is a painless one, taking just a matter of minutes, which is really just as well considering I've been offered no sedation. When Doctor Block emerges from underneath the white sheet draped across my thighs as a temporary screen, I am greeted with a reassuring thumbs-up. This universal sign that all is well lifts a weight from my shoulders that I briefly forgot was there and for the first time today, I begin to feel something close to relaxation.

I ask the nurse to keep the ultrasound running for a little while longer so that I can study my little dot of life for as long as possible. To some, it will probably seem underwhelming, but to me, it is quite the opposite. It bears a similarity to a tiny star floating somewhere deep inside the solar system, lost and indistinguishable and yet precious to the eye of the beholder. It strikes me instantly how overpowering the grief would be should this star just fade away now, disappearing somewhere into the abyss that surrounds it. I have spent hours of my life reading stories posted on the fertility forum from women who have been in this very same position and I have shared in their excitement in a vain, vicarious spirit. Theirs are the tales that I remember because there were other stories too from women who have gazed at that dot on their ultrasound screen, hoped as I do now and then lost everything. I have managed to convince myself that they are the unlucky minority because I can't bring myself to empathise with them. I don't want their suffering to be my suffering because if I fail at this now, I doubt whether I will be capable of articulating the pain. The thought of coming this far and then still falling short is inconceivable and if I was to do that now, could I honestly say that this arduous journey has really been worth it? In two weeks' time, I will finally be able to answer that question.

41

KIM

I recognise my mother's hand immediately as I collect her letter from my pigeonhole and take the lift up to my apartment. I notice how it isn't her usual heavily corrected scrawl (the product of a mind incapable of form) but a legible composition of a clear and conspicuous type and it's because of this that my sense of foreboding goes straight into overdrive. Historically, my mother will only communicate with me in this way whenever she deems the level of admonishment to have somehow exceeded the constraints of verbal delivery and so I know instantly that this doesn't bode well.

Dear Kimberley,

It is a common belief that challenge lies at the very heart of the Bible and God challenges us daily to battle against temptations that sometimes even we ourselves cannot recognise. With His love and guidance I have overcome a litany of tribulations that one without faith would surely fail to do, but Kimberley, I have to confess that one particular challenge has felt far more insurmountable than any other I can think of and that is being your mother.

Perhaps first I must explain by making an admission – your father and I raised you by liberal methods and this we did knowingly. We catered for your material wants, indulged your whims and never rationed anything that we could deliver to you plentifully. We gave you too much freedom my dear, too much love and because of this, you never understood the triumph of accomplishment nor the harsh consequences of foolish actions. In truth, we sheltered you and in admitting this I now acknowledge my failure and share in (at least) some of the blame I am about to direct.

You may recall how I once expressed my opposition to this ungodly insemination idea of yours and a part of me had hoped that my arguments against this had finally resonated with you. This (I now learn) is not so, but I remain unwilling to simply forego my stance on this simply because of your impatience and unwillingness to accept His will. It is unhealthy, it is unnatural but most of all, it is ungodly. And yet no doubt you have already wasted thousands of pounds on this project of self-gratification, lining the pockets of others who feed this desperate yearning of yours without any obligation towards the sanctity of human life. This decision you have purposefully hidden from me my dear, which compels me to assume that you recognise your guilt and see the shame in the path that you have taken.

My advice is not something that you value, my respect less so, but I always felt that in Simon you did at least have a moral barometer, someone who would stifle your flippancy and counter your selfishness and so you can imagine my surprise to learn that you and he are no longer together. At first, I assumed that the term 'separation' was merely overstatement but I have since learned otherwise. Not only are you estranged but it is my understanding that you have been so for quite some time, during which you paraded him around at your father's memorial as if you were still very much together. Really Kimberley, I will never understand your methods, but deception for the sake of it is truly quite sinful.

And so, if I'm to assume that Simon will not be fathering any child you may have (not that God will grant you this of course) then it leads me to believe that the identity of any such father would not be known to you. This means that your intention is to bring a fatherless child into this world, one who will never understand why he or she is the focus of ridicule, exclusion *and dedicated prayer. I, your own mother, will be forced to find explanations to things that I cannot abide by to my friends and neighbours without the loathsome recourse of lies. Oh Kimberley, why is it that you never think of me, you selfish, selfish woman? You have always been so wasteful, wasteful of every opportunity in life that your father and I afforded you, but one thing that we never encouraged was the motive of greed. And yet, it has now become apparent to me that you have been trading your late father's possessions without either my knowledge or consent. Ever since his death I have left his many possessions untouched, the alcoves that he inhabited about our home unencroached upon, and all of this in respect of his dear memory to me. And now what do I find as I conduct a solemn and lonely inventory about the house in preparation for the move? Well the answer is very little. Material things I grant you, but material things that you did not own and material things that you had no right to sell, and material things that had a value attached to them that far exceed your rapacious needs. I would pay anything to have these items returned to me, but I'd pay a greater price to save your soul from the contamination of greed and selfishness that has seemingly absorbed you. How did this escape my notice? How did your degradation as a human being and a daughter not register with me? I cannot say. Me, your mother, the one and only that you will ever have and yet one that you barely deem worthy of a visit or a moment of your time.*

When I think of your brother Declan and all of the struggles he has overcome compared to the gifts that were bestowed upon you without any application of your own, I can perhaps best begin to measure your true character. Declan, your very own brother who has so little and yet seldom complains, one who has never asked me for anything even though he knows how I would probably agree to it. He was a joy to our lives Kimberley when God blessed us with his presence and though you may not be blood related, I always hoped that you saw yourselves as siblings in everything but flesh. Perhaps I didn't see it at the time as clearly as I should have but the way you wrestled an inheritance away from him in your father's death was truly shameful. How you manipulated me in my preliminary mourning and fought with a ferocity that I did not recognise to keep him from a financial heirloom that he so rightly deserved. How you did all this so that the spoils would be yours and yours alone, well, it was nothing less than utterly abhorrent of you. I did not see it then like I did not see it since, but I was complicit in this theft by way of the weakness that you observed and knew so well, and the apologies that I offer to him will never amount to what he truly deserves. I cannot change what has been (though how I wish I could) but I can have some bearing on what will come.

This morning, I sat with a cup of tea in one hand and a cheque for forty-five thousand pounds in the other. That cheque, as you will know, I had promised to you as a gift from the sale of the house. Promises are a virtue of the godly Kimberley, and to break such a vow would never be something that I would dare to contemplate without good reason, but my dear, you will understand that your behaviour merely validates my decision to forego my cherished principles. More importantly, it is for your own good that I have decided to withdraw my financial offer to you because I cannot trust you not to squander it on frivolous things, and in truth, Kimberley, you are simply undeserving. This will be a severe lesson to you, I know, but my mind is made up – that money can never be yours.

It may be for the best that you do not come to visit me in my new home for it is quaint and sweet and my happiness seems to work in parity to this. Even though it's smaller than what I'm used to, I now prefer to live without clutter as I no longer have the strength to clean and polish and sweep all the floors as I once did. I have a small garden out front and a slightly larger one out back. The neighbours appear friendly and we've exchanged pleasantries and cakes already, and it makes me realise how much I missed that sense of community living in the family home as we did for all those years with nothing around us but space and silence. You will note how I am telling you all this for the first time because you do not know my address, nor have you ever enquired as to where I will be living. This is naturally disappointing to me, though not in any way surprising, and when compared to your past transgressions, I consider this the lightest.

May God forgive you, Kimberley, seek His love for only He can return my daughter to me.

Your Mother.

Once the content of this letter is fully revealed to me, I renege on my initial assumption that my mother is its true author. Instead, I marvel at the skill of imitation as such vitriol does not belong to her nor does this edge of character and it's impossible to believe that such traits have managed to elude me in the (near) three decades that I have known her. But closer scrutiny reveals otherwise. The level of clear recall, the intimacy in the delivery and the certainty of detail, all of it pointed towards an authenticity that is difficult to deny and no motive could I find for a suspected masquerade. And so, if it is my mother who has composed such a letter, then it leaves some room for conjecture as to who really was the true source of the revelations that it contains, for there are details within it that she does not know nor could she ever have known. That is to say that she has clearly been in league with someone who has performed a measured betrayal, someone who wants to see my downfall and knows just how this could be accomplished. That there are candidates for this I cannot refute but what did anyone stand to gain from my demise and what would they be likely to do with the coveted spoils? In two pages of scornful words, my future has been stolen away from me and it really doesn't matter what possessions are now left for me to sell because nothing will go as far as to compensate for the loss of a second parent. My father had never said enough during his life and I had been powerless to prevent his passing and now my mother is effectively relieving herself from her duty as parent for what she considers to be valid reasoning. Perhaps it is time to accept the fact that at twenty-nine years old, I am now essentially an orphan.

Maybe it is for the best that my mother ignores the six voicemail messages that follow, where my voice no doubt vacillates between plea and protest. The rebuke is obvious and less cutting than her words but if she craves the truth then I am willing to offer her this. I will tell her everything and omit nothing, from the promising career that I've lost to the mountain of spiralling debts that I've accrued. I'll talk of the apartment that I can no longer afford to keep and then reveal the long list of personal effects that have been hawked to stave off penury. I can also tell her just how much Simon now hates me and then move on to the man in the same apartment block who doesn't love me and then I can top everything off by saying how my last shred of happiness now rests in the medical hands of Doctor Block and tenuous chance. Yes, my mother may have discovered some truths but the details that link all of them together are still far from her comprehension.

I call her again and this time she answers but her response is atypical for one noted for her eloquence. 'Oh do stop begging Kimberley, it is simply unbecoming.' After she hangs up, I am left with an engaged tone that seems to resonate with the utter numbness that usurps my mind and body. Further, visual details of the letter I am holding now start to make themselves known to me, the son of God, bearded and austere, is positioned at the head of the page, towering above the text with a look of cruel endorsement of the bitter content. At the foot, a solemn church steeple, a telephone number and with it, a request for kind donations.

42

KIM

I wait patiently for Ricky to pull out of the car park at Gaddis Avenue from my secreted position that lay adjacent to the ramp which took all cars out of the complex. He may have noticed that my car had not been parked in its regular space and maybe he'd deliberated as to why this was but it's doubtful he'd suspected that I'd been trailing him for the past four nights. In doing this, I'd quickly discovered that I possessed little talent for surveillance and I managed to lose sight of him on the first evening after about a mile when he jumped a red light and the distance between us meant I couldn't do the same without risking fatal injury. Second and third attempts followed but these too provided no answers, for there was nothing for me to glean from his visit to the gym and then a local supermarket and so I returned home with a feeling of deflation.

I cannot confidently rationalise this behaviour but I'm certain that there's an element to Ricky's life that he is keen to hide and the only chance I have of finding any closure rests on my discovering this. That my methods are questionable I can readily admit but in the absence of any real intelligence, my hand has been forced and I cannot just confront him with simple accusations that he will only deny.

Protecting my anonymity remains imperative which is why I allow two cars to ease out ahead of me and join the flow of traffic behind Ricky. Because of this, I am able to follow him without issue before the road meets a large T junction about a mile ahead and the traffic splits left or right at about an equal share. Then, it is simply a matter of keeping him in sight, preserving a safe distance and rehearsing what I'm to say should I be detected. In this case, a set of my father's old golf clubs reside in my boot and these should form an ample excuse if I am questioned, even if the buyer is not expecting their delivery until tomorrow.

It is after around three miles of pursuing him that I realise we are heading for a new destination and not too long after that, we begin to encroach on the roads of suburbia. Through a process of natural elimination, I am now directly behind Ricky with the traffic having thinned considerably and while I do not recognise my surroundings, the speed of Ricky's driving suggests that he does. He spends several minutes gliding down numerous leafy avenues (each without distinction from the next) before easing to an eventual stop and pulling into a small driveway on a sleepy, provincial street. I pull up about fifty yards short of this, steering my car onto the side of the road and quickly take in my environment. The street itself is quiet and vast and it resembles a lesser version of the one that I grew up in. My view of the house is somewhat obscured by a row of tall conifer trees that form a long, green curtain next to the oblique front drive and I notice that another car is already parked there ahead of Ricky's. I turn the engine off and wait for him to emerge, squinting because of the distance even though I can faintly make out that he's still sitting in his car and is holding a mobile phone to his left ear. I consider edging further forward but there is no way of doing this discreetly and little evidence to suggest that gaining a greater vantage point is likely to tell me anything that distance couldn't at this stage.

What am I expecting exactly and how has it come to this, I think to myself as the absurdity of the situation begins to unsettle me for the first time. Why am I sitting in a stationary vehicle, stalking a man with whom I am infatuated, in search of clues that even should I find them, may not be connectible? The Kimberley Pleydell of five years ago would not have dreamt of doing this, in fact, if anything, the situation would be very much in reverse, with Ricky pining after me while I went about my daily business, vaguely indifferent and unmoved. As I look into my rearview mirror, it is clearer still that that woman is no more and that she will never be resurrected. If anything, I look older than my years and the emergence of my mother's features is now apparent in every curve and contour of my face. This hasn't crept up on me of course, it has just become harder to conceal, much like the excess weight that I have gained, protruding from parts of my figure that I never used to have to hide.

As Ricky steps out of his car, I consider leaving as my view is too obscured and I've no way of combatting this without revealing my presence. Perhaps another chance will present itself in the future if I'm patient enough and I can't discount the notion that maybe there isn't anything to discover about Ricky's life after all and it could be just as dull and monotonous as everybody else's. Hayley could well have exaggerated in the way that she is prone to do and if Ricky is to see me, then I know I'll never get this chance again once he's been alerted of my propensity to spy on him.

But still I cannot conquer the curiosity and so I decide to stay and wait it out, figuring that even the faintest of clues may give me something to work with. Already I can see that something or somebody has halted Ricky's progress to the front door and so I take the key out of the ignition and try to decipher what he's doing. I'm still at a side angle to him but can make out that he is crouching down and offering his attention to something in front of him. He looks playful in his manner as if petting a small dog but even with my window rolled down, I cannot make out the canine interaction. The front door is now open too and Ricky is mouthing words back at someone who is stood on the other side and whose identity is concealed from me by the obscure window glass of the porch. It is then that he hoists the object of his original interaction high up in the air, whooping as he does so and catching it in his hands amidst a din of satisfaction.

The boy is young, maybe around four years old and clearly enamored with Ricky, who responds to this obvious affection with a matching adoration. It is the same way that my father looked at me when I was a child and I too had returned that proud, paternal gaze with spellbound eyes and trusting touch. Like all proud parents, Ricky is basking in the idolatry of his son and clasps the boy's arms about his neck with an ease of command that looks totally innate. The boy responds in kind, resting a wispy blond head upon a broad shoulder, hushed and contented by his father's tactility.

Almost as if on command, the obscured figure from the doorway then emerges to complete the familial trio. She treads lightly towards the two of them before linking arms to form a communal embrace, receives a light kiss on the cheek from Ricky and gestures for them to go inside. I do not recognise her but then there's no reason why I should but it certainly isn't the woman I saw him with that morning in the Gaddis Avenue car park, who had sat in the passenger's seat while he returned Hayley's scarf to me.

Although I remain mere yards away, it doesn't feel as though the scene that has just played out in front of me is in any way tangible. It feels more like an elaborate ruse, a spiteful double bluff designed to punish me for cynically believing the very worst in people and longing for sinister conclusions. The very notion of Ricky being a father doesn't advance beyond the perplexing and although I've spent so much time striving to understand him, I clearly never have. The man I thought I knew treated intimacy with a suspicion close to fear and yet here he now is doting on another human being and brimming with a love of which I didn't deem him capable. I flit between shock and bewilderment, cursing my naivety while finally accepting that I have no more excuses left to offer him. This isn't the closure that I sought and yet, had I not always known that whatever I discovered was never likely to placate me? Of course I had, but then again, this gruesome truth still seems preferable to the void in my life that Ricky has created because my sense of distrust can now at least be validated and no longer dismissed.

Maybe in isolation I could get over what Ricky has done to me by attaching all fault to him and obtain my revenge by just getting on with my life. This is what happens in the books and the movies that are designed to make you feel better but it will be impossible for me to maintain that charade as I'm just not strong enough and his proximity to me will make it harder still. And it isn't just about Ricky either, everything in my life is falling apart and he is simply another component of that, a mere embodiment of my perennial failure. There is nobody to share this indignity with and that makes everything bleaker because all of this is the pitiful result of warnings unheeded. Collectively, it is just too much, sitting here in a car still waiting for repair in the midst of an expensive gamble to bear a child I can't afford while a man that I love hides the very existence of one from me. I then think of my mother and the lifeline she has snatched away from me, of the job that won't sack me despite another afternoon's truancy and of the golf clubs last touched by my father that now sit in the boot.

I get out of the car. After a brief examination, I settle for one of the larger clubs of the set and close the boot. With a thick, cast iron, triangular head, it feels surprisingly lighter than it looks, though is unquestionably sturdy enough for the task ahead. Never having played golf before, I have no idea what the name of this particular club is nor do I know how one should carry it correctly as I stride over to Ricky's car. Once there, I hoist the club above my head and hold it at a right angle before swinging with as much power as I can muster at the window on the passenger's side. On impact, I recoil instinctively, fully expecting the glass to shatter into a million pieces but rather disappointingly, the blow leaves nothing more than a large indentation at the point of contact with a series of slighter ones circling around it. Undeterred by this, I readjust both my grip and standing position and then swing once more, directing my strike at the tiny cleft I've created. This second attempt proves more successful as I manage to punch a hole through the centre of the window, leaving the clear shape of the head of the club. As if fortified by this success, I swing wildly at what's left while shattered pieces of glass spray inside the car, spreading themselves over the dashboard and onto the seats in a glittering mess. In the space of seconds, I feel exultant as I work to the rhythm of a blaring car alarm which simply adds to the growing, cacophonous din. Every breakable component becomes a target now as I move swiftly to the wing mirrors and then on to the headlights which fragment submissively without much effort. When the windscreen offers a stern resistance, I simply climb onto the bonnet and continue the onslaught, hammering away with all that I have and using the heels of my boots to puncture the resistant shards. Stray splinters of glass continue to fly everywhere, ricocheting back at me and affixing themselves to my clothes and hair, the club now bending slightly due to the repetition of impact. My adrenalin is now something close to frenzy and it feels as though I'm committing this act ethereally, watching from above while someone else takes possession of my person. There is liberation and empowerment to every blow now and months of anger, weakness and inadequacy pour out of my body with every swing of the club.

It isn't long before my exertions start to fatigue me though and I'm forced to step down and survey the damage in its totality. Small cubes of glass crunch noisily beneath my feet as I circle the car and the wreckage is so severe that it resembles the aftermath of a collision with another vehicle. I'm not exactly satisfied but still impressed with my own handiwork because as anecdotes go, no one would ever believe this despite the cuts to my hands and the crystal remnants that are wedged into my boots. And as I start to contemplate this, I sense that someone is standing directly behind me now, imploring me to stop and questioning the whereabouts of my sanity.

Looking back at the house, I see that the front door is now ajar and although neither Ricky nor the woman are there, I sense some movement. Faces of random people who have gathered at the scene now stare at me blankly, all looking visibly hesitant as if waiting for each other to intervene and so I hastily return to my car. There is nothing further for me to gain by delaying my exit any longer and I want to avoid a physical confrontation with Ricky if I can help it.

Once back inside and at the wheel, I notice that my hands are slipping from everything they touch due to a greasy perspiration and the adrenalin has started to descend into a sobering sensibility. Feeling for my accelerator, I take a quick look left to see if my route of escape is without obstacle but my attention is distracted by another small disturbance back towards my right. The same circle of people who had stood by tentatively while I embarked on my wild rampage are now dispersing and withdrawing themselves towards the opposing pavements. This leaves just one man, who stands alone in the centre of the road, ignoring all pleas from either side of him to step away.

Ricky's demeanour is one I do not recognise, his face a fiery blend of fury and perplexity and his stance defiant as if challenging me to confront him. That he has reason to feel aggrieved I cannot dispute but he isn't the real victim here and so I feel he has little right to exude the level of disdain that now emanates from him. To simply speed away would only serve to acknowledge the wound that I have dealt him (his being a mere scratch in comparison to mine) and if guilt lies on my horizon then I don't feel it yet.

I tell myself that I haven't sought this stand-off between us as I begin to change course and pull the car right, heading straight in the direction of Ricky. At first, I edge towards him no quicker than a crawl and then slowly start to bring my foot down a little heavier on the accelerator. As I begin to gather pace, I hope to induce his moving from my path but instead, he starts to walk towards me with a resolute gait and keeps on coming as if daring me to desist. I resolve not to blink first having finally secured his undivided attention after months of futile pursuit, regaining that same sense of control that I had felt with that golf club in my hands. With this in mind, I slam my foot to the floor and as the engine roars, the car surges forward, hissing and spitting out clusters of debris from beneath the tyres in a shower of dusty sediment. The sheer force propels my body backwards, free from the restraints of the discarded seatbelt, as I hurtle towards Ricky at a pace that continues to build with every yard that I gain. In mere moments, I reach a speed that will prevent the possibility of braking within a safe distance and my eyes close involuntarily, preparing for impact.

I hear a flurry of gasps coming from the crowd of onlookers positioned either side of the road but with the car still running smoothly and it is clear that I've avoided any contact. I'm relieved at this because I didn't want to hit Ricky and then allow him to assume the role of martyr in the aftermath, which he would surely have embraced had I sent him to the hospital. That is too good for him and would not replace the satisfaction gained from having successfully called his bluff when he no doubt expected me to lose my nerve at the very last moment. I still take a look over my shoulder to make certain of my assumption and sure enough, a rather disheveled-looking Ricky is now being helped to his feet by one of the bystanders. Luckily for us both, he must have dived out of the way just seconds before I passed and in doing so, had saved himself from serious injury or a fate possibly even worse. The consequences don't need thinking about just yet though as I speed my way out of that sleepy suburban street with a sense that victory, however slight, somehow belongs to me.

I drive around aimlessly for about an hour before my composure fully returns having visited several points of reference along the way, including the fertility clinic and the recently sold family home. It isn't clear to me why I do this and I don't want to conduct a deeper analysis but my initial restlessness seems to stem from realising just how indifferent I am to facing any potential consequences to what I've just done. I don't care whether Ricky retaliates and if he does, what form that retaliation will likely take. Report me, accost me, tell Simon everything, it doesn't matter in the least because I have nothing of any value left to take. The day-to-day subterfuge that is my life is now beyond tiresome, so maybe allowing others to discover the facts for themselves will be preferable to my offering a series of confessions that I don't care to give.

Recalling my original errand, I locate the address of the intended buyer of my father's golf clubs who on my arrival, seems only mildly peeved by the fact that they are now one short of a full set and have been delivered a day earlier than expected. Over tea and cakes in his living room, I break down into a weeping, emotional mess in front of him and his wife, who both take pity on me and agree to pay the full price for the clubs despite their numerical shortfall.

43

SIMON

I haven't seen or heard from Vanessa in over a week when I receive a letter from her addressed to me at my place of work. As letters go, I am happy to receive this, even if its content makes little or no sense to me and I'm unsure exactly as to what has inspired it.

Simon

I thought it would be easier to write rather than rely on the confines of a text message or run the risk of our emotions gaining the better of us in a telephone call. You have assumed correctly though, I have been reluctant to answer your calls and messages, partly because you call me at inconvenient times, mostly in the evening when it's often hard to judge your state of thought. Even so, you seem relatively contrite and I do care about you so I am prepared to see you again.

I want you to be aware that I've spent the last week pleading with Sebastian in your defence. He doesn't understand my loyalty to you and cannot reconcile this, but he has promised that he will not be pressing charges against you and I know him to be a man of his word. As a condition of this promise, he has insisted that you must never be present when I am in his company and so I urge you to respect and abide by this.

I'm also relieved to say that I've not heard anything from the other person that you assaulted at the party that night and as nobody seems willing to take this any further, I hope that this matter can also be left to lie.

Simon, it will never make any sense to me why you did these things as the last that I remember was of your caring for me and putting me to bed. Why you chose to return to the party and act in such a violent way is a source of much confusion to me and I'm sure to anybody that knows you. Sebastian admits that he acted indiscreetly towards me and I have forgiven him as I forgive you. I take responsibility for my own actions and acknowledge my part in what has happened and I apologise for dragging you into my personal affairs. I still want you to be a part of my life but I will not tolerate the side of your character that displayed itself that evening. You are someone that possesses a beautiful soul after all. I promise to call you soon.

Vanessa.

44

SIMON

I didn't remember suggesting to my ex-girlfriend's little brother that we meet up for a drink some time but if I did, it was probably more through sympathy than the intention of actually following through with it. Because of this, Declan's text message had caught me off guard but seeing as I was in the pub already, I hadn't been able to justify refusing him. My instinctual apprehension was probably validated as he's never been one disposed to loquaciousness and he hadn't disclosed his motives for the meeting beforehand. During which, he alluded to Barney and to Kim but I didn't really see where I fitted in to the Pleydell family narrative and knew from past experience that my involvement seemed to help neither side. I simply endeavoured to steer the discourse away from that particular subject matter but with common ground so hard to find, an incoming call from Vanessa had given me the opportunity to politely excuse myself and take it.

After receiving her letter this morning (the contents having only provided faint clarification to incidents I loosely remembered) I decided to wait and not respond immediately. There was something about the letter's plaintive tone that had troubled me all day and that tone had been further amplified in its telephonic form, which enabled me to visualise that weakness instead of merely sensing it. She was reluctant to elaborate on the events that had kept us apart other than to say that Sebastian's wounds were superficial and while I offered no apology, tellingly, she hadn't pressed for one either.

I knew that she would ask if I would see her tonight and that I would say yes, feigning joy at the prospect of our reconciliation. Maybe it was due to the short time that we had spent apart but somehow it felt too late and I no longer saw her as the woman I first formally met in the Plough & Trinket and I'm certain that her perception of me must also have changed significantly. If it hadn't, then she was perhaps more discerning then I'd originally credited her for but it would still change nothing, I simply didn't love her and now I knew for sure I never would.

When I returned to the bar, Declan had vanished and in truth, I was relieved. Nothing about our brief encounter had felt quite right and with so much weighing on my mind, a seventeen-year-old boy was never likely to be an appropriate sounding board. I ordered another (strong) drink and imbibed it rapidly to steady myself for what was about to happen.

45

SIMON

It felt a tad undignified to be creeping across the courtyard of a halls of residence at four in the morning or perhaps unbefitting of one on the cusp of thirty. I'd left Vanessa sleeping and splayed across the makeshift double bed in her room with the serenity of one unused to such a privilege. This was the benefit, she had told me, of sharing a dorm with a mostly absent roommate who had a serious boyfriend who lived somewhere across town in more salubrious conditions. I sensed that when she did wake up, she would first see the violin removed from its case and maybe somewhere deep down, she would also see it as the metaphor that I did. It was symbolic of our relationship and although whatever we shared may have sounded pleasant to the ear, the truth was that it was always going to end this way.

Last night, she had whispered that she loved me and told me that she wouldn't have slept with me otherwise. And I admit that I was horrified because I believed her and not because I didn't and although I could've stopped it at any time, I simply didn't feel inclined to. Perhaps she was trying to convince herself of something or to impress the significance of this maiden undertaking upon me so that I would value it all the more. I smiled rather dumbly, faintly concealing a sadness that she wouldn't understand because she obviously grasped the importance of the moment but had made a clear misjudgement as to who to share it with. She couldn't love me because she didn't know me and if she did, I doubt she'd have felt anything for me other than contempt.

What followed was sex without feeling, a sensual act lacking desire and truth, two bodies jarring against each other without any kind of cohesion. Where I was used to the grooves of another feeding into a rippling harmony, here it had felt like a physical dissension, like the sparring of two souls playing out a gross display. My discomfort went beyond just being her first but still I felt chagrined at her plea for tenderness, unsure of if she felt compelled to say this or whether some inherent selfishness had been attached to my character. By the time I fully understood everything, it was too late and I realised I'd never done this before with one I didn't love.

It didn't matter that she was undeserving because I too had been undeserving once and it hadn't changed anything. That she'd briefly invigorated me for a time I could not deny but it was a feeling that would never last long enough to validate me in the way that I needed and there was little left to gain by pretending otherwise. As harsh as it may sound, I think I'd probably intended to hurt her all along, to punish her for the crimes of others, people whose paths she'd never cross and who would be forever ignorant of their culpability. I wanted to leave an indelible mark, one by which all others after me would be judged against like a rite of passage that would only become clear in time. It was vain and it was cruel but the knowledge of this took the emotion out of it and had easier enabled me to sever all ties.

For Vanessa, the aftermath will be long and a little unforgiving and I wondered how the regret would eventually manifest itself. It will become easier (because it always does) but she'll never eliminate those faint but tangible traces of anguish and humiliation that will inform her decision-making in the future chapters of her life. There will be others, better men than me who she will meet with cynicism and distrust when their intentions are honest, still hampered by the decision to lose her virginity to a man that simply hadn't cared for her. And then there will be those who treat her disinterestedly and although they too will not care for her in the way that she deserves, I am sure that they will be rewarded by virtue of their honesty. Such are the complexities and repercussions of a once broken heart.

Everyone has someone in their life for whom they possess a deep, irrational love and in many ways, it's that irrationality of feeling that substantiates that love. It's in behaving beyond your logical boundaries or the voicing of feelings that you keep innermost by which it presents itself and once recognised, it can seldom be suppressed. It's when you don't hold such feelings or when you dare not act with that reckless abandon that you know it isn't nor can it ever be love. Goodbye Vanessa, it was strange while it lasted.

46

KIM

My manager looked unwilling to accept the extenuating circumstances that had contributed to me arriving for work over an hour late this morning. At first, I felt this unfair (even though it really wasn't) before it became clear that she didn't understand the meaning of the word extenuating. She'd have to inform my supply agency (she warned) but I couldn't stress strongly enough how that was the least of my concerns right then. It was the insurance company's fault I explained, as they had passed me around from pillar to post for longer than I cared to endure and it simply wasn't an option to just hang up. 'My car's been stolen!' I had seethed at them. 'I'm not a criminal, I didn't plan any of this so why are you treating me so unsympathetically?' That had been met with a nervy silence and after several uncomfortable seconds, the man on the other end of the line simply responded with, 'but you no longer have insurance with us Miss Pleydell, in fact, you failed to renew your policy three months ago.' I said I didn't remember doing that and yet I couldn't deny being reminded of this previously when I last called the company to enquire about their covering the cost of the damage to the front of my car. That decision, like many others made in the last six months or so, had been motivated only by the need to reduce my financial outgoings but insurance companies aren't famed for their clemency and this one had no intention of bucking that trend. The fact remained that last night, while I slept soundly in my bed, my car had been taken from the Gaddis

Avenue parking bay and there was nothing that they could do to help me with this.

The footage provided by the drowsy security guard sat in his booth at the entrance to the car park had proved inconclusive and I left feeling guilty for having taken up so much of his 'valuable' time. He opined that the face at the wheel was that of a man but I couldn't detect any prominent features from the grainy recording and so my only form of evidence was rendered useless. What had baffled him however, was seeing how the culprit had somehow acquired a fob that enabled him to lift the parking barrier at the exit of the complex. These, he'd explained, were like gold dust, of which the occupants of Gaddis Avenue were allowed exclusive ownership. Thankfully, I still had mine though it was of little use to me now.

Just what was I supposed to do without my car and perhaps more pertinently, no means of replacing the one I'd lost? Already I suspected it was probably beyond recognition, dumped in a field somewhere with its engine burnt out and four battered tyres. This I considered while I wept in the toilet for twenty minutes after my manager's tongue-lashing before the demand for my cubicle became impossible to ignore and I vacated it, albeit reluctantly.

My late arrival into work forced me into staying much later than usual and being the last to leave the office also meant that I couldn't catch a lift with any of my colleagues. My only way of getting home was to catch a bus (something I hadn't done since my semi-rebellious youth), only I wasn't sure which one to get and ended up jumping on the number 228 for no other reason than it matched the number of my apartment. Fifteen minutes into the journey, it became evident that I was heading in completely the wrong direction and that the only way back would be to alight at the next terminus and make further enquiries there. I reluctantly did this but if anything, my second trip proved more arduous than the first as I was forced to stand up all of the way home with seats being at a premium. My only light relief came in the form of a conversation I overheard in which a young lady sobbed to her friend about how some selfish moron had slept with her and then instantly broken off all relations. Of course, I could've interjected at any point but I figured there was little benefit to be had from my experience, as recent events had seemingly proved.

As I approach my flat, with all that behind me, I can only be thankful that today is almost over. All I'm ready for right now is a long, hot bath and maybe a very small glass of gin and tonic which I will easily acquire from Simon's not-so-secret stash, hidden inside an empty guitar case in his room. Perhaps focusing on this a little too much, I fail to notice that my front door is ever so slightly ajar and when I go to insert the key, it slowly recoils back and opens up into my living space. I tentatively call out for Simon as I press forward slowly but I am only met with silence. I figure he may have worked from home today seeing how he'd managed to wake me up at five o'clock this morning, buzzing on the intercom and unable to gain entry to the flat. Usually, I'd be fuming at such carelessness but I was already wide awake by that point and deeply uninterested in his apologies and completely unaware of what the morning was about to bring.

As I fumble for the light switch, it is already clear that Simon isn't home and I'm left trying to reassure myself that it would be impossible to be the victim of a second crime within the space of twenty-four hours. I flick the switch in a semi-alert pose, ready to face the tackle of a lurking intruder, which thankfully doesn't come, and then I begin to survey my surroundings. I quickly note that nothing has been damaged and nothing has been taken, the door, like the windows, shows no signs of forced entry and all of my belongings assume the very same position in which I left them this morning. Had it been any other morning, it would've been possible to believe that I rushed out of the flat with my mind on other things, leaving the door wide open in my wake but that wasn't so today. I clearly remember returning to the apartment after discovering that my car was missing to dig out the insurance details and I left Simon in the flat after asking if he knew anything of its whereabouts. Incidentally, he denied all knowledge of course but then he didn't really have a motive to steal something that he often made use of himself and so I'd quickly discounted him from my suspicions. Satisfied that all looks as it should do, I head towards the front room.

"I think you better slow down there Kim, last time you had that look about you, you almost killed me." It was Ricky who was casually addressing me from my sofa, looking not in the least bit discomfited. "You'll forgive my lack of manners but the scars will probably take a week or two to heal." He says this while nodding towards his right leg which I notice is raised on the coffee table like a patient would use a sling in a hospital. Flippant though he sounds, his face does not convey this and the shock of seeing him takes valuable reaction time away from me. At no point since the incident had I found the time to envision quite what I was going to say when this moment arrived. I didn't expect it now and I didn't expect it here.

"How did you get into my flat?" I ask, with an anger that is perhaps a tad misplaced.

"Would you believe I walked? My usual means of transportation is somewhat out of action."

"I'm being serious Ricky."

"You know, that's really not even close to an apology Kim, try again."

"I cannot give you what I feel you don't deserve. Now tell me, how did you get into my flat?"

"Oh the door was open, or at least it wasn't locked," he begins, while pulling himself up from the sofa gingerly, a painful wince spreading across his face. I notice for the first time how his hair is tied back into a small, half ponytail and there are remnants of neat, grey stubble about his chin and neck. This look is new to me and despite the pain I deem him answerable for, in moments like this, I still feel powerless around him. I curse myself inwardly and hope that this weakness will not present itself.

"Anyway," he says, "let's not worry about the moral high ground here as you're hardly one to wait for an invitation before entering someone's flat now are you? You're lucky Daisy didn't call the police."

It didn't matter now but I wasn't shocked to learn that she had told him about my entering his flat and I probably should've thought of an excuse for this transgression much, much sooner. The fact that Ricky had waited until now to even mention it suggested that he hadn't felt particularly concerned about this but in light of recent events, this revelation had perhaps undermined me even further.

"Look, it was you who stole my car Ricky so you're hardly averse to the idea of revenge. First you take my car and then you break into my flat so I'd say we're about equal now." Although I try to sound forthright in saying this, Ricky looks neither perturbed nor exposed.

"I have literally no idea what you're talking about, why on earth would I steal your car? And for the last time, I didn't break into your flat. I came to see you yes but the door was unlocked so I thought it pointless to just stand around on ceremony waiting for your return. It's actually a nice place you've got here, a little on the small side but I suppose that way there's less for you to damage."

"I *really* can't handle your levity right now Ricky."

"You nearly killed me you mad bitch!" He screams violently, fully upright now and grabbing both of my arms just above the elbow. The sheer force of his grip causes me to momentarily rock backwards and so he counters this by pulling me closer to him. There is a small but discernible flesh wound that I can now see just below his right eye. "I had to dive out of the way of you in order to save my life. What would you have felt like right now if you'd have succeeded Kim? Would you have satisfied your anger by maiming or killing me, a father, a man that you professed to have feelings for? Is that what you wanted?"

"No, it wasn't, I mean, I was never going to, I would've stopped…"

"You vandalised my car! You took a golf club to it and smashed it to pieces like some crazed lunatic. There were people at your side pleading with you to stop, there were children crying and yet you just continued."

"I was angry with you Ricky and I'm angry with you still. Your words are meaningless to me and I've no reason to believe anything that you say."

"And how exactly did you find me? How was it that you just happened to be in the neighbourhood that night?"

"I followed you."

"You *followed* me," he says, before releasing me and heading back towards the sofa, "well of course you did. Tell me, did your behaviour that night come close to reaching sanity at any point?"

"Yes I did," I cry, interjecting quickly as if claiming the upper hand, "and I'm glad that I did. It was the only way of finding out about your double life, the one that you have hidden from me and I dare say others. Just how long would it have taken you to admit the truth? To tell me how you spend your weekdays here in your sordid little bachelor pad and then the weekends in the suburbs playing happy families? In absolutely and every sense of the word, you're a fraud."

"A fraud? Oh don't be so melodramatic," he responds with a rhetorical disbelief. "Look, it was you who pursued me remember? I didn't encourage you, I offered no promises, and I will not be held accountable for your warped delusions. What we had was never a relationship and if you misjudged it as such then that's on you, not me."

Ricky appears to stop himself from elaborating further but I can't decide if he feels he's said too much already or is just being careful about how he steers this. My own hesitation is caused by a stinging sense that he has landed the first real blow of the contest and a strong concern that any rightful injustice will portray itself now as vitriol.

"Well maybe it wasn't a relationship in the eyes of the world but it was to me. I opened up to you physically and emotionally and instead of respecting that you just exploited me."

"And what about the relationship you did have when we were first intimate?" He re-joins, instantly. "I'd guess that Simon knows nothing of that or any of this and let's not even pretend that I was the first or even the last for that matter."

"That's completely different," I fire back at him, "Simon and I have been finished for a long time and on the night that you mention, we were over in everything but status. I didn't sleep with you until the two of us had split."

"You didn't think of him once, but then, you seldom think of anybody but yourself. You're just as selfish and as self-indulgent as I am but you can't admit that because it forces you to accept that you are everything that you are trying to hide." He pauses to focus on me more clearly, looking me up and down in a manner close to disgust. In a voice sneering and practically contemptuous, he resumes his diatribe. "There's no romance to any of this, you have no right to moralise and you shouldn't sleep with anybody if you can't control your emotional attachments."

I feel the venom in his words, in fact, I feel it deeply. Gone are the monosyllables and glib responses and in their place is a scorn so cutting and so direct, that it comes across as though it is rehearsed. He is punishing me not for what I've said but for my proximity to the truth and although I am unwilling to descend to such a level, I begin to sense that I am left with little choice.

"So tell me, how did I compare to Hayley then? I assume you do remember her, right?" I toss this question out and it draws a look of confusion from him as if a name once buried in a recess of his mind has been dragged back into the fore. "I mean, I'm not going to hazard a guess at how many women you've had sex with recently or if you even bother to take their names but in case you've forgotten, she was the friend of mine you spied on through my Congrelate page, hounded like some sex-starved adolescent and then slept with. To top it all off, not only did you hide this from me but you confused the two of us when you returned her scarf to me."

"Is that what she told you?" He responds with an air of disbelief that is, if anything, a little too dramatic. "Oh come on, it really wasn't like that."

"Yes, she told me, although you did everything in your power to conceal it from me."

"No, I didn't. Listen, I don't know what she's told you but it really didn't happen like that, she pursued me and it's evident that she has lied to you. Look, either way, whatever did or didn't happen, that was between the two of us and it had nothing to do with you. I can't understand why you would feel so upset about it."

A clear perspective suddenly dawns on me that maybe he wasn't lying after all. It wasn't improbable to believe that a man who attached so little thought to the consequences of sex would likely assume that all others did the same and although it was no excuse, it did seem credible. But even as I contemplate this, the images remain vividly and excruciatingly clear and I'm unable to dislodge them.

"You gave her an STD Ricky! She told me all about it. Do you know how dangerous that could be for someone in my medical condition right now?"

"Kim, you're being irrational. That would not have come from me, Hayley could've picked that up from anybody. Still, I'm sure that blaming me makes all this just that little bit easier for you. You know how careful I was when we were together, you can't deny that, I took *precautions* like I always do. Anyway, what medical condition are you referring to?"

I've inadvertently revealed too much but his point about his use of contraception is at least a valid one. Even so, I can't fully believe him and maybe I don't want to and his refusal to acknowledge his own wrongdoing isn't serving to pacify me.

"Deny it?" I say, with the advantage of clear recall. "You gave me the impression that it was because you were petrified of impregnating me so you'll forgive me for not taking the time to thank you for considering my sexual health."

Ricky takes a step towards me again with his index finger pointing in my direction, weighing an answer between his lips. Before this is delivered though, he seems to obey a second thought, recoils the finger back into a fist and adopts a ruminative pose. The delay is long enough to temper the ferocity of our dialogue but what I am about to say next is interrupted by the ringing tone of his mobile phone.

"I, er, well, it could be, you know?" He mumbles while waving the phone around somewhat apologetically.

"Just answer it," I say, dispassionately, "there's really no need for any secrecy between us now."

He excuses himself into the hall where a brief and inaudible conversation starts and ends within the space of a minute. When he returns, I make a concerted effort to pretend that its content doesn't interest me. I fail comprehensively.

"So was that her?" I ask, petulantly.

"Kim, please don't do this," he pleads, scratching his left temple.

"After all this Ricky, I still don't know her name."

"But why would you want to know?"

"Just tell me her name."

He takes a deep breath before replying. "It's Harriet, her name is Harriet."

"Can I see a picture of her please?"

"Is it really going to help in any way? It's not like you haven't seen her before."

"Yes," I insist.

Reluctantly, he unlocks his phone and hands it over to me. It is a simple photograph, the two of them standing on a bridge somewhere with a canal and woodland behind them, Ricky looking notably younger and Harriet with a clear glow about her. She really is incredibly beautiful in this picture (I have to concede) and my jealousy is valid even though she looks just about as far removed from the idea of a nemesis as one could possibly imagine. Deep down, I know that I am searching for something that really isn't there and trying to rouse hatred for someone who's done nothing to deserve it.

"That was the day we found out that she was pregnant with Bobby," he adds proudly, but he is somewhere on the periphery now and no longer in my line of vision as I bow my head to face the floor. My chest begins to tighten as I pass the phone back to him, hoping that he doesn't notice how the intensified resentment is causing me to shake or how the source of this has switched to Harriet.

"Ricky, I want you to tell me what she has that I do not."

"Kim, please, don't ask me to…"

"No Ricky, I *have* to know this because I don't think that I can move on until you tell me. I need to know what qualities she possesses that set her apart from me and everybody else in your life. What it is that makes you want to protect her from your infidelities and why you return to her time and time again. But I mostly want to know why you couldn't picture having anything like that with me." Although I can't bring myself to look at him as I say this, I do hear him sigh and try to compose himself.

"I don't love her Kim and I can't lie to you and say that I do but one day I could and hope that I will. I love her just about as much as I am capable of loving anyone and that's not something that I can explain or justify but it's something that I want to protect because she brings out feelings in me that tell me I'm human. Our relationship isn't perfect, at times it can be volatile and challenging and so I use the apartment here just to offer us both a bit of space when things become strained. There's really nothing sordid about it, despite how it looks. I always come back to her because the truth is that is where I feel safest, with her and my boy."

"But you're still living a lie Ricky," I say, "and I feel like you've made me complicit in your deceiving her. Nobody deserves to be lied to like that and there's nothing to stop me from dragging her out of this pit of ignorance that you've deposited her in."

"Well, Kim, I suppose that's up to you," he returns, calmly and confidently. "I'd rather you didn't but I know that I can't stop you. We have an understanding, our relationship works because of that and although we may have separate lives to some degree, I don't want to ruin what we have. Now, if you want to end all that and focus on making the mother of my child hate me then that's your call but if you know what it's like to grow up in an environment devoid of love, split between two parents who just resent each other, then why would you wish that on anyone else? Surely nothing could be more selfish than that?"

He attempts to apply a conciliatory hand to my shoulder but I flinch away instinctively. It is a bold and daring move, pleading to protect his family's unity like that and doing so with confidence, knowing how I recognise the family environment that he alluded to.

"I just wanted us to be together," I resume, with my back now to him. "I used to have visions of the two of us and it made me so happy that in some way it felt like it was destined. You had a duty to tell me not to invest so much emotionally and you failed to do that."

"That night when we slept together Kim, I opened up to you and told you how I was everything that your ideal was not. I thought you understood but now I think it's clear that you didn't want to understand."

"But you don't even know me Ricky, you've never wanted to know the first thing about me so how can you be so sure that you are not the man I love?" I concede this is a question that he cannot answer but somehow the answers don't seem so important anymore. I feel a number of different emotions but strangely enough, the predominant one appears to be defeat and his growing lucidity isn't helping matters.

"Who really knows anybody Kim?" As he asks this, I turn around to face him for what could be the last time and note that the grip of his hands on my shoulders is devoid of intimacy. His face, now seemingly on the verge of a confession, is as beautiful as ever but there is something foreboding about him and his eyes are now wanting of their once-mysterious value. He withdraws his hands from me. "I could never get to know you because the truth is you wouldn't let me. You would only let me know the person you claim to be, the person you think I want you to be and you'd convince yourself that you could change a man who doesn't want to change and is incapable of it. I've tried to put distance between the two of us Kim and now you need to do the same before others are dragged into this and they end up being hurt as well. The truth is that I don't love you and more importantly, I know that I never could." He doesn't wait for an invitation to leave nor does he say goodbye and just seconds later, as the door shuts conclusively behind him, I know and feel finality.

The sense of grief will dissipate and heal itself eventually, at least to a point where it is manageable but not the sense of loss. I say this because just like my father, it was loss on the terms of another, something that was beyond my control, an outcome that could not be rewritten. Mortality and love unrequited, two things that have defied the logic of man for centuries and still we seek a remedy, settling instead for whatever we can find to soothe the suffering. You are told that when you fall in love you will know. Nobody can tell you how you know this but every person to the next agrees and when it happens to you, you become a part of that knowing consensus. But if one expects to fall in love at least once in their lifetime, then one must also accept the danger of love in its purest form and the possibility that the strength of such feeling will determine the depth of your downfall. This is the gamble that we take no matter how steep the odds but how many of us would truly take the risk had we experienced the fouler side of the experience beforehand? And who of us could plead 'not guilty' to the charge of denying our misgivings when the bad in one you love far outweighs the good? The truth, in answer to those questions, is the great mystery of love, the fugitive of reason but whatever love is or is not, we will never come close to attaining it until we understand that what we capture is always less than what we yearn for.

47

SIMON

"You don't look too well," observes Malcy, who by sharp contrast looks as well as I've ever seen him. I neglect to mention that I've barely been home in twenty-four hours. "After I talked to you on the phone the other day, well, I gave a lot of thought to what you said and decided that perhaps you were right after all."

"Listen, Malcy, please…" I bid to interject but he isn't having any of it.

"Maybe it was the money that clouded my judgement, I don't know, it's been difficult to think straight recently, but I know that this decision will impact many others. I've got to think of my team and Judy and the company as a whole, to see what's best for everybody and not just me. This is way bigger than I initially thought."

"Malcy, you really need to listen to me…"

"No Simon, I think you should listen to me."

Having won my silence, he then steadies himself, confident under the misconception that I'm failing to see what's coming. "I'm here to tell you that I've changed my mind. I want to pursue this case, all the way to the very end if I need to and I want you by my side as I do this. You've always maintained that the truth will out itself and I don't doubt this anymore."

"Malcy! Stop talking, stop talking please!" I command, raising my voice above his and wringing my hands to illustrate the instruction. Naturally, this manages to secure his attention along with that of several other customers dotted about us in the pub and as I readjust my seating position, a thin stream of sweat snakes its way down from the back of my neck to the base of my spine. "It's important that you don't run ahead of yourself before you've allowed me to fully apprise you of the facts. As it turns out, things have developed somewhat since we last spoke and I wouldn't exactly say for the better. After you called me, I took it upon myself to consult the union about your case." This is a blatant lie; the union knows little if anything of the case and that is a miracle in itself. One sniff of the details and they'll most likely be pushing for a fair and thorough process which will in turn lead to an assessment of my conduct and mishandling of the whole affair. When you add the fact that Malcy still remains a non-member, my advising him outside of my role could lead to serious implications. "Anyway," I continue, "I presented them with the evidence we have and sought their opinion as to whether they felt we would achieve a successful outcome or not. Well, in plain truth Malcy, they were not optimistic."

"You mean to say that they think Mr Crockett would be believed ahead of us in spite of the evidence we have against him? That's incredible," he adds, bewildered.

"They said that it really doesn't boil down to truth against lies or fact against fiction as none of this has ever been about who is to be believed and who is not to be believed. The stakes appear far higher than we originally thought, senior management are implicated in this and they're already pulling together, fixing their stories and preparing for the long haul. You need to consider the implications on your career should this whole thing go against us. This could ruin you Malcy and although I can in theory still follow your instructions, the risk would remain entirely yours."

Conveying this in real time doesn't prove quite so easy as it did earlier in front of the mirror at home when rehearsing these lines without fear of recrimination. Then, my words carried purpose and fluidity but now that I am faced with a tangible threat of cross-examination, I appear to own no such resolve. Malcy, on the other hand, having just witnessed the one true stalwart of his entire campaign lay his guns to the ground in an act of surrender, looks utterly crestfallen.

"But I don't understand what's changed Simon, you seemed so confident before, when I was the one who wanted to accept the offer and you dissuaded me."

"I know what I said and I'm sorry."

"And you agree with this? Truly, do you agree with this?"

"Look, I understand your confusion, really I do but three months' paid notice is still a fair amount of money and you'll have the chance to put this whole affair behind you, to leave with a clean record and your integrity intact. No one can question your experience, so I don't think you'll struggle to find new work. Who knows, you may even find something better?"

"Let me assure you Simon that I have long lost sight of my integrity," he replies and that listless, pained expression returns, the one that belonged to the Malcy I first encountered in the coffee shop. The familiarity of this grieves me deeply and I try to look away, distracting myself with a series of jittery actions that emanate from my fingers, the nervous embodiment of guilt and shame. "And what about Judy?" He continues hopelessly. "Where does she stand in all of this?"

"Well I was just about to come to that," I say, while the ace up my sleeve begins to burn against my skin. "I didn't just confer with the union on this, in fact, their opinion on the matter is not solely what is influencing mine."

"So you have spoken to her then?" He begins, the melancholy in his eyes now giving way to a burgeoning optimism. "Well, how is she? I've sent her letters, lots of them, but all of them have gone without reply. That's really unlike her too because for all the years I've known her, I don't think I've ever gone a week without talking to her in some capacity."

"Yes Malcy, I have. She asked, no, she *insisted* that I gave this to you." I handed over a small envelope which contained a short note addressed to Malcy. My ace was now revealing itself.

Dear Malcy,

I do hope you are well.

I am writing to you in confidence and to ask that you consider the offer that the company has made you. I know that it isn't my place to try and influence your decision but things have taken a turn for the worse over this last week or so. It appears that Mr Crockett has become aware not only of your case against him but also of my intention to support you at his expense. He's a dangerous man Malcy and I do fear the consequences should I choose to testify against him in such a public manner.

I know that you will do the right thing (whatever that may be).

Judy.
xx

"And you say that Judy handed this to you personally?" He enquires incredulously, while fingering the note with clear distrust. I indicate confirmation, albeit demurely. "It just seems a little odd Simon. She never calls me Malcy, it's always Malcolm and why did she type this instead of handwriting it?"

I feign ignorance but as oversights go, this appears damning and it's very possible that I've given myself away in the very first line. I change tack quickly.

"Look, I don't know Malcy, maybe she was rushed into writing it or maybe she wanted to ensure whatever she did write wasn't traceable to her. You've got to understand what the environment's like at Tanner & Webbing at the moment, it's toxic and fraught with paranoia, it's literally the most unpleasant I've ever known it. And listen, I had to tell her about the offer you received and maybe that was wrong of me but I believed that she would be comforted to know about it. I don't suppose writing those lines was very easy for her but like you said earlier, the impact of your decisions will be felt by us all and Judy is not exempt from that."

He averts his gaze to the floor remorsefully as if it were a blow he was somehow expecting. While I should feel compassion, the knowledge that my passage into safety is getting closer overpowers that emotion.

"There is *some* good news that I can share with you Malcy, something quite important that may console you to some degree." I choose to pause at this moment but Malcy is predictably unresponsive now. I feel awkward but continue in spite of this. "Judy has applied for a new job in the Communications Team and I think she stands a really strong chance of getting it too, providing… well, you know."

And he does, I can see this in the way he nods back at me ruefully as if such hopelessness is familiar to him. He is just about to prove how much he really does love Judy.

"Did she say anything else Simon? Anything else at all?" He asks, searchingly.

"She's a remarkable woman Malcy but she's also very vulnerable. I know that you would not be able to live with yourself if your actions prevented her from bettering herself. It's clear how much she means to you, even I can see that."

Even though I wouldn't call us friends, he doesn't seem embarrassed of my exposing his affection for Judy nor do I suspect that he has ever tried to conceal this when in her company. This makes me resent her more than I already did because I know how such fondness is barely even respected, much less is it returned. That she has used this to her advantage over the years I have absolutely no doubt and although I perceived this and then capitalised upon it, I still pity him for it.

"Well in that case I guess I'm left with little choice. I'm

not going to fight this alone and even if I decided to, I couldn't do it in good faith. I'll write back to Tanner & Webbing in the morning to formally accept their offer. Thank you for everything you have done for me." He stands up ready to leave while extending his hand for me to shake. This time however, it is not the limp, lifeless grip that I initially attributed to him but a warm and vigorous clasp that takes possession of my hand. "She will remember what I did for her won't she Simon?" He asks, though I suspect he is trying to convince himself.

"Of course she will," I reply, and the irony seems bittersweet as our relationship concludes on one last fallacy.

As I watch him leave the pub, my head is spinning with a flurry of conflicting emotions and yet, I really can't tell you what I'm thinking in any meaningful way. I order another drink from the bar and then return to my seat, keeping my eyes on Malcy, who is stood patiently in line at a bus stop just over the road from where I'm sat. Immediately next to him, I notice a gang of five youths all behaving boisterously and clamouring for attention in the way the young do when thinking they're immune from reproach. When the bus arrives, these same youths wait for the very moment that Malcy is just about to board before brusquely pushing him aside and then rushing on ahead of him. Nobody does or says anything and once he's recovered himself, he is then forced to return to the back of the queue. A minute or so later, after he has boarded, an elderly lady enters the now heavily crowded bus and I watch while Malcy, in typically selfless fashion, offers to vacate his seat for her. When she accepts the offer gratefully, he trudges away solemnly, taking up the last available seat which just happens to be situated in the middle of the gang of rowdy youths. For a moment, I resolve to go after him but the impulse is fleeting.

My feelings towards Malcy have always been contradictory. At times, I felt him deserving of the injustice he faced because of his willingness to believe the best in others no matter how they mistreat him and yet sometimes, I secretly admire the man for his innocence and purity of soul. Despite his superior years, he has a heart that isn't stained with the cynicism and loathing that plague so many around him and although he probably recognises these flaws in his contemporaries, he chooses neither to judge nor to emulate. This alone makes Malcy better than most and it certainly makes him a better man than me.

It would be the easiest thing in the world to sit here and blame The Croc, Judy or 'the system' for what has happened to Malcy but in reality, I have committed the greatest crime. Nobody forced me into relinquishing my principles, the same principles I've always been at pains to exhibit and I've allowed my ego and ambition to take precedence above my integrity. These have been sacrificed for a career that I've only ever talked about with flippancy and indifference, distaste and disinterest, but it is too soon yet to say if it has really been worth it. Now, what hurts more than anything is knowing that I've gained the trust and respect of someone who should treat me with contempt and a man worse than he would see me for the hypocrite I am. The Croc had exposed me and now everything seems to thread back to the last words he said to me as I stood disconsolately in his office, beaten and bereft: *idealism is great but it doesn't pay the bills.* It has taken me until this very moment to realise that he merely verbalised a truth that I've been practicing for quite some time but haven't dared admit to. Whatever my ideals are, I do not deserve them and in life there is really nothing worse than a man who can say that about himself. I order another drink.

48

SIMON

I return to the office late in the evening having mislaid the keys to my apartment and finding myself now in a desperate search to locate them which leads me back to my desk. Early this morning, I fled from Vanessa's dorm while she slept and then found myself without any means to enter the complex at Gaddis Avenue. Figuring I may have left them at Vanessa's, I had little choice but to knock and ask to be let in by Kim, who struck me as remarkably calm for one disturbed so early. It didn't last long though, as I awoke around an hour later to find her screaming at my door and lamenting the fact that someone had stolen her car. Quite how anyone had managed to pilfer the vehicle while it was safely parked in a heavily secured and reasonably affluent apartment development was beyond me but sure enough, it happened. Kim didn't deserve that but still I was mildly comforted by the fact that something terrible had happened for which I could not be in any way at fault.

I'm not expecting to run into anyone other than a stray member of the cleaning staff so I'm somewhat surprised to find Agatha still sat at her desk in a gloomy reverie, a good two hours after she should've left for the day. Diligent though she undoubtedly is, this is out of character and I can only hope that this nocturnal act is in no way attributed to any oversight of mine.

"This is devilishly late for you Agatha," I begin. "As your boss, I really should insist that you go straight home." Already, this absurd choice of vernacular has probably betrayed the fact that I've been drinking and at a rate that accelerated in the wake of Malcy's departure.

"I'm just tying up one or two loose ends, there's a lot left to do with Marion not being around." She is right, Marion's workload has not been reassigned and if this is a subtle swipe at me for not fulfilling my duty as team leader, then it is a swipe that I deserve.

"Come on Agatha, you know you're not paid to do this. Leave it for me and I'll take care of it in the morning, it's my job after all." I try to take a look at what she's doing but she quickly minimises whatever she is looking at on the screen and leaves me with a sharp pang of guilt for the unnecessary intrusion.

"I really don't think that you could help me with this Simon," she utters meekly and I notice something about her that I have never previously seen. It is inhibition.

"Listen," I start, while trying to seat myself on the edge of her desk in an awkward fashion, "as from tomorrow, I've decided that I'm going to turn everything in my life around. I know it sounds trite and I know I've said it before but I want to be a better boss, a better friend and a better person and in all truth, I don't think it's going to be a very hard thing to achieve. I've prioritised badly and rewarded the wrong people but it's time to reward those who've invested their faith in me because it's well overdue." My impromptu speech doesn't seem to rouse her in the way I hoped it would and I can't quite figure out whether she's disbelieving or just unmoved.

"I believe you Simon," she replies with a tone of finality, a polite urging that encourages no continuation of discourse. Usually, I would grasp at such a chance to extricate myself from a difficult conversation and say something self-deprecatory to justify my reticence but here, I've already said too much.

"Look, I know something's up, so you'd be better off telling me now so even if I can't help I can at least say that I've tried."

"You don't look well Simon," she says, in the tone of one who is tired of repeating it and understands the futility of the observation. I note that she is the second person to make this remark today.

"On second thoughts, maybe this isn't the right environment to discuss things," I reply, while my eyes involuntarily drift towards the office of The Croc. "Anyway, I've been thinking that it's about time I took you up on that offer to join you and your husband for dinner some time. I know you've been asking me for quite a while and I've always made my excuses but you shouldn't have taken that personally because I did that through embarrassment and not ungratefulness"

"There's not going to be a convenient time for that I'm afraid."

"Well it doesn't have to be right away, I mean, I could take the two of you out somewhere if you'd prefer, my calendar isn't exactly busy."

"There isn't going to be a convenient time because Allan and I are no longer together. Our marriage is over. We're separated and have been so for around two months now."

Although I wish otherwise, I didn't mishear though perhaps I misunderstood. How is it that only now do I see the anxiety and defeat that is etched upon her face? Has she disguised this from me in her selfless way or have I overlooked the signs on my relentless pursuit of the things I always said I never wanted? I concede that it is probably the latter but I can't best judge, for everything now has stopped making sense.

I try to carefully consider my next response even though I understand the protocol for situations such as this very clearly. First, one must apologise and make empty offers of support before subtly trying to elicit more information, but this is way beyond those subtle pleasantries because this is Agatha.

"I don't know what to say. You've always seemed so happy, so contented. Perhaps if I wasn't so utterly self-involved then I'd have seen this coming or you could've told me about it sooner without fear of me turning everything back on myself."

"I'm sorry, I should've told you, it's my fault really."

But it isn't and it never has been for here is a woman that I've confided in more times than I can count, one whose advice I've acted upon and whose happiness I've secretly envied. And yet for all of that, the cruelties and the severities of life have not escaped her and if Agatha is not immune to that then what chance do any of us have? She is the second person in just a matter of hours today that has been dealt a hand that she doesn't deserve and she, like Malcy, is of an age where second chances are scarce. I can't blame myself for Agatha's marital troubles but the fact that I knew nothing of them points to an imbalance in our relationship and although I feel guilt at Malcy's plight, I've never considered him a friend, at least, not like I do Agatha.

We embrace, more to cover the embarrassment of silence than for consolation and maintain the attachment for a couple of minutes. In this time, I try to impart some words of solace to her in the hope that I can somehow reverse the trend of our relationship and take up the role of counsellor after years of being the counselled. She notices this and simply buries my head a little closer to her shoulder, muffling my words into nothingness. She doesn't need to hear what I have to say because she knows it won't help her.

There is a recurring dream that I often have in which I'm situated on the top floor of a burning building, looking out from the ledge for a route of escape. Beneath me on the ground there is a large safety net and people crowded round it urging me to jump. Every time, without fail, when I jump out of the window and begin to plummet, it is at first unclear if the net will be able to catch me or whether I have jumped outside of its perimeter. In the absurdity of dreams, a descent that should take a second or two does not abide by the standard rules of time and a minute or longer will often pass before I learn my fate. On every occasion so far, the net has secured my safety but with every night I have this dream, the margin of error seems to shorten and I know that before too long, my luck will finally desert me. Tonight, I sense quite strongly that this dream is likely to return.

49

KIM

I have taken three different tests and each of them has produced the same result. The second line hadn't been so clear on the first test but it is perfectly visible on the latter two which now leaves little room for uncertainty. The evidence is conclusive, I am outside the margin of error and am able to say without doubt or equivocation that I am now pregnant. But the euphoria that should accompany this moment is strangely absent and does not envelop me in the way I thought it would. Perhaps it is buried somewhere beneath the shock and surprise and just deciding how best to present itself. In reality, I hadn't pictured how this precise moment was going to look or feel and the failure to do so has left me woefully unprepared. I'm not sad, I'm not happy, I am somewhere balanced between the two and waiting for one emotion to take precedence above the other. Sat alone in my bathroom with three plastic sticks for company, I gaze at myself in the mirror and already it feels like I am staring at someone else. Surely, the culmination of all the heartache and toil is not supposed to look like this but when the elation comes, I will of course be ready for it.

It was Doctor Block who had warned me against the validity of home pregnancy testing but had said that if the urge became too strong, then the earliest to try this should be twelve days after my egg transfer. It was advice that I intended to follow but my restraint was eventually breached on the eleventh day of waiting when I awoke to cramps in my lower abdomen and the dread quickly conquered me. In the days and weeks preceding this, my hormonal imbalance had subjected me to a range of bodily malfunctions that were the obvious results of the toll I had placed on it but these cramps I recognised and instantly understood. They were the clear signs that I was starting my period.

Against my better judgement, I consulted the fertility forum but instead of reassurance, all I seemed to find was a host of conflicting accounts. Some posters pointed to the fact that pregnancy and period symptoms often carried a very similar form, while others encouraged me to trust my biological history and heed my intuition. Far from improving my mental wellbeing, this browse through the forum had merely worsened it and it was then that I decided that I just couldn't wait any longer. I took three from my plentiful supply of home pregnancy kits and tested to see if my fears were correct. As it happened, they were. All three were negative and I immediately posted news of this onto the forum.

It's difficult to piece together all of the events from the hours that followed but it's safe to say that I didn't react to the news particularly well. The first thing I did was make a rather teary and incoherent telephone call to work to inform them that I wouldn't be coming in for the rest of the week. As expected, a reply followed from my nemesis at the supply agency who left a ranting message on my voicemail, the gist of which being that the placement had now been withdrawn with immediate effect. I couldn't argue with that. I didn't care to explain how my various absences were due to a course of IVF or how nobody in the office itself knew anything about this. The job would now be offered to somebody who actually wanted it, she said, and again, she wasn't wrong. I hated everything about event management and always had.

Following the negative tests and news of my unemployment, I had to escape the confines of the apartment and without a car, I simply headed out on foot without a route or destination in mind. I drifted about for several hours like some floating hologram with cavernous eyes and dishevelled hair before my feet began to tire me as did the pitying stares of passers-by. Having found an unoccupied bench, I seated myself in an attempt to take stock without realising that the bench where I sat was located directly opposite a school. It had been purely coincidental as I didn't know where I was, much less could I have planned it and the respite didn't last long. After about an hour of sitting there and minding my own business, I was compelled to leave when a group of inquisitive teachers approached me from the school and talked of calling the authorities if I didn't comply with their request. Astounded and aggrieved, I protested ineffectually in the face of little sympathy before I rose to my feet and resumed my route to nowhere in particular.

Later that day when back at the flat, I loaded up the forum again and found a private message from jackiexx37. She had clearly read my latest post and told me to remain positive because the very same had happened to her and days later she'd discovered that she was pregnant with twins. With my patience exhausted, I found her sympathy galling and so I responded with rancour and unpleasantness. When she probably should've replied in much the same fashion, she simply said that she would pray for me.

In spite of everything, I slept relatively soundly last night but most of today had been taken up reeling from yesterday's disappointment with my mood only softening after a visit from Claire. Without planning to, we shared a lazy morning in bed with a vast array of chocolates for company and a bottle of cheap wine for her. As part of this diurnal vigil, we watched movies that took us back to the height of our adolescence, ordered takeaway cuisine that was mildly repulsive and made childish prank telephone calls to unsuspecting recipients. Claire didn't dwell on my disappointment and that was just what I needed because we both understood that the relief would be temporary and her solace wasn't worth as much as her company. She left me this afternoon walking unsteadily from my apartment with a stash of my pregnancy kits to prevent me from further testing. I solemnly vowed to wait for the blood test at the fertility clinic before giving up hope entirely but I didn't really mean it. I would venture to say that she probably knew this and also knew that I was going to test myself again (using one of my array of hidden tests) so the pretence was neither elaborate nor necessary.

I took the second round of tests earlier tonight with an air of despondency because the odds had never really been in my favour. Not only was I looking to become pregnant on my first course of IVF, but I was hoping to do this with the aid of an anonymous donor whose selection I owed to a network of tenuous links. Additionally, I had vandalised a car, endured an incurable heartbreak and watched my mother steal my future away from me, all during a period of time when I should've been taking it easy.

Perhaps I am an anomaly and the six parallel lines that I now hold up in front of me are the very real proof of this. I slowly start to realise that my present sombre condition stems from my having allowed perspective to govern my emotions instead of the reverse, which I'm often prone to do. Maybe I'm not 'woefully unprepared' at all, nor have I ever been indifferent to the news, it is simply that I've realised how in no time at all, lonely evenings of longing will be replaced by sleep deprivation and dirty nappies. That craving for motherhood which had dominated so much of my thinking in the last six months will be replaced by the reality of it and perhaps deep down inside, I fear I am going to miss the yearning. It doesn't mean that the horror of my natural infertility is going to stop gnawing away at me but I can't help but feel that it will somehow make that moment all the sweeter when I hold my baby for the very first time. That day is still relatively distant of course and I know that complications with my pregnancy could still arise but an innate confidence that all will be okay has now displaced the crippling worry that had formerly resided there.

While every mother will say that the bond with her child is truly unique, in my case, I believe it will be bolstered by the disappointment that has preceded it. I will cherish that bond and think back to the times I cradled numerous babies belonging to others, convinced that it was something that I could never dream to possess. I will think of the silent suffering that I concealed when all of those around me talked unknowingly about how my time was still to come and how I secretly died inside. For all of the anguish that I had suffered that was directly or even indirectly linked to my infertility, not one day would go by for the rest of my life where I would not appreciate for one second the beauty of what I was to own.

As an addendum to this, I begin to reflect on the time I'd spent at the fertility clinic and the mixture of emotions that had absorbed me when entering that building. Fear, embarrassment, perplexity, all of these feelings seemed to jostle for position but one seemed to override them all and that was loneliness. In between waiting on various appointments with Doctor Block, I had looked on enviously at the couples I had seen there, doting spouses and expectant mothers whose faces were aglow with apprehension and excitement. They, like me, found themselves on the precipice between the joy of their attainment and the harrowing descent into barren disappointment but unlike me, whatever should occur, they would at least have someone to share in their grief or their happiness. Claire remains the only person in my life to know the real details of what I've endured but I'd be lying if I said that this was through choice rather than necessity. I love her dearly of course but sharing the jubilation or the agony with her is never going to be enough because deep down, I too want a doting partner, maybe one day a husband with whom I could build a family. After all, it is what most women want (don't listen to the subversives) and I feel this never stronger than I do right now. My mother (who now seems to know something about this but far from everything) will grow to love my baby (yes, my baby) when she holds him or her for the first time and her religious prejudices will no doubt evaporate before my very eyes. It's inevitable, she's inevitable and maybe even in a weird sort of a way it could even bring me closer to my brother Declan. Babies can do that you know and let's face it, if it's a boy then I'm obviously going to call him Barney.

I try to call Claire to pass on the good news but for whatever reason, whenever I go to dial her number, I instinctively pull away. There was somebody else that I needed to tell first, one who did not deserve the secrecy that I had subjected him to and that was Simon. Despite my mental trauma these last two days, I'd still managed to get a birthday card to him before he left for work even if it was, as I now realised, a day earlier than it should've been. I felt bad for his ignorance of which he was undeserving and for lots of other reasons too but chiefly because it all stemmed from my own cowardice. I knew that if I told him, he would react in one of two ways, either he would offer to stay with me and raise the child as his own or he would leave my life entirely. The truth is that I have feared the latter more than the former but only now do I seem able to accept this. Instead, the burden of my secrecy had presented itself through curt small talk and scathing silences for which he probably blamed himself when I could've eased the pain for the both of us. This dream of mine had at one time been ours and although I accepted that maybe I had wanted this more than him, I know that he would've made a wonderful father then as he still would now. He, above all, is the one person in my life that has a right to know what is about to happen to me, maybe even to us and if it breaks his heart then I know that I am capable of winning that love back. The Simon that I loved was the Simon that deep down, I still love now and although some would say that we have failed in severing our lives from each other, I would say that we never did try hard enough.

I reach for my phone and decide to call him. It feels

impulsive but it doesn't feel wrong and the adrenalin surges through me like an electrical current. One ring, is it really fair to tell him this way? Two rings, I guess it doesn't really matter how I tell him, he just needs to know. Three rings, where exactly do I start? Four rings, is there anything I can say to make him understand and temper the inevitable shock? Five rings, of course there isn't but he is stronger than I give him credit for and always has been. Six rings, oh Simon, for once in your life please pick up the phone.

And then it rings off to answerphone.

50

SIMON

She introduces herself as Katya and I have no idea why she picked me. Perhaps if she explains I still won't understand for her broken English and scrambled syntax make deciphering what she says a little difficult. Katya, I am certain, is really nothing more than a character, one inspired by the fantasies and predilections of a host of former customers. I don't mind that, in fact, I think I probably prefer it and she knows of me as much as she wants to know, which is practically nothing. We are both playing roles here in this den of falsity and I like the idea of being someone else, being someone better, because I need this to feel like a transgression and not like something that makes any sort of sense.

I have drifted in and out of consciousness for several minutes, lulled by the dangerous blend of heavy drink and banal conversation. It's a stupor that is only broken when I start to feel a hand making a slow ascent, edging up towards the top of my thigh from its original position at the top of my knee. I quickly detect this light-fingered pursuit and this she notices, forcing her to reposition the hand and then move it across into the area of my crotch. I glare back at her with a look of vague admonishment for which she cares very little and tries to convey that she has taken this circuitous route intentionally by a feigned, innocuous smile.

"You pay up front, yah?" She says, posing a clear demand in the guise of a question, knowing already that her forceful seduction will not be met with resistance.

I try to piece together how all of this has come about, why the shadowy figure picked me when I was ambling down the semi-busy high street and why I followed him into a murky side street without care or question. This man (whose features were buried beneath the hood of his jacket) demanded nothing from me other than discretion while he punched six digits into the keypad of a door without light or number and left me to ponder what waited on the other side. Moments later, the rattling and shaking of the numerous locks and bolts had ceased and I crossed the threshold, certain in the knowledge that my friend of the shadows had already returned to the streets, probably in search of his next lost soul.

The welcome I received however, fell somewhat short of my brief expectations and was to prove far from cordial. The reason for this was the imposing figure that met me on the other side, one who stood comfortably above six feet tall and didn't seem quite so willing to cater for my wants as had my previous chaperone. He introduced himself as 'Hex' and the rules of the establishment were then imparted to me in a manner designed to suppress any desire for further clarity. Failure to comply with the rules, he explained, would see me leave with fewer parts of my anatomy than I had entered with and I quickly sensed that the power of reasoning would certainly be lost on him. Lacking in elaboration (as one would probably expect of a man in his position) this was an environment that seemed to suit him, the resident muscly mammoth that probably did this sort of thing for fun before payment. Dressed from the lengthy distance of head to foot in black garb, his jacket was arrayed with an abundance of pockets and zips which seemed to bulge ominously, packing nothing but threat. His features were difficult to discern as his face was screened by the peak of his cap and although I'd detected a sharp and rugged jawline, it was also partially obscured by sprouting facial hair. As he led me towards a vacated sofa, I muted his menacing directions in favour of a burgeoning character assessment, slightly intrigued at this gargantuan character. He spoke to me without direct focus, not in a supercilious way but more as if the script was embedded within his retina and could be delivered just as well for the lack of verbosity. Intimidation was a mere recourse for Hex because it probably came naturally to him and I didn't doubt he knew that this was far greater than any violent reproach that he could muster. Careers, reputations and marriages, all of these things were reliant on his discretion and power of recall and on the other side of that door, a word in the wrong ear could ruin a life for good. In this, surely, lay his greatest strength and like everybody else, my compliance was secured because of it.

From across the room there was little to suggest that Katya possessed either beauty or distinction, which may've explained my sense of apathy when she sashayed towards me in a manner that was anything but provocative. As she stood with hand on hip, trying to accentuate a figure that just wasn't there, I sat passively, aching for my indifference to animate itself but with limited success.

"Hay-lo, my name isth Katya," she had said, in an accent I didn't recognise and an exaggerated lisp, while she offered me a hand that carried the weight of my inevitable decline.

That same hand feels much colder to touch just minutes later when I remove it from my crotch and use my other to take the money from my wallet that she has already attempted to procure from me. Without unease or inhibition, she counts out every note, performing a mental calculation before waving to Hex, who then strides over from the door to collect it from her. True to his disposition, he offers an audible grunt, clearly displeased at having to remove himself from a duty he excels at and then he too totals up the amount. At this stage it's difficult to ascertain which of us he distrusts the most but I can't help but feel relieved when he solemnly returns to his original post at the door, pocketing the cash as he does so.

There is nothing alluring about Katya and I say this with some regret having spent great efforts in trying to find something during what has been an uncomfortable dialogue so far. She doesn't lack beauty per se but her features are embellished to the point of over-elaboration as if to steal your attention away from a secret layer of the ordinary. Her hair is ash blonde, pale at the tips but sharply contrasting with the darkness of her roots which seem to sprout from her cranium rather wildly. The face that stares back at me is oddly misshapen and is, I consider, a phrenologist's dream, for it is broad at both the ears and chin and then inwardly curved at the point in between. Her mouth is thin and crimson and stretches across two sallow cheeks making her expressions look brief and interchangeable. Two skeletal and ungainly arms reach a long line of nails protruding from the ends of emaciated fingers that stroke at my forearms in an encroaching fashion and fail in their sensual intent. The dress that she wears looks inexpensive and gaudy and doesn't so much reveal her milky flesh but actively yield to it, balancing perilously on her shoulders and breasts. And yet, there is no ugliness about her that I would call innate and in the embers of her burning veneer, one could argue that there is poise and maybe even beauty. But what I notice above all else is an air of distance about her, a disconnection from the scene that we are acting out together and that she doesn't appear quite so at ease with herself as she probably thinks she does. And this perception becomes clearer when I snatch a glance or two into those narrowing eyes of hers and see that very same look of utter abstraction that stares back at me in the mirror every single morning. It is these orbs of vacancy that humanise Katya and lift her above the air of reticence that precedes our impending intimacy. They make me want to know what her story is and how she ended up here, to learn if this is how she escapes from the drudgery of her life or if this is in fact the drudgery. Could she articulate in words what her eyes are yearning to express and could she understand me in the same way I think I understand her? I want her to tell me what I'm doing here, seeking distinction and companionship via this accidental encounter and if I differ from the many men that she has met before, sitting as I am now.

"You drink upschtairs?" She asks, pointing to the bottle of beer in my hand that has already been procured for me from the makeshift bar on the opposite side of the room. While motioning for me to rise and join her by the gentle tilt of her head, I notice that she is missing an earring.

The lights grow dimmer as she leads me towards the rear of the building and although I detect presence in every murky corner around me, I have little time to verify my instinct. We reach a small stairwell which we then begin to climb, Katya's high-heeled shoes clashing against the stone flooring ahead of me with an ominous clamour. It is here that we begin to pass others on their descent, girls that Katya greets (often in foreign tongue), trailed by men that look neither shamefaced nor discomfited and do not offer me the sort of scrutiny that I expected. We cover three flights of stairs before we reach our destination and then all I can see is door after door lined across a landing without detail or decoration, each of them identical to the next. Katya selects a key from a chain containing several dozen, inserts it into the lock and beckons for me to follow her inside.

The room is unashamedly basic with just a mattress and a small divider behind which Katya makes hurried preparations. After around two minutes of staring at bare walls, trying desperately to find a detail to focus my attention on, she re-emerges in a satin dressing gown that is beltless and loose-fitting and leaves little to the imagination. For the second time this evening, she positions herself alongside me, now rubbing her right breast against my left shoulder as her gown softly undulates across her chest to the steady rhythm of her breathing. This preparatory act signifies that things will now move along at a pace that she is comfortable with and that I'm no longer in control of any of this (if indeed I ever was). There is a steeliness about her and gone is the desire to assuage my hesitations, dislodged by carnal duty and subjugation to the natural order of things. As she leans in closer to me, I try to fight the apathy and induce anatomical elevation, mulling over every method that I have used in the past. With my attention quickly drifting, I spot Katya's dress now lying spread across the top of the divider, creased and redundant and then something else draws my gaze away from that, glistening limply on the floor not five yards in front of the bed. It is Katya's missing earring.

This discovery alerts me to the reality of what I'm facing and I suddenly feel cornered and desperately out of place. Katya clearly doesn't sense this though and just continues on completely unperturbed. When she touches me, I want to feel warmth in the grip that meets my palm and not the ice-cold friction of compulsion. As she removes her gown slowly and seductively, I want to feel something primitive and lustful and when the contraceptive is slung into my lap in routine fashion, I want to recall whatever the feeling was that had brought me here in the first place. Where is my sense of guilt or the squalor and the scandal that is ordinarily supposed to litter such a scene? It is missing or illusory at best because no matter how hard I try to convince myself otherwise, my perspective and my position are not as elevated as I imagined them to be. Instead, I feel chagrined, thwarted by the disinterest that had been shown to me from Hex on the door to the customers on the stairs and most of all from Katya, a prostitute who mixes faux-servility with sexual control and who, in just a matter of a few hours, will not recall my name.

She doesn't scream at first which is perhaps explained by the sense of shock and this slight but clear delay in her response buys me some valuable time. I can't really explain how it happened other than to say that when her hands had followed their natural route towards my lower half, the inevitable occurred (despite her best efforts) and she found me to be physically unresponsive. This useless pursuit wasn't entirely her own fault but that mattered little and when her incompatible mouth shot back a sound of what I deemed to be contempt, that all-too-familiar sweeping mist descended. The next thing I knew, my right hand was stinging and Katya was lying on the floor.

Instinct returns quickly though and I head straight for the door where I'm accosted by a howling Katya, screaming wildly and incoherently having quickly recovered. Her face is already a savage imitation of what it was just seconds ago when lying prone across the floor and along her right cheek, I can see a throbbing abrasion at the point of impact. I capitalise on the speed of this attack by taking her momentum and spinning myself out of the way, using the force of her own bodyweight to toss her aside. With the pathway clear, I shoot straight through the door and race back towards the stairs.

The speed of my escape looks to have caught everybody off guard and it is not until I reach the foot of the stairwell that I am forced to face any sort of attention. Katya, in her panic, appears to have raised an alarm which roars out at ear-piercing volume from wall to wall, the shock of which temporarily impairs both staff and clientele so that nobody really knows where to look. I take advantage of this while others head instinctively away from me in the opposite direction and back up towards the room in which the distress signal has originated. I speed towards the exit and my sense of relief is palpable when I find the main door to the building completely unmanned and my pathway to escape unhindered, free of the boorish giant and his subtle threats of violence. Instead, I see him far out of the way, stood behind the small bar to the side of the front room, changing an optic. He sees me of course but I am many yards ahead of him, so once I'm through the door, a combination of distance and darkness should see me safe if I can flee swiftly enough.

The side street is gloomier than I recalled it to be from around half an hour earlier and far from the shield that I expected and the darkness now has a deeply oppressive feel to it. I turn on my heels and take a sharp left, heading towards the lights of the high street that I can faintly make out in the near distance. Only moments ago, my senses were so numbed that I found myself incapable of mustering a simple biological reflex but this impulse to survive has unearthed a far stronger stimulant in me. Terror now drives me forward along uneven ground as my reliance upon instinct grows with every stride, but as I continue to train my limited vision on the lights straight ahead, I suddenly notice that the light is dwindling. Gaining closer still, there is really no doubt about it and if for a moment I briefly consider it a mirage, the reality is about to prove much worse.

Fortunately, my directional sense hasn't let me down and I find myself heading along the correct course of escape. This time however, there is a detail that emerges which must have escaped my notice on entry and it is one that seems quite glaring now. Two large metal gates stand either side of what is now my exit, which must've been in a recoiled position when my nocturnal chaperone guided me through them earlier. They are anything but that now and not only are they conspicuous, but they appear to be closing right before my very eyes by mechanised instruction. Within seconds, all remnants of light become completely obscured and I reach the gate just at the point where both wings meet in the middle of its structure. I search desperately for a handle, a lock or a cleft in the metalwork, seeking anything that I can grab hold of in order to force it open, but there's a growing futility in every heave and despite my best efforts, it doesn't even budge. Frustrated but undeterred, I then try to mount the gate and haul myself above it. I locate a hinge to the right hand side and use it as a makeshift rung, launching myself into position, ready to vault myself over. The hinge lacks width, forcing me to balance precariously on one foot and after steadying myself for several seconds, I make a feeble attempt at a jump, catching my hand on something sharp on the summit of the gate as I do so. As I instinctively withdraw my hand to nurture the wound, the momentum pushes me backwards and I fall from about six or seven feet in the air all the way onto the ground behind me with a sickening thud. The pain between the impact of the fall and the warm, fluid sensation now streaming down my hand seem to cancel each other out and I gaze up helplessly at this insurmountable structure. Lined across the top of it in clear formation stand a row of sharp metal spikes that were previously obscured to me and these are what have caused the deep laceration to my hand. Knowing that any attempt to scale the gate again will bring with it the very real risk of deathly impalement, I content myself by looking for an alternative route of flight. I start to think that maybe the gates closing in on me like that is the clearest indication yet that I have not been sighted and that the aim is to contain rather than pursue me. Although hard to understand, in the minute or so since I struck Katya and fled the building in a manner that was anything but discreet, I've been met with no obstruction and the silence that now surrounds me seems eerie rather than portentous. It is possible (though certainly improbable) that in the height of the melee, I have escaped unnoticed but even if true, it still leaves me trapped and cut adrift from actual safety.

To the right of the gates there is really nothing more than what appears to be a row of disused garages that run all the way back behind me, heading towards the door through which I originally bolted. I decide to turn in the opposite direction and pace adjacently to the left wing gate using both my hands as fumbling guides. After several slow, tentative yards, I can feel a wall to the side where the gate once was but still nothing ahead of me. The ground becomes firmer underneath my feet and so I start to quicken the pace, striding forward with a burgeoning confidence. Logic insists that I cannot be too far away now from locating another boundary of this prison-like enclosure but just as I consider this, I am temporarily floored by a grasping human hand which is then followed by an almighty collision.

I know instinctively what it is (or should I say who it is) but the impact is not as great as it really could've been. The hand barely makes contact with my left shoulder as it brushes by me but such is the size of this limb that it needs nothing more to knock me from my feet and send me tumbling towards the wall. All of a sudden, there are lights shining above my head, glaring at me, seemingly from every angle and shedding clarity onto the scene surrounding me. A fire door is now swinging on its hinges while audible gasps emanate from within and I can also discern small security cameras presiding meekly above the carnage. Just on the other side of that door, I can see the bar in which I last left that menacing ogre helplessly replenishing the alcoholic stock while I fled for freedom, he who is now an unmoving heap about five feet away from me. I quickly deduce that Hex must have intentionally contained me within the grounds and had been monitoring my progress via the aid of those numerous security cameras that line the building from front to back. Once he closed the gates, he probably knew that I would head in this direction, bringing me back alongside the very building that I was desperate to distance myself from and then timed his attack accordingly. The security cameras are likely operating under a slight delay with the footage being screened a second or so behind real time, so when he leapt at me through the fire door, he had unknowingly mistimed the pounce. Instead of tackling me from the side and launching his assault, he had barely laid a glove on me and had instead propelled himself with an alarming velocity into the wall opposite. The impact was colossal with his six-foot frame crashing against the concrete wall and had my body been used as the intended buffer, it is safe to assume that I could've been killed.

There is little option but to pick myself up and then continue in the same direction, spurred on and amazed in equal measure by just how quickly the human brain can recover itself with physical recrimination so close at hand. I eventually reach a point where the wall adjoins itself to one much smaller and far easier to surmount and haul myself above it with my right leg first. In this position, I can survey the scene around me for the very first time, gather my thoughts and try to recover my strength both in body and in mind. On the other side of the wall beneath me there is a garden that looks neglected and unkempt, backing onto a small terraced house that looks much the same. It isn't perfect but is certainly enough and as I begin to lower myself onto the shrubbery below, I take a last glance back at the wounded giant and see that he is there no more.

Stunned, I try to process what I'm seeing or more accurately, what I'm not seeing. How had he managed to recover himself so quickly after a collision such as that and without my even noticing? It seems impossible when just seconds ago he lay so numb and lifeless that I wasn't even sure if he was even conscious and yet, he had succeeded in dragging himself back inside in order to recuperate. I opt not to dwell on this any further though while picking rough foliage from my trousers and then brushing the earth away from the cut to my hand. If the occupants of the house are to see me now, stood in their garden in full business attire, the last thing that they'll assume is that I'm trespassing with the intent of larceny, for after all that has happened, I still look vaguely respectable. To others, I simply look like the victim of office high-jinks and in truth, the thought of their detection is far less troubling than that of the colossus who has just tried to maim me. With that said, I still can't help but flinch at a sign of movement in the hedge alongside me and I spy a rat shuffling languidly towards me. Clearly, this is his domain and certainly not mine but I become momentarily transfixed by the twitching ears, the inquisitive snout and the pebble-like eyes. It is ugliness personified but not exactly horrifying and it is not so much fearless but more disinterested in my presence and when it starts to scurry back towards the bush, I begin to feel guilt for my infringement. It is difficult not to feel anything other than a million miles away from home right now, away from my apartment block where the residents go into meltdown over the slightest of infractions and mere inconveniencies. Mock them though I do, the safety of their trivialities is comforting to dwell on right now as I stand in the middle of a predicament that as anecdotes go, will never see the light of day.

I exit the garden via a wooden gate and then creep along a small passage that connects the house to its neighbour, bringing me out onto the street. Eerily enough, I am greeted by neither light nor movement when I emerge onto the residential avenue and the fitful hum of city traffic is the only thing of note that seems to break the stillness. I turn right to walk back towards the high street which is about five minutes away from my current position and where I should still be able to find a taxi to take me home. Checking my phone, I can see that Kim has left me a voicemail (and a number of missed calls) and I figure that it has to be something serious for her to call so late. Nocturnal messages can often carry with them the scent of something fatal and so vain is the hope that this is simply news of a broken water main or a misplaced front door key. The automated voice coldly states that the message is five minutes long and a shadow of foreboding seems to encircle me instantly. But this shadow is not simply figurative, it is breathing, it is sentient and perhaps most significantly, it is vengeful.

Hex's recovery is so transformative that it leaves me in awe and momentarily suppresses my sense of terror. He is stood about fifty yards ahead of me now, his features shrouded by the very same darkness that had duped me already and somewhere above my head the stars are now retreating, complicit in the betrayal. I contemplate a plea for mercy but with little money left and no real grounds on which to negotiate, I know my luck can only stretch so far. As he starts to edge towards me, tentatively at first like a feral beast circling its prey, I try to match his pace in a backward retreat while training my eyes upon him. Minor details are now starting to emerge, the pulsing chest, a bloodied brow and two clenched fists, wounds that look merely superficial on his giant frame. Once again, I turn on my heel and run.

The street in which I find myself offers very little in the way of protection and much less in the way of escape. A seemingly continual line of rough, terraced houses flank either side of me, dictating my path and forcing me onwards, desperately in search of any sort of junction that will lead me back into civilisation. When I try to scream for help, the sound barely escapes my throat before it is abruptly nullified, as if confined between these lifeless residences and cobbled terrain. The brief stoppage has also worked against me and already I can feel my chest begin to tighten and the breath exiting my lungs via the route of my mouth in a rhythmless fashion. This is a pace that I will not be able to sustain and this realisation isn't helped by the murderous grunts that are pursuing me which are ominous, sinister and worse still, they are only getting louder.

I manage to generate a safe enough distance between us for around five hundred yards before the road finally starts to broaden and I spy a gloomy-looking expanse straight ahead of me. This then feeds into a small, winding incline which brings me out onto entirely new terrain several feet beneath the level of the street and briefly out of sight of my pursuer. Spurred on by this minor stroke of luck, I follow this course into a clammy, stone tunnel that reverberates to the sounds of my heavy footfall and then I emerge on the other side, out onto a gravel pathway and back into the open air. If anything, my line of vision is now even more impaired than it was before and I can barely see further than my immediate vicinity. Running headlong into a dusky vacuum, unknowing of where it may lead, I spot what appears to be my own feeble reflection running alongside me. At first, I consider this to be nothing more than a trick of the light or a minor hallucination brought about by a tiring mind and growing dehydration but in reality, I have inadvertently detoured onto a canal footpath. This would be okay had the unintentional detour thrown Hex off the scent but in the space of around twenty seconds, it becomes abundantly clear that it has not. Now, the grunting appears to have ceased and he's unnervingly muted instead, hidden somewhere outside the line of my peripheral vision and safe in the knowledge that he is gaining on me. The advantage of a clear head start has rapidly diminished and while his thunderous steps become louder in my wake, the time between each of my own is starting to lengthen. The seriousness of my predicament is now clearer than ever and in this battle of wills, my only hope is that he will somehow yield before I do, succumbing to the exhaustion or maybe halting to attend to the wound on his forehead. Between the line of trees running laterally to the canal path on my right and the lonely darkness of the water to my left, I have never cut such an isolated figure as I do right now. This is an environment that breathes criminality, one that I have entered of my own volition and gloomy imaginings begin to dominate my mind. I start to picture myself lying at the foot of the canal bed, bludgeoned and disgraced, waiting to be discovered by the police who will then endeavour to trace my final steps. And should they do so successfully, how the tributes will turn from maudlin to subdued when the ignominy becomes undeniable and stains my shortened legacy. These very thoughts are enough to keep me driving forward and although Hex's desire to slay me may be strong, I figure that the urge to survive will always be stronger and so because of this alone, I retain a slight advantage.

Despite my sapping strength and weighty limbs that work independently to my brain, I spot what could be my one last hope. While the trees to my right begin to thin in number, the far-off lights of the city start to surface upon the skyline. Although still distant, they are discernible and while my eyes gather focus, the line of the horizon presents itself, gloriously detached from the metropolis. This sense of recognition doesn't stop there as the sound of the humming traffic returns to my ears and as it does so, it dawns upon me that I am finally drawing nearer towards an area of the city that I know very well. Furthermore, if my calculations are right, then in around one hundred yards I will meet a small footbridge that will in turn lead me into a disused railway station that could well help secure my passage to safety. In fact, so much have I been consumed with my sense of panic that I lost all sight of where I actually am for a time, when in reality, I have walked this very route maybe a hundred times or so way back when. In the days that I had neither car nor licence, I would take a shortcut via this very canal path after seeing Kim home safely to her parents' house and now, if I can just reach that bridge before being caught, then history can yet work to save me.

All thoughts of mortality are banished from my mind as I reach the footbridge and follow it to the other side of the canal before I duck into the railway station. Once inside, I sprint along the deserted platform with a renewed pace and then ascend a second bridge that adjoins two opposing platforms. This then enables me to exit onto the second platform out on to the other side and then finally, I am back out onto the open street. This circuitous route has taken me out of eyeline of Hex but I still have only a matter of seconds left to take full advantage. Staking my life on the power of clear memory, I double back on myself and locate a small alleyway that runs parallel to the back of the platform and try to secrete myself there. With just the yellowing foliage to shield me like a canopy, I stoop behind a knee-height wall and then position myself as still as a sentry. From here, I now have the vantage point that I require of the main entrance to the station and if my plan executes as it should, I could be mere moments away from absolute salvation.

Just seconds pass before I hear the steps of my adversary again ringing like death knells in my ears as he descends the bridge onto the platform and then grinds to a halt on reaching the entrance. For the first time since our brief face-off in the street, I now have clear sight of him. Stood there like the embodiment of confusion, he strains his neck to survey the area, sensing something amiss, baffled as if the laws of the chase have somehow defied him. The instinct to maul and maim is everywhere about him, emitting itself through writhing limbs that seem to jerk and contort in the stark recognition of a pursuit now lost. So close is he now that I am able to perceive the outline of a small tattoo just below his left ear, the pattern of which is almost completely obscured by a thin line of blood escaping from the gash on his forehead. Palpitations disturb the flow of oxygen to my brain as I start to feel light-headed and while Hex sprints off into the night on an erroneous path that will only lead him further from me, my crippling fear eases in to self-pity. My eyes involuntarily close, the gamble has thankfully paid off.

I do not succumb to sleep but more to a temporary shutdown of the body and mind and when I come too, the oily discharge of sweat is all about me. This fleeting moment of slumber is hardly enough though and I find myself a shivering wreck with aching limbs and a methanolic odour seeping from my pores. Uncomfortable though I am in this dimly lit recess, I felt a debt of gratitude to the alleyway responsible for the preservation of my life, even though it would be a falsehood to say that I had found it through mere guesswork. It was one well known to me already as it was this very spot in which I now concealed myself that I had often escaped to as a child during days of truancy and adolescent cavorting. Back then, this was a safe space for me and one that I returned to on the cusp of my adulthood, seeking something that I was never really able to fully identify. As I fix my eyes upon the wall in front of me, I trace history with my fingertips, moving them across the grooves of the stone in a comforting regression. Sure enough, it is still there in between the various bits of scribble and illegible graffiti, a creation of my very own hand. This relic of former times takes me back in an instant, the ink faded and perhaps unclear to the untrained eye, but not to me. I can even recall the day when I wrote it and in addition to that, who I was with when I did so. In large black letters, penned within the confines of a heart-shaped bubble, a declaration of teenage love, the warmth of which has never left me. *From ST to KP, I will forever love you x.* That day, like today, was my birthday and the boy who had written this had been intoxicated with the dreamy notions of adolescence while on that seamless passage into my seventeenth year.

I detect the chill of the forthcoming morning now that the adrenalin is no longer in command of my senses as I follow the alleyway down to the opposite end and re-enter the platform from there. Still unwilling to risk detection, I take an unconventional route back across by stepping slowly onto the railway line and then rushing over the uneven track ballast in an unsteady fashion. When I pull myself up onto the first platform, I retrace my steps towards the original footbridge that took me from the canal path and then cross back over it. Brazenly, like a thief returning to the scene of a crime, I then wander back alongside the waterway (which nearly proved to be my own shallow grave) and divert my path towards the city once again. This time, my passage is significantly less eventful and before long I am stepping out onto the high street, ready to be immersed back into the familiar.

But the familiar is anything but this. There is nothing more than silence again everywhere about me now and something notably disconcerting as I begin to wander around the deserted thoroughfares of the city. Like a once-busy landscape in the aftermath of an atomic bomb, it is an urban masterpiece laid bare, stripped of its essence, leaving the architectural finery behind but rendering it useless. It is now ten minutes past five, and in just two hours' time, the sun will rise and bounce its rays off the many skyscrapers that tower above the speeding masses, none of whom will take the time to notice this detail. The shift from here to there will be quick and incredible, only I too will fail to absorb this because I, like them, will go about my business dutifully, serving as a mere component of this cyclical process. A new day might well be close at hand, but I'm not about to rue the repetition that will come with it anymore because I now see how all of these details are actually complexity dressed as the ordinary.

I catch a sight of my reflection in a shop window as I pass and do not fully recognise the figure staring back. The eyes looking back at me are lifeless, empty craters and a roll of skin protrudes from underneath my chin, making the edges of my face unclear. My stomach looks bloated, my hands shake violently and my kidneys ache with venomous ripostes. I notice how I have aged significantly over the last year of my life and while the blackouts are lasting longer, I have grown indifferent to the incidents that fill these lost spaces of time. It is masochism and really nothing more but I have to learn to control it before this numbness of body becomes a numbness of mind.

Today, on my thirtieth birthday, Agatha will place a card underneath my keyboard ready for my arrival into work just as she does every year. Kim has already given hers to me which is admittedly one day early but that mistake matters very little. What really matters is that she'd opted to remember because it signifies a constancy in her that she too often understates, as if the revelation will betray some inherent weakness. It is a trait that the two of us share, a tendency to self-reproach because it is easier to apologise for our love rather than admit it.

But that message inscribed in the alleyway is evidence at least that we haven't always felt inhibited in our strength of feelings for each other. Back then, we were gratified and confused by the power of our love but never reticent to express it and I miss the clarity of feeling that once existed. And truthfully speaking, I never wanted our lives to change from what they were at that time, just like I never wanted Kim to change from the sixteen-year-old girl that I fell in love with. When things did change, I resented the evolution of our lives and fought hard to resist it, clinging to the past in the hope that she would do the same. I stifled Kim and did it because I simply didn't know what I wanted from my life and that lack of direction always seemed to heighten in her presence. It's hard to explain but it felt for a time like the two of us were lost at sea and while I was trying to swim against the tide, Kim was drifting with it, trusting the natural course of the water as I tried to pull her back with me to the shore we had departed. I now know that that is when I lost her, at the point where her life had started to edge away from mine and I had tried to drag her back instead of floating with her.

I retrieve my mobile phone from the inside pocket of my jacket, amazed I haven't lost it during the pursuit and ready myself to listen to Kim's voicemail message. Somehow, it seems that regardless of its content, be it bitter or blunt, I will return to our apartment (having at least procured a replacement key for the door) and confess my epiphany to her before it is usurped by my resident self-consciousness. Greeted once again by the automated message, I wait patiently before th—

51

DECLAN

They told me that I was born addicted to crack cocaine. This was because the woman who gave birth to me used to take the drug regularly and it entered my system through hers when I was a baby in her stomach. She was seventeen when she gave birth to me which is the same age as I am now and I have never met her.

When I was born, I was very unwell for a long, long time but I've been told not to blame the woman who gave birth to me for this because she too was very unwell, so it wasn't her fault. I'm not very good at telling people how I feel and that is a symptom of autism. Autism is a condition that some people have and I am one of those some people. In a book that I was given as a child, it describes autism as 'an inability to ascribe emotions towards people or events that occur around you.' I know that isn't true or at least it isn't true in my case because I feel lots of emotions about people and things that happen to me or those closest to me.

I was adopted by Barney and Meredith when I was three years old and as far as I can tell, that's when my life really began as I have no memory of anything before that. I don't tell many people this because whenever I do, they either say that I'm lying or ask lots of questions that I don't know how to answer. Meredith has always told me that I'm special but I learned that special doesn't always mean good. There is bad special too and I think that's what I am because I often think things that make me very angry and do things that cause people to shout at me. I think what Meredith really wanted to say was that I was different but used the word special instead because she didn't want to hurt my feelings, the feelings that I'm not supposed to have.

I used to live in a large house with Meredith until she decided that we had to move out of there because it reminded her of times when she was much happier. I preferred our old house to the one we live in now as it was much bigger and I miss the garden and the fields beyond it where I used to play as a child. When I was younger, I spent most of my time building dens in the trees and alcoves there, laying traps for animals wherever I could lure them into. I like nature but I don't like every animal because some animals invade your space and kill the young of other animals who are usually much smaller and too weak to protect themselves. I mostly caught birds, frogs and rats but sometimes they would spring the traps at night and by the time I found them in the morning they'd be dead already and lying still with rigor mortis. Rigor mortis is a stiffness of the bones and muscles that happens after death.

When Barney died just over two years ago, Meredith cried a lot, in fact, everybody did and I felt out of place because I couldn't cry like they did. He died because of something called dementia which is a disease that lots of old people get and it makes you forget things before it eventually kills you. I know this is true because Barney often used to forget who I was towards the end of his life and sometimes when he did speak, I couldn't understand a word of what he was saying. Barney was my best friend and I loved him and I can still remember everything about him.

Meredith told me that Barney intended to give me some money after he died but that he had passed away before he had chance to write me into his will. A will is a written document that shows who a person wants to leave all of their possessions to when they are dead. Apparently, his first will had been drawn up just before they both adopted me and so he wanted to draw up another one that would include me as his son. I knew nothing of this but my sister, Kimberley wanted all of his money to herself and so she paid some clever legal people to argue that I had no right to any of it. Meredith cried lots of times over this and whenever I asked her why she was so upset, she told me that Kimberley had the devil in her and that I deserved the money that she had taken from me. The devil is the enemy of God and lives in hell which is one big, eternal fire and so I know how upset she must have been for her to say this because Meredith really loves God and talks about him all the time.

Kimberley was fifteen years old when I was adopted which is the same age that I was when Barney died. When I was nine, she moved away to live with her boyfriend Simon (I'll get to him later) and I was very happy about this because she had always been cruel to me and didn't treat me in the same way that I saw other big sisters treat their little brothers. It was Kimberley who told me that I was adopted and this made both Barney and Meredith really angry because they said that it wasn't her place to tell me this and she wouldn't say sorry. They said that I would always be their son no matter what and explained that Kimberley had only done what she did to make me feel inferior to her. That's what Kimberley does though, she tries to make everyone feel inferior to her and seems to enjoy doing it.

My favourite room in the old house had always been the study because that is the room where my memories of Barney are at their strongest. We would spend hours together in this room assembling our huge model train set and even now, I can describe every single detail of that little world that we created. Often, when the trains would stop working, Barney would let me try and fix them but I never could and so he'd always end up fixing them himself and then tell me that I'd done all the hard work. That was a lie but it was a good lie and not like any of Kimberley's because he said it to make me feel better about myself. The study was also full of artefacts and lots of dusty, old books with covers that used to fall apart when I held them so I had to be really careful when I did. Barney used to tell me all the time that his whole life was in that room and the objects inside of it were priceless to him before he got sick and forgetful. But now, our model train set is no longer in the study nor are most of the books and artefacts that once filled the space and I doubt that Barney would even recognise the room as it now looks. It is Kimberley who is responsible for taking these items and when I confronted her about this, she argued that everything in the room belonged to her under the terms of Barney's will and that there was nothing I could about this because I was never really his son anyway and he didn't love me as he did her. That argument made me really sad because I remembered how, in the weeks leading up to his death, he would often fail to recognise me but that he always recognised her and so maybe he did love her more than he ever did me. I get scared all the time now because already I am starting to forget things about him and if Kimberley keeps taking all the things that remind me of him, then I'm worried that I will end up dying like he did, with no memory at all of the things and the people that made me happy.

In the days that followed that conversation, I couldn't forget what Kimberley had said to me and how it made me feel and so I decided that the only way I could prevent any of my fears from coming true would be to retrieve as many of Barney's things as I could. So I took the spare key for Kimberley's flat (that Meredith always said was only there for emergencies) and walked all the way over to number 228 Gaddis Avenue. It took me thirty-seven minutes to walk there because I'd never been there before and I went in the middle of the week because I didn't want anybody to be home when I arrived. All I wanted to do was find as many of Barney's things as I could and then take them back home with me so that Kimberley could stop selling them. I turned the flat upside down that afternoon looking for Barney's things and couldn't find anything of his but I still made sure that everything I touched was put back in the place I found it because I don't like mess and I didn't want her or Simon to know that I had been there. I wasn't sure if she had sold everything or found a secret space to keep his things hidden that I just couldn't find but I did find a number of items that belonged to Kimberley. These included four wardrobes full of clothes, three televisions, several rows of shoes and two cabinets full of expensive-looking beauty products. On top of this, she even had an allocated parking space in the bay beneath the apartment block where she parked her expensive-looking car. It looked to me like Kimberley had everything that most people normally want but that she had bought all these things with Barney's money and by selling everything that he once treasured. That is called greed and Meredith told me that greed is one of the seven deadly sins in the Bible and a sin is something that only God can forgive you for and so if anyone commits a sin then we cannot forgive them.

I was just about to give up and leave when I heard the sound of somebody entering the flat and I realised that it was Kimberley returning home from work that day. I was scared that she would catch me and shout at me like she always does so I quickly ran into what I thought was the spare room and hid myself inside a cupboard. I couldn't really do much more once inside there other than stay very still and try to control my breathing but it did give me time to think about some of the other things that I'd discovered that day in Kimberley's flat. Firstly, I found paperwork that showed she was paying out thousands of pounds to a fertility clinic for IVF treatment. IVF treatment is when a woman who is infertile has to ask a doctor to help her have a baby because God has decided that she shouldn't become a mother. I don't know much about the mechanics of IVF but I remember when Kimberley told Meredith a while ago that she and Simon wanted a baby by this method and how alarmed Meredith was by this news. Kimberley always upsets Meredith in everything she does but I didn't understand why she was so keen to become a mother when she didn't seem to like her own parents very much and

I figured that God had probably made her infertile because of this.

A few hours later, I was still hiding in the cupboard feeling stiff and hungry when Simon entered the flat and headed straight into the room where I was hiding. Within minutes, he was asleep, lying face down on the bed and snoring really loudly. It was then that I realised something else. The room that I was hiding in was the only one in the flat that didn't seem to have any trace of Kimberley in it. It was messier and colder than the others and only had a single bed (like my own at home) and so it had to be that despite living together, Kimberley and Simon were living very much apart. I then thought back to Barney's memorial and remembered how they barely even spoke to each other that day and how unusual I thought that was at the time. It was clear that Kimberley and Simon had broken up but that nobody else seemed to know about this.

I had to wait for another two hours before the silence in the flat suggested that Kimberley had also gone to bed. Simon was still fast asleep when I crept out of the cupboard and tiptoed out his room and I had to be really careful not to step on any of the empty bottles that were left lying at the foot of his bed. I then entered Kimberley's room (although I'm not really sure why) and as I stood over her while she slept, I thought about how easy it would be to just take one of the stray pillows beside her and smother her with it while she lay asleep. I had seen someone do this in a television show once and remembered how easy it looked and I thought if I could do the same to Kimberley, then everybody's life would probably be much better for it. Doing that to someone is called suffocation and suffocation is when air is prevented from leaving the lungs and people can die because of this. It can also be called strangulation. But I couldn't remember if murder was one of the seven deadly sins and so I decided I couldn't do it and so instead, I helped myself to a handful of Kimberley's possessions (in replacement for Barney's) and crept quietly out of the flat.

When, in the course of moving house, Meredith stepped foot in the study for the first time since Barney's passing, she saw for herself how empty the room had become. Because she was so confused about what had happened to Barney's things, I didn't want to lie to her and so I told her absolutely everything. I told her how Kimberley had sold all of Barney's possessions to pay for expensive things in her flat and that she was using the money to pay for a baby through IVF and then I told her how she and Simon were no longer together. Meredith was angry and confused at hearing this and vowed that she would make things right by giving me a share of the money she'd received from the sale of the house that was originally intended for Kimberley. I said thank you because that's what you're supposed to say when people give you things or they're nice to you but I didn't like seeing her upset again because of Kimberley and I didn't know whether to feel bad for telling her what I had in the first place.

What happened over the next few days was something that I didn't really plan but still it happened anyway. It had all started when Simon gave me his telephone number on leaving Barney's memorial and told me to call him if ever I felt I needed to. I'm pretty sure that he was drunk when he said this because he kept repeating the same words over and over again before he hugged me, which he knows I do not like. Although I've known him all my life, I've never really spent much time alone with him as I've always been convinced that Kimberley has probably told him how much she hates me. I still wanted to learn more about where I could find Barney's things though and thought that he could help me in this after what I'd learned from my secret visit to his flat. So when I met him in a pub not far from where he works just a few nights ago, I was really hopeful that I'd have some good news to take back to Meredith but I was quickly disappointed. Even though he knows how I don't like being surrounded by lots of people, he turned up late and was drunk again and had only remembered because I'd reminded him earlier that day. I could tell that he was drunk because I'm able to remember things better than anyone else I know and I remember every word he said to me that night and none of them make much sense to me still. He said that he was about to do 'two really terrible things to two of life's better people' but he didn't want to explain what that actually meant when I asked him to.

I was angry because I was starting to feel scared by all the people around me and when I asked about the whereabouts of Barney's things, he claimed he didn't know of them. It was obvious that he wasn't really listening and I thought that he was lying because he lived in that flat with Kimberley and probably enjoyed all of the things she had bought with the money just as much as she did. And then I remembered how a few nights earlier, he had driven right by me at breakneck speed at the wheel of Kimberley's car and had failed to acknowledge me as I walked by on foot. That car, like so many of the possessions that now cluttered up the flat in which he lived, had been bought from what Kimberley had stolen from Barney and that made Simon complicit in all of this. Complicity is when someone knowingly aids another person in doing something wrong. This made me angry to think about because Simon was less entitled than anybody to steal from Barney (and Meredith) and Barney always really liked him when he was alive. I waited there much longer than I wanted to just hoping that Simon would tell me something or maybe even apologise for what he'd done but he didn't and so when he stumbled towards the toilet, I reached into the jacket that he had left behind and helped myself to his set of keys and a fob. I had been in his company for less than half an hour.

The car seemed like the obvious thing to take and because of Simon's drunkenness, this became a lot easier than it should've been. I was really nervous at first because I hadn't driven a car that size before and although my driving instructor says I'm one of the best he's ever taught, he still manages to find fault with the way I drive sometimes. But once I was at the wheel, I didn't really know what to do or where to drive to, so I headed to my old house and parked it in the garage there because the people who have bought it from Meredith are yet to move in. With the car safely parked, I wanted to use that time to decide what to do with it and it was then that I realised how I should've thought it all through beforehand. I first considered selling it but thanks to Meredith, I didn't much need the money now and even had I sold it, I probably wouldn't have asked for the right amount anyway. I then thought about holding onto it for a while and gaining some valuable practice at the wheel before my driving test in two weeks' time but figured that Kimberley would soon report it missing and if the police caught me, I wouldn't know how to answer their questions without lying to them. I am terrible at lying and always have been which is another symptom of autism (I am told). This caused me a dilemma and a dilemma is a situation where every option available to someone is difficult to choose between because all of them are equally bad. So I decided that all I could do was return the car to Gaddis Avenue a couple of days later when nobody else would be around to see me. Or at least, that was my intention

He didn't see me coming but even if he had, I was driving at such a speed that I doubt it would've saved him. I don't quite know what Simon's reasons were for walking all alone at that time of the morning with a mobile phone pressed to his ear and looking just as drunk as he had been the last time I had seen him but as I sped towards him, I didn't much think about it.

The impact was so severe that he somersaulted right over the top of the car and landed several metres behind me. When I checked my wing mirror (as my instructor always tells me to do), it looked like he wasn't moving and although I probably should've stopped to see how injured he was, I didn't. The car itself had barely suffered any damage other than a sixty-seven centimetre crack in the windscreen, a bump on the front bonnet and a slight crack underneath the front light which I'm pretty certain was there already when I originally picked it up. Other people would've turned around to check on him, good people like Barney or Meredith, instead of driving away like I did but I knew I couldn't do that. If I had, I'd have ended up apologising to him and I've never liked lying to others and pretending I feel guilt about things when I don't. Kimberley and Simon do that all the time and do not mean their apologies and Simon had even confessed to me himself that he was going to do bad things to good people before I had left him in the pub and taken his keys. But even though I didn't feel guilty, I didn't feel happy either because there was no sense of catharsis, only a slight regret that it had been Simon who had been stood in front of the car at that time and not Kimberley. Catharsis is a feeling of relief you get after you have done something bad or significant. Maybe it was God who had placed him front of the car because God has divine powers and can do that when he wishes and maybe Simon deserved it too because he had loved Kimberley once and probably still did and if I'm honest, Kimberley does not deserve to be loved by anyone.

I don't like to read books because stories never really end and when I do, I can never stop myself from thinking about the characters and their lives beyond the final page. Do the good people turn bad? Do the healed become sick again? Do the people in love with each other fall out of love with each other again? It seemed like every book I read as a child had a central character who always saw the error of their ways by the end of the story and they were always forgiven for the bad that they had done because of this. But I think that the reasons why people do good things are much the same as those who do bad. They want to be feared, loved, admired or rewarded and sometimes, all of those things at once. But I'm not one of them and neither was Barney and now, as I look up at the stars above my head, I hope that he'll remember me when we eventually meet again, somewhere way up there.

52

SIMON

FOUR MONTHS LATER

I awoke from a coma two weeks after the accident, lying in a hospital bed with a tube down my throat and Kim at my side. At that point, I remained in a precarious state and my survival was by no means guaranteed. I had suffered numerous injuries, the most serious of which being multiple bleeds of the brain which had, in the short term, made me verbally deficient and unable to recall what had happened. The physical toll on my body was unpleasant but manageable, I had broken my pelvis, tailbone, several vertebrae and bones in my neck, not to mention the internal lacerations and swellings. The result of which (I am reliably informed) means that I'll never recover full fluidity of movement and although I'll be able to walk unassisted one day, it'll be fairly visible to most that I'm a survivor of trauma. I have spent the last four months in and out of surgery and know well that there are more operations to come, while simultaneously, the focus is on my cognitive recovery. In terms of the latter, my support team say that I'm making excellent progress while stressing that my goal of full recovery remains attainable if I continue to engage with them. In truth, I find the mental probing far more invasive than the physical and yet, conversely, far more rewarding.

They tell me that I was lucky and I agree with them but for entirely different reasons. No one seems to understand my lack of fervour for identifying the culprit that did this to me and can't quite decide whether I'm protecting someone or suffering from post-traumatic stress. The fact is that should I ever meet the man or woman who drove into me that night, all I would have to say to them is thank you. Thank you for helping me win back everything that I had lost and aiding me in reclaiming everything that I ever wanted. I've spent much of my life blaming others for my failings so it is perhaps ironic that now I have genuine reason to hold someone else responsible for my condition and yet, I choose not to dwell on it.

My hospital bed became a point of confession throughout much of my recovery with my near-paralysed state breaking down many of the barriers that had once existed between colleagues, friends and family. The Croc informs me that the Area Project Manager role will remain open for me for as long as I need it which is reassuring, although I haven't decided yet if that's what I want or if I'm even going back to Tanner & Webbing at all. Agatha is still as loyal to me as ever and blames herself for what has happened and it's stark how many people have said that they foresaw tragedy in my life but felt unable to prevent it. I've reconnected with my parents and through the medium of therapy, I hope to harness this relationship in a productive way so that I can enjoy what others are granted without asking. But the most comforting thing of all has been to learn that I am to become a dad.

Kim is on first-name terms with all of the medical staff around me which suggests that her bedside vigil preceded my return to full consciousness. She was the platform on which my recovery was built, filling in the blank spaces of recollection and nursing me through my physical hardships. The patience and softness that she exhibited revealed her maternal secret to me quite some time before the delicate bump had started to protrude and I had spared her a blushing disclosure as soon as I realised this. We could be happy as a family, she proposed, and the child would be mine regardless of my genetic exclusion. As I looked at her while she said this, I no longer saw Kim as my teenage love but instead saw a doting mother-to-be, my life partner.

Whatever Kim and I now have, it isn't what it was nor would I ever want it to be. The baby is developing well and other than the regular, largely unfounded concerns that plague first-time parents, we're not facing the prospect of paternity with unnecessary trepidation. Plans have been made to sell the apartment in Gaddis Avenue which we decided would be an obvious impediment to our lives moving forward, for although it contains some happy memories, it isn't a home fit for a family. Now, we are slowly detaching ourselves from the idealism that once drew us both together while relishing the banalities and domesticities that lie ahead. It will be a challenge I'm sure but I can quite confidently say that I have overcome much bigger.

I used to think that there was nothing particularly noble in just existing, in the getting by from day to day and because of this misapprehension, I grew to hate myself for failing on the terms of others. I now know that this battle was unwinnable and if I'd died as a result of that car ploughing into me, then in the grand scheme of things, nothing would really have changed. After an initial period of mourning, everything would return to being just as it once was, the sights, the sounds, the smells, and nothing would lose any of its beauty for my not being there to share it. Those things, like life itself, are frail and transitory and for that reason, I will never tire of celebrating them.

THE END